EMERALD DECISION

DAVID GRANT is the pseudonym of a bestselling thriller writer with Welsh connections who describes himself as an unenthusiastic and very occasional jogger, and who lists as his recreations writing books, listening to music, reading, and writing more books.

Available in Fontana by the same author

Moscow 5000

DAVID GRANT

Emerald
Decision

FONTANA/Collins

First published in 1980 by Michael Joseph Ltd.
First issued in Fontana Books 1981

© 1980 by David Grant

Made and printed in Great Britain by
William Collins Sons & Co Ltd., Glasgow

for BRYN,

who talked of the minefield that
led to the decision

and

In Memoriam

E.R.D. and L.B.B.

Friends

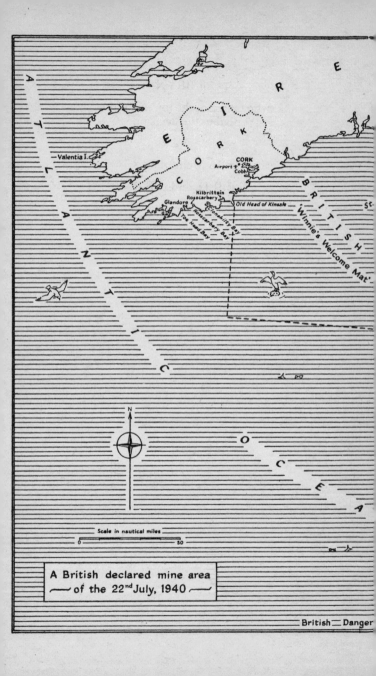

A
T
L
A
N
T
I
C

E I R E

C O R K

Valentia I.

CORK
Airport
Cobh

Kilbrittain
Rosscarbery
Glandore
Clonakilty Bay
Rosscarbery Bay
Toe Head Bay
Old Head of Kinsale

B R I T I S H

'Winnie's Welcome Mat'

St.

N

O C E A N

Scale in nautical miles

0   50

A British declared mine area
— of the 22ⁿᵈ July, 1940 —

British — Danger

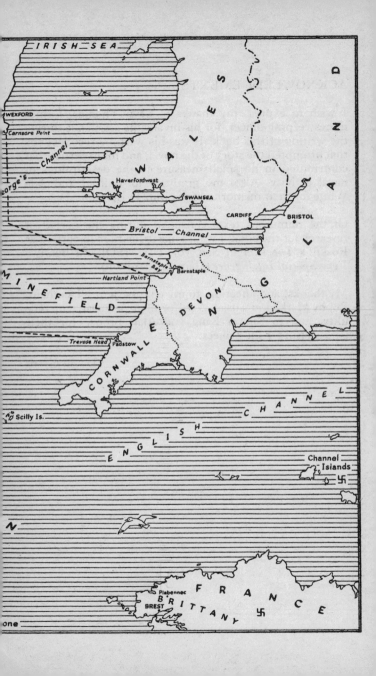

ACKNOWLEDGEMENTS

I wish to express my thanks to Bryn Thomas, former minesweeping officer, for his invaluable assistance during the writing of this book. It was his wartime recollections that prompted the story of the novel, and his expertise that contributed in no small measure to the descriptions of naval activity. Also, my gratitude to Wilfred and Ada White for their memories of the Blitz in London.

Of the numerous texts consulted during the period of research for the book, I would like to mention in particular Roskill's *The War at Sea,* vol. 1 (HMSO) and Beesly's *Very Special Intelligence* (Hamish Hamilton).

My thanks, and affection, to my editors, Jenny Dereham, Bobbi Mark, and Susan Watt for their persuasive incredulity, and to Simon King and Alan Brooke for their enthusiasm for the project.

David Grant

PART ONE

ANCIENT HISTORY

Chapter One

A VISIT TO THE OBERST

October 1980

McBride had spoken to many former Wehrmacht officers, all of them reduced to scribbled private shorthand in his notebooks, or become disembodied voices on cassette tapes. Yet Menschler was different, if only in that he was more intensely reminiscent of a former self than the others. He was different, and not merely because he was blind; the lines of visible scar-tissue were like pointing accusations, lines of perspective drawn to the dead eyes. Menschler was complete in another way, in the entirety with which he chose to inhabit the past, to walk corridors long disused – even the final corridors of the Führerbunker. His almost total recall promised well for McBride, chilling and fascinating him as they sat in the blind-man's living-room in the wooden house on Norderney, in the East Frisians.

McBride was seated facing the window, perhaps two or three yards from the desk where Menschler sat, his back to the window and its square of grey sky and choppy sea nibbling at the stretch of beach below the house. The house had seemed an outpost as he had approached it on foot along the beach road. It was a summer house – Menschler lived there all year, and had done since the early 1950s, when his prison sentence was commuted by a West German court. It seemed to McBride that he had chosen this flat, windy splinter of the Bundesrepublik out of a total disapproval of post-war Germany. Hermitage, or place of exile.

The furniture in this main room was old, heavy, dark. Polished by his caresses rather than by creams or waxes. Even the way in which Menschler gripped the arms of his chair at that moment suggested both possession and defiance. And he had the trick of looking directly at his visitor's face as he listened or spoke, and not in a vague direction over one of McBride's shoulders. His blind eyes seemed disconcertingly aware in the room and its fading early evening light.

Smaragdenhalskette – Emerald Necklace. *Smaragden-halskette* –

McBride's thoughts pushed impatiently, nudging him into speech. For the moment, he resisted the temptation to broach the real subject of his visit, while Menschler spoke of the last days, when his Germany had gone up in flames with two bodies in the grounds of the Reichschancellery. McBride wished, half-attentively, that he had obtained Menschler's first-hand impressions for his previous book.

'The Führer surrounded himself with SS trash in those last days – ' They were speaking in German, a language in which the American, McBride, was fluent. The contempt, the hatred of the army's displacement by the SS was undimmed by the slow blind passage of forty years. 'Even while their glorious leader, with his bowel trouble and his belief in sorcery, was doing away with himself like a rat taking poison – '

Four days before, in the Bundesarchiv in Koblenz, McBride had found the most tangible reference to Emerald Necklace, in a private letter written by Menschler to his cousin, a Junker Generalleutnant on the Oberkommando der Wehrmacht staff in Berlin, whose papers had been bequeathed to the Koblenz archives on his death in the early '60s. And unlike the memories of other men to whom he had spoken, or the official records, there had been no OKW censorship or editing. A private letter which referred to a top-secret army matter had survived intact, been waiting for him at the end of a long and fruitless search for a proposed operation that had never received the usual *Fall* – Case – designation used by OKW for France, Russia, Britain, Poland, Crete, Africa.

His book had begun as a sober treatise designed to enhance his academic status and reputation. *The Politics of Invasion: the Führer and his Wehrmacht, 1939-42.* Sober enough for any narrow-minded, conservative faculty board. McBride shrugged the image away. That was all before *Gates of Hell,* eight weeks on the *New York Times* list in hard-cover, half-a-million copies in print in soft-cover –

And he'd returned to his treatise, seeking to inject it with popular appeal, dynamism, something *new*. And Emerald Necklace, a name in a dusty Pentagon file of agents' reports from 1940, a name overheard or dimly remembered by a handful of Germans still living – and a reference in a letter dated October 1940 from Oberst Karl Menschler, a name he already knew dimly from his researches on *Fall Gelb,* the invasion of France, and from the planning group of *Seelowe,* Hitler's proposed and abandoned invasion of Britain.

McBride knew the war held few beneficial secrets to ambitious historians, especially those who had chosen the market-place to make their mark rather than the groves of academe that had seemed to slight and undervalue him for so long. All the bodies had been dug up – Babi Yar, the Cossacks handed over to Stalin's mercy, Katyn, the Final Solution, the atom bomb, had all received their popular historical exploitation. But – Emerald Necklace. If it was real, then it was new. No one had done it, no one even *knew* of it –

His hand had quivered, his breath seeming to be held throughout, as he read and reread Menschler's letter to his cousin.

Now, Menschler seemed to subside like a kettle gone off the boil. He sat stiff-backed in the chair, staring at McBride's features as if he could read their expression, or as if demanding that he make some comment on what he had heard. McBride coughed, watched a seagull lifted then plucked from its course by the wind off the sea, and picked out the painted dark strip of the German mainland subsiding into shadow five miles away on the horizon.

'Herr Menschler, thank you. Perhaps I could take you – unless you're tired – back to France in 1940?' McBride wondered whether his voice betrayed his excitement, his anxiety. Menschler's face was partly in shadow, but he was certain that the head moved slightly, a small flinch at the tone or subject.

'Yes, Herr Professor?'

McBride paused on the edge of the moment. His journey in a rented blue Audi from Koblenz up the Rhine into flatter and flatter northern Germany the previous day had effectively depressed his tension and anticipation. The short ferry journey, leaving the Audi on the jetty at Norddeich, in the company of a few late holiday-makers from Hamburg and the Ruhr crossing to Norderney for an off-season, cheap-rate ten days, had increased his sense of possible foolishness, of chasing after a whim and looking very, very dumb. The flat, uninteresting Frisian island held no promise as the ferry neared the old village and its tiny jetty.

Yet Menschler was real, and alive, and he had written the letters in the Bundesarchiv. He could be a few minutes away from the new heart of his book, and its probable status as a best-seller – including the six-figure, maybe seven-figure soft-cover advance –

On the edge of the moment, he indulged the comforting, comfortable prognostications. Print-runs, contracts, sales figures. *A new, unknown invasion* – a rewriting of history? A strange, bubbling excitement in him was compounded by the clear memory of his telephone conversation with Menschler two days earlier; the Oberst had been frostily polite, but reluctant, as if for him, too, the proposed meeting was heavy with significance.

'You were on the support planning staff for *Fall Gelb*, and later for *Seelowe*?' Menschler nodded, but after a pause. Had the facts come back only slowly, or did he anticipate what might follow the slightest admission? 'What happened, Herr Oberst, after *Seelowe* was postponed indefinitely on October 12th, 1940?'

'What do you mean, Herr Professor, what happened? We did not invade England, that is what happened.'

'I mentioned a letter you had written – one of three or four – to your second cousin, Generalleutnant Alfred von Kass on –'

'The 23rd of October.'

'Yes. Could I ask you about that?'

The silence seemed to continue for a long time, and the room's weight of furniture and memory pressed upon McBride with a tangible presence. He felt enclosed.

'Why? It was a private letter. Much better to ask concerning *Fall Gelb*, or *Seelowe* – I can give you many insights, my memory is excellent.'

14

'Yes, Herr Menschler. I appreciate that. But I'm interested in *Smaragdenhalskette,* the Emerald Necklace you referred to in the letter. It wasn't a family heirloom.'

Menschler's face remained unmoved at the remark.

'Perhaps not – '

'You said, and I quote – '

'I recollect exactly what I wrote.' The voice placed McBride, made him a reporter, an amanuensis and nothing more. It cancelled the inbred German esteem for his academic title. Now he was little more than a busybody from the gutter press.

'Why are you reluctant, sir? It's forty years ago.'

'Reluctant?'

'There is something – but you won't talk about it.' McBride suppressed a rising irritation sharp as bile.

'This is the first time you have come across this, this – *halskette?*' McBride was certain of a fervent hope in the question.

'No, sir, it is not. I have maybe another dozen references to it, always by the same name, verbal and written. In files in America, and here in Germany. Maybe in England, too, though I haven't checked it out. But at second, third, fourth hand, I admit. You were there – '

Menschler shifted in his chair. A parody of relaxation, yet McBride sensed the German had removed himself further from his guest, and from emotions that guest might initially have aroused. A thin cut of a smile on his face, giving the accusing lines of scar-tissue a more recent vivacity on his white face.

'Ah, I am to be impressed by such notoriety as you imply in your tone, mm?' The thin smile broke the planes of his face again. 'You suggest that I – *tell all?* – to you, you will create your sensationalizing book around it and make, no doubt, a great deal of money. Who will play my part in the film, Herr Professor McBride?' The blind man had perceived the ego lurking behind the mask of the bland, sober historian. Probably knew of *Gates of Hell.*

'I am pursuing only the truth, Herr Menschler.' It sounded palpably untrue, impossible, pompous. McBride wanted to laugh at himself, but Menschler did it for him, a sharp, barking sound, something long unused.

'And the truth will make you rich, mm? I believe there is a vogue for such books at the moment. My daughters tell me so. They are very often surprised to discover that my tales to their children are not merely an old man's dreams. They are products of the Socialist *wirtschaftwunder,* of course. *Who was Adolf Hitler?* And so on.' Menschler waved his arms, dismissing his descendents perhaps for generations to come, but not for ever. McBride felt it was unfair for an ex-Nazi to be so perceptive about *his* world. Especially unfair in a man blinded by a shell fragment in the Chancellery grounds and who had exiled himself – probably on his state pension – from the post-war Germany.

'And they show such a thing as *Holocaust?*' Menschler continued, his face entirely perspective lines towards the blind eyes. He was deeply angry. The hands polished the wooden arms of his chair in deep, massaging movements. 'The filthy lies – these new Germans accept them, spit on the past as if it had nothing to do with them –'

McBride was appalled. He was losing Menschler.

'Very well, Herr Oberst. You wrote from Guernsey in the Channel Islands, from France, and from Belgium to Alfred von Kass during the second half of 1940. What were you doing in the support planning staff after the postponement of *Seelowe?*' McBride leaned forward in his chair towards the blind man, urging him to answer, wishing for a loose senility of tongue or an avarice that might take a fee as bribe.

'I was acting the part – rather well – of a German staff officer, Meinherr. That is what I was doing.' McBride was incensed by the lordliness of the response, angry that the man was determined to retain secrets to which McBride felt he had some admissible rights of acquisition.

'What was Emerald Necklace?' he almost shouted. '*Was ist Fall Smaragdenhalskette?*' He felt hot and angry and blocked in that cold room. The man would *see* nothing, give nothing away –

Menschler was smiling with superiority.

'It was – nothing at all. As you admit, there are no records, Herr Professor, and no one will tell you. In fact, you will never prove that the *halskette* ever came out of the jeweller's window.'

'Why in God's name won't you talk about it?'

'Why – why? Is there a *right* that you have to know?' Menschler seemed to know that McBride had risen from his chair, and had adjusted his head so that the blind pale eyes still looked into McBride's face.

'Tell me, damn you, tell me!'

'No. I choose to remain in the conspiracy of silence. My motives are not important, and they would not be understood by someone as – *crass* as you. One of my daughters tried to ask me questions about your book, *Gates of Hell.*' Menschler held up his hands, and closed them into claws. 'I tore the book to pieces, Herr McBride. You have dirty hands, and you will never touch the necklace with them. I *choose* not to tell you – and there is nothing you can do about that!'

The Rt Hon David Guthrie, MP, HM Secretary of State for Northern Ireland, had flown by helicopter from Stormont Castle to Aldergrove airport, then on an RAF flight to Northolt, and been driven into London by a Ministry driver. Now, in the office of Davidge the Home Secretary, preparing for an urgent meeting with the Prime Minister, Guthrie still looked at his ease, and to Davidge, as if he were appearing on television. Moving with the grace of an athlete or an actor, using his profile, marking off the room like his territory as he moved about it or stood looking out over St James's Park in the autumnal mist that had persisted all morning. Though Davidge knew that the territory he really wished to appropriate was the office where they would lunch with the Premier.

The press considered almost everything Guthrie did and said as a piece of canvassing for some future election, some anticipated occupation of 10 Downing Street – but the press was usually kind, and more than normally impressed by the promised all-party conference, under Guthrie's chairmanship, to decide the power-sharing future of Ulster. Davidge, as he watched the man he could not be like and could not, therefore, like or admire, sensed the electricity running between the reports on his desk and the man at the window.

The Provisional IRA had detonated five hundred pounds of explosive at Aldershot, and a lot of soldiers and their families were dead and injured. And a second bomb had been defused at Catterick. In the wake of bombs in Birmingham, Leeds, Liverpool and Southampton. Yet Guthrie appeared at ease.

For Davidge, to whom the same school, the identical university and a parallel political career had not given the same ease before the cameras or the same overriding self-assuredness, Guthrie was habitually an irritant. He was still the man's fag, after all the years that had passed.

'What is the PM's feeling about the latest mainland bombings?' Guthrie asked finally, a look of frank distaste souring his features. As if he had spotted a weakness within himself which the words embodied.

'Distress – I think one may use the word unreservedly.'

Guthrie turned to face Davidge as he sat at his desk.

'Two bombs in Dublin, another in Waterford,' he snapped, as if he were the intended victim. 'Fires all over Belfast and Derry. Those bastards are worried, Davidge – *really* worried!'

'But will they succeed, Guthrie – that is what you will be asked this afternoon – can they succeed?'

'In wrecking the conference, you mean?'

'What else? That, I take it, is the object?'

'I should presume so.' Guthrie rubbed his chin, and stared across the low mist shrouding the park. It looked cold out there; figures moved through the mist as little more than dancing spots tiredness might have brought to his eyes. He'd seen the growing apprehension on the faces of his PPS, and the Parliamentary Under-Secretary. Even the GOC's staff were apprehensive, and felt unfairly restrained in a low-profile response which Guthrie hoped might keep the SDLP and the Unionists firmly committed to the Leeds Castle conference.

It was within his grasp, was still within it, even though the Provisional Sinn Fein seemed to drink the latest outrages like a cordial, and were backing away from the conference table.

Soldiers' wives, in the last couple of days when he had visited stations in Germany – *campaigning*, the press had called it, and he would not give them the lie on that – looked doubtful, apprehensive, faces closed to their husbands doing a third or fourth tour of duty in the province. It was all there, spread out like cards on baize or – more clichéd still – his was the final throw of the dice. He believed he could still win.

'The middle ground's still secure,' he murmured as if to himself. 'Paisley is holding back like a virgin at a party, but he's the spokesman for a tired people. The UVF and the rest of the Protestant lunatic fringe have been alienated, and he knows it. The Protestants are prepared to give – ' He shook his head. 'All the conditions for success are there, Davidge,' he turned to the Home Secretary, one hand before him in an upturned fist, 'which is why the Provisionals are *now*, and why it's their last, desperate effort. Lashing out blindly – '

'Provisional Sinn Fein haven't dissociated themselves from the violence – '

'No, they're more likely to dissociate themselves from the conference, unless you can make arrests.'

'Special Branch are hopeful – another sprig of the Braintree growth, they think. I shall authorize a number of raids for tomorrow.'

'You must – ' Guthrie could say no more. Davidge felt uncomfortable under his glance, and distinctly irritated that he was being made to serve Guthrie's self-seeking. 'There's an uncommon closeness of mind between the Provos in the Sinn Fein and the IRA just at the moment. Among the younger, wilder elements, at least. They're doing what they can south of the border, but the Provos are not coming out of hiding. We have to have *these* bombers, the ones on the mainland, if we are to maintain credibility. *Everyone* is so much closer than they were at Sunningdale – we can't have the cement blown out of the brickwork at this late date!'

November 1940
It was raining, and there was a wind sweeping across Guernsey which spattered the hard drops against one side

of his face. The left side, which was now almost dead to any feeling, ached with awakened blood vessels whenever he rubbed it. Minor discomfort. He was far more concerned with the duration of the shower and the time he was wasting keeping to the roadside ditch. It was already after dark, and after curfew.

Yet there was the same elation, familiar rather than self-betraying. They had told him, years ago when Drummond had first recruited him, that a lot of the work was sheer and unadulterated boredom. *A pain in the backside,* one senior instructor had drawled, dismissing espionage much as he might have done other people's boils. Michael McBride – currently Lt Commander McBride, RN – had wondered at the virginal excitements of training, at the persistence of such feelings during early operations immediately prior to the war, and then grown accustomed and accepting. Apparently – he smiled even now as he formed the thought – he was made to be an agent. He had found his *métier*, his vocation.

He climbed out of the muddy ditch, pumping his hands against his arms, flapping himself warm. He took out the pencil torch, flicked on the thin beam for a second, and nodded. He was half a mile outside St Peter Port, on the main road from St Sampson and the cove north of Clos-du-Valle where the submarine had landed him. The S-class submarine could not navigate between Herm and Guernsey in safety – could have brought him no further south and nearer St Peter Port. He was making reasonable time, but he was impatient to arrive in St Peter Port, as a lover would be for a rendezvous.

He could not be certain of the currency of his forged papers, which were designed to get him down to the main harbour itself – certainly through and past the patrols in the town. He had been ordered to go nowhere near any of the contacts among the occupied islanders – Admiralty Operational Intelligence Centre had made that the strictest parameter of his job. He was not to be known to be on Guernsey. Even at the risk of the papers he carried being days, even hours, out of date.

He crossed the coast road, looked down over Belle Greve Bay briefly, taking in the new ugly groins, the barbed wire rolls along the strip of deserted beach, the titled signposts, the empty beach huts falling into disrepair almost in a single glance. He'd been to Guernsey before on minor jobs – nothing like this one, from the tight-lipped briefing and the solemn faces that made him want to smile – but this landscape of fear and occupation was *déjà vu* simply because it was a scenery natural to him and his unusual occupation. Curtains blacked out the windows and lights of the newish retirement bungalows that straggled out along Les Banques from the old town in an effort to ribbon-develop St Peter Port and St Sampson. Some of them were empty, and some – he moved back across the road as he let in the thought – were used to billet Wehrmacht officers of the forces of occupation. And he must get on – it was strictly a one-night-stand, my darling. He dropped back into the ditch, and began moving more quickly along it. It was coming on to rain harder, and he did not worry. He was a passenger, moving too quickly for slow German minds and slower hierarchy of action.

Ten minutes later, he climbed out of the ditch, stood up, and kicked the mud from his boots. At the crossroad ahead, there was a German patrol, and a couple of arc lamps. Pub, tram sheds, bus garage. He could see the street plan of St Peter Port with vivid clarity, almost perceive his own route as a dotted line traced on it – much more clearly than the muzzy aerial pictures that had sent him here. Long low sheds erected in the strongly-fortified Albert Marina, intended to conceal as well as protect. Like submarine pens, the briefing officer had observed unnecessarily.

He worked his way behind the pub, where thin edges of light framed the blacked-out windows, paused to listen to the noises of a German song, tossed his head in amusement and in the superiority of moving secretively past, crossed Grand Bouet in a long-striding spring, and ducked down in the shelter of a hedge. Moving through a changed but still somehow pre-war suburbia on a holiday island. The bus garage was patrolled, but minimally.

He kept to the shadows of the buildings, listening with satisfaction to the silence of his passage. He climbed a rickety fence out on to First Tower Lane, took a fenced, grassy lane through to the Rue du Commerce, and rejoined Les Banques, now the esplanade.

Anti-aircraft guns pointed north, sandbagged against the sea-wall, incongruous opposite the boarding-houses which were mostly now billets. He began to walk openly, hands in pockets, humming softly. Dock worker, curfew permit and ID card in his breast-pocket, walking to join the night shift. He passed the first AA emplacement, and nobody took any notice. Coarse Berliner dance-band music floated occasionally to him on the wind. He skipped in time to it once or twice, because he was enjoying himself and the small part of his personal life which his pregnant wife occupied was dormant for the duration of any job they sent him on.

Along St George's Esplanade – he recited the names on the pre-war map, aware of the imposed German names, feeling the excitement curling like a drink in his stomach, or a cat contented to be warm and asking no more. The AA emplacement on the Salerie was betraying light, and the smell of cooking. Something with onions. A truck with a canvas hood was parked alongside the sandbags and the hut. Someone laughed, and he heard in a side-street a bus cough into life. Workmen's bus, heading for the harbour, then he was on Glategny Esplanade running along the north beach.

There was a barrier and guards at the crossroads. Other workmen by this time, and the checking of papers more perfunctory, as he had expected. He would have been more interesting to the patrol near the pub, coming from outside the town. Now, he was part of the nightly traffic to the harbour, and he joined the little queue of islanders and Frenchmen who had descended from a bus. Inevitably, someone spat in the brave darkness after a guard had passed, machine-pistol slung at the ready, boots splashing in the rain. McBride watched the men in front of him, and the manner in which their papers were checked by the officer in the Kreigsmarine greatcoat and the 'Security' tabs at collar and armband, and felt an intenser excitement. The guards were from no special unit, but they were alert, bristling with guns and purpose – the kind of charade McBride knew was habitual and which replaced real security when it passed into uneventful routine. The body-searches on the way off-shift would be thorough, but he would take nothing away.

He came level with the officer, adopted a careless, indifferent silence, and his papers were passed immediately. He had not even considered that they might be spotted as fakes, or betray him by an error. Some other part of the organism had shifted him half a yard closer to the nearest soldier, taken in his youth, his build, and the ease with which the machine-pistol would come away from his hands. McBride did things for his own survival without caring, with a thorough instinct.

He was waved through the barrier, which swung aside, and kept a couple of steps behind the two men in front of him down the North Esplanade, past the Victoria Marina, then through another barrier on to the Albert Pier. Here, there were more guards – the tabs of a special security unit clear in the white arc lights, the Kreigsmarine officers more numerous, the check more thorough, longer. He passed through, and dismissed the tension that had knotted suddenly in his stomach. The long, low sheds were ahead of him, each one marking a berth or berths. Closed doors, noises from within, lights slitting beneath doors, bursting from cracked windows or torn black-outs. Fuzzy aerial pictures.

He looked around him, slowing his pace so that the men ahead of him increased their distance. The man behind him was catching up. McBride slipped on the wet concrete, cursed in French, and rubbed his ankle under his boot.

'Hurt?' the man enquired as he drew level. McBride shook his head, swore and blamed the Germans for the weather, and the man walked on, laughing. McBride looked back at the barrier, lights fuzzy in the rain, and then slipped into the shadow of a warehouse. The sheds were fifty yards from him. He watched as a judas-door opened to admit the men who had been in front of him – the clatter of repair, bright leap of welding sparks, then the door closed. There was an armed guard there, too. McBride rubbed his hands, not entirely to keep warm, and began to wait.

*

Three in the morning. He was stiff with cold, and the single draught of rum had traced a slow, leaky passage like warm snow down his gullet, dissipated and might never have been. He had concealed himself between two of the coal-bunkers near the warehouse, at the end of the narrow-gauge track for the steam-crane which unloaded the coal Guernsey still imported for coal-burning coastal vessels. Like switched-off machinery, he had waited. Now, in the tired small hours, it was time to move. The cold was stiffening, annoying, but bearable because it was one of the conditions of the job, like his false papers and the swift row on the incoming rough tide from the slippery deck of the submarine. He was wearing three thick sweaters, long johns, two pairs of trousers – what did he expect?

He stamped his feet, slapped his arms, shuffled and blew, then moved along the wall of the warehouse – once hearing a rat scurry on the other side of the corrugated iron as he paused. The rain was falling almost vertically since the wind had dropped as he carefully emerged on to the pier again. He studied the terrain like an animal, then ran. His boots began what seemed a hideous noise, his breath roared in his ears as if he were unfit and exhausted, then he was in the shadow of the first low shed – a hundred and fifty yards long, he estimated. The noises of repair and service dinned through the corrugated wall as he pressed his cheek against it. Vibration quivered. He paused only for a moment. He had selected the window he wanted, and moved swiftly. He had declared his presence – a line of bootprints in the mud from warehouse to shed – to any patrol. They moved around the pier frequently, but he expected laxity this late in the night. He had perhaps fifteen minutes.

He moved along the side of the shed. The windows were high up near the sloping edge of the roof, for ventilation more than light. Pricks of light came from most of them. The ladder was at the seaward end of the shed.

He climbed quickly and silently, up into the wind that had changed its mind and sprung back. The handholds were icily wet. He paused at the top, surveyed the area around him. Guards tended to huddle round fires in huts, but he wanted to be certain. Nothing moving. He eased himself on to the roof, and moved in a waddling crouch along its edge. It took him whole minutes to reach the window he had selected, but he did not slip once, holding his feet as he moved them against the bolts that fixed the roof to the walls, resting his heels in the corrugations. His thighs and the backs of his legs ached when he reached his goal. Here, he tested the roof's edge, and the guttering, took firm hold with his now unmittened hands, the cold of the iron a shock that ran in a shudder through his system – then lowered his body over the edge of the roof so that he hung against the window, the weight of clothing and boots sudden and painful in his shoulders and arms.

The tear in the black-out cloth was thin, and long. He shuffled his handhold until he could lean in against the dirty glass, and see –

The submarine being worked on almost directly below him was a bloody mess, there was no doubt about that; only amazement that it had limped back for repairs. Most of the crewmen in the forward section of the hull must have died, or been badly torn up. The bow bulged open like a crusted sore, and the deck-plates had been shuffled like untidy cards. McBride estimated that the sub had lost ten or twelve feet of its bow. *Internal explosion? Torpedo? Mine? Depth charge?*

A big U-boat, and another beyond it, being checked over for plate-wear, hull-strain. Two of the biggest class of German U-boat, men hurrying about them. If each shed contained even one, then there was a pack of ten here – *on Guernsey?* These were submarine pens, but not like La Rochelle, Brest and St Nazaire and the rest of the Normandy and Brittany pens – no concrete, no massive servicing back-up, no – *permanence* – ? It had taken the Germans no more than a couple of days to throw up the corrugated sheds – which could only be for concealment, then.

These boats were either 'milch-cow' refuelling subs, or they were long-trip, ocean-going boats, designed to bite the jugular where it was exposed, far out in the Atlantic – not around the North Channel where the convoys turned for the Mersey and the Clyde. Why here? For God's sake, he told himself sternly, as if lecturing the general staff of the Kriegsmarine, it's like keeping old silver in a pillow-case under the bed. He smiled, shifted to test the weariness of his arms, then continued his surveillance. His hands were beginning to go dead.

The damaged submarine in front of him carried no deck-gun. He could not see a single torpedo-trolley, not even the necessary hoists to lower the torpedoes on board. *They were going out unarmed?* His arms weakened with the shock, he felt as if struck. The mysteriousness of what he had found assailed him like a punch that simply went on happening, almost for a minute. He could find no answer, and his ignorance was like an impotence. *What else, what else?* he prompted himself. *Concentrate.*

At the stern of the submarine – and the one beyond it – he saw the strange, out-of-place pillars, curved and jointed like insect mandibles. The men working at the bow of the undamaged boat were erecting stanchions, and he assumed that the missing bow-section of the other sub had borne a similar, inexplicable mounting.

There was nothing else, nothing he could take in as clearly as before. Fact had been deadened by speculation. He was wasting his time now, it might come back later, just as if he had caught it on film, when he was debriefed. Once the resolve had gone, it was hard to hang on for sufficient time to take in the scene once more, repressing the selectivity of speculation. He wondered whether he could haul himself up with the frozen hands and aching arms.

One thing more – his angle of vision had precluded sight of them before, but now they moved nearer the stern of the damaged sub, as if to inspect the mountings. Two senior officers – one wearing a Wehrmacht greatcoat, the other in naval uniform. His weariness, the aching muscles in his arms, seemed to go away to a great distance. He was a spectator of some adult drama he could not comprehend. There was a familiarity, a common cause between the two senior officers, so unlike the Intelligence proclamations of intense and unceasing rivalry between the Wehrmacht and the Kreigsmarine; all the way up to the General Staff and the Führer. *What in hell were they doing?*

Their conversation went on for minutes, then the two men shook hands, there was much self-congratulation, and, as they walked out of his view, he groaned with the return of awareness to his arms and shoulders. He didn't think he could pull himself back up –

The voice from below him settled the matter.

'You – drop to the ground, at once!'

McBride did not look down, nor did he pretend not to understand German.

October 1980
Thomas Sean McBride parked the mud-stained Audi in the hotel car park, collected his room key and mail from the stiffly-polite clerk, whose words he brushed off as if they came between him and the indulgence of his weary disappointment, then took the lift to his third-floor room with its view across the Moselstrasse to the river and the suburb of Lutzel on the opposite bank.

When he had closed the door behind him, draped his raincoat over a chair, and slipped off his shoes, he poured whisky from an almost empty bottle into a tooth-mug, and stood at the window looking across the darkening river, occasionally shifting his half-seeing gaze to his right, where the Deutsches Eck promontory marked the confluence of the Moselle and the Rhine. His eyes were gritty with a bad night's sleep in the *gasthaus* in Norden, after the evening ferry journey back from the island, and aching from the whole day's driving back to Koblenz. His mind creaked through the grooves of disappointment and frustrated rage the blind Menschler's words had worn.

A barge passed slowly across his vision towards the confluence of the rivers, from his vantage hardly seeming to move. It possessed an apt, facile symbolism. A woman collected washing at its stern – that didn't fit the symbolism, and he smiled, sipped again at the whisky, almost shrugged off his mood. The first street lamps were coming on along the Moselstrasse, and the brake lights of the cars sprang out as red globes as the cars pulled up at traffic signals. Behind him in the unlit room his scattered – now *useless, fatuous* – papers, which he had enjoined the maid not to dust or tidy, and the leaning heaps of reference books subsided into gloom. Even so, his mind could not ignore them; an inward eye focused on them more clearly than his retinae registered the passage of the barge.

He had had it in the palm of his hand –

He'd blown it, crapped out on a blind man. The Woodstein of World War Two had gone down without throwing a punch!

He knew he was easing himself into a better mood – the bitterness was gone from the self-mockery, which might have been an effect of the whisky. Still, a blind man! His innate self-confidence, the blooming ego under the sun of his best-selling status, his greater potential, combined to prevent him from long periods of self-condemnation, self-awareness. He no longer had anything to fear from the less-clever men who eased past him into the grandly titled chairs of study or into the plush administrative grades. Menschler, therefore, was not an interview board of one, turning him down; without enemies, real or presumed, McBride was unable to categorize Menschler with them, and thereby retain an anger towards him. He was the dead, keeping the grave's secrets.

There'd be others –

He turned away from the window, put down his glass on the writing-table, ignored the open notebooks, the last pages of his trace of Menschler through army pension records and the telephone exchange, and fanned out instead the letters he had collected from the desk.

His eye was caught by the smallest notebook, but only momentarily, in which on three neat pages he had summarized his knowledge of Emerald Necklace. Little more than the faintest trace of an old perfume. He picked up the bulkiest letter, feeling through the envelope another, enclosed letter.

Gaps in Wehrmacht records, in the Führer Directives, in the papers of the General Staff. And a tight-lipped silence –

He shrugged off a returning investigative mood, and ripped open the outer envelope, from his university and presumably forwarding the other letter. He was seized – perhaps in compensation for disappointment – with a childish mood, with the eagerness of discovering of a child from a home where mail seldom came.

Excitement became self-mockery until he had carried the letter to the window. An air-mail letter. And he recognized the handwriting? Yes, strong, small, neat. Gilliatt's hand. Peter Gilliatt, who had helped his mother out of Ireland in '41, and got her to America, had written to her in New Jersey, but whose mail had lost the cold trail after his mother had moved them west, to Oregon. Gilliatt must be an old man by now –

McBride savoured not opening the letter, the little childish excitement warm as the drink in his stomach. An old, familiar world was coming back with that handwriting, the red-blue edging of the envelope. The handwriting retained the secret of Gilliatt's age. He'd found out that McBride was in Portland, and written to the faculty – McBride nodded in self-compliment. *Gates of Hell* – Gilliatt had read it. Had he written about that? After all, his mother had been dead for nearly four years, and he'd never even met Gilliatt –

He'd entertained the fantasy, when the letters used to come to Jersey and his mother never seemed to tire of talking about Gilliatt, that the Englishman was his real father, despite the disparity of name. At first, the fantasy possessed romance – until his accidental consulation of a dictionary for the meaning of the word *bastard* in a book he was reading under the bedclothes with a torch. Then the fantasy had become shameful and secret, and he'd gone back to believing in the fact of Michael McBride, dead and buried in Ireland.

A long preamble, compliments on *Gates of Hell,* references to Michael, an invitation to visit him – and, certain as signposts, the change of tone. The hushed, secretive tone, and the sudden temptation to look over his shoulder communicated to the reader. The wrist adopting a nervous twitch as if to turn the letter's contents away from eyes that might be watching behind the double-glazing.

My visitor told me you were in Europe, but not where, hence my writing to you at your university. He seemed inordinately interested in your current field of study, and to smile as if he possessed prior information. He suggested – in a very oblique manner – that your work might have a bearing on the events of 1940 in which your father and I were together involved. I should welcome an opportunity of talking to you on this subject – your mother knew little, and I have no doubt would have told

29

you nothing. I, too, have felt bound by certain security restrictions. Until now. I have been bluntly warned not to help you, without being told why. I am irritated by the presumption of it all!

Therefore, if this reaches you, and you have the time, come to me and we shall go over some very old times together. I doubt you have ever known what happened to your father, and perhaps it is time you did

It was as bald and provoking as the trailer to a mystery film. McBride was amused, intrigued and disturbed in a complex moment of emotion. Instinctively, as soon as he had read the signature he moved away from the window and laid the letter carefully on the writing-table. Gilliatt had deliberately constructed his story with a novelist's sense of having to grab his reader. Half a dozen mysteries were hinted at, and strangers moved at the edges of the page, concealed in shadow. McBride felt himself enmeshed, as it was intended he should be.

The room darkened as he revolved the last paragraphs in his mind, and sipped the last of the drink. When the telephone rang, it startled him out of his reverie, but with the shock of cold water, or a threat. He shrugged, smiling away the insidious effect of the letter.

'McBride.'

The voice was distant, official, clipped.

'Herr Professor Thomas McBride?'

'Yes, who is that?'

'The Embassy of the Deutsches Democratisches Republik.' McBride felt an irrational chill, an aftermath of his day-dreaming, then recollected his hoped-for outcome of the call. Yet now he was impatient *not* to go to East Berlin, just as over the past weeks he had pestered the DDR authorities for a 'scholar's visa' for the chance to inspect archives on the other side of the wall. He tried to shake off Gilliatt's unspecified claims on his time.

'Yes?'

'Your permission to visit Berlin to consult certain historical records has been granted, Herr Professor.' A pause into which McBride should have dropped his gratitude like a silver collection.

'Thank you, but I'm afraid I'm very busy right now – '

'Herr Professor, the visa and the other papers are valid only for a few days. Besides, the importance of the papers you wish to see – '

'Yes, I see – '

'You wish to refuse this excellent, unique opportunity, Herr McBride?' There was academic demotion in the mode of address. 'Herr Professor Goessler of the University, our leading expert on these documents returned to the Democratisches Republik by our Soviet friends – and one of our leading authorities on the Fascist period – ' A slight pause, as if the sentence had escaped him in its own complexity, then: 'He has agreed to place himself at your disposal – ' It was not an inducement; rather, quiet outrage.

'I see – ' Gilliatt's letter was indecipherable on the table in the darkness of the room. *Smaragdenhalskette.* Who could tell?

Why in hell should Menschler get the last laugh? It was as if the writing on the pages of the letter were in secret ink, and the warmth applied to its revelation had now gone, and the symbols were disappearing once more. He shrugged.

'Sure – and thanks. Thanks. I'll drive up to Bonn tomorrow and collect the papers.'

'Good. But that is not necessary – they have been put in the post to you today. You may book a flight for tomorrow afternoon. Good hunting, Herr Professor.'

The official broke the connection. McBride was left with the return of an older and more powerful scent than the fate of a father he had never known. He did not for one moment consider why the East German embassy should be concerned with his unimportant documents at eight in the evening.

Chapter Two

ARRIVALS

November 1940
Don't freeze, don't freeze –

Awareness running through his body, concentrating for split-seconds in the soles of his feet, his hands, the centre of his back where the rifle or machine-pistol would be aimed, the back of his head. The moment of silence after the soldier had given his order, and McBride listened for the first step back, the adjustment the German would make to let him drop at a safe distance. No scuffle of boots –

Drop!

His hands seemed to come unstuck from the icy guttering very, very slowly, and his body drop through the air much too unaffected by gravity – he was floating, it wouldn't work – and his body could see the gun, the white upturned face backing away – then his boots hit the soldier a glancing blow, his fall was broken, he struck the concrete heavily, winded, rolled over, tried to get up and knew he was moving as awkwardly as if his legs were under water, then saw the German down on one knee, trying even more slowly to bring the machine-pistol to bear. He'd been caught by McBride's lack of delay, but he was recovering. McBride's arm and shoulder hurt from impact with the ground as he thrust up into a crouch, and hurled himself against the German, felt the rough serge of the field-grey against his cheek, the cold metal of collar-tabs, the edge of the helmet against his head – heaved rather than cannoned against the soldier, knocking him backwards. He heard the explosion of breath, the sharp clatter of the machine-pistol, as he rolled over the German, raised his upper torso and looked down into the young, scared face, its mouth opening much too slowly to yell. McBride pulled at the helmet strap, and jerked the head back. The mouth contorted, remained silent except for a gurgle, then McBride struck the German with his fist, below the ear. The head lolled when he let it free.

Immediately, he climbed to his feet, aware of the shadows alongside the shed, sensing the rain-blown night, aware of the silence beyond the muffled noises from inside. Then he dragged the unconscious – possibly dead – soldier up against the corrugated wall and left him, moving away immediately towards the pier-end of the shed. When he reached it, he paused. There was another hour and a half before the shifts changed, and he could not wait. The German would be unaccounted for inside five minutes.

He was surprised at the manner in which his mind sought the amusing, the unexpected, solution, even as he looked at his watch and some more urgent part of the organism collected swiftly the few sensory impressions along the pier. A radio, muffled hammering, the spit of welding equipment, the patter of the sleet against the wall of the shed. He turned round with deliberate calm, and walked back to the unconscious German.

He bent over him. There was breathing, tired and quiet. He lifted the head like an easily bruised fruit, and removed the helmet. Then he tugged the German out of his greatcoat, the back of which was sodden, and removed his boots. He removed his own donkey-jacket and boots, became in seconds a German soldier. He buttoned the greatcoat right to the throat, picked up the machine-pistol, and returned to the pier. He paused only for a moment, as if patting mental pockets for required and necessary equipment, then began walking with a tired, bored shuffle towards the warehouse and the barrier.

And with each step the nerves increased, as he knew they would however much he attempted to disguise them in confidence, in indifference. He was aware of his heart-rate increasing, of his body-temperature rising; employed deep-breathing to calm himself, gripped more tightly the stubby barrel of the machine-pistol.

He was past the warehouse, and the barrier at the end of the pier was the only thing in his vision, when someone spoke in German, and he knew the voice was addressing him. The man he appeared to be. But he caught the note of uncertainty, too, just as clearly as he heard the footsteps coming from the side of the warehouse, closing on him.

'Friedrich, where the devil have you been? Friedrich – ?'

The puzzled tone hung on the air like frost. McBride was a hundred yards or so from the barrier, and a man he could not turn to see was coming from behind him. Each footstep separated in time, almost to the rhythm of the dance-music he could hear from a radio. He half-turned, and slipped, sliding on to his back, his greatcoat billowing like a skirt. The soldier behind him burst into laughter.

'Friedrich, you're pissed, you bastard! Where is it, where's the drink, you selfish little – ?'

McBride rolled on to his side, propped on one elbow, the machine-pistol pointing up into the German's face.

'If I kill you, I'll attract their attention, I know that. It just won't do you much good, old friend,' he observed in German. *Drink, drink* –

It was coming to him. The German's mouth kept slowly popping open and closed, then he began sucking his cheeks to wet his dry throat.

'What's your name?' Puzzlement almost approaching the catatonic. 'Just tell me your name – it might save your life.'

'Willi – Willi Frick.'

'Well done, Willi.' McBride stood up, leaned against the German with a smile, and pressed against the nerve below his ear, just behind the chinstrap. Willi slid against him, gently declining. McBride pulled the rum flask from his pocket, and spilled liquor into Willi's mouth, down his chin and on to his coat. He let Willi lean unconsciously against him as he checked his own papers again – Friedrich Bruckner, and his rank, unit and number.

'Come on, Willi, you're going on a charge, and me with you.'

He slipped Willi's right arm round his neck, hefted him upright, his own arm round Willi's waist, and walked him towards the barrier, making an exaggeratedly slow approach in the shadow of the warehouse, stepping out into the light only at the last minute – but by that time a Kreigsmarine Leutnant was already calling him.

'Soldier, what the devil are you doing? You, there!'

McBride snapped to attention, and Willi began to slide to the ground – McBride grabbed him, straightened the body. Someone laughed behind the officer, who seemed suddenly to consider it all as simply another scheme to make him appear foolish. His face contracted as if he had sucked a lemon and he marched across to McBride, who tried to adopt peasant stupidity as his habitual expression.

'What's going on – ' Nose wrinkling, suspicion gleaming in his eye. 'This man's *drunk*!'

'Sir – '

'No excuses – breathe on me, you dummy!'

McBride exhaled. The Leutnant shook his head in obvious disappointment. The guards behind him had formed a knot of eager spectators – one or two of them trying to make McBride smile or laugh by mimed antics and expressions. They were fifteen yards away – too far to hear his replies, his claims to identity. He kept a rigid face as the officer continued.

'Where did you find him?'

'Heard someone singing behind one of the warehouses, sir!' he snapped out.

'Him?' The Leutnant was disgusted. McBride nodded. 'And now he's passed out – you weren't going to report this, were you?' Again the gleam of realization and superior understanding. McBride looked guilty. 'Trying to sneak him back to his billet, weren't you?' McBride swallowed, nodded. 'What's your name?'

McBride barked out his assumed identity.

'Him?'

'Frick, sir.'

The Leutnant made a note (with a gold-encased pencil) in a little notebook contained in what might have been a slim cigarette-case. He put them away with a quiet triumph.

'Both of you – report to me in the morning. Now, get that disgusting clown out of my *sight*!'

'Sir.'

McBride grabbed Willi's body more securely, kept his head down as he half-pulled him past the barrier, to the raucous laughter – soon quietened by the Leutnant – of the rest of the guards. He could hear them discussing the likely charges with the Kreigsmarine officer as he moved beyond the cold splash of the light above the barrier and the guard-hut. He heaved and pulled at the unconsciously-resisting Willi, a chill bath of perspiration covering his body from the effort and the bluff. He couldn't control his body's relief, and it irritated him. Eventually, he was in the shadows of a seaman's church opposite the Albert Pier, and he thankfully dropped Willi into the shadows by the wrought-iron gate. He looked up. A chill, unwelcoming little church, the rain like a shiny skin on something gone cold. He shivered, and moved swiftly away, the machine-pistol over his shoulder, the sweat drying on his forehead at the line of the helmet and under his arms. He wasn't quite ready to smile. He hurried up the Quay to the North Esplanade, out of the centre of the town.

October 1980
McBride wondered whether it was courtesy on the part of the attaché who met him at Tempelhof, or the habit of security, that the man acquired his papers and ushered him through Customs and passport control in the terminal building. McBride had flown in on a Trident to Tempelhof, West Berlin's principal airport. He wondered briefly why the Cultural Exchange Committee of the Democratic Republic had bothered to send an escort to the airport, and was more surprised at the deference with which he was treated, and the obvious and studied compliments on his book, *Gates of Hell* produced like mottoes from Christmas crackers by Herr Lobke. The young man seemed anxious to please, yet almost too aware to be the pleasant, rather naïve, person he exuded in McBride's direction.

'Professor Doktor Goessler is, I know, very anxious to meet you, to offer his help – it is a remarkable compliment – ' McBride almost sensed the unspoken addition of *to someone like you*, but opted to accept the enthusiasm, the desire to be merely helpful.

Outside the terminal building, a black Lada saloon drew alongside them almost in the instant that Lobke raised his arm. There was even a uniformed chauffeur – one or two arriving passengers glanced at the little tableau, then disregarded it as if dissatisfied with the size or make of the car. McBride slid across the bench seat at the back, and Lobke climbed in beside him. The chauffeur pulled the sun-visor down, and accelerated away from the terminal doors.

They picked up the Tempelhofer Damm, pointing north like an arrow at the city. Lobke seemed impressed and distracted from him by the passage of the mumerous Mercedes saloons, the Porsches and Datsun sports cars. McBride indulged the immediate excitement of the urban autobahn, the tall buildings, the neon silent but endlessly boastful. The advertisement of the *wirtschaftwunder*, a slick, affluent stranger in a peasant economy. West Berlin, he sensed immediately, postured like a glamorous, bejewelled model against the temporary *chic* of a ghetto or a slum. The city shouted at him, demanded he accept its image as reality.

They crossed the Spree on a high arch of pale concrete, to the Friedrichstrasse. McBride had been to Berlin before, researching *Gates of Hell*, but then the city had evidenced to his tunnel-vision the remnants of its battering in 1945, its German-ness, its foundation of ash rather than its post-war substance. Now, he had no preconceptions – he was there to study documents, follow an old, cold trail, and the city leapt upon his senses.

There was a short delay at Checkpoint Charlie, on the American side. The guards seemed uninterested, in the late afternoon sunshine, in McBride as an American, but they checked Lobke's papers thoroughly, even though he had obviously crossed from East to West earlier in the day. On the East German side, the barrier was up almost immediately, and there was a smart salute for the car from the guards. The grey breeze-blocking of the Wall was almost obscured from the consciousness by the ceremony, the swiftness, of their arrival in East Berlin. Except that the Wall was suddenly high enough to cast a long shadow, out of which only after a few seconds did the car emerge into the slanting sunshine of the Friedrichstrasse again.

One of the Vopos on the checkpoint telephoned the arrival of McBride and Lobke less than a minute after their crossing.

McBride, ringing from Koblenz, had booked a room at the Hotel Spree, an ugly block of pale concrete on the Rathaustrasse near the river and the Marx-Engels Platz.

The porter seemed entirely respectful, the desk staff willing and welcoming. The hotel foyer was modern – polished dark wood, greenery and thick carpet, a coffee shop open-planned to one side. He could have been in any modern four-star hotel in the world.

Lobke left him in the foyer, shaking his hand with a formal warmth, and promising that Professor Doktor Goessler would be certain to contact him. Lobke watched him get into the lift behind the porter carrying his bag, waiting until the door sighed shut, then placed his ID on the desk in front of the clerk.

'Where's the secure phone?' he said. The clerk seemed unsurprised, nodding to a row of four plastic globes sprouting from the wall alongside the coffee-shop. 'Second from the left,' he said.

Lobke crossed the foyer, watched by a woman in a beige coat and boots who was sitting in the foyer in order to be noticed. Lobke thought he recognized her from the television-news programmes. Lobke didn't like the Hotel Spree and its spurious Westernism. He disliked it because it was part of a façade – behind it the grimy dullness of the DDR waited to displace fantasy. To jump out and remind the dreamer that it was a joke, nothing more substantial. On the contrary, he liked West Berlin, liked any messenger-jobs to the Federal Republic, or the rest of Europe. The shiny toys were real there.

Meanwhile the stupid cow in her Italian boots and West German coat waited for her dreary friends from East German TV or the pretend-glossy magazines. He dialled headquarters. Asked for Goessler after identifying himself.

'Chief?'

"Rudi, how did it go?"

'He's booked in. Seems to be enjoying himself – I think he'll go all the way with you, Chief.'

'Rudi, what TV stations are you watching these days?'

Lobke laughed. 'Ours, naturally.'

'OK – well done. I think I shall call Herr Professor McBride at once, and introduce myself.'

'Goodbye, *Professor* – '

Lobke put down the telephone, winked coarsely at the

woman in the beige coat who turned her head away immediately, and then he went out of the revolving doors into the evening sunshine, to walk along the Rathaustrasse to Marx-Engels and the Unter den Linden. He liked to look at the Brandenburger Tor with the low sun coming through its columns. It seemed to hold out a vague promise, made to him personally.

McBride unpacked methodically as soon as the porter left, with the tip in dollars that he was not, by law, allowed to receive at all. He always staked his claim to possession of any temporary home by spreading his things around – the toiletries on the bathroom shelf especially helped to establish his claim. While he was still putting socks and pants into a drawer, the telephone rang.

'McBride.'

'Ah – a call from Professor Goessler of the University for you, Herr McBride.'

'Put him through, please.'

McBride straightened at the telephone, as if before a superior. The window of his room looked over the shop roofs on the Rathaustrasse, towards the cathedral. He was pleased it did not face in the opposite direction, where he would have seen, beyond St Hedwig's, the Wall.

'Professor McBride?' The voice of a jolly man – an image he would not have connected with an East German Marxist historian. He shook his head at his own misconceptions.

'Professor Goessler, good of you to call me, sir.'

'The pleasure is mine. Please, you are comfortable at the Hotel Spree – it is suitable?'

'Sure, fine, Professor.'

'Good, good – if you had given us time, I would have booked your room for you. However, you have not made a mistake with the Spree. Tell me, my friend, are we to get right down to business, as you would say?'

'I'm in your hands, Professor. I haven't changed my ideas since I wrote you – '

'And you expect to find what you are looking for here in Berlin, in our archives?'

'What do you think my chances are, Professor? You've been through all that stuff the Russians gave back in the sixties and seventies.'

'My friend, I have only scratched the surface, I assure you!'

McBride felt a thin, needle-like sense of satisfaction that Goessler seemed ignorant – and a disappointment at the work in front of him. Needles in haystacks.

'I see – but you'll give me freedom of access?'

'*Naturlich* – oh, I'm sorry. No, but you speak German, of course. My friend, perhaps we can have dinner together this evening?'

McBride looked at his watch. Six, almost.

'Sure. Here any good, Professor?'

'A rather bland cuisine, but it will not hurt us. Yes – shall we say eight?'

'Sure. Ring my room when you arrive, Professor, and I'll meet you in the bar.'

'Excellent. Goodbye.'

McBride put down the telephone, and crossed thoughtfully to the window, recognizing the process of revising prejudices going on inside him. How could he complain at the treatment? He stared at the cathedral, blackening in the shadows and the low streaming sun.

He suddenly received a curious image of himself crawling over the face of that cathedral, checking each of the figures and gargoyles carved on it, looking for a piece of paper with its secret message stuffed up one stone nostril of one of the hundreds of stone saints and devils. He laughed. If *Smaragdenhalskette* had dropped a couple of its stones in East Berlin, then he would find them.

November 1940

McBride hunched down between two rocks, jammed in as if afraid he might lose some precarious hold. The greatcoat – which he had wanted to abandon half a dozen times – now kept out the searching wind that moaned off the sea, moaned against the low cliffs of the cove. The tide had just turned, and the sea – because the wind was from the north and against the tide – was choppier than when he had rowed in. It would be harder for him to pick out the submarine when it surfaced bow-on to the cove. The deflated carlin float was hidden only yards from him.

He'd returned the way he had come, avoiding the guardposts since, despite his uniform, he had no movement order or excused-duty chit. It had taken him almost three hours. He looked at his watch again, then took up the signal-lamp. If the submarine was out there, he wouldn't know it until it surfaced. He was early, and all he could do was to signal periodically and hope they were using the periscope.

He flashed the morse-signal, *M,* put down the lamp, and listened. He'd heard a couple of cars and a truck pass along the road above him, but nothing had stopped. Yet he knew that by now they must be searching for him – someone would have found either Willi or Friedrich or both of them long before, and they would have been able to describe him and what he'd been doing when Friedrich surprised him. And they'd want to finish him off, deducing that he'd be taken off by submarine before light. And from one of the narrow, sheltered coves at the northern tip of the island, near l'Ancresse Bay.

He listened. Impatient, he picked up the signal-lamp again, hesitated more out of pride than caution, then flashed his morse *dash-dash* identification out to sea. The rain had stopped, but the wind was colder now, angering the sea as if to provide another barrier to his escape. He hugged the lamp to his chest while despising its use as a comforter.

Then, almost involuntarily, he flashed out the ident once more, gripped by a panic he could not laugh at or depress. He put back his head, and breathed as deeply as he could, inhaling and exhaling regularly for a minute or more. When he looked at the choppy, threatening, empty sea again, he could hear the sound of engines; identified them almost at once, and waited until the German S-boat rounded the low headland, its searchlight sweeping the tossed surface of the water, then – more in hope than expectation – flickering and dancing along the cliff-face, off the huddled groups of rocks. The tide on which he had come in had removed all traces of his arrival.

The S-boat – he watched it in helpless fascination – moved inshore and he could just make out the toy-like figures in caps and duffle-coats behind the coaming, the sailors at the bow operating the searchlight, or waiting armed with rifles and machine-guns.

He thought he detected the sounds of vehicles from the cliff-top even as the searchlight bounced away above his head, but the noise of the S-boat's twin diesels boomed off the cliffs, magnified and drowning any other noise. He felt his body-temperature drop, the wet rocks press on him. Then the searchlight moved on, sweeping back out to sea. The S-boat moved away, and in less than another minute had rounded the opposite headland, and its engine-noise dropped away.

Then he heard the shouted orders from above him. He *had* heard a truck stopping. He fumbled with the signal-lamp, adding to its shielding with his cupped hand as he flashed his signal on and off, again and again. The S-boat would be back, or another might be following, and in minutes – when the troops sent to search the cove had descended the cliff-path – he would be unable to signal.

'Come on, come on – for Christ's sake, come on,' he muttered over and over like an incantation, flashing the ident out to the rough, empty sea, listening to the banging of the truck's tailboard, the scuffling of boots and the clink of metal which some freak of the wind brought to him clearly. He might even hear them click on their torches.

'Come on, come on, come on – '

October 1980
McBride wondered whether the *crêpes suzettes* after the richly sauced venison was for his benefit, or whether Professor Goessler was indulging himself in the surroundings of the Hotel Spree's dining-room and its cuisine. McBride felt full, and impatient. Goessler – florid, large, beaming, grey hair swept back into wings at the peripheries of a bald pink dome, bulbous nose and full lips – was someone who spoke little while he ate, except for pleasantries concerning the meal. Who would settle the bill had not been decided, but McBride – with some quiet amusement – considered it was more likely to be American Express than the University Bursary.

When Goessler had finished his *crêpes*, he sat back, dabbed his mouth with his napkin in a tidy little gesture that would have suited a smaller head and more delicate hand, and beamed once more on the American.

'Not for your goodwill, you understand,' Goessler said with unexpected perception. 'This is what they serve here every night, not just when Americans are resident.'

McBride laughed, put down his fork. The *crêpes* were beginning to pall on him, possessing a certain unmistakeable Germanic heaviness, richness.

'Coffee?' Goessler nodded, and McBride summoned the waiter. 'Schnapps?'

'Bring me an Asbach brandy,' Goessler told the waiter without replying to McBride, as if he had been irritated. There was also a barely masked *casualness* of authority, as if it had been long-accustomed, about the way he addressed the waiter. 'And you, my friend?'

'I'll pass – just coffee.'

'Bring a pot, and leave it,' Goessler instructed, and the waiter nodded. 'Large cups,' Goessler called after him. He beamed on McBride, as if reassuming a role. 'Now, of course, you wish to talk. Go ahead.'

Permission to speak? McBride was puzzled by Goessler, and resolved the German academic must be interested in his work. Perhaps too interested – then again Goessler, interrupting him as he was about to speak, said: 'Do not worry, my friend, I am not concerned to steal your work – ' Again the broad smile, and the mouth almost overfilled with dentures. 'No, I can imagine what you must think of me. Softening you up, mm?' He indicated the plates before them, looked with passing regret at the remains of McBride's *crêpes*. 'No, I am at present at work on more *dialectical* material – the official history of the German Communist Party, from the beginnings. I don't think any work of yours is likely to throw up new material for me, eh?' He put back his head, laughed, then smoothed the wings of grey hair flat against his head. 'No, no, not that I would not perhaps change places with you – ' He leaned forward confidentially. 'To be truthful, much of *my* research is extremely dull. I do not suppose yours is, mm? What is it – what invasion plans are you wishing to discover?'

'Illuminate, you mean? Each one of the *Fallen*, every

invasion up to and including *Barbarossa*.' McBride
returned the unblinking stare, the slightly fixed smile
Then Goessler nodded, as if releasing him from a
hypnotic control.

'Very well, but I warn you, the bones have been well
picked by the Soviet Historical Academy.'

'But for their purposes, not mine.'

'Ah, true – they weren't writing for the American mass
market.' Goessler laughed disarmingly, and McBride felt i
impossible to be nettled by the implied slight. 'Anything i
particular, my friend?'

McBride had weighed the moment in advance, whil
showering. He could get nowhere without Goessler
Goessler might know *people*, as well as documents. He ha
decided to tell him.

'A little-known invasion plan without a *Fall* designatio
– called *Smaragdenhalskette*?' He turned the remark to
question on the last word. Goessler crinkled his shin
forehead, then shook his head. The grey wings of ha
loosened their grip on the sides of his head. He brushe
them back again.

'The name means nothing to me – but, we can put som
of my postgraduate students to work with you, Professor
to save you time.' He clapped his hands together, possibl
at the arrival of the coffee and brandy. 'Yes – we shall d
that for you, certainly. Your own little research team – an
we will see what turns up, mm?'

David Guthrie sat in one of the beige PVC chairs with
tubular steel frame common to many current affair
programmes. Opposite him sat a renownedly belligeren
interviewer, a low glass table between them. Guthri
always insisted on this staged informality when he wa
interviewed on television, rather than become a talkin
head and trunk behind a desk. He was never pedagogic i
his manner, eschewing all suggestion of lecturing o
hectoring that a formal setting might convey.

Red light – a camera moving in on him, the interviewe
aware of the director shouting in his earphone and the link
man's voice across the studio. Guthrie felt the slightes
pluck of tension, adrenalin sidled through him. He smile

in the general direction of the interviewer, half-profile to the oncoming camera. Behind the cameras, beyond the meagre area of carpet, the bareness of the studio suddenly impressed itself upon him – he kept the smile, but deepened it as if prior to serious thought. His little circle of bright light, himself spotlit – and the rest of it nothing more than a façade. Was he pretending that the Leeds Castle conference was a substance, a reality? He made almost as if to protest at this pushing, uncomfortable prevision.

'Secretary of State, we've heard on the news tonight of a further spate of fire-bombs in Belfast, of two bombs being defused in Birmingham, and an explosion in Glasgow. What do you say to those people who tonight are worrying for their safety?'

Guthrie did not clear his throat, but leaned slightly forward, talking to the interviewer but at points of emphasis turning to the camera.

'I wish there was better news – I can only tell you that the Government, in co-operation with the police, the Special Branch and the security forces in Ulster, is committed to hunting down and removing into custody the people guilty of these hideous crimes – ' His eyes glittered, and the interviewer, who knew Guthrie as well as anyone in television, suffered the familiar moment of doubt as Guthrie seemed to shift into a higher gear of response, of emotion. He could not decide – ever – whether it was a political or a human response. 'I *saw* the film of those people being carried out of the wreckage of that super-market in Belfast – just as your viewers did. We want this business *finished.*'

'But, Mr Guthrie, many people may well consider you to be one of those guilty men. Is it not your conference on Northern Ireland that has directly led to these latest attacks – here and in Ulster?' The interviewer disturbed his papers, as if checking his own question.

'I would understand that, except that I'm sure that the people of this country – of the United Kingdom – understand by now that the conference which is scheduled to begin next week *is* the answer to the bombings, the killings and the violence. It is not the cause – ' He smiled at the camera soberly, with *gravitas*. 'All the parties except the

IRA *want* the conference to succeed. They are frightened – showing their fear openly. What we must not do is to lose resolution. We can win – we will win – '

'Mr Guthrie, you say that we can win. Have the Provisional wing of Sinn Fein or the Reverend Ian Paisley agreed to attend the conference?' Bullying the answer out of him.

'As to Sinn Fein – official Sinn Fein will attend. I have the strongest private assurances, also, that no prominent body of opinion on the Protestant side will be absent – ' Smile, suggesting discretion rather than evasion. 'The bombers, as we might expect, will not be there. They do not represent *anybody* – this conference will be attended by every party which seeks a peaceful solution. And every *representative* party in the province wants peace.'

'Now, if we can move on to the area, Minister, of the agenda of the conference – ' Guthrie nodded, sitting back in his chair. 'Are we to understand that attendance at the conference by all responsible parties implies an agreement with your power-sharing proposals in Northern Ireland?'

Guthrie paused, weighing the question. 'I won't prejudice – or pre-judge – the outcome of the conference by outlining demands or even suggestions. The kind of political power-sharing, the kind of government in Ulster is what the conference has to decide.'

'Just one moment, Minister – ' The interviewer touched his earphone, listened, and his face became grave, pressing into its most belligerent lines. He nodded, then said bluntly: 'We've just received news of an explosion in a restaurant off the Charing Cross road – there may be as many as thirty dead and wounded.'

Guthrie looked appalled, as if some direct and violent attack had been made upon him. The studio appeared no longer bare; more it was insulated, safe.

'We'll go to the newsroom for more details – ' the interviewer added, almost unnecessarily. Guthrie appeared unable to speak.

Not one arrest – not a single arrest. People would be frightened, would contemplate drawing back. He knew he was poised upon a critical moment, yet he was unable to speak, to reassure, to offer solutions. His conference, his career, lay with the bodies and the broken glass and the walls stained and scorched. The Provos had brought their war to him, and they could yet win. The red light winked off on his camera, and he rubbed his face as if trying to remould flesh grown suddenly loose, shapeless.

November 1940
He had perhaps two minutes in which to get the carlin float down to the waves, inflate it, and begin rowing out to sea – to nothing and no rendezvous. The sub must have moved offshore, dived deeper, when they picked up the S-boat on asdic. Another truck moved along the cliff-top, stopped, and he could hear the soldiers being disgorged. What he had seen he was not to be allowed to report.

What had he seen, then?

Get on, get on – There was no time to debate the significance of the sheds and what they concealed. He was simply a camera, film waiting to be developed by an expert.

He could not hope to mingle with the searching patrols when they reached the beach, no chance that they would not find the deflated carlin float hidden in the rocks. Yet as soon as he moved, even on that dark beach, he would be spotted. Time was to be measured in strokes of a paddle, and the range of a German rifle.

He flicked the ident twice, then sent the emergency distress code. His head wavered between the cliff-top – crunch of boots on the loose gravel of the cliff-path – and the empty sea. Then he moved, crouching his way to the float, hoisted it on his shoulder, and began running, labouredly and reluctantly, down the beach towards the water. Even the wind resisted his efforts, it seemed, and his feet began to sink into the newly uncovered sand, slowing him. All the time, he listened behind him and looked ahead, waiting.

They must have seen him, must have –

He splashed through the shallows, flung down the float, knelt by it in the bubbling white foam, and released the stop on the compressed-air canister. The air roared, and the yellow float bucked out of his grip, writhing as it inflated automatically, growing like a nearing target.

Shouts?

He looked out to sea – black shape against the darkest grey? No.

He experienced a moment of paralysis close to panic, until the first hopeful shots from the cliff-path could be heard above the noise of the waves and the wind, and he was startled into looking back. He could see torch-light wobbling and hurrying down the side of the cliff, see the headlights of the trucks as they backed and turned seaward to illuminate him. Torches flashed uselessly out to sea. He stumbled through the surf, cursing himself and tugging off the restraining, soaked German greatcoat. The wind cut through him as he let it go and clambered into the float which seemed to want to rush back towards the shore, then tumble away from him out into the cove. He unhooked the paddle, began pushing at the water, desperately over-coming the onrush of the water, waiting in a space full of shouting and gunfire, then feeling the retreating tide grip his float more severely, lifting him out to sea. He paddled furiously as soon as its grip lessened, fighting the next incoming wave – water splashed into his face, froze his hands almost at once, drenched his body through the three sweaters. He yelled, struck, yelled, struck – driving the bobbing, wild float into deeper water.

Bullets plucked at the water to left and right – one cried closer than the wind, and he instinctively ducked. Nothing, nothing out to sea. The signal-lamp had gone, with the greatcoat or with the water slopping in and out of the float. The wind palpably restrained him.

Radio – there must be a radio in one of the trucks in touch with the S-boat, to bring it back to pick him up.

He looked back, fleetingly, as if ducking from the blow of the next wave and the slosh of stinging, icy water the wind whipped off its crest – saw the figures on the shore-line, in the stance of riflemen.

It would take one bullet. He ducked into his next stroke, renewing the frenzy of his activity, his vision confined to the bottom of the float, which was gradually filling, and to the next wave. Hearing above the wind the buzz of bullets, the shouted orders now far behind him, and with no sense of the futility of his escape –

He looked up.

Black shape, bow-on. A submarine surfacing, blowing its tanks, the conning-tower running with water, decks awash – perhaps five hundred yards from him. Increased firing, but he was suddenly invulnerable. He struck madly with the flat paddle, heaving the float through the waves, his arms and shoulders protesting and his hands dead and fixed vice-like by the cold to the paddle.

He was up to his waist in water suddenly, having heard nothing of the bullet's passage through the float, with no sense of impact or deflation. But the carlin float ducked almost shamefully beneath the next big wave, and the paddle remained too deep in the water to make its next stroke. He unclenched his hands, and was at once at the mercy of the waves, flung under then up as he struggled, then under again. The sweaters and his stolen jackboots seemed impossibly heavy – he struggled out of the boots, swallowing water, coughing, let the boots drop away through the water, tried to pull off one of the sweaters, but could not tread water to do so.

He looked ahead – the submarine was still five hundred yards away, but he could see the dinghy they'd launched, and began to swim very slowly, furiously, towards it.

He was in the water for a long time, aware of the recurring drag of the tide taking him out, but seeming always weaker than the water that heaved over his head with each incoming wave. He drove forward with heavy arms, legs kicking feebly, the weight of his clothes increasing; dead-weight. He was not certain, but there seemed to be short black intervals between successive strokes, between the times he lifted his head to try to spot the dinghy – a view through a lens-shutter, alternating, the black moments elongating, swallowing reason.

They dragged him in, unceremoniously, head-first so that his face was plunged into the slopping water in the bottom of the dinghy. Two men in oilskins immediately began to pull back towards the submarine, and a third pulled him into a sitting position. He was grinned at in the darkness.

'All right, sir?'

He nodded, retched but brought none of the swallowed water up, then nodded again with more affirmation.

'That S-boat – ' he began hoarsely.

'Skipper's watching out for it, sir, don't worry.'

And McBride simply nodded, and retreated a little into his sense of relief until the dinghy banged against the hull of the submarine, and hands took hold of its ropes, and the Petty Officer in the dinghy handled him like a child being lifted up to see some passing sight above a crowd of heads. Other men in oilskins – the smell of them was omnipresent – assisted him along the swaying, unsteady, awash after-deck towards the conning-tower.

'Ditch that dinghy! Our friend's back,' he heard from close to him. Two young faces under caps, one of which nodded to him, and round the headland he had a momentary glimpse of the reappearance of the S-boat, searchlight trained ahead of the craft to pick them up.

'Shake it up down there!' someone barked. McBride was bundled down the conning-tower ladder, stumbling and weak. 'Clear the bridge!' he heard the same voice call above him. Seaboots thumped over his head, and then his rescuers dropped one by one into the confined space. He was aware of faces watching him intently, then the captain closed the hatch, and dropped at his side. The klaxon sounded. 'Dive, dive, dive!'

After someone had thrown a blanket over his shoulders, no one took any more notice of him. His rescuers disappeared, and each man but himself seemed to have a task that precluded all other activity or sensation.

'HE at Green Nine-Oh, increasing, sir,' the asdic operator called.

'Starboard thirty, steer Three-Two-Oh – full ahead together.'

'Three-Two-Oh, full ahead together, sir,' the coxswain answered. Then there was a sudden strained silence, punctuated only by the pinging of the asdic as the S-boat closed on their position. McBride was suddenly entirely apart from the men in the control room – the cause of their danger. McBride glanced from face to face – the captain alert beside him near the periscope column, the first officer at the diving panel, the two men at the hydroplane controls, and the coxwain the wheel

McBride heard the throb of the S-boat's screws, beating

on the thin hull of the submarine like drumbeats or someone forcing entry. Eyes sought the hull above them, and the silence intensified as the screws faded.

'HE fading, sir, and now bearing Green One-One-Oh.'

Something scraped on the hull, as if sliding past it.

'Christ – ' someone breathed.

'Not yet, I hope,' the captain murmured. 'Hold tight, Commander,' he added, as if aware of McBride for the first time. McBride clutched himself to the periscope housing, feeling slightly ridiculous, very weak, and dizzy with tension. He was shivering with cold. Then the muffled explosion beneath them and behind, the lurch through the length of the submarine, the flicker-douse-flicker back of the lights, water running from a slight leak, and the sense of people picking themselves out of a ruin and shaking themselves like wet hounds. Everyone grinning as the second depth-charge roared like a breath some distance away.

'Take her down, number one – to the bottom.'

The first officer looked away from the diving panel. 'It's risky, sir.'

The young-faced lt commander replied: 'We'll sit this one out. Jerry will be buzzing around up there like a blue-arsed fly. He's only got small depth-charges, but even they could make a hole in our nice submarine – ' He grinned. 'If we sit still, he'll get cheesed off.'

'Sir.'

McBride felt the submarine settle gently on the bottom a moment later. A slight list to port. Silence. The pinging from the asdic seemed a long way away. The water had dribbled almost to a stop from the strain-leak.

'Silent routine.'

The captain looked into McBride's face, as if assessing some prize he had won. When he nodded, McBride felt he had passed some test successfully. And was able to smile.

'Thanks.'

'Your pal's in my cabin, wants to talk to you – if you're ready. Better change first, mm?'

McBride nodded. The asdic increased its tempo once more, but McBride felt calmed by the confidence, the almost alien superiority these submariners exuded like a gas. He was out, and on his way home.

The next brace of depth-charges shook the submarine, and the lights merely flickered. Someone cheered quietly.

'Silly cunt – '

'Bloody awful shot.'

He followed the lt commander out of the control room.

October 1980

'Why won't you tell me now, Goessler? Why do I have to play this elaborate bloody game which amuses you so much?' Goessler's companion was young, dark and broad-faced. The expression of the face was angry, creased into lines such as a bad-tempered child might display when denied some treat. It was a face that could have been pleasant, open, vivid with pleasure. But perhaps something of its secret life had grown on it like a patina, rusting the intensity of its emotions, restricting its expressiveness. Moynihan, sitting in Klaus Goessler's office in Abteilung HQ in East Berlin – a grey Trade Ministry building on the Wilhelm-Pieckstrasse – was being made to feel younger than his twenty-eight years, and distinctly inferior in mind and position to the academic who was Deputy Director of the Abteilung's Foreign Directorate.

The Operations Commandant for the Belfast Battalion of the Provisional IRA writhed in silence under the unctuous yet steel voice of the balding German. Now, in answer to his blurted, sulky question, Goessler smoothed the wings of hair flat against his head, and smiled, leaning back in his leather chair. He looked over Moynihan's head at an oil painting of the pre-war Unter Den Linden that hung on his office wall. Only after almost a half-minute did he speak.

'My dear Sean – ' Moynihan's face winced at the pretended equality, its superiority sticking through like a broken bone. 'I have explained to you. We must not be seen to be involved in this – the scandal must emerge *naturally*.' His hands imitated a growth, an explosion, on the top of his desk. 'Naturally, also, you have the impatience of all youth – ' A slight shake of the head. 'As impatient as Professor McBride in his more academic way. If I told you *what*, you would want to take the *how* into your own hands. Like a mad dog – which is what I sometimes think you are.' A glint of contempt in Goessler's eyes. 'You would go for the throat. You would lose, like a poor actor, your sense of *timing* completely.'

'God, do you think you're running our show, or something, Goessler?' Moynihan was holding one hand with the other on his lap, afraid to make them into protesting fists. But he could not control his tongue. 'You've got the bloody bomb we need, you bastard! Give us the bloody thing and we'll blow Guthrie and his fucking conference sky-high!'

Goessler banged his hand flat on his desk, once. Leaned forward, and said, levelly, each word weighted: 'That is exactly why you will not be told, but will do as you are told. You are bomb-happy – real or metaphorical. You could not be trusted to exploit the situation to its maximum advantage. And, since you require an answer, I will reply *yes* – we do run your show. We sell you the guns, we provide the explosives, the funds, the false papers, the escape-routes – the knowledge that any enterprise needs that its investors are powerful, and loyal.' Goessler smiled. 'Thus, you are here simply to *see* McBride – when he moves on to England, you will go with him. When he reaches Ireland – as he no doubt will – you will take him over. *He* will provide you with your explosion, without your help. Just let him do so –'

'Time is short,' Moynihan snapped.

'This will not take long, Sean. In a couple of days, at most, McBride will find what he needs here, and be on his way. A man has written to him from England – we will point him in that direction.'

'It's all too coincidental!'

'*No it is not!*' Goessler saw Moynihan blench, as if he sensed himself on enemy territory and without allies. '*Wait!* It will work for you, and for us – and we will not be blamed for the collapse of the conference. Clocks will go back five years in Northern Ireland, and this time you will win.' Goessler assessed that his instructions would be obeyed, then added, 'Now, get out.'

Chapter Three

UNPOLISHED GEMS

November 1940

The light on the breakwater, the South Ship Channel, the
bulk of Portland Castle were ahead as the submarine
altered course, the lights of Fortuneswell flickering before
people remembered the black-out; dusk advancing over the
island. McBride saw it from the conning-tower of the
submarine, standing alongside the young lt commander,
dressed in a borrowed duffel-coat. Overhead, the two
Hurricanes who had provided escort droned away towards
Weymouth, mission accomplished. The destroyer which
had rendezvoused with the submarine at dawn when it
began its ten-knot surface-run across the Channel, was a
slim, knife-like shape behind them, having preceded the
submarine with an asdic sweep until they were only a
couple of miles from Portland.

McBride felt drained, and reluctant, even though the
view of Portland harbour was familiar, even comforting.
He had felt little of the tension, the strain, of finally slipping
away from Guernsey underwater, or of the silent routine,
the submarine resting on the bottom outside the cove
during the remainder of the night. His tension had been of a
different kind, leaning forward like a sick man, whispering
out his initial debriefing report that had occupied most of
the night – coming out of what seemed like a light, self-
induced trance at the distant occasional concussions of
depth-charges. As soon as he had settled in the captain's
cramped, neat cabin, the curtain drawn between it and the
companion-way, he had begun to respond to the quiet,
teasing, unceasing questions of the lieutenant RNVR –
commissioned at the outbreak of hostilities from civilian
intelligence – which had seemed to fall on his awareness like
a constant, defeating drip of water. The lieutenant was little
more than an amanuensis, taking a shorthand account of
everything McBride had done, seen, thought during the
hours he had been on Guernsey before he could forget, or

ignore, or arrange the material according to his own speculations. The professional agent had made no comment, offered no speculation. The submarine had surfaced, after coming to periscope depth and given the captain the relief of a choppy, empty sea, and then begun its run of sixty-odd miles for Portland.

The submarine docked alongside the fat bulk of a depot ship, suddenly cramped and made insignificant. McBride, looking down at the jetty from the conning-tower, could see the two figures waiting for him. Then the lieutenant joined him next to the submarine's captain. McBride shook hands with the captain.

'Thanks.'

'Almost a pleasure.' The submariner tossed his head towards the jetty. 'Have fun.'

'Are you ready, Commander?' the professional asked, not so much in impatience as with due attention to time and required expertise. McBride nodded, rubbed his face as if massaging it, and took off the duffel-coat. 'I'll go down and check the arrangements.' The lieutenant climbed over the side and down the ladder.

'I'm glad to say not all RNVR chaps are like him,' the young lt commander observed after the head had disappeared. 'Cold fish, I should think?'

'Professional,' McBride observed.

'And you're an amateur?'

'Sure I am,' McBride replied in the broadest brogue he could summon. 'Thanks again.'

He climbed lightly over the side of the conning-tower, and down the ladder. He jumped the narrow space of oily water on to the jetty. One of his reception party, almost to his surprise, was a Wren – his driver, he presumed. He grinned at her, but she ignored him. The commander, RN, of NOIC staff, Portland, seemed to expect him to salute, then appeared to lump him with the lieutenant as a professional agent to whom naval discipline was an unreality.

'Shall we go?' he asked.

'Where's Walsingham?' McBride asked, suddenly not wishing to clamber into a car and sit out some unlit night drive along the south coast.

The commander seemed to sense his reluctance at once, and said with a smirk: 'You haven't anything against women drivers, have you, McBride?'

McBride felt suddenly irritated, unreasonably so. He supposed it to be the aftershock of his escape, or simply his weariness.

'Where the hell is Walsingham? I want this debriefing over so I can *sleep*!'

'Walsingham's at the Otterbourne house – you're being taken there.'

McBride raised his hands, as if to wring them in protest and frustration, then he seemed to subside, grinned tiredly, and merely said, 'Very well, your honours, let's get on with it, shall we?'

The noises of the submarine releasing its crew behind them seemed safe and familiar to McBride as they walked to the Austin at the end of the jetty. A jeep was parked behind it, with an MP sergeant leaning on it, and a driver and two more MPs inside. Armed escort. After Guernsey, it all seemed piffling and unnecessary to McBride.

'The prisoner leaps to loose his chains – ' he sang softly. The Wren, standing next to him, looked up into his face and smiled.

They left the commander standing watching their departure, McBride and the lieutenant in the back seat of the Austin, the jeep ahead of them, and turned out past the depot and along the short stretch of Chesil Beach to Ferry Bridge and the outskirts of Weymouth. The intelligence officer seemed disinclined to converse, as if his task were accomplished. McBride surrendered to the expertise of the driver as she tailed the jeep. He tried to sleep, dozing off occasionally, waking often and catching the moonlight glinting like steel on Weymouth Bay, the trees along the A352 like sentries, the snail-like progress through blacked-out Poole and Bournemouth, the darkness-moonlight alternations of the New Forest, the stop-start and sense of a bigger, more frightened town as they passed through Southampton.

And came awake at the burning, the smell of it in the car and the light playing disturbingly on his closed eyelids. There had been another raid on the port. The Wren had to thread her way behind the jeep through undamaged side-streets to the north of the city centre, which seemed a chain of fires linked by darkness. There were fires, too, down in the dock area. McBride, half awake, saw them from a seaward vantage, Southampton Water reflecting the glare down as far as Hamble and beyond.

The car jolted over fire-hoses, paused at hastily erected barriers – McBride saw in the light of a fire begun by a stray bomb a bath hanging crazily out of the torn side of a house – and moved slowly on until they turned on to the main Winchester road. As if he had felt obliged to witness the damage to Southampton, he now slid down in the seat again, and began to let the thoughts of his village, Leap, and the cottage and his wife, Maureen, repossess his dreaming. There had been something stinging and salutary about Southampton, diminishing his own previous night on the run in Guernsey. It was no great matter beside the dead and burned in the seaport behind them. Reflected firelight still shimmered just above his head on the roof-lining.

Whenever he finished a job, there was time for the slowness of Ireland, for the cottage, for his wife and the gleam of moonlight on the ceiling of their bedroom and the frame of the brass bedstead; and the water jug which was frozen over on winter mornings. He settled to the work of memory, hardly noticing as they turned off the A33 just south of Otterbourne, entered lodge-gates, and passed down a drive lined with oaks, finally drawing up before a small eighteenth-century country house which seemed to disdain the modern encroachment of a guard-hut on its gravel drive.

The Wren parked the car, and McBride was shaken awake by his companion. He groaned, stretching and feeling stiffer than he had done between the coal-bunkers or the rocks. Maureen slipped away from him, smiling, and he felt intense irritation with his companion. He climbed out of the car, nodded to the occupants of the jeep who were already at ease and smoking, then saw Walsingham on the steps of the house, waiting for him.

He consciously prodded himself forward, wanting nothing more than to return to sleep.

*

Lieutenant Peter Gilliatt, RNVR first officer of HMS *Bisley,* hefted his grey hold-all down from the carriage and over his shoulder. He had got as far as Cardiff, and the variety show at the New Theatre and then a pub called The Moulder's Arms where some of the female customers had inspired anxiety rather than desire – before the local police had caught up with him. He had put aside the thin, warm Welsh bitter almost gratefully, surprised more that the PC had found him than by the order to return immediately to Milford Haven and his ship.

But it had been relatively easy for the police, he had decided during the slow, late-night train journey through south and south-west Wales into empty, unbombed Pembrokeshire. He always went as far as Cardiff on his forty-eights, preferring it to Swansea, he always went to a show or the flicks, and he always got half-tight in one of half a dozen pubs at the back of Queen Street. One day he would change his routine, and they wouldn't find him.

Some of his crew had been on the train, all noisy and most of them angry; reluctant to believe that he was as ignorant as they as to the reason behind the summons back to the minesweeping flotilla. Gilliatt, amusedly considering that an officer's pleasures were less vivid than those of his men, had no great sense of being cheated out of leave, and therefore no great expectation of dire necessity attached to their sailing orders. The Jerries had probably sewn a new net of mines in the Bristol Channel or outside Swansea harbour either by minelayer or aircraft – nothing more or less than routine.

Milford Haven station was in complete darkness, and Gilliatt let his crew members roll and grouch ahead of him down the wet platform, curse their mislaid tickets and their officers, then go out into the light, soaking rain to find their way down to the docks. The ticket collector saluted as he took Gilliatt's ticket, and Gilliatt touched his cap. The Moulder's Arms and the other back-street pubs in Cardiff were no great loss. He liked being at sea – which was why he had resigned from the navy in '37, fed up with Naval Intelligence and a desk-bound life. And why he'd re-enlisted, in the RNVR, as soon as Hitler invaded Poland. He'd been quite well aware that there would be a war in

Europe when he resigned, and he'd known he'd be trapped in Intelligence unless he temporarily broke his career ties with the Royal Navy.

He carried with him the constant satisfaction of having outwitted the Admiralty. Their Lordships had decided, it seemed, that his university background and his facility in French and German shaped him for only one role in the navy –in Intelligence. With the first hints of the reorganization of Admiralty Intelligence to prepare for another war, Gilliatt had gone to work for a small boat-builder in Appledore until September 1939.

He was a happy man as he passed through the dusty-smelling booking hall of the station, his shoes clicking on the wooden floor, and out into the soft Pembrokeshire rain, insinuating and persistent. Pulling up his collar, he set off in the wake of Campbell, Howard and the others he had recognized. As he walked down the hill from the station, past the NOIC HQ and the Lord Nelson pub, he could see, through the rain, the harbour and bay laid out before him, across to the mouth of Angle Bay. Escort ships ready to fuss over their charges, and another convoy building up. Cardiff –and the less immediate past –faded behind him; he was a shallower, more contented man.

A D-class cruiser emerged from the wet, murky curtain of rain, a light high up on her superstructure the only spot of colour in the greyness. From the vantage point of one of the three British merchant ships, there was something piled and slabbed and sinister about the cruiser's bulk; and something worn, and tired – an air of making do, of potential defeat. The greeting in the signal-lamp's message was hollow, almost threatening. The American cruiser had already vanished back into the rainy mist, heading for the neutrality of Roosevelt's America.

They were fifty miles east of St John's, Newfoundland, sailing from Halifax, with two thousand miles of the North Atlantic between them and the Clyde or the Mersey. On leave in New York, before they sailed, the strangeness of a country not at war had seemed welcome, shallow, and even something to be despised. Women well-dressed, arms full of packages from early Christmas shopping at Macy's; taxis to be had by raising an arm; Manhattan garish and alive with light when darkness fell; the skies quiet. Now, as the British cruiser – their sole escort – emerged from behind the weather, heaving with the effort, it seemed, it brought with it the smell of war, of Europe.

The cruiser signalled each of the three twenty-thousand-ton merchant ships in turn. There would be complete radio silence except in the utmost emergency. All communication was to be by means of signal-lamp, as it had been with the American cruiser.

America was now impossibly distant, infinitely desirable, and incapable of being disdainfully looked down upon, veteran upon rookie. Between them and their destination, as they zig-zagged their way across the Atlantic, were the U-boats. Their imagined presence was more potent than the grey, insubstantial bulk of the cruiser.

The cargo – grain, machine-parts, aircraft spares – was no longer important, nothing more than a futile gesture of help by the Americans, and a single drop in a bottomless bucket to the British. And the idea of it being a trial-run for new convoy tactics seemed now only the unenviable prerogative of the guinea-pig. Some of them knew the figures for shipping losses the previous month – 103 ships, 443,000 tons. Britain was dying, being starved to death. And that did not seem to matter so much now as the garish safe lights on Broadway and Fifth Avenue, the coffee-shops, bars, restaurants where they were a strange and welcome species.

October 1980
McBride had agreed that Goessler should be paid the equivalent of five per cent of the advances and royalties of the book, when it was written – Swiss account, dollars or Swiss francs did not matter. McBride was gratified in discovering Goessler's motive for helpfulness, and accepted the demand without question. He was paying no one else, and the agreement was unwritten and conditional on the discovery of some striking and convincing new material.

It took the four students that Goessler had subverted temporarily from their postgraduate work two days to assemble a slim folder of evidence for the existence of Emerald Necklace. Goessler had only occasionally appeared in the room off the main university library that he had caused to be set aside for the work, like a nanny periodically checking upon her charges. He claimed – to McBride's anxious anticipation – to be tracking down some of the names that had been thrown up by the documentary material they unearthed. Five per cent had galvanized Goessler – he seemed slimmer, less jolly, sleeker of mind. McBride enjoyed the cupidity displayed by the East German Marxist academic. It made him feel more justified in depising those American professors guest-reviewing *Gates of Hell* as a bad badly-written book.

McBride handled the collected documents with a reverent delicacy, and returned to them compulsively again and again – reading the German slowly, caressingly, and with a catch-breath anticipation that he might have misread, mistranslated, read into.

As the girl student, Marthe, brought his coffee in a lumpy brown earthenware mug, and he nodded his thanks, he was reading the movement orders of two infantry divisions, dated late in October 1940. The two divisions, XXXII and XLV, had not been stood down when *Seelowe* was cancelled by the Führer – except very temporarily. A leave-pass record had survived with the movement order, and there had been little leave – unlike other divisions in France initially required for *Seelowe* – after the cancellation. A number of senior officers had been summoned to Berlin – regimental and *abteilungen* commanders – but for junior officers and other ranks only compassionate leave. After a very brief bivouac in the Cherbourg area they had been transferred to Brittany, to the Plabennec-St Renan area north of Brest. Here, they were to establish a temporary headquarters. The temporary nature of their headquarters was attested to by the surviving requisitions of building materials and billets.

In the same fortnight after the cancellation of *Seelowe* – *Sea Lion* – on 12 October, certain units of the XIV Panzer Division, the division's Panzergrenadier Brigade and the Panzeraufklarungsabteilung – the armoured reconnaissance unit – had also been moved from Holland to the Brest area of Brittany. Lastly, the recce company, the three parachute rifle regiments, and the engineer-signal units of a Fallschirmjaeger – Parachute – Division had been detached from their headquarters in Poland and been reassigned to guarding certain airfields in northern France on behalf of the Luftwaffe. Such a wasteful employment of highly-trained, élite troops that McBride had lumped it with the other evidence.

What he had gathered was sufficient proof that a small, highly mobile invasion force had been assembled in Brittany during late October, 1940. *Smaragdenhalskette* was a reality in terms of the deployment of units.

It remained without a target, an objective.

This was not something that disappointed McBride. Just as he accepted that what lay now under his hand had come spilling out of dusty files when required, so it would go on. He knew that somehow he was meant to find the documents relating to Emerald Necklace, and that it would all be in his book, and that the book would be a big one. One slight regret – he would have liked an eye-witness, or more than one.

He sipped at his coffee, the warm liquid spreading like the warmth of self-satisfaction in his stomach. Goessler, when he popped his head round the door of the room, found McBride still studying the documents as if they were already fine-print contracts, and sipping at his coffee.

'Herr Professor McBride – ' Goessler seemed so much more bumbling at moments, yet so much sharper at others now that he was in on the money side, that McBride wondered what kind of mind kept slipping in and out of focus behind the rubicund, smiling face. 'Working on the unit designations – ' He sat down beside McBride, hand on the younger man's arm immediately in a conspiratorial gesture, voice lowered. For five per cent, Goessler was apparently only too willing to subordinate himself to McBride. McBride nodded, amused. 'I have so far traced one man living in Berlin here who was with XLV division in France during the – *critical* time?'

'You're sure of this?' McBride smiled, saw a moment of calculation in Goessler's eyes, dismissed it, and added: 'Can I meet him?'

'That is being arranged – by my secretary. Possibly this afternoon. The records are very sketchy. I think we are lucky to find this one man. There may be others, of course.'

'If he knows enough, it may not matter –'

'Of course – your visa terminates tomorrow –'

'Shit, yes.'

'You can rely on me to continue – *our* work, Thomas.' Goessler smiled at the introduction of the Christian name. For him, it seemed to seal something.

'I'll get this stuff duplicated, Klaus.' McBride indicated the documents with a wave of his hand. 'Thank you.'

Goessler bowed his head in a bird-like eating movement towards McBride.

'It is exciting – and it will be remunerative, Thomas. Much more interesting than the early years of the German Communist Party, I assure you.'

Goessler's laughter – which caused the beavering team of students to look up in unfeigned surprise – seemed to bellow in the quiet of the Archives Department of the university library.

He was a janitor for a block of flats out on the Greifswalder Strasse, well into the north-east suburbs of East Berlin. A fifties built, unrelievedly grey area of workers' apartments in ugly, duplicated blocks. No trace of history prior to the war and the peace and the Communist Party of the DDR, as if the erasure of the past had been deliberate, final. He had been a Funkmeister – a Signals sergeant-major – with the Signals Abteilung of XLV Infantry Division, and his name was Richard Kohl and he was now an upstanding, clean-nosed member of the Communist Party – and undoubtedly an Abteilung 'unofficial' set to monitor the behaviour, visitors and domestic life of the occupants of his block of flats – having been an eager member of the Nazi Party since 1936. He'd transferred from the Wehrmacht to the Waffen-SS in 1942, and ended up at Leningrad for his pains. A short prison sentence after he was caught on the outskirts of Berlin by the Red Army, a process of 're-education', and he was fit for service in the new DDR.

He was thin, in his early sixties, and with a padded, complacent mind. As he talked of 1940, however –

undoubtedly remembering forward through the remainder of the war – a gritty quality of survival seemed to emanate from him and McBride could no longer simply despise him.

'Yes, we were transferred to the Brest area late in October – if you say the twenty-sixth, sir, I won't argue. Near Plabennec, sir, that's correct.'

Goessler had insisted on accompanying McBride, but remained carefully silent during the interview. McBride and Kohl might have been alone in the simple, comfortable janitor's apartment. Kohl's wife had been sent shopping. Pictures of party leaders on the wall, a small TV set, patterned carpet which clashed with the flowered curtains, a solid, plain three-piece suite, a square-edged, dark dining-table, the flimsy chairs of which were covered with the material from the curtains. Flowered wallpaper. McBride allowed one part of his mind to indulge itself seeking an analogous room. He finally found it in British films of the 1940s – there was something old-fashioned about the room, as if the consumer-boom of the fifties and sixties simply hadn't happened. It hadn't here, he reminded himself.

'I remember those weeks – we were taking it turn and turn about in tents and billets, sir,' he added, smiling with the recollection. Then he shook his head. 'Officers had billets in the villages around – we had tents a lot of the time, or barns, or outhouses, sheds.'

'Why were you there, Herr Kohl? Wasn't such temporary billetting strange for France at that time?'

'Yes, it was. But we were just told – *special assignment*. And that meant you didn't ask questions, just did it.'

McBride restrained the temptation to glance in Goessler's direction. Kohl seemed unaware of the German academic in one corner, perched on a dining-room chair, occasionally making his own notes.

'What was that assignment – what did you do during those weeks?'

'Played around with radio-gear, ran signals exercises – as we always did.'

'Nothing – *special?*' McBride's disappointment was evident.

'No, sir. More intensive practice, a whole new range of codes to learn – though we didn't use them in practice – but not much more than that.'

'Your briefing – what was your briefing?'

'I – sir, I never had a briefing. I was in hospital, caught influenza sleeping in those tents. Hospital in Brest – '

'How long?'

'Late November – perhaps even early December when I rejoined my unit.'

'And where was your unit then?'

'Stood down, sir. Rest and recuperation, regrouped around the Rennes area. Proper billets – '

McBride's face screwed up in frustrated disappointment. Then he said very slowly: 'And what happened while you were away?'

Kohl thought very carefully. 'XLV Division never moved – no, they did, sir. One of my pals told me they'd all been shipped down to Brest, by lorry. Now, when was that?' He screwed up his thin face with the effort of recollection, rubbed his pale forehead beneath the thin grey hair, tapped his pursed lips, then said: 'Sorry, sir – late in November, but I don't remember – '

'That's all right,' McBride said hollowly. 'Go on, what happened?'

'They waited in Brest for two days, then got shipped back to Plabennec, every man in the division.'

'No rumours, nothing like that?'

'Everyone thought it was England, sir. Our new codes were in English, I remember.'

'England, with two divisions and a Fallschirmjaeger Division's rifle regiments?' McBride laughed, concentrating his sudden absence of enthusiasm in the mocking sound. 'The Isle of Wight, maybe, Herr Kohl – '

'I remember, the Fallschirmjaeger left a couple of days before the division was shipped to Brest. Just weren't there in the morning, so the lads said. Never saw them again – and there was a lot of aircraft activity that previous night, heading for England.'

'They all disappeared?'

'Three rifle regiments, recce company, signals, the whole lot. There was even a Parachute Artillery Abteilung that came in at the beginning of November – with the ten-o-five recoilless guns – they'd gone as well.'

'Where, Herr Kohl – flown out or transferred?' McBride leaned towards the former Funkmeister. Goessler coughed, making Kohl shift slightly in his chair, aware of his fellow-German again. He shook his head.

'I don't know, sir. But I do know that Third Fallschirmjaeger Division were short of signals when they went into Yugoslavia in March forty-one – they wanted me to transfer, but I had an application in for – ' He glanced keenly at Goessler, and his voice was only just audible as he added: 'Waffen-SS, and I didn't want the job. Can't stand heights – ' He laughed, a brief, mirthless sound.

'And, as far as you're concerned, these units of parachute troops vanished – in England?'

Kohl nodded. 'Yes, sir. They couldn't be anywhere else – could they?'

McBride shook hands with Goessler once more, the German clasping both hands round McBride's hand, pumping vigorously as if to restore circulation.

'It is both more and less of a mystery, eh, Thomas?' he said, smiling like a cut melon. 'Do not worry – I will continue the work here. You must now go to England in pursuit of our mysterious parachutists – anything I learn will be sent to you. That part of it will be simple.'

McBride nodded.

'Klaus, thank you. I confess I was disappointed – but there was enough there to make me go on, track the whole story down. Maybe it's even better than before – the disappearing Fallschirmjaeger, uh? Everyone likes a mystery. Maybe the book will change its shape if I can get hold of more – ' His lips compressed as he realized he was walking away from East Berlin, from papers he might not have seen, people he might have been able to interview. 'If I apply for another visa, you can smooth it, mm?' Goessler nodded. '*People* is what we want, Klaus. Men who served in those units with Kohl – records of those night flights late in November – ' The avenues of investigation bubbled out of him now, as Lobke from the Ministry opened the door of the Lada and made him aware, by looking at his watch, that his journey to Tempelhof could not be longer delayed. McBride nodded at Lobke. 'OK, OK.'

'Go along now, Thomas – and leave everything with me. You'll be hearing from me very soon, I am certain.'

His hand was released, and McBride climbed into the car. As it pulled away from in front of the Hotel Spree, McBride looked out of the rear window. Goessler was waving enthusiastically after the car.

November 1940

The morning was crisp, cold, clear, a sky washed of imperfections except for the smudge on the southern horizon which was the effluent of Southampton's bombing. McBride nevertheless felt invigorated by the air, the frost crunching like powdered glass underfoot, the chill on his wan, tired face. He rubbed one hand through his hair, tousling it. Walsingham walked beside him, deep in contemplation of the debriefing, of the notes he had studied and the tape-recorded dialogue with the weary McBride.

McBride liked Walsingham, effectively his special operations controller for OIC for the past year. Walsingham was a few years younger, not even thirty, though his rank of Commander, RNVR, seemed to belie his age – his age belied the sudden rank, McBride corrected himself. He had been drafted into OIC by means of an RNVR(S) commission at the outbreak of war, by Rear Admiral Godfrey – Director of Naval Intelligence – himself, from his job in civilian intelligence. By general repute, Walsingham was brilliant, painstaking, thorough, imaginative – and ruthless. McBride liked him as much for the suggestion of that latter quality that always seemed close to his eyes and mouth as for his more acceptable qualities. He was what McBride could accept, and admire, in his operations controller. And Walsingham respected his qualities as a field-agent.

A rook called from a bare tree, hunched above its great lump of a nest. Both men looked up at the noise, smiled.

'Well, Charlie-boy? Have you learned what you wanted? You're being remarkably silent, even for you.'

'And your sudden brogue isn't having the slightest effect on me, Michael-*lad*,' Walsingham observed, looking down at his shoes, rimed with the frost on the lawn in front of the house.

'*Touché!*' McBride stopped, facing Walsingham. 'What's it about, Charlie? I'm not an idiot – even I could smell something big – what is it?' Walsingham wandered a few steps away, then turned to face McBride. He was suddenly boyish rather than donnish as he rubbed at his fair hair, making it stand up away from his pale forehead.

'I wish I knew, Michael, I wish I knew.'

'Listen, Charlie, it's a two-way process. *You* talk to *me*, now.'

Walsingham, as if ignoring McBride's demand, walked away from him, seeming to study the bare trees, the last curled leaves on the lawn – scuffing some of them with his foot, a sharp, cracking sound. McBride was surprised not at his reluctance, which he considered only apparent, but by the intense mental agitation that Walsingham's young face clearly evidenced. Walsingham looked up.

'I discount, of course, your remarks concerning the *cameraderie* of the Kreigsmarine and the Wehrmacht – at least, I want to ignore it, perhaps simply because it's so tantalizing to speculate on it.' He smiled, almost in a hurt, defensive way. He thrust his hands in the pockets of his brown jacket – Walsingham was rarely in uniform – as if to limit the dramatic emphasis he might bring to bear on his remarks. 'Your drawing is quite inadequate, you know – your skill with the pencil, I mean – '

'Charlie, are you trying to tell me something?' McBride grinned. 'Go for your gun, Kincaid,' he observed. Both men stood, ten yards apart, hands in pockets.

'Don't joke.' It was said with the affronted dignity of a lover.

'OK – talk me through it, then.'

'I guessed the sheds concealed submarines, but I couldn't understand why they were so – so *flimsy* – ' He surrendered to emphasis, waved his hand briefly at his side, replaced it in his pocket. He looked like a schoolboy trying to explain a breach of discipline. 'And the submarines in there – Raeder and Dönitz don't have that many submarines, so this use of Guernsey is quite out of character, and ties up a lot of boats – look, they must have been

building these big U-boats at the expense of other vessels!'
He looked up at McBride, as if for confirmation, and
McBride realized for the first time that Walsingham was
rehearsing an argument; or was repeating one that had
already failed to convince other people.

'Go on, Charlie,' he said.

'Let's cut over this way,' Walsingham said quietly,
pointing towards a grove of trees that ran down to the
stream that crossed the estate around the house. McBride
nodded, and they walked in silence until Walsingham
pursued his argument, the cry of another rook seeming to
galvanize him into speech.

'Those boats you saw – you *think* they were ocean-going
big boys, right?' McBride nodded. 'But they might have
been milch cows, right?' Again, McBride nodded. 'And
again, they could have been a new type – what do you think
they were doing? Had been doing?'

McBride walked on in silence for a time, listening to his
own footsteps and those of his companion.

'I don't know, Charlie, I really don't. Your eyes lit up
when I described the stuff on them – you tell me.'

'I'm going to have to talk to the Admiralty – to confirm
my suspicions. They weren't loading, refuelling, anything
like that?' McBride shook his head. They emerged from the
trees, and the narrow stream was filmed with grey ice. It
appeared remarkably forlorn, evocative. The grass along
the bank was stiff, sharp-edged, with rime. Beyond the
stream, the countryside to the edge of the estate – where it
was bordered by a farm – was dulled, rendered vacant and
inhospitable by the grey air, the trees fuzzed into rounded
lumps of frosty branches. In the distance, cows picked their
way, painfully slowly, across a white field.

'No, they were repairing the damaged sub – but I had the
sense of *mission over*, rather than mission *ahead*.' McBride
stared into the distance, seeing the Friesians taking and
losing shape against the background. 'What had they been
doing, Charlie?'

Walsingham looked at him, and seemed to judge that the
moment was right.

'By the way, you're going back to Ireland via Milford
Haven, with a minesweeping flotilla – it should be

illuminating!' He chuckled. 'Sorry – I want you to see for yourself, then tell me – via Drummond or the captain of the minesweeper, of course.'

'Just tell me, simply – what are the Germans up to?'

'Drummond's crying out for your return, you know – there have been several reports of submarine activity, and of at least one agent landing west of Cork – '

'Charlie, don't be irritating – '

Walsingham flung his arms wide like a magician. He looked more like a schoolboy than ever.

'I think the Germans are going to invade the Republic of Ireland – and I think they're going to do it soon!'

October 1980

Heathrow was conspicuously neat, and orderly, and cool. With the kind of meticulous, fastidious care that a bomb-disposal expert might give to an inspection of his equipment, and his opponent. McBride had used the airport many times before, either travelling to England or in transit for Europe. The limited chaos that he always perceived by comparison with Kennedy or Dulles or Logan – those long cool corridors, the quiet, the whisper of luggage-conveyors and escalators – had disappeared; he had always regarded Heathrow as the triumph of desperation, perhaps the apogee of the British capacity to make do as a way of life. Yet now the busiest airport in the world was creeping about its business.

Because of the soldiers.

The terminal was full of them, armed, and the baggage search seemed endless, and his passport was checked with a thoroughness perhaps more appropriate to Dusseldorf – in fact, he realized as the passport controller, with a soldier standing armed and bored behind him, held his passport face-down beneath his desk that the British had imported, and put to use, the German computerised passport system they used at Federal Republic airports.

It was almost an hour and a half after he disembarked from the Trident 3 that he emerged with his bags into the lounge of the terminal. He looked immediately for a telephone, found one near the bookstall, and dialled directory enquiries.

He was eager to work in London, go over all the wartime records he could lay hand on, and therefore he had decided to get Gilliatt out of the way quickly. Gilliatt and his own father seemed impossibly distant figures, unreal beside Kohl and Menschler and others that Goessler might unearth, given time. If he could arrange to see Gilliatt – hire a car and drive down in a day, and back – listen to the old man, thank him and walk out of his life, so much to the good.

A soldier paused near him, looking with exaggerated suspicion at his bags. McBride smiled, edged them closer to him with his foot. The soldier – who appeared sixteen behind his straggly fair moustache, acne belying his manhood – nodded, and moved on, the 5.56 Sterling LAR over the crook of his arm looking modern and plastic and completely, unnervingly deadly. McBride watched him move on. The guns on the belts of German policemen had become familiar but this – because a rifle and carried by a soldier *in an airport* – disturbed him.

Gilliatt's number was supplied by the enquiries operator. McBride scribbled it on the back of the folded letter from which he had supplied the address – outside Sturminster Newton in Dorset. His Michelin map had indicated on the plane that he could drive there and back in a day.

He dialled.

Emerald Necklace, he thought, grinning helplessly as if he had been given an expensive, long-desired present. It was in his hand now, in his hand. The phone went on ringing for a long time, and then it was picked up.

'Yes?' A woman's voice, and he was instantly aware that the voice was weary of answering the telephone; someone expecting the same wrong-number call for the tenth time.

'Is that Sturminster Newton eight-eight-two-six – Peter Gilliatt's home?'

He'd had better transatlantic calls. A long pause, then: 'It is.'

'My name is McBride – '

'Michael McBride?' the woman asked. 'No, I'm sorry – Thomas McBride, you're his son, aren't you?'

'Yes – to whom am I speaking?'

'Peter Gilliatt's daughter.'

'Hello – is your father available to talk to me?'

'I'm afraid he isn't – '

'I see. When will I be able – '

'You don't see at all, Mr McBride. My father is dead – he died last week of a heart attack.'

Chapter Four

WESTERN APPROACHES

October 1980

Gilliatt's cottage was on the northern outskirts of the village of Sturminster Newton, beside the road to Marnhull. It was white and pretty and very English to McBride's eyes as he approached it, checked its name against the sign on the three-barred gate, and crunched up the gravel drive. The last roses round the trellised porch to the door were puckered with a slight over-night frost, but more than that they carried an overtone of mockery to McBride. As if, in some medieval woodcut, a skull grinned out of the heart of each flower.

Thatch, leaded windows, brass door-knocker. McBride, as he shook off the ironies of the cottage's appearance, almost expected Mrs Miniver to appear in the doorway. Instead, Gilliatt's daughter was small and neat and dark, and her face was wan, strained, without make-up. She gestured him inside without a greeting, and he noticed the wedding-ring on her hand. She was aware of his glance, and rubbed one hand with the other.

'I'm staying here for the moment, though I don't like it – since the break-in. Through there, please – ' Rugs covered the flagstones of the hall. He ducked under an exposed beam, and went into the lounge which overlooked the garden behind the cottage. Dark wood panels, bright prints on the old, substantial furniture, french windows out on to the terrace.

He said, shocked awake: 'What break-in? When?'

He turned on her, even as she was gesturing him to sit down, and she flinched as if struck. She sat down, brushing

72

her full tweed skirt smooth, then plucking at the collar of her blouse. She was in her late thirties, McBride estimated, and normally a self-composed, assured woman. Worn down by grief? Or something else?

'It was last week – Just after the funeral. I came down at the weekend to find his papers and stuff everywhere – ' Her hand swept vaguely across her skirt, indicating the carpet. 'It – seemed more terrible because he was dead, can you understand?' He nodded. 'And so ridiculous here – my father had lived here for years, it couldn't be anyone from the district – ' He wondered whether she was reassuring herself. 'I've stayed here this week – my husband's coming from Bristol on Friday.'

'You're frightened,' he said bluntly. 'Why?'

'I don't know – ' She frowned, the broad clear forehead running into furrows, her small mouth pursing. 'Perhaps – puzzled, and that's become fear. Nothing was taken, you see. My father had a small collection of jade, and a few items of silver. I'd packed them away – but that wouldn't have stopped a thief, would it?' Her hands were fidgeting now, stabbing in emphasis, or lying irresolutely, unrestfully, on her lap. 'Anyway, I decided to stay – there were things to do, his solicitor in Sherborne – ' She smiled, nervously. He sensed she had been happy here as a child and a young woman, and she wanted to absorb something of it, for the sake of the years ahead – but what had once been a good, if maudlin, idea was now making her nervous, afraid, and vulnerable.

'Why are you afraid – they won't come back. Burglary isn't like that – '

'I suppose not. It's just that – ' She seemed to scrutinize him, as if to check her impulse to spill the whole story into his hands, make him share its oppressive weight. 'My father, last time I was here, when he wrote to you – was certain he was being watched – he said, *under surveillance*, and laughed, actually.' The memory warmed her for a moment, then the tears stood at her eyes, making them glisten. She seemed determined to ignore them. 'He claimed it was the most interesting time of his life, since the war – '

'Why did he write me?'

'He explained – didn't he?' She seemed to have little patience to talk about his concerns.

'He wrote me like a novelist – full of mystery – ' He consciously employed his most disarming smile, and she responded slowly. He noticed her nose had reddened with the restrained tears. 'He said he had a visitor – did he?'

'I wasn't here that week – ' In the way she spoke, there was something that made him not envy her husband. He was vying with a worshipped father who would now be beatified by memory. He hoped her husband in Bristol had learned to cope. 'But I believe my father. Someone came – he said *from the government* in his most mysterious tone – ' A slight, almost luxurious smile. 'Interested in you, and your work. But he didn't explain – the visitor, I mean – and made my father very angry that he'd been warned not to talk to you – '

'What did he want to say to me, Mrs – ?'

'Forbes,' she said simply, announcing something of minor significance. She talked of her father much as his own mother had talked of Michael McBride, and he wondered about two men so easily, casually capable of inspiring love.

'Mrs Forbes, your father's letter intrigued me, I have to admit. But it didn't tell me anything – do *you* know anything?'

As he asked, he was aware again of the break-in, and the fact that the jade and silver wasn't missing. She looked thoughtful.

'It was the work he and your father were involved in – in nineteen-forty, I think. He didn't talk much about the war, funnily enough – not until this happened.'

McBride realized his mouth must be open, and his eyes furiously active. She seemed frightened, as she might have been of a harmless but retarded person in the street, suddenly encountered.

'Papers – what about his papers? Were any missing?'

'I can't say – there was a mess, and I tidied it all into cardboard boxes, but I didn't know what was there. Nothing of any importance, I'm sure. My father didn't hoard things, never kept a scrapbook, or took a lot of pictures, even when my mother was alive. He was always clearing out cupboards and drawers, throwing things away. He had a very good memory – perhaps he was just careless about who and what he once had been – ?' The thought seemed to have just struck her, and she evidently found it uncomfortable.

'So you wouldn't know?' She shook her head. McBride was beginning to believe the unimportance of the burglary; it retreated in his consciousness, though he knew, dimly, that he wasn't finished with it. 'The man who came to see your father – was your father frightened in any way?' She laughed out loud, then clapped her hand to her mouth as if caught in an irreverence. But she was still smiling when she uncovered her mouth.

'Of course not. My father thought him stupid, and impudent.'

'And he didn't threaten your father?'

'No, why should he? Official secrets? My father hadn't learned any for forty years, Mr McBride. Would you like coffee – some lunch?' He shook his head.

'No to the lunch, yes to coffee.'

While he listened to her making coffee in the kitchen, he pondered Gilliatt's death, and the frustration of this minor part of his visit to England. *But, 1940?* It was too coincidental.

When he had taken the delicate china cup with the heavy rose-pattern in the deep pink saucer, sipped and complimented her, he said, 'Your father didn't mention exactly what it was he wanted to talk about, I suppose?' He was resigned to it being idle speculation – her answer had a startling clarity.

'He was still laughing when he told me. He said that your connection with it was the best irony. It put the wind up the people in Whitehall, he was certain of that – the same name, you see, and the blood connection. The man from London told him that you were interested in the operation my father was part of in late nineteen-forty – '

'Emerald Necklace?' he asked in a hoarse voice, the cup tilting in his hand as his attention was forced from it.

'Careful,' she warned. 'I'm sorry – I don't know what you mean – '

'The operation was called Emerald Necklace.'

'I don't know – was it? My father didn't refer to it by name. He simply said it was to do with a German plan to invade southern Ireland, late in nineteen-forty. Are you interested in something like that?'

Sean Moynihan handed over the papers he was required to carry under the Prevention of Terrorism Act, as Peter Morgan, visitor to the Republic. He'd filled a sheaf of forms at Heathrow which attempted to stop people like himself from travelling freely in and out of Eire.

The passport official at Cork Airport accepted the papers and the Welsh accent that Moynihan had assumed, and the single suitcase and the false passport. Outside the tiny, almost empty terminal building, Donovan was waiting for him with his car.

When they were on the L42, driving back towards Cork, and Monynihan had maintained a deliberate silence in order to irritate Donovan, the driver said, 'You had a satisfactory trip, I take it?' He wiped a hand over his thinning hair, as if nervous at having trodden on some private grief.

'I did, Rory, I did.' But his face portrayed only the mirror of his angry frustration at the hands of Goessler. 'Herr Goessler was his usual smiling, fat, bloody self.'

'Well – what did you get from him? What can we use?'

'Nothing – nothing yet.'

Donovan was emboldened by disappointment. 'But you promised – look, Sean, I've got the committee on fire for some startling piece of usable information, and you come back with nothing?'

'Shut your gob, and drive, Rory – you do that best.'

After a silence which seemed to mist the windscreen slightly, Donovan said, 'I'm sorry, but the committee is pressing. It's a matter of image, now – if we don't agree to be represented at the conference, then we – '

'Fuck the image of Provisional Sinn Fein, Rory!' Moynihan snapped.

'Our point of view is only *just* in a majority, you know that! And that's with the promise of something really good to blow the conference down. What if I tell them they'll have to wait – what good will that do? The old sods on the committee will get their way – the tired old buggers! You *must* have something for me!' His voice cracked into a whining plea.

'I've nothing for you – not yet. Goessler has us by the balls, Donovan, you know that. That lot would cut off the guns and the bombs *tomorrow*, if we don't do as they say.'

'What's going to happen, then?'

'Goessler's set his elaborate scheme in motion – '

'McBride?'

'Yes. He's in London now. Soon, he'll be coming here, following an old, old trail – '

'How long is this going to take?' Donovan's round eyes blinked behind his thick spectacles as he looked almost desperately at Moynihan.

'Watch the cart,' Moynihan said, and when they had swerved to avoid it, added, 'Not too long – damn you, Donovan, I can't help it, and I don't like it, either! Sinn Fein will go to the conference – OK, so they go. That conference will last weeks – it'll all be out in the open before then!'

'You hope,' Donovan said quietly.

'Shut up and drive.'

November 1940
For McBride, the bridge of HMS *Bisley* was of no special significance. He was being delivered back to Drummond and to his home in County Cork by the most convenient route – as part of a minesweeping flotilla. Another borrowed duffel-coat, a cap picked up at Otterbourne, someone else's seaboots, his dried roll-neck sweater – Walsingham had brought McBride's jacket, but the cap had been mislaid. He was amused at his own amateurishness, and felt no superiority of function to the first lieutenant of the minesweeper, Gilliatt. A mild discomfort at being amongst a ship's officers and crew was always just below the surface, as if he were some sort of ignorant civilian guest – but it was a feeling that was in himself, not in those around him. They accepted his uniform as proclaiming the man, and enjoyed the mystery and shadows that seemed just beyond his physical presence.

The flotilla consisted of just seven ships, moving out of Milford Haven harbour into the sound down towards St Anne's Head It was a grey early morning, the sea already alien, inhospitable. One of the flotilla was having her boilers cleaned, so six ships would sweep and one would act as 'spare sweeper'. McBride had no interest in their objective – the Germans might have sown a new minefield by aircraft or submarine across Swansea Bay or Cardiff docks, or at Bristol. Routine, par for the course. The two dan-laying vessels had already left port to rendezvous, presumably, at the location of the sweep.

He smiled as he remembered Walsingham's words. The m/s davits, kites and floats on each side of the quarter-deck of the *Bisley* had indeed informed him of the purpose of the big U-boats on Guernsey – minesweeping duties. They had been rigged out to sweep a minefield on the surface, he suspected now, carrying the sweep along behind them. He presumed it had something to do with keeping the U-boat pens along the French coast clear of the mines the Navy and Coastal Command had started laying. Its importance had already diminished, and the small mystery of their function, being solved, led him to o further interest. He was anxious now to get home.

'Cigarette?' Gilliatt offered him a Capstan Full Strength from a battered packet. Then he and McBride lit up. McBride sensed the proprietorial affection the lieutenant felt for the bridge, now that the captain had left it and gone below to his cabin. Gilliatt was to join him when the flotilla had passed St Anne's Head and turned away to starboard. McBride had not been invited, so he presumed it would be some kind of briefing. 'On your way home, sir?' Gilliatt added casually as they stood behind the helmsman, watching St Anne's Head emerge from the early mist. Rain-squalls spattered the bridge screen. The young sub-lieutenant who was officer of the watch was in effective command of the bridge. It was therefore Gilliatt's indulgence to engage McBride in conversation.

McBride nodded 'I am. And you – you're already home?'

Gilliatt looked startled and very young, then he smiled. 'You noticed,' he said

'A friend told me you were once in Admiralty Intelligence?'

'Once – a long time ago. I ran away to sea.'

McBride laughed. 'I try not to stay at my desk,' he said. 'And, before you ask, I'm *Anglo*-Irish. My sainted mother, God rest her soul, was a Dublin girl, and my father worked for an English firm of paper-makers. Now, does that much careless talk cost me anything?'

'The helmsman's a German spy – aren't you, Campbell?'

'Sir – Glasgow branch,' the helmsman replied without turning his head.

St Anne's Head slid alongside them as they passed down the west channel. Gilliatt looked once at McBride, and nodded.

'Excuse me, sir, the captain wants me. Good luck,' he added in a quieter voice. McBride saw a moment of envy, a reassertion of satisfaction, and smiled.

'Rather you than me,' he offered, indicating the bridge of the minesweeper with a traversing gaze.

Gilliatt went below. The curtain was across the captain's door. He knocked on the bulkhead.

'Come in, Peter.'

Gilliatt entered. The flotilla commander, Captain James Ashe, nodded, returned his gaze immediately to the papers on his folding desk.

'Close the door, Peter,' he said. Gilliatt closed the door of the tiny, cramped cabin. 'Find a seat – you may need it.' Gilliatt's face retained the grin of ignorance. Ashe looked set, determined. Secretive. Gilliatt glanced at the Admiralty chart held open on the desk. A spread-legged compass lay across the St George's Channel, its dog-leg minefield marked in red – officially laid in July 1940. When Ashe picked up the compass, and tapped at the minefield, close in to the coast of Ireland, Gilliatt felt a sudden, inexplicable pluck of nervousness. He even wondered for a moment whether the presence of McBride had been somehow explained to him – then dismissed the idea.

'Bloody minefield's only been there just over four months,' Ashe grumbled, as if deploring impermanence, shoddy workmanship.

'What is it, sir?'

'We are on a special job, Peter. What we are going to do is to sweep a thousand-yard passage through the St George's Channel minefield – Winston's Welcome Mat, as they call it in the Admiralty.'

Gilliatt was stunned. The minefield ran in a huge dog-leg from the Eire coast to that of north Cornwall. It followed the coast from Carnsore Point south of Wexford to the Old Head of Kinsale, west of Cork, and ran along the Cornish coast from Hartland Point on the southern arm of Barnstaple Bay to Trevose Head beyond Padstow. It protected the St George's Channel, the Irish Sea, the Bristol Channel from enemy ships and submarines, and the coasts of Ireland, Wales and Cornwall and Devon from enemy invasion. It was – with the development of radar, RAF Fighter Command, British escort vessels and the American convoys – more than anything else responsible for the survival of Britain into the hard winter of 1940.

'Sir – why?' Gilliatt waved his hands loosely, at a loss to explain the orders to himself, disqualified from comment upon them.

'Ah, I presume their Lordships felt called upon to give a reason – in case we refused to carry out the order on the grounds of its insanity!' Ashe could not quite conceal his sense of satisfaction at being privy, as mere flotilla commander, to Admiralty thinking and strategy. 'They're not ready to let the German Navy come sailing up the Bristol Channel – ' His laughter barked like a gruff hound in his throat.

'Thank God for that,' Gilliatt breathed, staring at the red-marked minefield lying across the chart like a peppering of attendance marks on a school register.

'A convoy is on its way from Halifax – ' Gilliatt looked up. 'Nothing special – except for the fact that it's three big merchantmen and a single cruiser escort. Its route is special – it's ignoring the North Channel and the Irish Sea and coming by the southern route – the one we'll open for it.'

'What – ?'

'It's the loss of ships – over a hundred last month – ' Again, Gilliatt appeared stunned, and a shadow passed across his features, an uneasiness as if ground beneath his feet had become treacherous marsh.

'That many?'

'That many – and more expected this month. By January, I don't think we could go on.' Ashe's face was stiff with feeling, each line carved. This was a conclusion of his own, rather than something he had been told. Gilliatt realized that his captain had been shunted out of his natural habitat into a place which reeked of power, and of impotence and despair. He shuddered, because in Ashe's face he could see the Admiralty staring out. 'Certainly February – more U-boats all the time, whole packs of them waiting out in the Atlantic, clustering round the coast of Ulster, as the convoys funnel into the North Channel – hopeless.'

'And – this is the *answer*?'

'They hope so – it's an experiment, a new operation on a dying patient, Peter. A narrow passage, marked, through Winston's Welcome Mat for a few ships sailing line astern – they'll have run a fast zig-zag across the Atlantic, slip through as near the coast of Ireland as they dare, into Swansea, Cardiff or Bristol.'

'Can it be done?'

'Dammit, it's got to be done. If it works, then it can work again and again.'

'Until the Germans get wind of it, catch on – '

'But they'll have half their U-boats to the north, half to the south. We could still hang on, with the odds rearranged like that – '

Ashe seemed to be telling himself, convincing an invisible audience. Gilliatt remembered he was from a moneyed family, and there was a cousin high up in the Admiralty. What he was hearing was a private conversation rather than a briefing or a digest of sailing orders. Ashe had been put in the picture, and wanted to retreat from it, or share it so that it was not so immense a burden. He hadn't wanted to join the club, be in the know – if the knowledge was close to despair.

Gilliatt recognized his own reluctance to digest what he heard; even his own attitude to desk-work, to Intelligence. Perhaps he had wanted to be at sea, in the lower echelons where no one carried responsibility for more than his own ship, his own men.

The air seemed hot, constricting, in the small cabin.

'Close to the three-mile limit, and they'd be in sight of land all the way, and on the unexpected wing of the minefield, not down near Cornwall – any ships could make a course alteration at the last minute, outpace the U-boats – ' Ashe was speaking more softly now, calmer. Making sense of his orders, limiting their implications.

'A thousand yard channel, dan-buoyed, all the way from Carnsore to Old Head?' Gilliatt asked.

Ashe nodded. Looked up, his eyes clearing, his face less firmly, more habitually set; familiar lines, familiar strength.

'That's it, Peter. Another sweeping operation.'

'What about that McBride chap?'

Ashe shook his head. 'We'll transfer him to the spare sweeper, they can drop him off inshore of the minefield. He has nothing to do with us.'

'Lucky for him.'

'My cousin told me how vital all this was for the war effort – *et cetera*,' Ashe said, standing up for the first time, his big knuckles resting on the chart – directly on Kinsale and County Cork. 'I could hardly tell him I didn't want to know we had our backs absolutely to the wall, could I? That I didn't want to know we might be going down the bloody sink at any moment!' Ashe was growling now, but he patted Gilliatt on the shoulder. 'Sorry to let you in on it, Peter. I'm afraid I couldn't carry it around inside me any longer – ' His eyes became inward-looking, filmed. 'They're all drifting round the Admiralty with grey faces, Peter.'

'It's all right, sir, thank you for telling me.'

'Polite – but you don't mean it.'

'No, sir, perhaps not. We're hanging by the merest thread, it looks like. Not a pleasant thought – '

Ashe seemed guilty at having burdened Gilliatt, yet there was also relief, the shoulders were straighter.

'God,' he said, as if in consolation, 'we may already be beaten, Peter – do you think it could be true?'

'I hope it's not, sir. I hope to God it's not true.'

Both men seemed to have agreed, unspokenly, that to remain in the commodore's offices in the Admiralty building in Whitehall was too covert, too removed from the battered London around them which now, indirectly but more urgently than ever, concerned them.

Walsingham had gained an interview with the Director of Minesweeping as soon as he returned to London from the house outside Southampton. The smudge of the city had been visible to him, hanging like a pall against a pale winter sky without other cloud, for miles before he had reached the Surrey suburbs. Then it had taken him hours to make his way through Wimbledon, Wandsworth, Battersea, across the bridge and through Chelsea. Streets wet with fire-fighting, coated like a new surface with broken glass, heaps of smouldering – or rescued – furniture piled on the pavements, little groups of stunned people, the occasional ambulance, and other small groups who knew what they had lost already and had abandoned hope, holes in the lines of terraced houses in so many streets – heaps of rubble over which firemen and ambulance men clambered for the sake of relatives who watched them dumbly.

They were walking now in Hungerford Lane, near Charing Cross Station, the gaunt skeleton of the railway bridge black against the sky, sombre. The station roof, too, appeared charred by recent fires rather than sooted by time and the steam engine.

'Commodore – would it be a reasonable supposition, then?' Walsingham asked at last, as if he had wearied of visual impressions, wanted now a renewed sense of purpose. He felt himself coming out of mild shock.

The Director of Minesweeping, to whom the damage of the previous night, and the prior weeks, had been a narrow burning perception of the enemy's vileness, looked at his young, small companion. Walsingham seemed troubled by doubts, but the commodore could not decide if that was a deferential pretence or merely the visible reminders of the air raid.

'I would say – ' Someone passed them pushing a handcart into which were piled office chairs. The spiky, tumbled legs seemed to threaten, or defy. 'Yes – yes, Commander, it would be a *very* reasonable supposition.'

They turned down towards the Victoria Embankment, passing under the railway bridge. A train rattled over them, and out across the Thames. The noise silenced them, but the shadows under the bridge were cold, and the sound hammered down at them so that both men flinched as if deep, traumatic memories had surfaced. When the train had gone, both men smiled.

'Yes,' the commodore continued. 'The kind of stanchions and other new fittings you describe would certainly most likely be minesweeping equipment. It's probable that they would operate as a team of six -- linked in twos, and rigged out to employ an A-sweep in a "C" formation.' Walsingham appeared confused, irritated at his own shallow knowledge. 'The U-boats would be linked in twos, the first two in line, then the second two, then the third pair, in a "C" formation. It would give them as near as possible a one hundred per cent clearance of the channel they were sweeping.' Walsingham nodded. 'I can't think why they'd be based at Guernsey. Naturally, we drop mines outside their harbours, and the submarine bases in Brittany and Normandy, but Guernsey isn't especially well-placed as a base for sweeping subs, and we don't make a fuss around the Channel Islands. What is going on?'

Walsingham was not prepared to lecture the DMS on security.

'I'd rather not say at present, sir,' he murmured deferentially. 'It's only a theory – '

'Those bloody U-boats aren't a theory, young man. I hope you're not going to play silly buggers with this information, keep it to yourself or something equally stupid?'

Walsingham knew it was bluff. He would not tell the commodore, because he had to conserve the element of shock and surprise for his own masters in Whitehall.

'Sorry, sir, but I will be seeing my own superiors in OIC later today – and they will decide what happens next.'

'Politely telling me to mind my own business,' the DMS snorted, looking studiously ahead at the approaching bulk of Waterloo bridge. He laughed, an abrupt, loud noise like indigestion. 'Very well, but let me tell you this – '

He turned to Walsingham, stood with his hands on his hips like some more piratical ancestor.

'The Kreigsmarine doesn't have U-boats to spare,

Commander. If there are as many as you suggest engaged in minesweeping duties, then they are sweeping to some very exact, and vitally important, purpose.'

'That is exactly what I was afraid of,' was all Walsingham would say in reply.

October 1980
McBride had wanted to stop for a while in Salisbury – the white cathedral spire across the fields summoned him from photographs and prints – but he felt energized by a restlessness of mind that prompted him to find the A338 on the other side of the city, and head towards the M4 and London. The spire flicked in and out of the driving-mirror for a time, so that he hardly attended to the news item on the car radio.

' . . . a police spokesman said that two men were being held in custody at Braintree police station, where it was expected that charges under the Prevention of Terrorism Act would be brought against them later today. Our reporter believes that the two men are among those wanted in connection with the London restaurant bombing . . .'

He switched channels as the news items of a country he hardly knew continued. Vivaldi sprang from the two speakers behind him, and he tapped at the wheel in a comfortable state of half-attention while he considered what Mrs Forbes – Gilliatt's daughter – had told him.

His own father had been in Ireland, and with Gilliatt, late in 1940, and in connection with a German invasion of Ireland. Emerald Necklace – his father had been part of it.

He had encountered few moments in his even, academic life which possessed such naked shock. Few things had impinged upon him so directly, the halting, recollected sentences of the woman in the chair opposite him beating on him rather than seeping into his consciousness. He was in the presence of events – an alternative *present* – rather than hearing of some dim time beyond his own experience. A curious sense of predestination assailed him, almost as misty and illogical and assertive as a religious experience. He could not cope with the information, almost ignored the name and whereabouts of the man his father had operated under – Drummond, he'd fixed it like a photographic image, the chemicals of repetition coming to his assistance – in his desire to get away from the house in Sturminster Newton and come to terms with what he had heard.

'*What happened to your father I have no idea – my father would not say, though perhaps he didn't know. But they were together in Ireland, working for Drummond, who was some kind of secret agent –* '

She had smiled with apology. She believed her father, naturally, but had no sense of what he might have been doing. Certainly not figuring in some drama she might have read in a fiction.

His own reaction – now in the warm car, the Vivaldi moving crisply through its slow movement – was of a similar unreality. He was ignorant of his father's war record, but the secrecy which may have surrounded it too easily toppled into melodrama. Except that his father was connected with *Smaragdenhalskette*. His father was a proof of its existence.

It was growing dark by the time he reached the motorway and turned on to it. He began to make good time, looking ahead to a flight to Ireland, to meet Drummond – if he still lived south-west of Cork. It would be a simple matter to trace him, and perhaps as simple to interview him. An old man now, he would open his memory like a box of keepsakes. Somewhere under the years was his father.

McBride had no direct interest in his father – he had, during the drive, sublimated him in the publicity that would attend his new book, the son-of-the-father angle which was pure, dramatic accident. He was not on a quest for his father. Michael McBride, about whom he possessed a certain curiosity, was only one light among the decorations giving off a Christmas-tree gleam as he approached the warm room in which Emerald Necklace waited like a reward.

November 1940
The minesweeper lowered him into the water, in the ship's motorboat, half a mile offshore – though officially the ship should not have entered the three-mile limit of neutral Ireland's territorial waters – and in the company of the young sub-lieutenant and a stoker in charge of the boat's

86

noisy engine he chugged towards the unlit shore where Drummond would be waiting to pick him up. There was no element of danger, and there would be no protest from the Dublin government. Naval vessels had collected fruit, eggs, even alcohol from the coast of southern Ireland – he was just another item of barter.

He was conscious of the windless night, the almost calm sea, the fresh chill and the smell of land. He was aware of Guernsey and his frantic effort to escape, but now only as an occasion for smiling.

They slipped into low Carrigada Bay, the lights of two cottages a sighting and a welcome; the faintest glow of the village of Reagrove beyond. The lack of black-out so different from England, and – most recently – the dark, wet docks of Milford Haven as the minesweeping flotilla had forlornly set sail. Always that sense of emptiness behind the outlines of cranes, an empty country or city; and always the sense of lights, of scattered quiet lives being lived when he arrived home.

The stoker cut the engine to idling, and the boat immediately began to wallow. McBride slipped over the side, and the chill of the water struck through his sea-boots, the slopping incoming tide reaching almost to his knees.

'Good luck, sir,' the young sub-lieutenant called, and McBride waved one hand as he waded through the shallows to the beach and the motorboat's engine picked up again as it turned back to the minesweeper.

The incoming tide would remove his footprints – though most of the locals would have heard the engine of the boat and guessed at its passenger – and he lengthened his stride.

He grinned in the darkness as he moved on to the soft sand above the high-tide mark, and saw Drummond waiting, calmly smoking a cigarette. He was leaning on the side of the shed where a fisherman kept his nets, his tall, lean frame relaxed, unconcerned.

'Michael?' he asked quietly.

'No,' McBride replied in German. 'Admiral Dönitz – I'm here to look around.' Drummond laughed softly in the darkness, then shook hands with McBride. 'Welcome back.'

When McBride had lit the offered cigarette, Drummond

headed the Morris back up the track towards the coast road. McBride settled against the leather seat, contentedly drawing in and exhaling the smoke.

'You were of use to our common masters, I take it?' Drummond asked as he turned on to the road. Lights dotted the fields around them, small as hand-held lamps, each one an uncurtained window or an open door. McBride noted them like a Victorian parent counting heads and reassuring himself his family was entirely present. Not one of those lights would not be there the following night, or the night after that –

Unless Walsingham was right. As he thought that, he was aware, also, of Drummond's half-amused question, even of the nettled irritation far back in the tones which reminded him of Drummond's dislike of loaning one of *his* agents to London.

'I suppose so. I just went, looked, reported, and was told to keep quiet about it. I suppose it was of some use to someone.' Walsingham had told him that Drummond *might* be informed at a later date. For the present, he was to be told nothing. He did not even know where McBride had been.

'It's secret, of course?' Drummond asked lightly as he pulled up at the crossroads in the village of Nohaval. As expected, there were no other cars, in any direction. McBride wound down the window, and felt the cold air rush into the car.

'Apparently, Robert.'

'I've got another job for you, anyway. Your real work,' Drummond said as the car pulled away on the Kinsale road.

'Tomorrow, I hope – '

'Tomorrow will do. Reports of a German agent landing two nights ago by boat from a submarine – *reliable* reports, I hasten to add – ' Drummond chuckled. McBride studied his profile. A stereotyped British naval officer, that head above the white roll-neck sweater and the dark jacket that could have been mistaken for a uniform.

'No trace since?'

'Nothing.'

'Where was this?'

'Rosscarbery Bay – the other side of Galley Head. A couple of miles from your place.'

Drummond laughed. 'You'll have a look around, and let me know?' McBride nodded. 'Good. That's the third in two weeks. I wonder what's going on?'

'They could be deserting from their submarines,' McBride offered before he settled back into the seat again, lighting another cigarette from Drummond's packet on the dashboard.

The tiny hamlet of Leap lay almost in darkness astride the main Clonakilty-Skibbereen road as Drummond's car pulled up outside McBride's cottage. There was light coming through flower-patterned curtains in the kitchen. Drummond's own house was a spacious, prosperous-looking white farmhouse near Kilbrittain, twenty-five miles back the way they had come, inland of the Old Head of Kinsale. Drummond had officially retired from the Royal Navy in 1934, in company with a great many officers who, at that time, believed the Royal Navy would never rearm and thus rob them of careers, and moved to Ireland, selling a small family estate in order to buy a farm in County Cork. Here, he had continued to work for Admiralty Intelligence, setting up a network of coast-watchers and intelligence gatherers along the south coast of that weak defensive flank of Britain, neutral Eire. McBride had been one of his first, and most successful, recruits.

McBride got out of the car, slammed the door for the pleasure of making a noise that would betray his presence, and walked round to Drummond's window.

'I'll get on with that in the morning,' he said, and Drummond nodded.

'Good. Let me have a report in a couple of days. And take care of your health, Michael.'

'I will. Thanks for the lift.'

'One day you must tell me all about your trip,' Drummond said lightly, then switched on the engine, and turned the car round towards Clonakilty again. He tooted noisily as he drove off, a white hand waving from the still-open window. McBride threw away the rest of his cigarette, and approached the door of the cottage.

Maureen would never come out to greet him if Drummond were there – McBride could never decide whether it was because she was Irish rather than Anglo-Irish like himself or whether it was because she simply resented the man who took him away, placed him in danger. But then, he reminded himself, Maureen didn't like what he did for all sorts of reasons, not least of which was her father's lifelong acquaintance with the IRA. He smiled as he pushed open the door, latched it again behind him – but the smile was saddened, as if he were suddenly burdened with an unpleasant freight of unwished-for complications amid his homecoming.

Maureen emerged from the kitchen into the lamp-lit gloom and warmth of the living-room, her arms white with flour, apron on. She wore her domesticity like an irritant or a disguise; a posture of which he was well aware. She seemed to desire to be nothing much to come home to, have no special place in his mind or affections. *The little woman*, he told himself as he stood watching her and she did not move from the kitchen door. Since the war, since he had begun working for Drummond and the British – not so much a reproof or disapproval; rather a slight distancing, more in case he got killed than because she objected. She was more comfortable inside an unpretentious outer covering – nothing overwhelming would happen to a woman like her.

'Hello – you're not cooking at this time of night, surely?' he said, taking off his coat and throwing it on to a chair. He moved to the fire, rubbing his hands, then turning his back to it as if chilled, waiting for her to move to him.

'I expect you can eat it,' she offered grudgingly. He watched her inspect his body, seeing through the clothes, for new marks, new contours violence might have drawn. He remembered her horror at a knife-wound across his ribs that had bled badly – and she hadn't asked what he'd done to the German, ever. It had happened on a beach east of Cork, early in 1940. Even now, she avoided looking at him as he washed or shaved stripped to the waist, and when they made love her hands hovered near, but never caressed, the scar.

'I can. What is it?'

'A pie.' She wiped her arms with a towel, removing the worst of the flour as if she were removing a disguise. Then she came to him in front of the fire, and put her face up to be kissed. He looked down at the small features, the auburn hair which framed them, the parchment skin that looked somehow raw-boned and stretched, typically Irish. He bent his head, kissed her, squeezing his arms so that he pressed her body against him. He felt suddenly guilty as he stroked her hair as she leaned against his chest. He had been a painter when they met, just finished art school and with a few small commissions from rich dog-owners and one or two advertising companies trying to encourage cheap new talent. There was a studio upstairs, next to the bedroom, and an exhibition of unsold landscapes and portraits of Maureen in the loft. But he had found himself a natural spy, an adventurer, almost in the first days after recruitment by Drummond – one slight pang as if he were betraying his past, or his wife, and then he had leapt into the secret life. Each time he measured her smallness in his arms, he felt guilty again for what he had discovered of himself. He had lain in the room of his own life like an unused weapon until another war required his services. A natural.

'I love you,' he whispered, and she pressed her cheek closer to his chest. He stared at the furniture of the room as if appraising its value.

October 1980

Rear Admiral Robert Evelyn Drummond, RN Retd, still lived at Crosswinds Farm, County Cork. It had taken only a couple of telephone calls, and a visit to a branch library in Bloomsbury for a Cork Area telephone directory, to locate him. The Admiralty were pleased to confirm his continued existence in good health, though they would not immediately release his address without some personal details.

McBride had determined not to telephone Drummond before he reached Cork, but instead simply to visit him as the son of Michael McBride – letting surprise and perhaps even pleasure spring the lock on the memory-box. He anticipated no difficulties with Drummond.

As he changed flights at Dublin Airport for the flight to Cork, he was unaware of being watched. When he left the Aer Lingus Viscount at Cork Airport and passed through Customs, he did not see Moynihan sitting at the cramped and tiny snack bar, reading a copy of the *Cork Examiner*. But Moynihan saw him, logging his arrival with a nod to two other men in the passenger lounge who followed McBride out, watched him pick up his Hertz car, and drove after him into Cork.

Later, Moynihan drove down to Kilbrittain and booked into the one small hotel in the village. The next day, he expected McBride to call on Drummond and his daughter at Crosswinds Farm.

Chapter Five

OPEN DOOR

November 1940
McBride squatted on his haunches, staring at the seaweed wrack, the splinters of wood, the old bottle, the shells where he had brushed his hand across the soft white sand above the reach of the tide in Rosscarbery Bay. He smiled, squeezed the wrack so that one of its dry pods burst with a flat cracking noise, and wished that Drummond's reported German agent had left an evident, unmistakeable sign of his passage. McBride was working his way from Galley Head and Dundeady Island west around the bay. The stiff little wind rustled and whisked the sand, and carried the smell of exposed mud now that the tide was well out.

No, he didn't wish it. Perhaps just the slenderest clue, the momentary glimpse as if through a door-crack into the agent's mind – and then the slow, building pursuit. He breathed in deeply, engaged in something more fierce – more enmeshing – than his love-making with Maureen late in the night. Maureen had been tidied to one part of his mind again, her habitual and appointed residence, fuzzy and localized like a snapshot of some place in the past. Yet he loved her as he had loved no other woman, and would love no other. He never discussed with himself the *weight* of that love, or its importance in the entirety of his awareness.

He had pondered, at first, whether the war had distracted him from his marriage; but, remembering the caged days in the studio-attic in Cork, the search for this cottage in Leap, the restlessness of the days in the bedroom he then used as a studio – he knew that perhaps the war had saved his relationship with Maureen. She had become only a necessary fraction of his life, placed in proportion; he thought that she, too, had accepted that he was somehow disabled from accepting the completeness of a life that centred on the domestic, on a relationship.

The bed thy centre is – He stood up, shrugging the Donne from his mind. The German agent – if indeed one had landed three nights before – would have left no traces, unless he was somehow careless. The float would be buried or hidden inland, and if he was anywhere in the area still, he would have registered at an inn in a plausible disguise or be staying with one of the fellow-travellers who expected a Nazi victory.

He walked slowly through the soft sand, head down, eyes casting about for something out of place. The smoothness of sand where the belly of a dragged float had passed, one half-erased footprint missed in the night –

McBride was a hunter. Something kept in a kennel until there was a man who needed hunting down. German agents had been landed in southern Ireland, along the Cork coast, since 1937 or '38, most of them taking the quick route north either to Dublin to cross on the ferry as native and neutral Irish to Liverpool; or into Ulster and from Belfast to England. In either case, the object was the same – spying on Britain.

Until perhaps three or four months ago, when McBride had found a dead body on the beach – drowned when his float capsized in a rough sea – carrying papers which gave his nationality as Irish, and which would not have fitted him to cross to mainland Britain, but rather would have suited a resident of the Republic.

Since then, rumours, traces – in one case a killing – of agents who were staying in the Cork and Kerry areas, possibly being taken off again by submarine the way they had come. Rumours of men with assumed English identities – painters, bird-watchers, travellers, students. Swallowed by the damp, musty County Cork earth, for all the hard evidence.

The sun was well up – the day bright, hard as steel against his face, the low hills behind the bay sharp in the dry, frosty air, the sea smooth beyond the exposed mud flat – by the time he reached the point where the road bordered the beach, which itself narrowed to a thin, grey strip. He had found nothing, and wondered whether he might temporarily abandon his search and check Ross Carbery itself, sprawled haphazardly on the far bank of the bay's narrow inlet at the mouth of a lazy river. An agent with the right papers might have gone into the village – they were walking up to the front door these days, after all –

He climbed the steps up to the sea wall and the road, his eyes alert as if he expected to see an unfamiliar ornithologist or cyclist. He walked up to the main road from Clonakilty, along which he had been driven by Drummond the previous evening. He felt almost light-hearted, in spite of his wasted morning, and he whistled to himself, hands thrust for warmth in the pockets of his donkey-jacket. He was happy in his work, and he was working again. Walsingham and his concern with Guernsey had receded in his imagination.

A pony-trap caught up with him just before he reached the bridge across the inlet to Ross Carbery. He turned, and his face darkened as he saw the driver was his father-in-law, Devlin, the principal grocer in the village. Devlin, who must have recognized his walk, his posture, still adopted no conciliatory face. He'd been delivering to the farms, perhaps, and was as reluctant about the encounter as McBride.

'Good day, Da,' McBride said, squinting with the sunlight and perhaps with irony.

'Michael – good day.' McBride observed Devlin's thick neck, the squat body which he could never decide was actual or merely the visual exaggeration prompted by his dislike of the man. In the end, Devlin's Republican politics, his short-changing, his bully's air were little alongside the man's voice, gestures, shape. 'How is Maureen?'

McBride climbed up beside the man, acting out their mutual parody of propinquity. Devlin clucked the pony into movement, shaking the reins on its back.

'Maureen's fine.'

'You've been away, then?' Devlin continued as the cart moved on to the narrow road bridge. A bull-nose Morris squeezed past it.

'My aunt in Dublin – sick again. You know how it is, Da, when they get old – ' Neither of them believed, but both normally accepted, the fiction of his behaviour. Devlin certainly knew that McBride worked for the British, and despised him for it. McBride, for his part, had nothing but contempt for the narrow, bigoted, unrealizable aspirations of the IRA. Sometimes, he wondered when some of Devlin's more outspoken, and less cowardly, acquaintances would get around to an attempt on his life – as a traitor to something-or-other.

'Ah,' was all Devlin replied.

'Any strangers in Ross Carbery in the last three days?' McBride asked, studying the pony's rump intently.

Devlin was silent almost all the way across the bridge, then he said. 'I haven't heard.'

'The lads about as usual, then?'

'They are.'

'All of them?' Devlin steered the pony into an alleyway off the main street of Ross Carbery, to the yard behind his shop. He grunted as if it took all his physical strength to control the docile animal. He did not look at McBride, who suspected he was lying.

Devlin provided him with information as readily as if McBride threatened his daughter in some obscure and violent way. He did it, however, simply out of his own fear of Maureen's husband – perhaps even out of a fear of Maureen herself. The IRA, for some strange reason, did not frighten him. He did not inform on them, anyway, and the British had lost interest for the moment. McBride had never threatened or coerced. There had been no need.

'Now, Da – *anything*, anything at all?'

Devlin reversed the pony and trap, then climbed down. He looked up at McBride. His eyes shifted guiltily.

'Someone – ' He cleared his throat. 'Someone is buying groceries for two – ' He choked off any amplification of the bare fact.

'You're sure?'

'I am – twice as much bacon, eggs. Isn't that enough?'

'One of the lads?'

Devlin shook his head vehemently. 'No!'

'Da – I don't want him, just his guest.' Devlin swallowed, shook his head again. 'Come on, Da. His guest won't be Irish, he'll be German – '

Devlin erupted in unaccustomed defiance. Someone had recently warned him about talking to his son-in-law, evidently. The truce was over, and McBride wondered at the reason behind it.

'No, damn you, no! No more than that – find the man yourself, if you want him that much!'

McBride skipped down from the trap, stood before Devlin.

'It's all right, Da – I'll look after you.' He felt no reluctance in saying it. Devlin he disliked but the threat encompassed him, Maureen and her father alike. Devlin hesitated, then nodded. McBride understood his relief. Somehow, just as he was more afraid of him, Devlin regarded him as stronger, more powerful than the IRA men he knew. It wasn't much like respect, but it was a recognition of superiority. 'One of the lads, Da. OK, I'll find him – ' He frowned. 'And what do the silly buggers think they're up to, Da – playing with the Germans? They'll get their fingers burned.'

But Devlin, reassured, retreated from a moment close to intimacy. He merely shrugged and readopted his habitual sour face.

Walsingham paused outside the door of Room T of the Admiralty main building, as if to take a deep mental breath. He tucked the buff folders more firmly under his left arm, yet his hand still refused to turn the door handle. The green stripe of the RNVR(S) between the gold on his cuff now mocked him. At the bottom of some great steep mental slope, he looked up, daunted. He felt little more confident of success than some harmless crank who continually reported the landing of creatures from outer space to the local police.

Then he opened the door, and went in. Rear Admiral March was waiting for him, seated at the far end of the long polished walnut conference table of Room T's main office – other, smaller rooms waited behind the half-dozen doors off this main room, where March's Section II of Admiralty OIC seemed to lie in wait for him. March smiled at his entry, gestured to him to join him at the far end of the table.

'Charles – sit down, my boy.' Then he immediately looked at his watch, as if impatient of missing another appointment elsewhere. 'What can we do for you in Section II?' A distance was marked between them. March was Walsingham's superior, Walsingham was on the strength of Section II, but now he was being made to feel an outsider. His civilian intelligence background, the green RNVR(S) stripe, was again a matter of importance, and being used to dissociate him from the naval staff with whom he worked.

'My – Irish business, sir,' Walsingham began, sitting down, opening the top folder. March looked bored almost at once, hardly glancing at the aerial pictures he had seen before or the reports that lay beneath them.

'You've been talking to DMS, I gather,' March said in a spirit of surprised offence. 'Interesting?'

'Sir, the Director will submit a report to this office as soon as he can, based on our conversation – '

'And you led him by the nose, I suppose?' The Admiral's face creased in a humourless smile. A narrow face, the pitted skin of which was leathery, blue-jowled. Dark, probing eyes, thick grey eyebrows which seemed perpetually lifted in disbelief. 'Come, come, Charles, no pouting. I know you. DMS no doubt supports your cock-eyed theory simply because he doesn't know any better.'

'Sir,' Walsingham said in a tight, smoothed tone. 'DMS agreed that what my agent had seen was quite probably a group of minesweeping submarines in Guernsey – '

'This agent – Irish, isn't he?'

'Anglo-Irish, for all it matters. He is reliable – '

'Charles, look out of any one of these tall windows. It is

November outside ' As if in sympathy with Walsingham, weak sunlight bloomed on the carpet on the other side of the elegant room, revealing its faded pattern. But, almost immediately, a heavy cloud removed it. It would rain before the afternoon was over. It was cold in the room, despite the huge radiators and the coal fire. 'No seaborne invasion plan – such as you propose – would be seriously entered into by the Germans. When we knew Hitler had cancelled *Sea Lion* in October, we also knew we were safe from the sea. The invasion you suggest is *impossible*.'

Walsingham's boyish face narrowed as if he had sucked a lemon. In a moment, he would again be reminded of his lack of expertise in naval matters. 'Sir, I admit it is unlikely. But not that it is impossible.'

March looked at the folders, the original aerial pictures of the newly erected sheds in Guernsey harbour, and the digest of McBride's debriefing beneath them, clipped to them.

'I see. Your man has provided *fresh* evidence, I take it – hence your persistence?'

'Sir, I request you read his report, and my account of what the DMS had to say.' Walsingham realized his knuckles were a strained white as they rested on the table. He removed his hands.

'Very well, Charles, I'll read it. But you're wrong, you know. Utterly wrong.'

October 1980
Crosswinds Farm was an easy house to find on the southern side of the hamlet of Kilbrittain. Solid, white, almost Italianate with its red roof and surrounding fruit trees. It was situated on a knoll, looking north to the hamlet and the hills towards Bandon, south over Courtmacsharry Bay and the Old Head of Kinsale. McBride turned the rented car off the narrow, hedged road, up the track to the farmhouse. Friesian cattle watched him over a newly painted wooden fence. As he pulled up before the house, a woman was waiting for him – presumably Drummond's daughter with whom he had already spoken on the telephone.

She moved confidently towards the car, extended one hand and shook his in a firm grip. Mid thirties, he estimated, some instinct making him study her hands for rings. No wedding ring. When he looked up again, she was smiling sardonically, blue eyes amused, yet appraising. Then she brushed her dark hair away from her cheek, and beckoned him towards the house. She was dressed in denims and a pale green sweater over a blouse. A green scarf knotted at her throat. McBride found her immediately attractive, and somehow off-putting, as if a great deal had already passed between them, and her judgement of him had already been made. He had been expected for a long time in her life, and she might already have defined and placed him.

He followed her into the house – dark wood panels, a heavy staircase that turned out of sight, polished floors with splashes of bright rug. She led him through the square hall into a large room that looked north towards Bandon and the low green hills where the shadows of clouds chased across their contours, swallowing sheep and cattle, white farms, trees. The view became sinister in an unexpected and inexplicable way the moment he saw it, and Drummond rose from his chair at the side of the big window, hand out. He smiled.

'Admiral,' he said. Sunlight on the scene again.

'No formalities,' Drummond said easily, waving him to a chair opposite his own, sitting down again himself, at ease, comfortable. Drummond was tall, grey-haired, clean-shaven. The skin was mottled with age, as it was on the backs of his hands, but it was drawn tight on the fine bones. His eyes were clear, his gaze steady. Though McBride knew he must be close to eighty, he appeared still vigorous. Only the ebony cane with the silver fox's head which he had used to get up quickly marked age, infirmity. McBride could understand how the man had successfully run an intelligence network in Ireland forty years before.

Then he was struck by the sense that this man had known his father. Not just Gilliatt, and Emerald Necklace, perhaps – but his own father. Drummond's disconcertingly complete appraisal of him, imitating his daughter's intent look, reminded him of it. Drummond was looking for a likeness. He nodded.

'You are like him, Mr McBride – your father, I mean.'

Then he seemed to notice his daughter for the first time. 'Drink, Mr McBride? Claire?'

'Coffee would be fine.'

The woman went out of the room. McBride's smile stretched, became strained under the continuing close scrutiny. Eventually, Drummond's gaze released him.

'I'm sorry, McBride. You do remind me of him, very clearly. I am being made aware of how damned *old* I've got, and how long ago it all was! Forgive me.'

'You knew my father well –' It was not a question, and it was not the conversation that McBride had wanted to begin. Yet he sensed the life of memory in the upright, preserved old man, and something reached out to meet it, comprehend it. He suddenly had an intuition that the old man would tell him nothing without being asked.

'Yes, I did. He worked for my little organizationfor some years, until – ' Drummond shook his head, watched his daughter bring the fine bone china, the coffee. She served McBride with sugar-lumps from a silver bowl, with small silver tongs. He studied her strong hands, caught her perfume as she moved away again. She and her father disconcerted him, but he could not say precisely how or why. Formidable, perhaps?

'Thank you,' he murmured, and attended to Drummond, silently urging him on. 'What happened, sir?'

'To your father?' Drummond replied, watching his daughter pouring his coffee with the greediness of the old.

'Yes.'

'You don't know, then? Your mother, I mean – ' He sipped at the coffee, took two of the biscuits and rested them in his saucer.

'My mother –' He looked at Claire Drummond, who had seated herself on the sofa, crossed her legs, and taken up the posture of an intent spectator. Disconcerting. 'My mother told me nothing about my father, except that he died before I was born. How and why I don't know.'

'And you never bothered to ask?' Drummond supplied quietly. 'But now, in front of a mummified old man – ' Claire Drummond smiled – 'you are reminded of your ignorance, and intrigued to know more. Mm?' He sipped again at his coffee. McBride heard his dentures click against the rim of the cup. He felt taken over, subordinated, by the old man and his daughter.

'Do you know what happened, sir?'

Drummond shook his head. 'I was in London – one of my rare trips, I'm glad to say. There was one hell of a flap on – '

More to reassert himself than to raise the matter, McBride blurted out: '*Smaragdenhalskette*, you mean?' Drummond's eyes narrowed, more than anything at the German, McBride surmised.

Drummond nodded.

'I thought you must know quite a bit of it, when you rang,' Drummond observed. 'The German invasion plan, eh?' McBride nodded. 'Yes, your father was mixed up in it, in a way. So was I – and young Peter Gilliatt. But I'm not the one to be able to tell you – ' He smiled at McBride's complete and child-like disappointment, his comical expression. 'I wasn't privy to all of it, by any manner. It was masterminded – if you can call it that – from London by a man named Walsingham in Admiralty Intelligence.'

'But my father – ?' The remainder of his coffee had grown a skin and he put his cup on a delicate side-table the woman had moved close to his chair.

'Your father used to run off and do errands for Walsingham – and I was told nothing, I'm afraid. I know we were running around here like mad things during late November – about the time your father died – scared stiff the Germans were going to come, agents landing on every side, that sort of thing, rumours of parachutists and so on, but nothing ever came of it, I'm afraid.' McBride looked devastated. 'I'm sorry about this, Professor McBride. You seemed to want to talk about your father when you rang – I was glad to be able to help, meet his son. But this other matter – I'm in almost as much ignorance as you, I'm afraid. I don't really know what happened here for almost a week before your father – died. I was in London, advising the Admiralty on this Irish thing. Without being told very much, I'm afraid.'

He finished his coffee, put it down, bit a biscuit in half.

'My father, then – ' McBride asked, his disappointment

evident, interest in his father minimal, mere politeness
'What happened to him? Do you know that, sir?'

'My investigations – on my return here – led me to the
conclusion that he was murdered by the IRA,' Drummond
said levelly. Claire Drummond's head twitched as if her
father had slapped her face.

At seven-thirty McBride was waiting for Claire
Drummond in the bar of the one small hotel in Kilbrittain.
The impulse to ask her to join him for dinner at the hotel
had been simply that – a way of retaining some contact with
Drummond rather than with the woman. Drummond had
closed the conversation soon after the revelation of the
manner of his father's death. He had ascertained as much
from his network; the body had never been found.
McBride's father had had more than one brush with the
local IRA, who sometimes helped German agents hide out,
fed them, sent them on their way to Dublin and the British
mainland. Presumably, they had exacted the price of his
interference, his contempt and animosity towards the
Republican movement. Drummond had warned him
often, but McBride had always disregarded the threat
posed to him by the IRA.

Drummond had been – forty years later – visibly moved
by the narrative of Michael McBride's demise. Yes, Gilliatt
had later helped his pregnant mother over to England,
thence to neutral America where she claimed to have
distant relatives. Drummond knew no more of her than
that.

Nor did he know anything more of Emerald Necklace.
McBride was absorbed by the news of his father, and
pressed few questions on Drummond during the rest of
their conversation. He felt almost helplessly drawn to his
father by Drummond's ignorance of the manner and detail
of his death. The mention of *IRA* brought images of a
hands-bound, kneeling figure, head hooked, being executed on a barren spot of country, bones growing white in
passing seasons, namelessness –

He could not take his book, or himself, seriously. His
own ignorance, his mother's silence, seemed exaggerated
and derided by Drummond's lack of knowledge.

Somehow, he felt they had all let his unknown father die, were all responsible for the namelessness of it.

Men in London, Drummond had added. He must pursue his researches in London. Many of them were dead, but Admiralty records might turn something up, Walsingham was still at the Home Office, so Drummond believed –

But London was distant. Within maybe even ten – twenty? – miles of where they had talked, where he now sat, his father had died. He felt immeasurably sad, weighted with emotion that seemed to be attempting to catch up with itself, make up for lost time – to apologize for the years of light, dismissive feelings towards Michael McBride. He did not expect to be able to do anything; he expected only not to return to London. He felt he must not leave County Cork just in case his present, ennobling, emotions deserted him with a change of location. But, what to *do*?

Claire Drummond walked into the bar, brushing at her heavy dark hair, dressed now in corduroy jacket and pale green skirt, and long boots. He smiled, was about to rise, offer a drink before dinner, replenish his own whiskey, when she transferred her smile to the only other man in the room, the studiously-reading man at the bar.

'Sean!' they embraced, kissed lightly, studied one another in an acquaintance from which he was excluded. 'How long have you been in Kilbrittain?' she asked disapprovingly. Before he could reply, however, she turned to McBride. 'Mr McBride, this is Sean Moynihan, an old friend of mine.'

Moynihan smiled, extending his hand.

November 1940
Michael McBride was drinking in a bar in Clonakilty – the uncarpeted public bar of a grey, delapidated building that presented itself, rather unsuccessfully, as a residential hotel. The bar was sparsely populated in the early evening, the rain sliding down the uncurtained, grimy windows behind his head, the spilled beer gleaming in wet rings on the stained wooden table. He felt a covert excitement simply in being there. The hotel was known as an IRA meeting-place, had been since the twenties, and he was awaiting the arrival of a man called Rourke who was a

known and vociferous Republican. He lived in an isolated cottage north of Ross Carbery, but had lately been doing his drinking in Clonakilty.

And McBride knew, by a process of elimination that had taken him the best part of two days, that Rourke was the man with the sudden increase of grocery purchases. Words picked up, rumours, friends who had not seen Rourke for a couple of days, changes of habit, a stranger who was a cousin from Killarney – McBride had narrowed the field until there was only Rourke. And his stranger-friend-relative.

If the man was German, then McBride would have him.

He studied the barman's bald head in the Guinness-advert mirror behind the bar, watched him move into paler reflection of the glass in front of a cigarette advert framed and hung like a work of art. The barman was aware of McBride's unwelcome status as a stranger. A heavy-set man had come out of a back room, at his invitation, and studied McBride malevolently for whole minutes before disappearing again. McBride enjoyed the silent encounter, the ripples he was causing on this Republican pond. Other men studied him from time to time, but lost interest in his bland and silent exterior. He looked, sitting against the wall on a wooden bench, unthreatening. The possibility of his being a police informer could be decided by others.

As he was buying his third pint of chilly, flat bitter, Rourke came into the bar with another man. Short, dark, possibly Irish. McBride was immediately disappointed, until he corrected himself in amusement. No Prussian-officer-looking German would be sent to Ireland, anyway. He returned to his seat, the barman's eyes on him as Rourke introduced his *cousin Mike* to the regulars. It was a charade, McBride concluded, a small, intense excitement nagging at his stomach, making him belch quietly. The barman seemed concerned to draw Rourke's attention to McBride. Eventually Rourke turned his back to the bar, raised his glass while he studied McBride. He recognized him from Ross Carbery, and his connection with Devlin passed clear as a signal across Rourke's broad, lumpy face. His eyes narrowed.

'Good evening to you, Mr Rourke – and to your cousin,' McBride said amiably, raising his glass. The barman seemed to relax at once, then become more suspicious.

'McBride,' Rourke replied, putting down his glass, seeming at a loss. Almost visibly searching for a bolt-hole. Then the familiar territory of the bar seemed to reassert itself. McBride was on his own, impotent. The 'cousin' seemed puzzled yet cognisant of some unease, even danger. He studied McBride, met his eyes for a moment when mutual professionalism passed between them like some Masonic recognition, then turned back to the bar and began whispering to Rourke.

McBride stood up, his drink half-finished, and headed for the lavatory at the back of the hotel. As he emerged into the wet night, he was immediately aware of the stench from the urinal, the path wet and slippery under his feet, the noise of a passing car, the screech of a fiddle from an upstairs room. He was more aware, had shed a skin, felt the night dangerous and close around him. He went into the concrete urinal, feeling for a light-switch he suspected was not there, his hand scraping lightly across the rough brick of the wall. The poor light of one distant round-the-corner street lamp. He stood, shoulders hunched, waiting.

The big shadow of a man, blocking the poor light at the corner of McBride's eye. The heavy-set man from the back room. McBride whistled softly, as if slightly embarrassed at his proximity. Then he made as if to pass the big man, who suddenly blocked his exit.

'Something troubling you?' McBride asked pleasantly, tensing himself as the big man stepped back, allowing him to pass out of the urinal. McBride took two steps, hunched himself suddenly, and stepped to one side. The kidney-punch caught him a half-blow in the side, and he gasped. Then the man was on him in the yard, reaching his arms round him, seeking to aim a blow head-against-head, knee moving to strike the groin. Dirty, untidy fighting, just in case McBride was an expert.

McBride felt himself losing balance, his feet scrabbling to retain purchase on the wet ground as the big man grabbed him, paining his ribs, making breathing difficult, noisy. McBride kept his head back, trying to avoid being stunned by a blow from the big man's forehead.

Smell of dried sweat, old unwashed clothes, a meal on the man's breath. McBride's feet came up from the concrete as the man lifted him.

McBride had gone into his embrace with one arm crooked against his chest, as if it were being carried in a sling. Now, as the man's head jabbed closer again, catching McBride on the chin and grinding his teeth together, he stabbed back as the nostrils moved into vision. He jammed his fingers into them, raking outwards. The man screamed in pain. McBride dropped to the floor, gagging for breath, then rose to one knee and drove his head into the man's abdomen, knocking him over. Noise of a gun skittering across the concrete, dislodged as the big man went down. McBride kicked him in the side of the head, carefully and weightedly, then leaned over him, recovering as if from a distance race.

When his breathing became easier, he dragged the unconscious man behind the urinal, and let him drop behind a heap of beer-crates. The man wasn't dead – McBride would have regretted the unnecessary force needed to kill which might have been forced upon him by sheer physical size. He did not consider the possibility of some vendetta having been created in this wet, dark yard between himself and the IRA.

He heard an engine start up, a car pull away. Rourke and his cousin, presumably, heading back to Ross Carbery. Then, suddenly, he knew what was on the point of happening, and he began running out of the hotel yard towards the motor cycle he had left in a ditch on the outskirts of Clonakilty.

Rourke was in the outhouse, with the scent of stored apples and a hidden *poteen* still and two sacks of potatoes. He'd been killed with a narrow sharp knife that might have served as an advertisement of the killer's nationality and profession. The blade had been inserted between the fourth and fifth ribs, and thrust into the heart. When it was removed, not much blood had emerged. Far less, McBride thought as he knelt over the body, than had drenched

Caesar or dyed Agamemnon's bathtub. But those two had been killed by amateurs.

McBride felt the short hair on the back of his neck rise, as if the German were still in the outhouse, or the cottage, or behind the nearest knoll. He assumed he'd be long gone, over the hills and far away, but he left the body and began a methodical search of the cottage. The stone walls seemed damp, the cottage long empty and uninhabited.

The German had slept in the one bedroom, Rourke on the sofa, presumably. Supplies – courtesy of Devlin – had been laid in for an extended stay, possibly two weeks or more, and there was drink in abundance which wasn't *poteen* but beer and Old Bushmills. The German had refused to drink the stuff Rourke made in his outhouse. No maps, no radio, no clothes – except a rolled-up pair of socks that had been missed under the bed – no sign that the German would come back.

Would he?

Surely not – not for his socks, and if he had a radio, it wouldn't be buried at the house. He was running –

Was he? Why? Because of one man, someone Rourke knew, seen briefly in a bar in Clonakilty and presumed to have been removed like a mote from his eye?

And then McBride knew that the German was outside somewhere, waiting. Had seen and heard McBride arrive, had hidden the evidence of his presence as casually as he had removed the body to the outhouse –

And was now waiting to move in.

McBride shivered. He knew it – *knew* it. This was too good a place to abandon, even when the terrified Rourke had been disposed of. He was out there, somewhere –

His head snapped round as he caught the light splashing on the cottage's stone wall – fiery red, followed by the *crump* of the explosion.

A theatrical announcement by the German, blowing up the petrol tank of the motorbike. The challenge issued, the threat made. He *was* outside.

Ashe could see Gilliatt down on the sweep deck of HMS *Bisley*, picking up the quarter deck telephone. He watched the sweep deck crew – the buffer, the chief stoker and another stoker, a leading seaman and four ordinary seamen – at their staions, then he very consciously cleared his throat into the bridge telephone. He felt the insides of his mouth dry and old like an uninhabited cave, and sucked spit from his cheeks.

'Number One, prepare to sweep in "J" formation to port. Set for deep sweep, twenty-five fathoms.'

'Aye, aye, sir.' Ashe watched him repeat the orders to the sweep deck crew, and in the moment before any man moved, Ashe envisaged the whole scene before him, and political horizons beyond. The *Bisley* was rolling gently with the swell in the grey dawn, the rest of the flotilla lying astern in echelon formation. *Bisley* would begin the sweep, moving ahead with extreme caution into a known mine-field. Each ship of the flotilla would follow astern, safe in an already swept overlap, sweeping a similar safe area for the ship astern of it. The trawlers with which the flotilla had made rendezvous were in the shadow of each minesweeper, marksmen aboard each one to destroy the cut mines by gunfire when they bobbed like shiny black snails to the surface. When the initial sweep through Winston's Welcome Mat had been made, the flotilla would turn and make another sweep back on a north-easterly course to widen the channel for the cruiser and its three merchant ships.

A more misty perspective, colder and more disheartening, lay behind the solidity of apparently unmoving men on the sweep deck, unmoving ships on a grey sea. Ashe's flotilla was opening a path to the heart of Britain, and he could not avoid the grandiose imagery because his fear, even despair, was similarly large, pressing down on his shoulders like grief or age. He tried to rid himself of his mood by shaking his head, but it persisted like a cataract over the eye, requiring surgery and not mere resolution.

Gilliatt heard the reluctance in Ashe's voice even in the tinnily distorted tones that came from the telephone. For him the horizon was bounded by the sweep deck, and the eight men on it with him. Beyond that, only the sense of the ship's bow moving through dangerous water, cutting deep enough to contact one of the black mines reaching up from its sinker on its thin wire towards the *Bisley*'s hull. The fear was suddenly bilious in his throat and then he swallowed it and it was gone. It was an almost controlled habit of fear every time they began a sweep – every man on the sweep deck, aboard *Bisley* and in the flotilla, shared it – but one which was familiar and transient.

The chief petty officer in charge of the sweep deck under Gilliatt stood next to him, his horizons only those of hands and procedures and techniques and implements. Gilliatt nodded to him, and he began snapping out his orders. Each man was suddenly aware of the forward movement of the minesweeper. The sweep wire, which would cut the wires holding the mines beneath the surface, was run from the port winch to the bollards, and then the port davit lifted the multiplane otter – looking like a child's elaborate sled – to the stern for the sweep wire to be shackled to it. Then the float wire was attached to the heavy Oropesa float, and a seaman checked that the float's flag was secure. In a calm sea, the men worked with the uninterrupted smoothness of a shore drill or of machines. Then the float wire was attached to the otter, which would move through the water, beneath the surface, controlling the depth and passage of the serrated sweep wire.

When they had attached the sweep wire to its companion implements, Gilliatt spoke into the telephone.

'Sweeping deck closed up and sweep ready for streaming, sir.'

Then he moved cautiously, like a factory inspector, around the float on its chocks, the suspended otter, the winches and tackle. One last look. He returned to the telephone. Ashe's voice was still tinny and insubstantial but less colourless and afraid. Oiled by routine.

'Stand by to stream, Number One.'

'Hoist float and turn outboard,' Gilliatt ordered the buffer, who bellowed the order.

'Stand by ready to slip,' Ashe ordered.

'Stand by, Chief Stoker.'

'All hands, clear of wires,' the chief stoker yelled, an excitable Londoner who enjoyed his authority on the sweep deck.

'Stream sweep,' Ashe ordered over the telephone.

'Watch your hands, Jarvis!' the buffer yelled at one of

the young seamen hoisting the Oropesa float. The calm sea had made him careless, or perhaps his nerves were worse because he knew for certain that the mines were there. His white face glanced thankfully towards the buffer. The float was now suspended above the side of the minesweeper, the crewmen reaching up, arms outstretched in supplication as they steadied the float, appeasing some god with this committal of the float to the sea.

'Aye, aye, sir.' Gilliatt yelled direct to the sweep party, 'Lower float and slip!'

The float hovered outboard, then moved gently, sedately down to the surface of the water.

'Float clear, sir!' the buffer called from the ship's side.

'Stream sweep, Chief Stoker,' Gilliatt ordered.

The otter rattled against the stern before it entered the water. The serrated sweep wire sped easily over the racing bollard, down into the green water after the float and the otter. The buffer stood near the sliding wire, which was marked at intervals, calling back the marks to Gilliatt.

'One hundred fathoms, sir.' The wire slid on, alive and eager. Removed and independent from them. The float was moving away and out from them suggesting the great and increasing arc of the sweep wire between it and the ship. 'Two hundred fathoms, sir.'

'Good. Check speed, Chief Stoker.'

The float bucked like a prancing thing, a whale's back or a porpoise celebrating life, then it settled and moved across the quarter in a wide arc to port.

'Another hundred fathoms, gently, Chief!'

The float checked again as the sweep wire slackened.

'Three hundred fathoms, sir!' the buffer yelled.

'Check, check, check, Chief.'

'Winch brake on, sir!'

'Very good, Chief.'

'Sweep wire taut, sir!' the buffer called.

'Lower away kite, gently, Chief.'

The kite was lowered over the stern. It was a second otter, to hold the sweep wire at the required depth, acting in concert with the otter beneath the float at the other end of the great arc of the sweep wire. The chief stoker called the depth of the sinking kite.

'Five fathoms, sir – ten fathoms – twenty fathoms, sir – '

'Easy, Chief.'

'Twenty-five, sir.'

'Secure kite wire, Chief.'

'Float running well,' the buffer volunteered.

Gilliatt lifted his binoculars and checked the distant float as it rode steadily out on the port quarter, ahead of the second ship in the 'J' formation, HMS *Knap Hill*. He knew just how the float should move through the water, and he had taken to the expertise of minesweeping gladly and enthusiastically after the deadening years of desk-bound intelligence work. The float rode like a thoroughbred – it was all right. Satisfied, he picked up the telephone.

'Sweep running smoothly at twenty-five fathoms, with three hundred fathoms of sweep wire streamed, sir.'

'Very good, Number One. Post look-outs and report immediately any mines cut. We're not even sure of the density of this field – the tide could have shifted a few, but they should be in good nick. Pilot will plot every one cut.'

'Aye, aye, sir. I'll stay on the sweep deck for this lap. We may lose an otter or a kite. Sweeping our mines *must* be different from sweeping Jerry's!'

Gilliatt watched *Knap Hill* steaming cautiously, safely ahead in the arc of *Bisley*'s sweep wire. He had no reluctance concerning his position as first lieutenant aboard the flotilla leader, admitting rather the subtle, almost febrile, nerve of pleasure because his ship led the sweep, every time. Something close to the edge.

The flotilla moved steadily into the field. Gilliatt kept his glasses trained astern for an interminable space of minutes – aware of the bulk of the minesweeper at his back, thrusting ahead as if throwing out some obscure and ill-calculated challenge – and then he saw a mine bob to the surface, winking in and out of sight with the slight swell. The solid evidence that they were into the minefield plucked at his breath now, and he heard his heartbeat loud in his ears, punctuated by the first rifle shots from the side of the trawler. He waited, but the mine did not explode. It disappeared in the swell and did not re-emerge. The water had washed into the holes made by the .303 bullets. When it had gone, Gilliatt remembered to replace his cap with the steel helmet that hung across his shoulders. The rest of the sweep deck crew had retired behind him already.

In the distance, there was a fount of white water as a mine exploded, but no thump of shock-wave reached them. Then a second fountain, and a third. The flotilla's sweep wires were cutting the first leg of the prescribed path with an uninterrupted regularity. A fourth fountain, then a mine bobbing perhaps a couple of hundred yards astern of the *Bisley*, almost immediately sending up its fountain of water like a signal of its release as rifle fire exploded it. A slight tremor ran through the deck plating, and the shock of water thumped against the stern of the minesweeper.

At the end of the first lap of the sweep, *Bisley* hoisted the signal to take in port sweeps and stream to starboard in readiness for the second leg. It was a quick turn around – the men on *Bisley*'s sweep deck working even more like automata, drilled, oiled, perfect – in the reasonably calm water, with sufficient breeze blowing off-shore to take the funnel smoke clear of the look-out's arc of vision. A flow of sightings and detonations continued to reach *Bisley* until the flotilla was some miles into the second leg – the grey dawn light had strengthened but the low cloud remained, diffusing the weak sunlight so that it rubbed against the eyes like an irritant – but then minutes went by for Gilliatt on the sweep deck without a fountain of white water and without *Bisley* cutting a single mine.

For over a mile, there was a preternatural stillness that was undisturbed even by the steady beat of the engines. No rifle fire, no detonations. The telephone rang and Gilliatt picked it up.

'Is the sweep running well?' Ashe asked.

'All in order, sir.'

'We haven't cut a single mine for more than a mile, Number One. Pilot has marked the area. Damned odd. We'll finish this lap then run another leg and check as we sweep. I don't like it – '

'Sir?'

'I don't know what I mean, Number One.'

'Couldn't it be the minelayers, sir? Or perhaps the mines laid haven't been released from their sinkers?'

'I'd expect that of an enemy minefield laid in a hurry –

but not of the *Manxman* and Co.! Stand by, Number One.'

Gilliatt remained puzzled until they had completed the second leg of the sweep. Within minutes of Ashe's gloomy, mystified comments, they began cutting mines again. When they had reached the end of the lap, another quick turn around was followed by the port sweeps being streamed again for the third lap. As the flotilla, trailing as before behind *Bisley*, moved towards the suspect area where they had cut no mines, Ashe sent a signal by lamp to the rest of the flotilla.

'*Watch sweeps closely. Indicate anything unusual and any mines cut from now. Report immediately with three siren blasts.*'

Gilliatt felt his body tense, as if a net had closed over his skin and was being pulled tighter. Instinctively, he seemed to know the moment when *Bisley* moved into the empty area, and found himself waiting for the lack of danger, a false and more dangerous safety.

On the bridge the pilot, an RNVR lieutenant, checked his chart as Ashe sat drinking a cup of cocoa, knowing that his own deliberations were matched by the more inexperienced guesses of the pilot. They were both thinking that they had stumbled across the beginnings of a swept channel across the British minefield running roughly from north by east to south by west.

Then three blasts on a ship's siren, followed by a detonation. Ashe looked up, and the pilot nodded.

'Just over a mile, sir,' he said.

Gilliatt watched the first fountain of water, then a mine bob to the surface which had been severed by their own wire. Rifle fire detonated it within another minute, and the fountain of water remained on his retinae, superimposed upon the long minutes of silence and calm sea. The double-image chilled him.

At the end of the third leg of the sweep, Ashe looked up from the bottom of his cup, held still as a chalice in his hands. He had come to a decision which pressed itself urgently upon his attention. He looked across at the pilot.

'Pilot, we'll detach from the flotilla, steam to the suspect area and make a search through it.' He paused, as if the next words were too difficult to utter in the same level voice.

'We'll check out your theory of another swept channel across our own. It's too important to wait until we've finished sweeping. The rest of the flotilla to continue with the sweep.'

He turned to the chief yeoman of signals. Having broached the subject, it was easier to continue. 'Ask the first lieutenant to come to the bridge. Then prepare to take a signal to the Admiralty.'

'Sir!' the chief yeoman replied, turning to the bridge telephone and passing on Ashe's order to Gilliatt. Then he moved across the bridge to Ashe, signal pad and pencil ready. Ashe rubbed his grey, drawn face, and then spoke slowly and steadily. 'Make to Admiralty. Immediate. Repeated to DMS, to C-in-C Western Approaches, and NOIC, Milford. "Intend checking suspect area in mine-field, apparently cleared, four miles into area from westward, running North by East to South by West and over one mile in width. Will report immediately search carried out." ' He looked up at the chief yeoman for the first time. 'Take that to Lieutenant Bennett and ask him to code it up and have it transmitted immediately. Confirm when signal has been passed. Then we'll signal *Knap Hill*, repeated to the whole flotilla.' Ashe was speaking like a machine, with a voice that stepped on thin ice beneath which dark, chilly emotions waited for him.

Gilliatt arrived on the bridge, pausing at the top of the ladder as if he had burst upon some solemn ceremony that could not be interrupted. Ashe went on, speaking now to the leading signalman whose Aldis lamp was already sighted back towards *Knap Hill* astern of *Bisley*: 'Make to *Knap Hill*. Assume command of flotilla for next lap. Am acting independently for special purpose. Will contact you at end of next lap with instructions.'

The lamp chattered in the silence as Ashe beckoned Gilliatt and the pilot to the starboard for'ard corner of the bridge. Gilliatt could see the marks of concern like scars on his captain's face but felt he was only looking into a mirror. Possibilities too huge and threatening to voice or con-template lurked just at the back of the forebrain. Ashe's whisper seemed entirely appropriate.

'I'm worried, Number One. It doesn't make any sense –'

He was moving backwards in time, reaching the shore of fact that lay over the horizon of speculation they could both see. 'If there was no major error by the minelayers, and all those mines don't have working release-gear, who's responsible for the hole in Winnie's Welcome Mat?' Gilliatt realized he didn't want an answer. 'I've told the Admiralty we'll carry out an independent search from north to south in the area Pilot had mapped. We'll steam ahead of the flotilla to the area on the fourth lap and then stream double Oropesa at the same settings – ' Ashe raised his hand against an interruption Gilliatt had no intention of making. Rather, he was allowing his captain to express authority, certitude at a moment when he needed such a reassertion of self. 'I know we'll be taking a chance of blowing ourselves up on one of our own mines – and with my luck it wouldn't be a dud – but we have to solve this, Peter.' His face darkened. Gilliatt had the impression of an actor reciting carefully rehearsed lines. The emotions were genuine, but they lay as a mask over other, less controllable, feelings. 'The Admiralty boffins and DMS will buzz when they get my signal.' The last words were a reassertion of wardroom manner, enclosing the self in safe, pre-war attitudes. Jolly good show –

Gilliatt wished he could re-enter reassurance's safe, comfortable room. He nodded, and added merely, 'Very good, sir.' Ashe studied his face as if for mockery for a moment before he continued.

'You prepare the double sweep, Number One. Pilot, make sure we sail down the middle of the suspected channel.'

'Sir.' The pilot rubbed his long sallow cheeks as if to smooth out the entrenched lines or rub away the habitual stubble of beard. He appeared about to say something but took his cue instead from Gilliatt's silence. Ashe dismissed them both with a curt nod.

Gilliatt returned to the sweep deck to organize the double sweep, while the pilot returned to his navigation table. Ashe stood morosely, wrapped in a tight net of gloomy prognostications now he was silent again, in the starboard for'ard corner of the bridge until *Bisley* approached the suspected channel.

'Five minutes, sir,' the pilot called from his table.

'Very well, Pilot,' Ashe replied in a rusty, unused voice. 'I want a course to steer to the northern edge of the suspect area, and then a course to steer down its centre.' As he finished, a seaman from the signal cabin came up on to the bridge and seemed immediately unsettled by the suppressed, intent silence. He handed Ashe the Admiralty's decoded reply.

'*As soon as check carried out to limits of area required in operation signal report back. If area is clear as believed detach from flotilla and proceed with all despatch to Milford where NOIC will give berthing and movement instructions.*'

Ashe held the signal in a hand he concentrated upon keeping steady for a long time. Then he dismissed the seaman with a nod. Ashe sat down in his captain's bridge chair delicately, as if his bones were made of glass. To Lieutenant Cobner, the pilot, he looked extremely old. Cobner dismissed his own surmises, shutting out everything except the chart under its table-light, the course he was plotting.

Eventually, he said to Ashe, 'Steer zero four zero, approximately two miles, sir, then turn to one nine eight degrees.'

'Aye, aye, Pilot.'

Cobner waited as he would have on some important, personal decision until Ashe gave the order to the officer of the watch, a young sub-lieutenant standing behind the yeoman. Cobner visibly relaxed.

Bisley reverberated to increased speed and to running across the swell as she changed course. Ashe said again to the officer of the watch: 'Warn the chief buffer that I want no one below decks unless absolutely necessary while we do the search sweep. Check all watertight doors and bulkheads. Warn the engineering officer, and every member of ship's company must be wearing lifebelts – you, too, Sub!' The little personal joke fell heavily, inappropriately into the deep pool of the bridge's atmosphere. The sub-lieutenant proceeded to transmit Ashe's orders.

'Ready to turn now and point new course, sir,' Cobner said.

Ashe raised himself from his chair and took over at the

ompass platform. Clearing his throat, he began barking is orders down the voice pipe to the wheelhouse where the oxswain was now closed up and at the wheel. The oxswain CPO had the gift of touch-steering, and Ashe lways used him for anything other than routine. But the nowledge that CPO Fenwick was in the wheelhouse gave im no confidence now. Every perspective of sense or hought rendered old routines, old comforts, illusory.

'Starboard fifteen!'

'Fifteen of starboard wheel on, sir.' *Bisley* leaned to port s she swung round to starboard.

'Midships.'

'Midships, sir!'

'Steer one hundred and ninety-eight, Cox'n.' Then he aid to the yeoman: 'Tell the first lieutenant to stream weeps.' The yeoman picked up the bridge telephone and ansmitted Ashe's message to Gilliatt on the sweep deck ith his crew.

Gilliatt watched the wake of their change of course issipate behind them, and the smoke from the rest of the otilla – small grey shapes sailing a different course – ragged into stiff, unreal shapes by the offshore breeze, and ut out reflection. There was a peculiar pointlessness in pening perspectives which were better shut off by a oncentration on the smaller futilities of routine.

'Stream sweeps, port first!' Both sweeps were in the ater smoothly and swiftly, veering out on to their uarters. When the kite had been shackled to each sweep ire, they, too, disappeared into the green water. The small rey toys of the flotilla had now passed astern of the *Bisley*. istant explosions, fountains of water, the pattering of unfire. Normality. 'Sweeps running smoothly,' he said to the telephone. He could feel the ship straining against e drag of the double sweep, feel the reverberation as Ashe creased revolutions.

Gilliatt moved to the starboard guard-rail, watching the vo floats, his eyes flickering between them like those of a nnis spectator. His hands gripped the rail unnoticed. He new they must now be clear of their own swept area. No ines rolled with the swell, bobbing up to the surface. A atery sunlight which hurt the eyes less than the cloud-cover had done gleamed weakly off the water. He saw *Knap Hill*, now leading the flotilla, flash a signal to them.

'*God be with you.*'

And Fraser's Scottish Presbyterianism no longer seemed overdone or antiquated but moving instead – and forbidding. He wondered whether Ashe would return his habitual signal: '*The Devil looks after his own.*' He didn't think so. Gilliatt turned his attention to the bridge, and smiled as he read the reply. Ashe must have recovered something of his confidence.

'*May the Lord lighten our darkness and unfold His mystery.*'

When he had sent his reply, Ashe returned to his chair and sat unmoving, minute after minute, making the bridge an electric, charged, cramped space where the pilot, the yeoman and the officer of the watch fidgeted, coughed, shuffled to dispel the mood he created. The humorous reply to *Knap Hill*'s captain, Fraser, seemed to have drained some last reserve of pretence or resolution from Ashe. The pilot, as he tracked their progress through what should have been a minefield, willed Ashe to look at the chart. It was a channel, it was –

Ashe continued to sit, carved or petrified by his own knowledge. The silence beyond the bridge deafened them. They all knew it, Cobner thought, there was no need to go on. Gilliatt down on the sweep deck would know it, the sea empty of cut mines, the coxswain would know it, subby knew, the yeoman – the men on deck, shuffled for'ard of the sweep deck like a transported herd. Come on, man, come on – And then Ashe was at his shoulder, staring at the chart. Cobner's finger rested on their position. Ashe breathed in deeply, once, then crossed to the voice pipe.

'Cox'n, reduce revolutions.' Then, galvanized, he was at the bridge telephone. 'Number One, stand by to take in sweeps – in sweeps!' He paused, then: 'Report to my cabin on completion, Number One.' He turned to Cobner, eager now to escape the bridge, as if a stranger himself to the atmosphere he had created and not yet dispelled. 'Take over, Pilot. Steam north again on zero two zero until we're heading east again, inform me and we can relax ship's company a little.' The brief smile that he tried to fit to his

nouth when he had finished speaking did not seem viable
nd he abandoned it.

As he went below, Ashe could think of nothing else,
eeling the realizations engulfing him like a wave of
ickness. It was a German-swept channel, running from
he edge of the minefield to the coast of Ireland, and it
neant only one thing –

Invasion.

The Germans were going to invade Ireland.

PART TWO

SMARAGDENHALSKETTE

Chapter Six

THE COMBATANTS

November 1940

McBride, suddenly aware of every corner and shadow of the single living-room of Rourke's cottage, was assailed not by a perception of his own danger, but a complete and entire sense of the links which bound together the German outside, the dead Rourke, the beaten-up thug in Clonakilty, Devlin, and Maureen. He felt her danger, and was as impotent against it as if he were tied in a chair and the German agent on his way to silence her.

The flames from the burning motorbike he had left down the track to the cottage flickered on the wallpaper, and he dismissed the sensation of threat to his wife. There was only the reality of the man outside and the threat to himself.

He listened, and the room and the night outside it were silent. McBride steadied himself with one hand on the deal table, absorbing the solidity of its wood, the lines of knife-marks. And listened.

Nothing. He had to move. The last light from the motorbike was dying down. He had not memorized the contours of the room's poor furniture, and it was slipping back into darkness. He crossed to the door pausing, breath held, as he caressed a stool with his shin, felt it move almost imperceptibly, bent and stilled it before it scraped on the stone floor – then he opened the door very slowly, anticipating the protest of its hinges. Silence. He breathed out in a controlled, choked way, then stepped out into the short passage to the front door. He closed his eyes because he could see nothing, and listened again. But he could hear only the beginnings of the blood moving in his head, like the rustle of the sea in a shell. He opened his eyes again, knowing he dare not open the door. A silenced Luger would end it in a moment.

Upstairs. He placed his foot on the first of the narrow steps, let it take his weight, then raised his other foot. One at a time, very slowly, he moved up the short flight, resting his weight gently on every one, anticipating the betraying squeak. At the head of the stairs, he listened. One bedroom upstairs, and a storeroom. He listened, the German more omnipresent now in his imagination, more skilled and deadly with every passing minute in which he remained hidden.

Noise –?

A mouse scurrying somewhere, over his head, the swift patter of its paws loud in the continuing silence of the cottage. He smiled dismissively and with relief, though the noise persisted after the mouse had presumably vanished. Could he dismiss the noise?

He cocked his head, listening back down the stairs, beginning to wonder whether he had not made an error in retreating upstairs. He had done the obvious. He listened for a window, or a door, knowing all the time that the German was using *his* imagination as a litmus of fear, a catalyzing agent. The longer he stayed outside, hidden and silent, the more he was to be feared, the more unnerved his opponent would become.

McBride could not help the tremor that was starting in his left leg, or the nerveless sensation which had begun in his fingertips.

The mouse moved again over his head, startling him, his breath loud and ragged. He pushed open the first of the two doors at the head of the stairs –it creaked, and he scrabbled to stop it, the creak loudening and going on like an uncontrollable yawn. He felt drawn to follow it, into the bedroom. He'd forgotten the creak of the bedroom door, and cursed himself for his error.

His nose was beginning to run with tension, he wanted to sniff and dared not. He began to fumble for his handkerchief, and the emptiness of his pockets – his unarmed state – as he searched for it, further unnerved him. Gun, knife he had used on Rourke, throat-wire, unarmed combat – which? The German suddenly possessed a hundred ways of killing him, and McBride remembered the clumsy, half-beaten way he had fended off the thug in the yard behind the hotel, and the tremor in his leg became more pronounced.

He backed into a corner of the small bedroom, next to the

window, an instinctive retreat. The darkness of the rainy, moonless night was almost complete, but gradually the vague shapes of the bed, the chest, the mirror echoing the paler square of the window next to him, the basin and jug, the now opened door, emerged. He pressed his back against the wall, feeling the dampness of his fear down his spine, round the waistband of his trousers. He was growing cold, forcing himself to remain still, to listen.

The house was humming in his ears now, the silence gone on too long for him to hear anything quieter than a whisper. The German was patient, patient enough to reduce his opponent to impotence before he made a move.

Cold air flowed from the slightly open window, sliding across his hand with the solidity of liquid. He could hear nothing.

His hand got colder.

The window had been closed when he entered the bedroom, not just now, earlier when he had made his search –

No, now, when he entered the room.

Mouse-feet above his head.

The window slid noiselessly up. The German had prepared an escape-route, easing the window on his arrival, now he was coming back in.

McBride saw the arms, in the same grey mackintosh from the hotel, the white hands, as the window was pulled very slowly, very gently, upwards.

His first reaction was to run. The German was lying on the roof, easing up the window. Then he would drop into the room –

McBride felt the room, the rest of the cottage, close as a bandage around his head, a thong drying out and pressing the brain. He wanted to get out, get away. The bottom half of the sash-window was up almost as much as it would go.

He stepped away from the wall, saw the arms and hands stiffen in surprise, sensed the German's face only a couple of feet above his own.

His left leg quivered uncontrollably.

Below the window there was a rising bank of grass behind the cottage and a heap of rotting straw becoming manure along with the kitchen peelings. He'd almost tripped into it on his search, before he found Rourke.

Microseconds. The hands moving gently, slowly and aquatically, away from the window. The cold air reaching his skin like lava, creeping. The metronome in his left leg at a different tempo –

One breath, then he jumped through the window, head protected by his hands, body flung outwards, turning over, feet coming down to be caught by the manure-heap, sucking him in, the pieces of the shattered window-frame landing beside him, banging painfully against his left arm, glass clinging in his hair and clothing and his hands, a voice swearing in German a long way off, his first stumbling foot-step out of the manure, lurching forward so that he fell against the bank of wet grass with the momentum of the jump still moving him.

The click above him, the shift of a body, someone standing up as he rolled on to his back and saw a figure outlined against the almost black of the clouds. He rolled to one side, flame at the corner of one retina like a thin pencil-mark, the absorption of the bullet by the ground something that he could feel through the cheek which rested against the bank. Then he pushed himself upright and ran to the shelter of the angle of the cottage wall.

He wanted to do nothing but breathe in, but he choked off the desire for air, listening now to the unguarded movements on the roof. The German thought he was panicked, would move into the open at the front of the house, running away –

He heard the German moving over the angle of the roof, his foot scraping on the slates, one shifting slightly. McBride's leg was still, his hands firm, his heart racing but under control.

A slate fell down the sloping roof, snapped with a hideously loud noise on the paved path between the cottage and the outhouse. Then silence from the roof, and McBride fed on the guessed-at mood of the German, suddenly unnerved in his turn. And he did not know McBride was unarmed.

Minutes. Then the first movement, a quick stutter of footsteps across the now treacherous slates, the drop to the path on the other side of the house, and the silence again – all advantage cancelled. The German knew he had not run, but lurked in the shadow of the cottage, as he now did himself.

And he had a gun.

Which way? He knew the direction of McBride's dash for cover, knew his approximate location.

Which way?

McBride eased silently around the cottage until he reached the front door. He paused, listening again, then opened the door quickly, banging it back against the passage wall, then slamming it shut again.

He retreated then as quickly as he could, back to the angle of the building.

He'd seen the German's outline. His threat was compacted into a frame of medium build dressed in a grey mackintosh. He was the man called 'cousin Mike' in Clonakilty, nobody more than that.

He listened as the German came round the corner of the cottage towards the front door. He heard his footsteps pause, undecided, trying to assess the element of bluff. He was less than ten feet away – nearer seven, maybe eight at most. The cottage shrank – it was three paces from McBride to the German.

Open the door, open it –

He had to look now.

The German, boot raised to kick open the door – as McBride had hoped, off-balance and gun on the far side in his right hand. McBride launched himself as the German kicked open the cottage door and regained his balance. He caught the German in a tackle, wrapping his arms around the man, reaching with his hands for the gun. The German tried to tear free as they fell to the ground – the gun fired, then again, and again, deafening McBride, before he could get his hands on it.

The German pulled his right arm free of the tackle, tried to roll over, attempted to strike McBride across the face with his left forearm. McBride shifted his concentration to the German's face, hit down with his fist and made contact, knuckles against bared teeth, so that he knew there was no power, no effect. The German heaved up at him, turning his body, and McBride felt himself rolling off the German. He raised his body, struck again across the German's face with his forearm, immediately groping in the darkness for the hand that held the gun. His hearing was returning, he could hear his own breath and that of the German, roaring as they struggled on the wet ground.

A blow across the side of his head stunned him, but he reached up, his hand sliding across the smear of blood and grabbed the gun barrel. He wrenched down, then away, hurting the German, freeing the gun. The German threw the rest of his weight off him, and got to his feet, reckless with the knowledge that McBride had the gun, secure in that he would be unlikely to kill, needing to interrogate him.

McBride wiped at his eyes with his left hand, fumbled the gun around with his right. When he could see again, there was the noise of heaving running footsteps. He fired off two hopeful shots in their direction as he knelt by the front door of the cottage, the blood seeping into his left eye again from the cut across his forehead. The footsteps diminished with distance, with undiminished pace. The German had got away.

McBride rubbed at the trickling blood again, cursing.

HMS *Bisley* was signalled to anchor off Milford Haven, and her crew, with the exception of the captain and first lieutenant, were to remain aboard. Gilliatt and Ashe went ashore in the minesweeper's motorboat, the grey water choppy across the half-mile to the dockside. Gilliatt was huddled in his duffel-coat, hood pulled over his cap, arms thrust down into the deep pockets. He felt peculiarly uneasy, almost disorientated, like some prisoner being transported from one confinement to another. It was a localized feeling, one he sensed he had deliberately though subconsciously induced. It alleviated the pressure of Ashe's presence, his mood of inward shrinking. Ashe had the Admiralty plague of looming defeat, picked up in Whitehall. And Gilliatt knew that was where he was to proceed.

On the jetty waiting for them, impatient to help them from the motorboat, anxious and desperate to hear their expansion of the one brief coded message they had radioed to Milford, were two commanders from NOIC's HQ at

Milford, Western Approaches Command, together with a captain Gilliatt did not recognize, and an armed escort. The prisoner analogy struck Gilliatt even more forcibly, but deeper anxieties broke through that surface. He could not shake off Ashe's gloomiest prognostications.

'We'll go straight to NOIC,' the captain informed them, assessing each of them swiftly then indicating the staff car with its driver. There was a jeep, too, for the escort. Gilliatt suddenly wanted to walk away from it all, get back in the motorboat and go on pretending that the war was winnable as long as he and others like him did their duty, carried out their allotted tasks.

He climbed into the back of the big Austin next to Ashe, who smiled at him like an encouraging parent, as if Gilliatt were about to vanish round the dentist's door. The car pulled away immediately the captain got in next to the driver, hurrying out of the dock area as if towards some emergency. Milford was grey and drying after overnight rain, scoured by a cold wind that whistled outside the car windows. The captain in the front seat said nothing. The Austin pulled up the hill – Gilliatt resisted a valedictory look back at the low hull of *Bisley* slopping in the bay – and into the drive of the imposing house that had become NOIC's HQ for Milford.

The captain ushered them through the door, upstairs to what once had been a drawing-room but was now partitioned by board into three or four small offices with impossibly high ceilings and strips of green carpet that were offcuts from other offices. Maps provided a temporary artwork, there was a paraffin heater for warmth, and a utility desk and chairs. One long window, which looked down towards the sound. Again, Gilliatt refused to acknowledge the image of *Bisley*. That, he knew with a sullen certainty, was part of the past already.

As if to confirm it, the captain's first words as he took their coats were to Gilliatt, and dropped heavy as stones.

'Admiralty Intelligence until a few years ago, Lieutenant?'

'Yes, sir.' The captain studied the tone for insolence, almost tasting it with a movement of his lips, then nodded, recognizing it as disappointment

'Captain Ashe, if you would describe exactly what you encountered during your sweep of the suspect area?' The Intelligence captain sat down behind the desk, his bulk threatening it, the braid of office folded like handcuffs in front of him. Ashe told him.

'What did you do, Commander, after the first profound shock?'

Ashe looked at Gilliatt almost resentfully, as if to protest the unfairness of Gilliatt not having to answer the questions. Ashe appeared to Gilliatt to be reliving the experience. Shadows, forebodings, hovered round him. His captain had grown older in the passage of hours.

'We – I ordered the sweep to continue – ' The captain raised his eyebrows, but nodded – 'then carried out our orders. I detached *Bisley* and we proceeded to check the channel that had already been swept.'

The captain's eyes seemed suddenly alert, demanding as those of an interrogator.

'Yes? How far did you proceed – what course?'

'An hour. The swept channel is at almost ninety degrees to the channel we were sweeping. I – did not think it necessary to proceed to the southern edge of the minefield to ascertain the full extent of the sweep that had been carried out – ' Ashe was picking his way through a booby-trapped area of emotive words, smoothing all evocation from his voice.

'Go on.' The captain was childishly impatient for the climax of the story.

'The channel is almost a mile wide, and we estimate it runs from the southern edge of the minefield – ' he began to pull a chart from his inside breast-pocket, unfolding it so that it crackled in the warm, temporary room. Gilliatt listened to a typewriter in one of the other partitioned cells of the drawing-room, and a saucer rattled in a cup. Ashe spread the chart, the minefield on it, a peppering of little red crosses. The captain leaned forward, touched it almost reverentially. Then Gilliatt saw it was nervousness like their own that made him hesitant.

Ashe continued, clearing his throat, 'Here it is – it runs north by east to south by west, from the coast at a point just east of Cork to the dog-leg here which marks the edge of the minefield – ' Ashe's finger traced carefully, as if across the surface of a still-wet print. His finger moved down, and as if to stop him, the captain spoke.

'North to south – Ireland to France. Very well, gentlemen – ' He looked at the chart again, at the hard black lines that denoted the discovered channel through Winston's Welcome Mat that Ashe had marked – a dotted line indicated the remaining area that *Bisley* had not searched. When Gilliatt studied his face, he saw that it was clenched tight around some indigestible fact or emotion. There was white along the line of the jaw, the lips were thinned and bloodless, the fine lines around the eyes had become creases. 'Gentlemen – the sooner all three of us get this to London, the better.'

As the D-class cruiser signalled each of the three merchant-men in turn to alter course on another leg of their zigzag route, the noise of the U-boat spotter – a seaplane – overhead faded into the murk of the coming dusk and the rain-squall. It should have stayed with the convoy for another two hours, to the limit of its range, but the weather was already closing in on its Gander base, and unless it returned immediately it would be unable to land either at the airfield or on the lake. And it did not possess sufficient reserves of fuel to outfly the weather.

The noise of its engines disappeared behind the gale-force wind which flung great sheets of green-white spray against the super-structures of the four ships. They would be alone now, without escort or spotter planes, for fifteen hundred miles of the North Atlantic. Perversely, the bad weather was almost welcome. No U-boat could operate at periscope or torpedo depth in the troughs and peaks of the sea that was now running.

The three merchantmen altered course in turn, shepherd-ed by the cruiser. Each man aboard assumed that, whatever his dreams demanded or envisaged, they were headed for the perilous North Channel and the Clyde or the Mersey, if they survived the wolfpacks that without doubt waited for them. Except the cruiser's captain and first officer, who had opened their sealed orders after they rendezvoused with the convoy, and knew that a passage was being swept for them at that moment through the St George's Channel minefield.

Those two officers also knew the nature of the special cargo carried on board the cruiser itself, more vital in its way than the grain and oil and machine-parts on board the merchantmen, more vital even than the experimental route of this special fast convoy.

October 1980

Goessler and Lobke were shopping in Oxford Street, the younger man with an almost child-like pleasure, sampling boutiques and department stores and record shops with the hurried inquisitiveness of a garden bird seeking food in winter. Goessler's attitude was parental, a mock reserve covering his own enjoyment. After a couple of hours, they abandoned the thudding rock music of the small boutiques for the encompassing, air-conditioned expanse of Marks & Spencer near Marble Arch. For Lobke, Oxford Street had already almost replaced the Kurfurstendamm as a place of dreams.

They had travelled to London as accredited personnel of the East German embassy the previous afternoon, registering at a modest but comfortable hotel in Bayswater. From their floor, there was a distant view of Hyde Park and Kensington Gardens.

While they shopped with the habitual comprehensiveness of East European diplomats visiting the West, Goessler answered Lobke's questions concerning the operation that Goessler had termed *Juwelier* – jeweller. McBride was the merchant who would handle the gemstones of *Smaragdenhalskette*. Their deliberately casual and interrupted conversation provoked no interest in the shoppers around them.

Piling two Shetland pullovers on to the heap of shirts he carried in the crook of one arm, Lobke said, 'Herr Goessler, I don't understand something – '

'Yes, Rudi?' Goessler replied pleasantly, the greater part of his attention taken up by a cellophane-wrapped pile of cardigans through which he was searching for his size. 'What would that be?' He seemed to reject the fawn-coloured sample in his size, and began rooting under the piles again for another colour. When he did not find his size in navy-blue, he clucked his tongue against his teeth.

'Why the Wehrmacht ever attempted to invade Ireland in November?'

Goessler smiled. He had moved on to the sweaters, and held up one with a vivid green lightning-flash down its middle. He checked the size, nodded.

'Pride, more than anything else. The Pact with the Bolsheviks, the cancellation of *Seelowe* – an army of occupation sitting on the coast of France, doing nothing.' He tucked the sweater under one arm, moving on to the underwear counter with a surprising eagerness. Lobke trailed after him, the racks of suits irritating the corner of his eye, making him impatient. He returned to his questions as to an anodyne against helpless covetousness. For a moment, he understood shoplifting.

'That's *all*, Herr Goessler?'

'Inertia – yes. The Wehrmacht had rolled over everyone except England – and that prize had been taken away because Goering could not subdue the RAF. They decided to enter through the back door. Sit in Ireland until the spring, threatening the mainland. A sort of second front which would also have the effect of dissuading the Americans from sending more convoys, increasing their aid to Britain – '

A woman with rinsed hair arranged to frame her narrow face looked up at the sound of Goessler's German, and Lobke wandered off towards the suits while Goessler answered her questions concerning the whereabouts of men's overcoats – a friend had bought a long leather trench-coat on her last visit for less than two hundred and fifty marks, were there any left? Goessler seemed amused by the conversation.

When he joined Lobke, the young man was already being instructed by a sales assistant not to leave his parcels unattended on the floor while he tried on a suit jacket. Goessler laughed, explained that he would stand by the heap of plastic bags. Lobke paraded in front of a full-length mirror, shy of Goessler's proprietorial smile.

'It was rather a good scheme – ' Goessler explained, half to himself.

'Why did the Nazis try to hide all trace of it?' Lobke asked, shuffling through a rack of trousers to find his size.

'Another failure was not to be admitted, even *remembered*, Rudi – besides which, I think it was hidden deep in case it was to be used again in forty-one, or maybe even as late as forty-two.'

'But it wasn't?'

'No – *Barbarossa* was on the road by then.' Goessler seemed tempted by the racks of suits, studied a conservative brown one with a small check, held it out from the rack while Lobke guarded the parcels – aware, briefly, of the irony of the IRA bomb-panic that inspired the assistant's concern. Goessler swiftly selected jacket and trousers, and returned to Lobke without trying on the jacket. An Arab passed them, carrying four jackets, followed by his veiled wife. Both East Germans watched the couple, shaking their heads, smiling.

'Will McBride be of sufficient use to us?'

'The good Professor? Of course. He will be back in London within a couple of days. Then he will begin to look at Admiralty records, and we all know what he will discover there – ' Goessler grinned in a way that was almost good-natured, kindly. He looked at his suit, nodded. 'I believe the Americans would call it *dirty for dirty*. Oh yes, my dear Rudi – and *how* dirty it all is!'

Someone who spoke German looked at Goessler then at a nearby Oriental, and nodded in complicity.

A bell began ringing. Neither Goessler nor Lobke heeded it, Lobke already collecting his parcels and unbought clothes and heading for the topcoats next to the suits. Goessler shook his head as the younger man walked away, followed him clutching his own prospective purchases. The bell went on ringing. People moved past them.

Lobke was pulling himself into a leather topcoat when the assistant approached them, the young woman who had reminded Lobke not to leave his packages unattended.

'I'm sorry, but the bell means you must leave the store,' she announced calmly. Goessler seemed to attend to the bell for the first time, cocking his head as if to hear it more clearly. Lobke, one arm hitched into the topcoat, looked stunned.

'I am sorry – ' Goessler said, watching the customers trooping towards the exits, canteen staff passing down one of the escalators, the blue overalls of the sales staff more evident than ever. The doors out into Oxford Street and Orchard Street were wide open.

'Would you please put down all the items you haven't paid for – just on the floor, and leave by the Orchard Street exit.' She pointed across the shop. The bell insisted.

Lobke looked betrayed, mocked. He let his arm sag back out of the coat, studied the mound of cellophane-wrapped garments on the floor by his feet, and looked to Goessler as to a parent, who would somehow reverse the logic of events. Goessler laid down his own unpurchased items, picked up the bags that belonged to both of them, and simply nodded.

'Thank you,' he said to the assistant. Their corner of the ground floor seemed suddenly empty. Lobke trailed after him, joining the orderly flow towards Orchard Street. He was sulking, pouting at Goessler.

'Damn,' he muttered. 'Shit and damn.'

'There is an irony, my dear Rudi – perhaps it serves us right, you know?'

'Will we be able to come back in?' Lobke asked eagerly.

'Not for hours – the police will be here to search the store thoroughly. That will take the rest of the afternoon. I suppose it serves us right. Dear Herr Moynihan and his friends. We must look on the bright side, Rudi.'

They came out into Orchard Street. Someone was holding a placard high, instructing the staff of M & S to congregate in the forecourt of the Selfridge Hotel, across the other side of Orchard Street. A swelling gaggle of blue overalls. Customers drifted away towards Oxford Street.

'Come, Rudi,' Goessler offered. 'We will try Selfridge's.' Lobke appeared unconsoled. 'After all, if there is a bomb in the store, you may have arranged its shipment to Herr Moynihan yourself!' Goessler laughed, slapping Lobke on the back.

Guthrie came out of the small private conference room into a suite of reception rooms, his hands clenched into fists above his head, his face contorted with unexpressed anger.

He waited until two doors had closed behind him and his PPS and the Under-Secretary of State before he called out, face lifted to the ceiling:

'Dear God-in-Heaven, that bloody *man*!'

The Under-Secretary smirked, a little at Guthrie's discomfiture by the Reverend Ian Paisley, more at Guthrie's justifiable anger. The PPS, an experienced politician from a safe constituency in the south-east, maintained an expressionless face.

Ballard, the Under-Secretary, said, 'You think it's an impasse, Minister?'

David Guthrie turned on Ballard. 'What's with the formality, Donald? Are you taking the piss, or something?' Chapman, the PPS, wrinkled his mouth into a small pout of disapproval. He knew Guthrie used vulgarity as an escape-valve, but he could never quite accept it. 'And don't be so prissy-knickered, Harold – ' Guthrie shot at him. 'It's all very well keeping your faces cold-cream smooth in there, but don't let's carry the pretence too far, eh?' He strode the room a couple of times like a caged animal, then said, 'Pour us some drinks, Donald, there's a good lad.'

As Ballard fiddled at the cocktail cabinet, Chapman said, 'I don't see how we can go any way to meeting his demand for an imbalance in recruiting for the RUC to replace British troops with a *suitably loyal peace-keeping force* – ' Chapman, as if to apologise for his previous disapproval, provided a precise imitation of the Protestant cleric and political leader. Ballard burst out laughing, and Guthrie smiled, wiping a hand through his head of grey hair.

'Thank you, Harold. No, we can't, of course, but I wasn't going to tell him that. Otherwise we'd have to keep him here in Leeds Castle under lock and key until the SDLP and the Sinn Fein entourages arrive.' He accepted the whisky that Ballard proferred. 'Thanks, Donald.' He took a deep swig at it, swallowed, and sighed.

'We'll have to toy with the bugger for a couple of days. I'm not having him walk out *before* we get down to business – '

'Suggestions?' Chapman asked, accepting a gin and tonic from Ballard, who then sipped at his own whisky.

'If you have any?' Guthrie said almost carelessly, a manner warmly casual rather than off-hand.

'We could bog him down in sheer numbers and statistics – ' Ballard offered eagerly. 'I could do most of that.'

'It's one way – ' Guthrie sounded unenthusiastic, rubbing his forehead as if to ease a headache. Then he got up, walked to the narrow windows looking out to the grounds. It was growing dark.

Torches of a patrolling police unit. Vivid bark of a dog somewhere out of sight. The camouflage overalls of two soldiers fading into the background with the loss of light. He could still see their rifles, at a slope across the crooks of their arms. He turned away from the window, weary of the sight rather than conscious of security.

'I think we could profitably spend an unprofitable session or two – ' Chapman began, looking over the steeple of his fingers, 'by arguing the appointment of a new Chief Constable, who would of course be Protestant, and perhaps the establishment of a department in the new Ulster Home Office responsible for *civil order* and nothing else – even talk about a Special Patrol Group – ' Chapman opened his hands as if to demonstrate their emptiness.

Guthrie nodded. 'It'll have to do – yes, we'll take the whole lot, item by item.' He paced the room again for a while, then stared at each of his companions, as if making some mental demand of them. 'Two days – two days before we really get this show on the road.' His face clouded. 'I'm not letting that bloody man ruin everything before it gets rolling!'

November 1940

McBride was sitting in an armchair beside the fireplace when Drummond arrived. Maureen was sewing. Looking up in occasional disapproval at the plaster adorning McBride's forehead. She had been gruffly solicitous when he returned the previous night after unsuccessfully scouting for the vanished German; then, when she thought him asleep, her hands had traced his face and shoulders and hair again and again in delicate butterfly-touches, something she would not do, feeling herself not permitted, when he was conscious. Waking was a barrier between them; he was never helpless enough when his eyes were open.

'You're all right?' Drummond asked while Maureen made tea for him. McBride nodded, seemed instantly to regret the motion of his head, and grinned tiredly.

'He wanted to kill me,' McBride observed without emotion. 'He could have run at first, but he wanted to kill me. And he was an expert.' He had lowered his voice and kept his eyes on the door to the tiny kitchen. 'Now, why do they send that kind of man, all of a sudden, do you suppose?'

'I wonder if the man they landed last night was of the same ilk?' Drummond murmured.

'Another one?' Drummond nodded.

'Oh, yes – becoming quite a popular holiday resort, the Cork coast. That's four we haven't traced, four in the last couple of weeks. Hardly a sniff of them, from Cork to Bantry, but they're all in the area somewhere.'

'Are they working as a team?'

'I don't know. Your chap was on his own – before last night. Perhaps the others are, too?' He spread his hands as if warming them at the fire. 'Whether they're here on the same job would be a more profitable speculation, perhaps.'

Maureen McBride brought in the teacups on a tray, and poured out tea for the three of them. Drummond was polite, but made no attempt to engage her in conversation while he drank. For some obscure reason, Maureen McBride disturbed him. Her silences were not abstraction so much as vivid, careful attention. He felt as if he were being spied upon; and he felt that too little of the woman appeared on the surface, a sense of her withholding herself to disarm his suspicions as to her opinion of him.

When he had finished his tea, he said: 'If you're fit, I think we should have our own scout about, don't you?' He watched Maureen for sighs of agitation, but she merely studied her sewing. Mending one of McBride's shirts, it appeared. McBride nodded in reply.

'You've checked out the cottage?'

'Oh, yes. I think he had a push-bike in one of the outhouses.'

'Yes. Let the tyres down with a skewer.'

'He came back for it. His puncture kit was on the floor, and the bowl of water to look for the bubbles.' McBride looked crestfallen. 'Don't worry. It just shows he wasn't going far, mm? He ran off, then came back after you'd left. Cool customer. He must intend staying on for a bit yet.'

He stood up.

'Goodbye, Captain Drummond,' Maureen said suddenly. Drummond nodded to her, and went out to wait for McBride in the car. McBride studied his wife as if he had just received a new and surprising insight into her character. He crossed to her, pulled her to her feet and kissed her quickly.

'Now, don't worry. Drummond will look after me.'

'I'm not worried. But, take care, just for a bit of a change, will you?' She touched his face, once, with her right hand. He did not seem to resent the gesture, kissed her again.

'All right, I'll be careful, Maureen.' He saw concern flicker in her eyes despite her control, and witnessed in that moment the small, important distance they had travelled back towards each other since the beginning of his work for Drummond and the British. He had acquired a mistress she could not rival, and she accepted that. To himself, he had emerged from some chrysalis state into a self his pre-war personality could not match. He kissed her again, more gently and in understanding, and squeezed her to him as if to erase all distance between them. Then he let her go as Drummond sounded his car-horn, and his attention, she could see, was instantly elsewhere. The moment had only a diminished and awkward meaning for him. 'I'll be back tonight,' he said almost guiltily, and went out. She watched him shut the door behind him, shutting her off.

She clenched her teeth, sniffed loudly once, began to clear the tea things. If she ever apportioned blame – rather than standing beside her marriage staring dumbly at it as if into a new, unnerving bomb-crater – then she blamed Michael and not herself. She had remained still, it was he who had travelled in another, and unexpected, direction.

October 1980

His parents' former cottage in the hamlet of Leap ha
crumbled by the side of the road. Nettles thrust throug
the remains of floorboards, infested empty windows, fille
the open doorway, while heavy trees leaned towards th
decaying, and partly missing, roof. It was impossible t
enter the house without difficulty, and pointless to try
Nothing remained. Tinkers had used it as a staging-pos
for a while, but periodic storms over the years and it
habitual emptiness had made it uninhabitable. McBrid
was sorry he had suggested that Claire Drummon
show him the place. There was nothing of his father there
except a sense that he might never have lived there, live
at all.

Their first awkward embrace in the front seat of the sma
MG – hood down on a day of fine, cool sunshine – ha
however, more than compensated for the empty cottag
that had lost its power to evoke even qualified melanchol
Claire Drummond had responded to his kiss lightly, bu
without reluctance, even perhaps with promise. McBrid
was enlivened, sensed himself at the beginning of some
thing. Claire was desirable, and pliable in spite of her self
assurance.

After she had driven up into the hills behind Leap, the
sat in the car looking down over the Skibbereen-Clonakilt
road winding below them and towards Glandore Harbou
its sound dotted with the low humps of tiny islets. The
shared cold chicken and a bottle of Moselle from th
hamper she had packed, and McBride began to luxuriate i
her proximity, the small airy space that enclosed them, an
in the prospect of an affair with the woman. There wer
only the briefest moments where a sense of his lack c
direction, his Pavlovian response to outside and immediat
stimuli, disturbed his equanimity; they occurred only i
the silences between their words.

'What will you do now?' she asked him, finishing he
wine and smoking a cigarette. 'What's the next step?'

It was as if she had awoken him to a less than perfect stat
of affairs.

'Go back to London, I suppose. Begin working o
Admiralty records, and try to dig up some harder fact

oncerning Emerald Necklace. That guy Walsingham, if I an get to him – '

She was surprised at his diffidence. 'You're still nterested in it, then?'

He looked at her carefully. She seemed to be appraising aim.

'I suppose I am. Look, it's like a light I can see in the listance, mm?' She nodded, prepared to follow the nalogy. 'It gets brighter and then it fades, and I seem to get loser then seem to be further away?' Again she nodded. Well, I guess that's this book of mine. I can see it on the est-seller lists, I can feel the money – yet I wonder vhether there's anything real out there, you know?'

'Do you want to write the book?'

'Maybe I should never have gotten out my doctoral hesis – should have started fresh on something else.'

'But this is leading you to this Emerald Necklace thing, sn't it? That's new.'

'You sound like my agent – ' He grinned. 'Sorry. Your nterest is appreciated.' He sighed, leaned back in his seat nd stared at the clouds moving above him. 'Yes – yes, your nterest is appreciated. And maybe *my* interest ought to get ff its butt and do some sniffing around!'

Claire Drummond seemed relieved, pleased. 'Perhaps it hould. For your sake.'

'I guess my father – distracted me?' He nodded, agreeing is supposition. 'Mm. Gilliatt and the old man may have een involved, but they're both as dead as that cottage lown there – ' He nodded in the direction of Leap. 'I never .new him, and maybe I have to get used to never knowing im.' He grinned disarmingly. 'I have a big book to write. _ondon calls – ' He let a theatrical regret enter his features. Claire Drummond smiled.

'I'll come with you,' she announced.

November 1940

McBride and Drummond had explored the coastline etween the western shore of Glandore Harbour down to Toe Head. The search had taken most of the day, especially ecause they had to wind north then south again around the nlet of Castle Haven. They were looking for some sign of

the landing of a German agent, to give them a more precis
area of search when they moved inland. Drummond ha
received a report of a landing the previous night which wa
no more than a sighting of lights on a stretch of beac
between Horse Island and Scullane Point – and lights fou
miles further up the coast. Either or both of them coul
have been a little smuggling, even an IRA attempt to lan
guns and explosives, but Drummond could not afford t
ignore any such report.

Drummond watched McBride from behind the wheel o
his car as the Irishman walked along the beach below hin
towards Scullane Point. The tide was out and he would b
able to round the headland to Toe Head Bay withou
leaving the beach. When he had done so, they would call it
day, and go back to the unrewarding task of pub-watchin
and shop-to-shop enquiries for strangers, for increase
orders of food and supplies.

Drummond jogged in his seat with the slow, carefu
movement of the car along the narrow cliff-top track, hi
patience almost as exhausted as his physique. He was cold
and uncomfortable, and frustrated. He could scent, with
certainty, a German preparation for something hithert
outside his range of experience and expertise. Yet stil
McBride had found nothing.

McBride was waving, yelling – was McBride waving? H
tugged on the handbrake, leaned out of the window. The
were past the few straggling cottages on the cliffs, almost a
the point. Yes, McBride was waving –

Drummond got out of the car, cupped his hands to hi
mouth, and yelled down at McBride. The wind from th
sea seemed to throw his words about like gulls, bu
McBride was nodding furiously, beckoning him down
He'd found something.

Drummond began running back along the cliff until h
reached the nearest path down to the beach. He scramble
down it, his shoes scuffing, almost slipping on the loos
gravel and rock. The cliffs were low, but he was out o
breath and almost dizzy by the time he reached the sof
sand. McBride was waiting for him right under the cliff
overhang, sitting on a large rock smoking a cigarette. H
seemed, after his frantic semaphore, relaxed and un

concerned. Drummond approached him as if he suspected a joke, and he its object.

'Well?'

McBride gestured over his shoulder. 'Behind me there, weighted down in a rock-pool. One very obviously German raft.' McBride was studying Drummond as if he expected an immediate explanation. Drummond scrambled over the rocks. Just as McBride had described it, a grey inflatable raft – now deflated – lay at the bottom of the shallow pool, weighted down almost carelessly with a few heavy rocks so that it would not drift back out to sea with the next high tide. It seemed undamaged. Drummond scrambled back to McBride, and sat down, lighting his own Player's cigarette.

'Well?' he said again.

'You know, I'm thinking that we were meant to find that thing there.'

'What?'

'It's never been so easy before. As if they wanted to tip us off they're here. Now, why would they want to do that? If we hadn't found it, someone who would have told us about it or might have done – we'd have come here anyway.' McBride looked about him almost with a sense of threat. He continued in a murmur, clarifying something for himself. 'There's a man in Castletownshend would help them, and there are more than a few in Skibbereen. He might have been met here – no, why didn't they take the raft if they met him?'

'It's really worrying you, isn't it?' Drummond's features were sharpened by cold rather than concentration.

'It is. They're landing more agents than before, and taking less care – at least on this occasion. Downright sloppy, if you ask me.'

The sharp plop of something in the rock-pool behind them was clearly audible before the flat crack of the Lee Enfield rifle came to them, muffled by the wind. The second shot splintered rock near McBride's left hand, and he felt the patter of tiny pieces on the back of his hand before he was able to absorb the sensory information, understand it, and begin to move.

'Get down!' he yelled at Drummond, who was far slower to react.

143

McBride began running, stepping from rock to rock with unbalanced speed, changing direction by instinct as he moved closer to the cliff-face, under its overhang. Two more shots, the bullets skipping like angry insects away from his feet.

Then, ahead of him, and with a clear view of his dodging almost hysterical passage across the rocks, a second rifleman opened up at him from Scullane Point. There was no shelter beneath the cliff-face from the second man, whose vantage looked down the length of the beach towards Horse Island.

The first two bullets plucked through the tail of McBride's donkey-jacket as it flew in the wind.

Chapter Seven

WEIGHT OF EVIDENCE

November 1940

McBride felt the tug of the bullets as they passed through the tail of his jacket as a momentary hand restraining him. Then he pitched, off-balance, across the rocks, scraping his shins and hands, but already adopting the momentum of the fall and rolling with it, sliding down the face of a boulder, his cheek dragging painfully against its surface. He came to rest half-sitting in the shallow water of a rock pool. He lay back as another shot splintered the grey rock, whined away towards the cliff-face.

He was out of sight – trapped, but temporarily safe.

'Drummond?' he called, and found his voice ragged and dry. 'Drummond, are you all right!' A gap of time that the wind filled and the cry of a gull; but there was no shooting.

'Yes, where are you?'

'In the rocks. Are you hit?'

'No, thank God, are you?'

'No.'

Then there was nothing more to say. McBride broke the contact that seemed as fragile as a long-distance telephone call. Drummond was, presumably, out of sight. McBride lifted his head, and began studying the cliff-face that leaned out over him, hiding him from either of the snipers who might walk along the cliff-top to that point. But as long as the second man remained on Scullane Point, McBride could not move.

A bullet screamed off the rock beside his head, and the flat crack of the rifle pursued it.

One of them would come down on to the beach – by the path Drummond had used – while the second man kept them pinned down. It was a simple task, like killing seals or seabirds. McBride felt infuriated at the helplessness of his situation, knowing even as he raged inwardly that he was wasting adrenalin, wasting rationality. But there seemed nothing he could do.

He raised his head again, in a different position further along the narrow pool. The water was chilly, seeping into him already, suggesting lethargy, insinuating inactivity. He was a hundred yards from the cliffs of Scullane Point, from their shelter. A hundred yards across outcrops of rock, fallen boulders, and loose sand. He could die a dozen times before he reached the shelter of the overhang. Again, his hands bunched into fists, and he hugged himself with the fury of impotence.

He had no other choice. Drummond receded in his awareness, as if he had begun clearing out the lumber of his life in preparation for dying. The man might already be coming down the cliff-path, might kill Drummond while he was still running for the cliff-face, but it could not be helped. He slipped out of his jacket, wondered for a moment about his boots but left them on, then began breathing deeply, easily. He lifted his head again, ducked back as the bullet whined across the rocks, waited a moment before turning on to his hands and knees – then thrust himself up and out of the shelter of the rock-pool.

The wind seemed to cut through his wet trousers, the noise of the sea was more ominous, omnipresent, a gull screamed as if to warn the sniper, he felt buffeted and unbalanced. He drove on, senses flooding with information, every inch of his skin alive with nerves that anticipated the impact, the dulling blow of the first bullet.

He jumped on to sand, a shot plucking up shells and sand near his boot, then began weaving in a broken run towards the point. A speeded-up drunk. He moved by instinct, the awareness of his body's paper-like fragility growing with each moment.

His mind chanted in chorus with each thudding footstep, come on, come on, *come on* – it chimed with the racing of his blood, the hideously loud heartbeat, even with the slowed-down breaths like an undertow. Each step was taking him closer, making the angle of the rifle more acute, more depressed. The sniper had fired only twice since he showed himself. He was waiting, lining up, had him now in the notch of the sight, his progress so much slower from that angle and height, his body bulky and unmissable –

He wanted to shout out, wave his arms, felt his nerve going finally as his sense of his own fragility all but overcame him. He knew his legs were going, slowing down, his breath catching up in pace. And the rifleman was waiting for that, waiting for the exposed fly to lose its nerve, crack. Anything else would be a waste of bullets. He was very close to screaming.

He stumbled into the overhang, felt the cliff at his fingertips, heard the rattle of rifle fire as the man on the cliff-top squeezed off four in rapid succession to express his frustration, the overconfidence outrun and baffled. McBride scuttled forward until he was sitting hunched into the rock, his back pressed against it, shaking, his arms hugging his knees, his breath roaring to drown every other sound. He could not believe that he had made it, even as he accepted that he had survived the gamble that the rifleman would wait just a moment too long for the optimum shot at a target moving towards him. McBride knew – an instructor somewhere had said it – that the first, second, even third man you killed could not be running towards you, could not be so easy a target, growing bigger in the sight-notch. It unnerved, but more than that it rendered complacent, expanded time until it ran out before you noticed.

McBride had never believed the instructor – not completely – until that moment. Now, he wanted to laugh, and vomit while he laughed. He kept his teeth pressed together.

The first man who had opened up on them was nowhere to be seen. Drummond's arm waved from behind some boulders, seemingly a huge distance away, then it went back out of sight. Drummond would have to take his chance.

Recovery time, *recovery time* –

He forced himself to his feet, and immediately felt light-headed and weak, his legs leaden and useless. He jogged a couple of yards, tried to feel better but didn't, then forced himself into an awkward, shambling run around the point, keeping drunkenly close to the cliff-face for shelter and support, his feet skittering and scrabbling in the loose shale.

He rounded the point, into a notch of rock with a pebbly beach which opened out further on into the cliffs of Toe Head. If he were simply running away now, he could keep on all the way round to Toe Head Bay, away from the two snipers. He moved along the bottom of the low cliff slowly now, eyes always flitting between the rock above him and the places where he carefully put his feet.

A split in the rocks, like a jagged knife-cut. His hand almost caressed it. He slid into it, back braced, boots wedged against the opposite side of the slit. Then he began moving up, using his back, his shoulders, his feet, his grasping hands – scuttling like a beetle or other insect as quickly as he could. The wind seemed to want to dislodge him. He did not look down. It was an easy climb, only difficult because he was climbing towards a rifle, he was already nervously exhausted, and because he was doing it in a hurry. His hands reached over two sharp lips of rock, and he heaved at the rest of his reluctant body – balanced – then raised himself by his arms until his head was just above the cliff-edge, his eyes level with the thin grass, with an old cigarette-end which lay right at the edge of the cliff.

The sniper was standing up, yelling to his companion a couple of hundred yards away – no, more than that, he corrected himself. Three, three-fifty even. He seemed to have temporarily lost interest in McBride, perhaps was even at a loss. His accent was Irish, and at the same time as that realization chilled McBride he understood that the local IRA were in the business of executions on German orders, and why the boy – he was little more than that from the back – was now puzzled. He was taking orders, and more orders were now required. Who was going down to the beach? When?

The boy had assumed that McBride – unarmed, insect-like McBride running brokenly, dementedly across the rocks and sand below – was evading him, not coming for him. He was confident his target huddled below him now, catching his breath and praying for rescue.

McBride balanced again, testing the strength of his arms and the toe-holds he would use.

The German voice was shouting something about making certain that McBride – *he knew his name?* – didn't escape by following the cliff-face around Toe Head, no, he couldn't see him against the cliff-face from where he was, and maybe the other one would take the same route, and he'd better get down on to the beach at once –

McBride heaved himself up on to the cliff-edge, scrabbling with his feet to push him beyond his centre of gravity then pulling with his arms, his legs swinging sideways and over, finally pushing himself upright. The German shouted and the boy began turning. The rifle came round, lifting towards him as he thrust forward, cannoning into the boy – who was impossibly thin and light as soon as he touched him – and knocking him down. He rolled over with him, the rifle sandwiched between them far harder than the boy's bones under him. He hit the boy once, hard across the jaw, felt the neck snap round as if it had broken as easily as a twig, and the boy's eyes closed, his head lolled. McBride solicitously joggled the head, knew the neck was not broken – then hefted the rifle into his own hands, taking aim while he still straddled the boy, wanting only the German now that he was armed, loosing off three shots, tearing his fingers on the bolt action of the Lee Enfield that might have come from the Rising, almost certainly from a Black-and-Tan and now a family heirloom.

The German ducked down, then began running, away beyond the car, down into a dip, then up again where McBride loosed off two more shots before the German disappeared again. Moments later, he heard the sound of an engine firing, held back and made distant by the wind from the sea but there, nevertheless, quite clearly.

McBride stood over the boy.

'Drummond, Drummond!' he yelled. 'Get up here – quickly. Get up here!' Again, he wanted to vomit with exhaustion. Instead, he hauled the boy to his feet, held him against him tender as a lover, the rifle under his other arm.

They'd get the bastard now – if Drummond was bloody quick enough!

Room T was familiar to Gilliatt, though he had hoped never to return to it. It was in no way sinister – no part of the Admiralty was that – but it had a deadening, musty, arcane quality he had long ago rejected; finally he had thought.

It had taken them hours to get this far, after the enervating train journey from Pembrokeshire. Swansea had been bombed again, and there had been a derailment that held them up. There was bomb rubble on the tracks just outside Paddington from the raid the previous night, and that had meant a further delay. Then the initial debriefing, then the waiting around while their reports were digested, then the summons to Room T, and a man called Walsingham and his superior officer, Rear Admiral March. The two men looked as if they had been quarrelling just before summoning Gilliatt and Ashe. Gilliatt had the uncomfortable feeling of someone intruding on a family dispute. Walsingham, Gilliatt noticed, was RNVR, and it was evident from his youth and rank that he was a former civilian intelligence officer drafted into the Admiralty. Gilliatt was silently amused at the idea that he might have taken his own place. The humour of the situation gave him a sense of superiority to the room and its occupants.

Ashe was tired, worn, drained. As if respecting an invalid, March concentrated his questions on Gilliatt. He snapped them out, primarily retracing the ground that lay tracked in the typed sheets in front of him on the table, supplementing with one or two riders to the initial debriefing. It took less than fifteen minutes, and nothing in March's voice or face indicated the weight he attached to what he asked or received in reply. Gilliatt was gradually assailed by a loss of reality surrounding what they had discovered in St George's Channel. Winnie's Welcome Mat was still out there, unbreached. March's strong, unmoving face suggested as much. The late afternoon sun behind his head haloed the white hair, tipped the ears with pink – an elderly rabbit. Nothing bad was going to happen –

Gilliat jerked awake. The questioning had transferred to Ashe briefly, then back to him.

'Sir?' he fumbled.

'What are your conclusions, Mr Gilliatt? As a former intelligence officer?' March snapped, scowling at Gilliatt and the debriefing report in turn.

'It has to be – well, it has to be to land troops in Ireland, from the sea – I suppose.'

Walsingham, who had said little, beamed and seemed suddenly much more aware. March looked at him, momentary puzzlement hardening into a more habitual authority.

'Very well, I'll leave Commander Walsingham to talk to you, while you and I, Captain Ashe, have our own discussion. You'll want tea sent in, Charles?' Walsingham seemed unconcerned.

'Please,' Gilliatt said.

Ashe left like an old man being taken to a hospital ward, disturbed as to what his forthcoming tests might reveal. March was erect, and did not look back as he vacated the high-ceilinged room, its tall windows spilling light across the carpet and over Walsingham's head and shoulders, so that he squinted. A mock seafaring look, Gilliatt observed.

Walsingham wandered over to the fireplace, and seemed to study the dwarfed gas fire that squatted in it. He leaned on the high, cream-painted mantelpiece almost in a deliberate pose of abstraction. Then he turned to Gilliatt.

'I believe you,' he said simply.

'Is it a question of belief?'

'It might be. No one here wants to believe it, of that you may be certain. To their Lordships, it would be the last straw. Tell me – how do you think the Germans would have swept the minefield?'

Gilliat studied Walsingham across the room. There was something almost obsessive about him, a barely-restrained energy. Obscurely, Gilliatt didn't like him, aware at the same time that he might only be disliking a former self.

'Submarine, on the surface, probably.'

'Yes, I have other opinions that would confirm that. How would they land troops, then?'

'Ship?' Gilliatt realized he was being led to ponder the darkest unpleasantries; invited to contemplate disaster by the bland voice. 'No – submarine again. Their biggest U-boats could transport eighty to a hundred men – *each*.'

'How many troops could they land in one night?' Walsingham was almost crouching towards him by the fireplace, demanding an answer that confirmed his worst suspicions.

Gilliatt considered. 'Close to two thousand if they had the subs – and the weather.'

'And what about the present weather, Lieutenant Gilliatt?'

After a long silence, Gilliatt, appalled, said, 'I would – would consider the weather good enough, at present.'

'Exactly!' Walsingham's glance at the ceiling was almost theatrical, his face slightly flushed, his body alert with nerves.

'Exactly!' He studied Gilliatt for a moment, then nodded. 'Lieutenant Gilliatt, I am familiar with your record, and you can be of use to me. You'll consider yourself reassigned, pending confirmation.'

Before Gilliatt could protest, Walsingham had gone, leaving Gilliatt to wander to the window and look morosely down at Horse Guards Parade and St James's Park. Walsingham's enthusiasm confirmed more dire prognostications than Ashe and March put together. He did not wish to become involved any closer with the fate of his country.

McBride bundled the IRA youth into the back of the Morris and climbed in after him. Drummond took the wheel, started the engine, and screeched off along the cliff-road looking for a junction with the track the German had taken inland.

'Come on, start explaining!' McBride snapped, his hand in the stuff of the youth's sweater, bunching it under his chin. 'Where is our friend heading?'

The youth shook his head. Carrotty hair, freckles, pale skin. Scared stiff, but stubborn. He'd taken oaths, *belonged* –

'Ask him which way – again,' Drummond offered.

'Where are *you* from?' McBride asked, leaning agains[
the youth. The leather of the bench-seat creake[
Drummond stopped the car, and turned in his seat.

'Which way?' he demanded.

'We are going to find out, you know,' McBride said wit[
a smile, letting go of the sweater, taking out cigarette[
'We'll all have a quiet smoke, and then we'll have a tal[
mm?'

The youth took the cigarette, McBride lit it, the bo[
coughed, looked defiant, then dragged deeply. Suddenl[
he appeared very vulnerable, and aware of the closeness o[
the car around him, the proximity of the two tall men muc[
older – and wiser and more ruthless, no doubt – than he. H[
coughed again.

'English cigarettes, eh?' McBride said, his accent slightl[
broader than before. 'Like everything else, they're not fo[
the Irish, eh, lad?'

'Why are you working for *them*, McBride?' the la[
snapped back, nodding at Drummond. 'We know a[
about you, McBride – ' He flinched as McBride's fac[
hardened.

'Now, that's not the way to get out of here in one piec[
lad. What's your name?'

A long hesitation, then: 'Dermot.'

'Pearse, O'Connell, Yeats, Gonne, Casement – which [
it?' The boy appeared puzzled, then realized he was bein[
mocked. 'You've joined then, have you?' The boy nodde[
'So, Dermot, you've got a bloody great gun, and you're tol[
to go and blow my head off – and you nearly did, mm? But [
isn't quite the same as shooting pheasants or crows, is it[
The boy disliked the turn of the conversation. 'How old ar[
you, Dermot?'

'Twenty – '

'Grow a moustache, Dermot. If you're over eighteer[
I'm a black-and-tan. And just say I am and I'll push a[
your teeth back down your throat, Dermot.'

The humour and the threats disturbed Dermo[
Drummond turned away on cue, just as the boy began t[
look to him as a silent, and therefore rational, being.

'Piss off, you – ' The flinch was just below the surfac[

the shudder one layer of skin too deep to show. But McBride knew Dermot was hanging on to his new identity in the IRA. The German probably meant nothing to him at that moment.

'That's a brave lad. They'll give you a martyr's funeral, no doubt of it. I'll tell them you were spitting defiance up to the last.' He paused, smiling, then: 'You little cunt, you tried to *kill* me! You're going to pay for that – ' He opened the door, and pulled the boy bodily across the back seat and out of the car after him. Without hesitation, he dragged him to the cliff-edge, then held him at arms' length, teetering on the edge, body inclined so that if McBride released him he would be unable to regain his balance, would fall. 'You've tried to kill your last Irishman, Dermot – your last *anything*!' The wind plucked at Dermot's grey mackintosh, at his red hair. His face was shining with a ghostly paleness. His eyes kept moving from the beach below to McBride's pitiless face. 'You think it's like the Boy Scouts, do you, Dermot? It isn't, lad, it isn't. You've joined the scum, the bombers and the assassins – the *comedians* of destruction! You're going over, Dermot. I'm going to save your soul, Dermot. Save you from yourself! There's time, Dermot – start saying your confession. *Absolution follows!*' He bellowed with laughter. Dermot screamed. McBride loosened his grip on the boy's arm, then jerked him backwards. Dermot collapsed on the grass in a faint. Vomit leaked thinly from the corner of his mouth. McBride turned him over so that he would not choke on it.

When Dermot regained consciousness, he found himself back in the car, a tartan rug wrapped round him. Drummond pressed a flask of rum to his lips. He coughed as he swallowed, but the drink seemed to revive memories, and his eyes darted in his head. He was obviously looking for McBride.

'I've sent him for a walk, to calm down. But, you did try to kill us, Dermot. It did make him angry.'

'He's mad,' Dermot mumbled, swigging again at the rum. 'McBride is as mad as a hatter, mister!'

'Tell me – why you, Dermot?'

A long silence in which Drummond could almost hear the fragile raft of Dermot's recent oaths tear itself apart, strain and break against the rocks of immediate experience

Dermot told Drummond everything – which wasn' much. He'd been available, had a gun – once his father's his grandfather's originally – and the German had neede help. He'd been ordered to give it. The German hadn' joined up with any other Germans, as far as he knew. Yes the Skibbereen Battalion was giving help to the Germans how many? Three or four since Dermot joined. Yes, the were still about –

Eventually, the little cargo of information had dimin ished to nothing. Drummond was certain of it. He said 'Right-ho, Dermot, on your way.' The boy was nonplusse and did not move. Drummond opened the rear door fo him, waved his hand in a gesture of dismissal. 'Go, and si no more,' he added, then: 'Dermot, you're free to go – g and tell them you got away from us, you told us nothing what the devil you like – but *go*!'

Dermot scrambled out of the Morris and away, soo disappearing behind a dip of the headland, coat-tails flyin behind him. After a while, Drummond lit a cigarette, an McBride rolled out from underneath the car, stood up an brushed himself off, and joined Drummond.

'Fat lot of use he was, our Dermot,' he observed. 'Quite good choice by our German friend. Young enough not t think of the consequences, and young enough, too, to kno nothing.'

'We'll not get anything out of the Skibbereen Battalion A dead end, if they're protecting German agents.'

'You know – I would have thrown him over if thought that way I could have done him the favour o keeping him out of their hands – and if I could be ruthles enough.'

'Michael – you mean it, don't you?'

'Yes. Oh, you didn't know they killed my father, did you No wonder it came as a surprise to you.' Drummon studied McBride, who was staring through the windscreen memory racing. He could ask no more questions.

'What do you think?'

'If they want to get rid of us, then I think they must b very close to whatever they have planned. It's so *out o character* for those Skibbereen clowns, they're being hard pressed by someone else. God, they think the Germans are going to help them unite Ireland! No, forget it – ' McBride was talking almost to himself. 'They must be scared stiff of us – not because of who we are or what we know, but just because of what they're up to! We're a danger just because we're here – now, tell me what it might be.'

Rear Admiral March was sufficiently alarmed by the debriefing of Gilliatt and Ashe that he allowed himself to be badgered into calling a consultative meeting in Room T which would consider OIC's response to the German sweeping of the St George's Channel minefield. The Admiralty's Operational Intelligence Centre had failed, during the first year of the war, to develop its resources of cryptanalysts and air reconnaissance to a degree which would provide the Intelligence Division and the Director of Naval Intelligence with an understanding of German naval intentions and planning. OIC had had to take its share of blame for the fiasco of the Norwegian operation in April of 1940, and had been among those most relieved by Hitler's cancellation of *Sea Lion* in October. Recent history made an uncomfortable extra presence in the room as Walsingham, with Ashe's chart pinned to an easel near his chair, rose to address the men he had been able to gather together for the early evening meeting.

March sat at the head of the table, Walsingham at his right, a Wren stenographer on his left. A lieutenant from the Tracking Room – an ex-submarine navigator and an expert on German-swept channels – sat nearest the betraying chart, and had been studying it since his arrival. A commander from the office of the Director of Minesweeping was deputizing for his chief, and Walsingham had managed to persuade a lieutenant-commander from the Anti-Submarine Warfare Division of the Admiralty to delay his date with an actress.

Walsingham looked once at March, who studied the reports and pictures in front of him studiously. Each man in the room had a duplicated set. Walsingham, looking at the mostly young faces, at the insufficiency of gold braid around the uniform cuffs displayed on the table, felt a momentary qualm. This was most definitely the sixth-

form debating society in terms of the Admiralty's hierar
chy. How long would it take him to get from there to th
headmaster's study?

The image daunted him, but it also amused an
challenged him.

'Gentlemen, you've all had time to study the reports an
photographs before you, albeit hurriedly. I think our firs
priority – ' He glanced at March again – 'is to establish tha
the St George's Channel minefield has been swept by th
Germans. Barry, your opinion?'

The young lieutenant from the tracking room seeme
startled out of his assiduous attention to Ashe's chart. H
blinked.

'Yes, sir. There are no orders for a British sweep – sorr
only that carried out by the *Bisley* and her flotilla. N
north-south sweep by us. And from Lieutenant Gilliatt'
detailed description, I think it's certain the Germans swep
this using submarines on the surface. At night. It has th
marks of a German sweep, much like one of their ow
swept channels – ' He glanced at the DMS's deputy, wh
nodded.

'Commander?' Walsingham asked.

'Yes, you've spoken to the DMS already. You know tha
it was swept by the German Navy, and how they did it.'

'Thank you, Commander. It would seem to be our nex
priority to try to understand the movement of Germa
naval vessels as they might be affected by this sweep
Chris?'

The lt commander from ASW Division said im
mediately, 'What you want to know is – did we spot thos
U-boats of yours on Guernsey, and where are they now?'

The Tracking Room lieutenant, Barry, chuckled
Walsingham nodded his head as if Chris had scored a nea
point.

'Did you?'

'We did. That many heavy-duty submarines wer
tracked from Brest to Guernsey. But we didn't know the
ever left Guernsey – this sweep was done at night, whic
would explain our oversight. Ask Tracking Room – '

'Barry?'

'We – don't know where they are now. When you came t

see me the other day, I got on to it. If they've left Guernsey, then they did that at night, too. They haven't emerged from any other base – not as far as we can tell.'

There was a sense in the room, Walsingham was aware, that those present had been carefully, cleverly orchestrated, and that they were reciting lines long prepared, like suggestions that Walsingham might have planted in them under hypnosis.

'I have information from Guernsey which suggests that the sheds are now empty. Would the U-boats return to normal wolfpack duty, Chris?'

'It seems likely. They must be back in Brest by now, then. Neither we nor Tracking Room have registered any of those designations at sea in the past four days.'

Walsingham nodded. 'We'll go on. What, gentlemen, was the object of converting those heavy-duty U-boats – which the German Navy cannot easily spare from North Atlantic duty – to sweep that channel?'

March said, 'You're preparing your ground here, Charles. But we already know what you think. Do you want us to vote on it?' The sarcasm was abrasive, crude.

'Gentlemen, I had a suggestion earlier in the day which made me think. It was suggested – by Lieutenant Gilliatt – that perhaps two thousand front-line Wehrmacht troops could be transported in a single night from the coast of France to the coast of southern Ireland, by submarine. Is that feasible, do you think?'

Chris from ASW Division was first to speak. 'Mm. It's a small force – but it's less noisy and a lot more efficient than dropping parachutists in large numbers. I'm not a military expert. Those subs you found in Guernsey could do the job – '

'Very well. When was any one of those U-boats *last* recorded on anti-convoy duty?'

Barry said, 'I checked those numbers off. Two weeks ago, U-99 was seen returning to Brest, moving on the surface at dawn. Spotted by an unarmed Coastal Command Anson. It dived, but they got the number. The others are earlier sightings.'

'And no one's seen them since then, until Guernsey, and not since then?' Heads were shaken, the commander from

DMS was now intrigued, converted. March remained with his head bent over the papers on the table, unwilling to accede to the slowly mounting barometric excitement in the tall room. 'Very well, where are they, and what are they doing? My man saw them in Guernsey stripped down – even the gun was missing – and rigged for sweeping duties. Those duties, we know, were completed. Now they are no longer in Guernsey – are they in Brest, and what are they doing there?' Walsingham held up two glossy prints. 'Air reconnaissance pictures of Brest, taken yesterday. The weather was good enough – '

'These don't even show the harbour, certainly not the U-boat pens – ' Barry objected. March nodded in agreement.

'No. But, if you look carefully, you will see an unusually large concentration of military equipment.' He tapped at each picture in turn. 'Other pictures record the same sort of movements – *troop movements* – in and around – Brest. An expert in this sort of thing from Army Intelligence is prepared to bet that there are at least two new divisions in the immediate Brest area, just on the basis of the transport he can pick out on these pictures. Unfortunately, we don't have other pictures of the area behind Brest. At present. But we should have some by tomorrow.' He smiled in March's direction, acknowledging a concession. 'If those new troops in Brest have any connection with the submarines we suspect are back in Brest, what can we conclude from that?'

The question elicited only silence, until March spoke. He stood up, and spoke slowly and distinctly, his teeth almost closed together. The veins stood out on his neck. All the time, he continued to look at the table in front of him.

'Gentlemen, this meeting is closed. Thank you for your time. I do not need to remind you that these matters are to be discussed with no one outside this room. I apologize for any sense of *anti-climax* you may now feel.' He glared at Walsingham. 'Commander, if you'll come with me – '

He walked out of the room, followed by Walsingham. The Wren finished her shorthand, and the three naval officers stared at the door through which March and Walsingham had retreated, then at each other. They appeared like children robbed of the ending of a new, and absorbing, bedtime story.

When March had sat down at his desk, and Walsingham had closed the oak door behind them, he barked at the junior officer with an anger that Walsingham had never seen unleashed before. He had pressured, even embarrassed, the Rear Admiral in a deliberately cavalier manner. And the Admiral knew he was being pressured.

'Don't you *ever* try to do that to me again, young man!' March's eyes burned. He let Walsingham continue standing like a recalcitrant in front of his desk. 'You tried to *force* me to side with you, fall in with whatever ridiculous scheme you have in mind! I will *not* be blackmailed into agreeing with you out of embarrassment! You arrogant young puppy!' Then March subsided into silence, staring broodingly at his blotter, at the papers he had carried with him from the conference room. Walsingham stood very still, staring at the portrait of the King that hung behind the Admiral's desk; George VI, King-Emperor, in full naval uniform. A little, thin gleam of patriotism came and went, ousting the arrogance of conviction, the personal quality of the course on which he had embarked. Then March spoke again, tiredly. 'What did you attempt to persuade me to do, Charles?'

'Sir, I'd like to put someone into Brest, immediately, to recce for those U-boats, even to look at the troop dispositions.'

March looked up as if slapped. 'Beneath your absolute conviction of your own brilliance, Charles, are you equally convinced of the reality of this German invasion?'

'Sir, I am.' Walsingham's cheek glowed at the accusation of arrogance. Its truth struck him as he went on staring at the portrait of the King-Emperor. 'Yes. Admiral. I'm convinced that the Germans are planning an invasion of Ireland – as a beach-head to replace the foundered *Sea Lion* venture. A second front against the mainland United Kingdom. And a means of closing, *finally,* the convoy routes. Just imagine U-boat bases in Ireland –'

March, surprisingly, nodded. 'We've been wrong, or

behindhand, or short-sighted most of this year. We can't afford to be wrong again.' His eyes were hard as he looked up into Walsingham's young face. 'God, Charles, I hope *you're* wrong about this!' Then he seemed to shrug off such speculation as useless. 'We'd better get something organized. You'll want experts, of course – '

'Sir, I'd like to use my man McBride, and Lieutenant Gilliatt, the officer who – '

'Yes, I know who Gilliatt is. Formerly of the Intelligence Division, yes.' March pondered it. 'You have a predilection for this man McBride – you obviously think him good.' Walsingham nodded. 'If you in your unbounded arrogance think him good, then he must live up to an impossible standard! You're ruthless in your *assessment* of people, Charles – ' Walsingham's features remained an inexpressive mask, and March brushed his hand across the desk as if to dismiss the ineffectual reprimand. 'Very well, get McBride here as soon as you can. Operation plan to be on my desk first thing in the morning!'

October 1980

'I see. Very well. If Mr Walsingham is going to be absent for the next few days, perhaps you could give him a message when he returns – would you inform him that the son of Michael McBride – yes, that's right, Irish spelling – his son is making enquiries into Emerald Necklace – ' Drummond chuckled. 'Yes, it does sound mysterious. Please tell him that, would you. Goodbye.'

Drummond replaced the receiver, and sat back in his chair, smiling up at the ceiling of his study. Outside, the evening was quiet except for a fresh little wind that had sprung up at sunset. The house, too, seemed silent, and empty. His face sagged into folds that mirrored his mental lethargy now he had delivered his message. Walsingham, no doubt, as head of the Directorate of Security, was supervising the intelligence and security effort around the Leeds Castle conference. It had taken Drummond some time to get through to Walsingham's senior aide. As Head of the DS (MI5), Walsingham had an official civil service rank as a Permanent Under-Secretary at the Home Office and was hedged about with the expected number of assistants, aides, secretaries, all of whom had needed placating before he could leave his cryptic message. A glimpse of Walsingham's face when he received it would have been worth having.

Drummond felt tired, and edgy, unrelaxed. He was disinclined to listen to the gramophone or Radio 3. Nothing attracted him to the television. On the ceiling, clear as pictures, his own past glimmered. McBride was roughly assisting him down a road he did not wish to follow. And the father lurked behind the son, the recollected smile a pain in his side. His stomach felt gaseous and empty, but he could not be bothered to cook a meal. He was nearly eighty, for heaven's sake, and these pictures bobbing unwilled out of the dark at the back of his mind were harsh and unwelcome.

He heard a small car approaching, and suddenly shuddered as if he had opened a window to the breeze. It stopped outside, and he heard the approaching footsteps with something like terror. The present wiped away the ceiling-images rudely, insisting with a contemporary nightmare of its own. The doorbell rang. Sighing, he got shakily to his feet and went to the front door. He switched on every light he passed.

It was Moynihan, as he had known it would be. He had recognized the car engine. Moynihan was grinning.

'You'll invite me in, then?' he said. Drummond reluctantly made way for him. Moynihan, familiar with the house, made for the study, warming his hands at the fire whose flames shimmered on the ceiling. He sat down in the easy chair opposite Drummond's own. With unwilling complicity, Drummond poured two whiskies and handed one to Moynihan. 'I suppose your coming was inevitable,' Drummond said, sitting heavily in his chair, swallowing at his drink.

'Naturally, Admiral.' Drummond winced at the rank, his face pursing. 'I made sure they got off all right from the airport.' Drummond appeared startled. 'Don't worry. McBride didn't see me. But, as I was saying to you, I saw them off, then came straight here – for a briefing.' Moynihan laughed.

'Claire will be all right!'

'Come now, Admiral. We know they're not looking for her. She's your daughter, dear God – how safe could she be?' He laughed again. 'No, just tell me what he'll be up to in London.'

'Admiralty records, for the most part. He'll find the sort of thing you need there – ' A swift passage of emotions across Drummond's face, to which Moynihan attended. Many of them puzzled him, and Drummond, he finally decided, was confused with age and senility. Fear, concern, sense of betrayal like repeating images. Claire had suggested her father was totally pliable, which he was. But she hadn't suggested an intense mental life surrounding what he had been forced to do with regard to McBride – point him back to London

'Gilliatt – ' Drummond began, then fell silent.

'Yes? Us, do you mean?' Drummond nodded. 'No, I think he died naturally – old age. Unless it was – someone else?' Moynihan thought of Goessler, but remained silent. He didn't know.

'God, it's a *mess*!'

'Your daughter joining us, you mean?' Drummond nodded. 'Ah, well, Admiral. Not your fault she's more Irish than a lot of the Irish are. She was born here.' Regret again on Drummond's face. 'I'll keep an eye on her in London, don't you fret, Admiral. She'll be quite safe. And you've played your part splendidly, haven't you now?'

Drummond, staring into the fire, regretted his call to Walsingham, regretted even mentioning his name to McBride. Claire had no idea that Walsingham was still in intelligence work; she thought of him as a civil servant. What had he done to her? Had he betrayed her?

He was horribly, inescapably caught in a trap. He saw that now. How could he save his daughter by betraying her? How would that get her out of Moynihan's hands? He'd led McBride on, played his part in McBride's betrayal, as she had wanted and demanded. But what had he done to her, telling Walsingham?

Even after Moynihan had left, indifferent to the old man's silence, he sat on staring into the fire, the empty glass still clenched in his hand. What had he done to Claire?

What would happen to her?

Even when he occasionally glanced at the ceiling, it was only a screen for the past. McBride's father. Forty years ago, what had he done to Michael McBride?

Chapter Eight

FRENCH LEAVE

October 1980

David Guthrie, getting easily out of the back seat of the Daimler, the camera moving into close-up as he walked from the car, then Guthrie turning and waving before going in. The security guards – including soldiers in camouflage uniform, rifles sloped over their crooked arms, heads moving constantly – evident, almost omnipresent. The Daimler pulling away, the camera focusing on the BBC reporter sombrely expounding the significance of the opening session of the Leeds Castle conference on Northern Ireland. The reporter consulting his clipboard of notes frequently, listing the parties present for the opening session – SDLP, Ulster Unionists, Sinn Fein, the government, observers from the Eire government –

Moynihan crossed the room and switched off the television. The screen flared down to a white spot which he watched as if mesmerized. Then, when he seemed satisfied that the images from the BBC news would not reassert themselves on the screen, he returned to his chair. The hotel room was thick with cigarette smoke, there were opened and empty beer bottles on the small writing-desk and the low table by his chair. The bed was unmade. The hotel in Bloomsbury had been his London base on more than one occasion; one of those anonymous hotels used by commercial travellers or football supporters and by members of illegal organizations. Moynihan was not a man the Special Branch or MI5 put high on wanted lists or whose movements they assiduously watched, and the hotel was one remove from the seedier refuges of terrorists and illegal immigrants.

He lit another cigarette, glancing distastefully at the

crowded ash-tray as he did so. He exhaled the smoke towards the ceiling. He felt that Guthrie and the British had gained an important initiative, had outwitted and outdistanced him. A furious, angry frustration possessed him, making his free hand clench and unclench repeatedly as he sat waiting for his visitor. He was impotent, in the hands of others. He wanted to hit back, make assertions of his own. Claire was in London with McBride, but the thought brought no comfort or respite from his anger. McBride, fiddling in forty-year-old records, could not, in Moynihan's imagination, successfully oppose the image of a smiling, casual, self-satisfied Guthrie at Leeds Castle. McBride was a useless dummy.

There was a knock at his door. He stubbed out the cigarette instantly, came out of the chair like a lithe animal, gun appearing in his hands from behind the cushion, and he moved silently to the door. Action, even this action, charged him with a subtle electricity. He almost wanted it to be Special Branch on the other side of the flimsy woodwork, flimsy as flesh and bone –

'Yes?'

'Lobke.'

Carefully, he opened the door on its safety-chain. The young East German's face smiled at him, saw the gun, and smiled more broadly. Moynihan unlatched the chain and let Lobke in.

'You're late,' he said, closing the door. Lobke seated himself almost primly in a chair opposite that bearing the impression of Moynihan's weight. He had shaken his head quickly at the unmade bed.

'I'm sorry, Herr Moynihan. Business, you know –' He raised his hands, let them drop, recollecting his purchases in Bourne's and John Lewis's.

'Making sure McBride dots his i's and crosses his t's, I suppose?' Moynihan sneered.

'You seem on edge, Herr Moynihan?' Lobke was looking at the beer bottles. He waved towards them with one hand. 'You have any that are full?'

Moynihan took two bottles of Guinness from the string bag under the bed, opened them and poured some of the black stout into a tooth-glass, almost deliberately letting the thick head overflow. He handed it to Lobke, who sipped, then said, 'I prefer the dark beer they make in Prague – you've tried it, Herr Moynihan?' He sipped again. 'It's very good – the Czech beer, I mean.'

'Bloody connoisseur,' Moynihan muttered, sitting down, lighting another cigarette. Lobke watched him.

'Count the stubs, Herr Lobke?' Moynihan invited. Lobke shook his head, smiling.

'I understand how you feel – like a caged animal.' Moynihan nodded, disliking even that much agreement with Lobke's analysis. 'Herr Goessler has sent me to tell you that we think McBride is making good progress – he is *refining* his researches just as we would wish.'

'God, this bloody game you and fatty Goessler are playing!' Lobke's nose wrinkled in disgust. Moynihan leaned forward in his chair, drawing deeply on the cigarette. Stout slopped from his own glass on to the thin carpet between his feet. 'You tied my bloody hands from the beginning, Lobke. I had no *choice*!' His fist clenched in front of him; the glass of stout appeared fragile and threatened in his other hand.

'You were like a greedy child,' Lobke observed, speaking almost with Goessler's tones.

'Mother of God, you take some beating, Lobke. Goessler offers me the chance to bring down that bloody conference and create the biggest mess the Brits could find themselves in – what in hell do you think I'd have done for that? You can have my right arm, Lobke, but for God's sake get something *done*!' Moynihan's upper lip was shining with sweat. His eyes were intense, burning as if with a fever.

'Calm down, Herr Moynihan. McBride is now clearly on the right track. He will soon bring to the surface the elements of the situation that you require. Then – you can have him.'

'Tell me –'

'No. Not yet. But it will ruin the conference, and Guthrie, it will discredit the British Government in Ulster, poison the atmosphere for future talks for perhaps ten years, alienate world opinion, especially America – what more could you ask, Herr Moynihan?' Lobke's smile was especially irritating at that moment. Moynihan wanted to hit him, but wanted more to remove from his own features the hungry eagerness he knew they displayed.

'So you say,' he said.

'We *know*, Herr Moynihan. What we promise, we deliver. Guns, explosives, papers – and Guthrie's head on a plate. But, patience is a virtue – '

'All right, all right. What about Claire?'

'She is doing her job, I believe?'

'Has she been to bed with him yet?'

'Soon, I believe. Another little sacrifice, Herr Moynihan. In the expectation of great things, mm?'

'Just deliver, Lobke – or I'll have your balls, so help me I will. In a specimen jar, and labelled.'

Thomas McBride considered, as he heard the key scraping in the lock of her hotel room next door to his, the last few days, since their meal in Kilbrittain. Moynihan had been a momentary irritation, having left after sharing a drink with them, walking out of their lives quite deliberately, it now seemed to him. She had explained him away as a friend, and he believed her. He listened intently, sitting at his desk, the day's notes in front of him, as she opened her door and entered her room. The kisses on the hill above Leap, and since, had promised without fulfilment. He did want her, yet more he attended to her noises in the next room as if to something loved through familiarity. He was prepared to wait for her.

He disregarded his recent sexual experiences, the few relationships with students of his – plus one brief affair with a feminist associate professor that had ended a year before – because Claire Drummond had placed them in an unflattering, immature light. They displayed themselves to his memory as pointless affairs of self-flattery, affairs of taking rather than giving. By ignoring or despising them now he understood himself to be more than half in love with Claire already, and entirely acquiescent to the idea of loving her.

Tourist things, they'd done mainly tourist things. The shops, the sights, a lot of laughter that shaded into smiles of promise and acceptance. He was – this he was prepared to admit because he welcomed the sensation – besotted with her. He wanted to make love to her; more he wanted to love her and be loved. He felt his breathing shallow and quick as he waited for her to knock on the interconnecting door between rooms 402 and 404 of the Portman Hotel. And when she came in, he wanted her arms to be full of parcels purchased with the money he had given her for clothes – she had her own money, enough for Liverty's and all the expensive clothes she wanted, but he had given her the gift of a blank cheque as a declaration. *No strings attached,* he had said, and almost meant it.

She knocked, and walked in. Her arms were full of bags, above which she was smiling almost apologetically, and she suggested a past and a context to their relationship which had remained absent until that moment. He felt a rush of gratitude in his chest.

She was wearing new boots, and a new dress. She heaped the packages on his bed, taking a winter coat from one of the larger bags, which she put on and paraded before him. She did not make the fashion show an occasion for titillation, nor did he regard her as an object of immediate desire. She seemed closer to him, better known, than that.

'You like them, then? You approve?' He nodded. She draped the coat over a chair, then sat down. 'Pour me a drink – shopping in London is murder.'

He poured whisky for them both, toasted her, then she came and stood by his side, looking down at his notes.

'Busy day?'

'It must be easier than shopping in London,' he observed, his hand wiping across his notebooks, the arranged scraps of paper.

'Are you getting anywhere?' she asked. He was aware of her thigh against his shoulder; aware too, of another mood suggested. He watched her parading her purchases now in a different way, replaying the images to himself – turn of the body, line of the thigh and hip he could sense through his shirt-sleeve, breasts only emphasized by the new dress.

'I – yes, I think I am. I'm looking at naval activity around that period, near the Irish coast and the French coast.'

'What have you found?' Her thigh pressed with an emphasis – he was sure of it – against him. He heard the rustle of the dress against the nylon of her tights.

'I'm not quite sure, yet. There are some important factors I know already, of course. The St George's Channel minefield, for example – ' He looked up at her. She seemed almost brooding, not looking at him but at his papers.

'What – ?'

'The minefield protecting the channel between Cornwall and Ireland. The Germans would have had to deal with it if they wanted to land between Cork and Waterford.'

'And – ?' Her hand on his shoulder was an almost absent gesture. He shivered, barely perceptibly, and she seemed not to register the reaction she had created.

'I haven't found any evidence of the minefield having been swept by the Germans. But a British minesweeping flotilla left Milford Haven – in Pembrokeshire – under sealed orders at just about the right time. I'm trying to follow their progress. I'd like to know where they went, and what they did.'

'Why?'

'I don't know – maybe it's just a hunch? I have some reports from Admiralty Intelligence about troop movements in the Brest area of Brittany about the time – ' He looked up at her. 'I *know* I'm close to it!'

She smiled with a peculiar intensity, transferring her gaze to her hand on his shoulder, then swallowing some of the whisky. She seemed intensely alert, expectant, and for a moment McBride thought her concentration had nothing to do with their physical proximity.

'Good,' she said, and it was obvious she had lost interest. Her hand rubbed the hair at the nape of his neck.

'That minesweeping flotilla lay at anchor on its return for three days – the flotilla captain was ordered to London – ' then he added, his voice thick and his concentration elsewhere: 'there's something about the time of return, and the sailing date – I almost realized what it was just as you walked in – ' Then he gave up the small, and quite uninteresting, spark of enquiry, putting his arm around her thighs, squeezing her against him. She moved slightly closer, then bent in front of him, putting down her glass on his notes. Normally fastidious, the wet ring created on his notebook did not irritate him.

He lifted his head, kissed her. Her mouth rubbed against his, her tongue prised open his teeth. There was something diametrically opposed to their earlier selves between them now, something uncomfortable, vivid, almost violent. She had retreated as a person, become merely physical. He stood up, pressing against her, moving her towards the bed. She stepped back for a moment, smiling, and undid the tie-belt of the dress, and the buttons, stepping out of it as it dropped to the carpet. The she pressed against him again, moving her hips, her arms pressing his sides, fingers splayed and slightly clawed against his back

He moved her slightly sideways, then they declined on the bed slowly, statuesquely, their limbs interweaving with a slow, rubbing passion, as if the skin of one savoured that of the other. He unhooked her brassiere, tugged at the restraining tights and panties with the same half-frozen, intense slowness, while she unbuttoned his shirt, unzipped his trousers.

She caught sight of their splayed, intertwined bodies in the mirror of the dressing-table, just once as they neared a mutual climax. His trousers were comically round his ankles, her tights and panties a silly crushed flower, brown and green, dangling from one foot. Then she lost all objective awareness for a time, even the awareness of engineering their love-making, of confirming her control of him. He thrust into her eagerly, hungrily even as she decided that in his case sexual passion was a sufficient substitute for love – he would, at least temporarily, believe himself in love with her, be malleable – and she gave herself to replying to his eagerness, lifting her hips so that her legs gripped his sides, ankles crossed at his back. The necessity of performance became an imperative she could not quite cold-bloodedly control.

Moynihan picked up the telephone with a lover's eagerness. He had sat on in the darkening Bloomsbury room long after Lobke had departed, waiting for one call, suffering the unwilled images coming out of the dark of her body twisted about McBride's white torso.

'Yes?'

'Claire – ' He caught his breath. He hated, now that she

had diminished his imaginations by calling him, the delight that had leapt under his heart just as she spoke; hated the sharp jealous pain the first ringing of the telephone had recalled; hated the dependence her body, her attention forced upon him; hated the superiority she seemed to acquire over him.

'Well?' He tried to sound casual.

'He's asleep.'

'You wore him out, I suppose?' The sarcasm didn't seem to have any ability either to hurt her or restore his self-satisfaction.

'Naturally. But I didn't ring you to tell you that.' He could sense the laughter, like a cold chill against his skin. He had no recollection of his own love-making with her, no physical identification with her. Even her voice was thin and distant.

'No?' Better. Lighter, surer tones now.

'Don't be stupid, Sean. Just listen. He might wake up, and come in.'

'Yes,' he snapped.

'He's interested in a minefield, in the St George's Channel, and in a minesweeping flotilla – he seemed to think it's leading somewhere. Are you any the wiser?'

'No, I don't know a damn thing. That pig Lobke was here earlier – '

'I've no time – he's awake. As soon as I have anything concrete, I'll call.'

'Take care – ' he began, even as the connection, broken, purred in his ear. Another moment, and he would have added something more revealing, more committed. *I love you –*

Stupid. He slammed down his receiver, the anger bubbling like nauseous indigestion or heartburn.

November 1940
The three men walked abreast along the glass-littered pavement, stepping carefully over the trailing hosepipes, averting their gaze from the occasional blanketed forms, preferring the grim neutrality of ruined buildings and the gaping dark interiors of shops. A naked tailor's dummy lay sprawled through the glassless window of one shop,

grotesque and mocking. McBride, alone of the three of them, seemed distracted from Walsingham's conversation by the rubble, the drawn and haggard faces, the lumps under the grey blankets, the stench of burning, the wet pavements. A stranger from a distant country, he felt out of place, disturbed and obscurely angry.

A typing pool sat in chairs arranged behind desks like a class of children. Behind them, their offices had crumbled in upon themselves, with grotesque diffidence and good manners only spilling a few crumbs of masonry and brick into the street. A balding, self-important man with half-glasses and a small, yellowed moustache was checking their work fussily between bouts of dictation to his secretary. His desk was larger than those of the typists, and virtually undamaged. The clatter of typewriters, the droning of the man's voice and the occasional rumble of traffic beyond seemed to satisfy Walsingham, and the three of them became a tight little group in animated discussion.

'Charlie, you're greedy, you want everything,' McBride said, his voice belying the grin on his face.

'Michael, my boy, you're the one to get it from the Germans, if anyone can – ' Gilliatt felt an outsider in the conversation, a visitor observing the verbal and facial games of a married couple, a semaphore he barely understood. He was taller than the other two, and this seemed a further distance.

'Hell, Charlie. Brest is tight as a virgin. Guernsey was easy – but not this. You want army and navy stuff, and you want it in twenty-four hours. It's not on, Charlie.'

'I think it is. You'll be picked up at the drop, ferried to the Plabennec area. All I want is proof that new divisions have been moved in there – in Brest, all I need is proof that the U-boats from Guernsey are sitting there, awaiting their passengers.'

A telephone rang, startling all three of them. The man in the half-glasses picked it up from his desk. He seemed suddenly aware of them, and turned his back as he answered his call. The telephone lead snaked away from his desk along the street, Gilliatt noticed for the first time. He felt the little incident to be quite unreal, and realized also that the dialogue between McBride and Walsingham was similarly lacking in reality. He had anaesthetized himself against it, unwilling to accept his situation.

'Charlie, you just haven't got the contacts in France to pull it off. This isn't a two-man bob rushing down the Cresta run. I need a team.'

'I have the contacts –'

'You trust them? You've tested them, tried them out?' Walsingham shook his head. 'Your honesty does you no credit at all, Charlie!' McBride grinned again. Gilliatt almost felt the man's facial muscles were completely beyond his control. Or perhaps it was mockery? Certainly, Gilliatt's impression of Walsingham was that he disposed of questions of human safety very easily if they came between him and his objective. Yet he knew that McBride was going to accept his orders, whatever qualifications he felt. He had not, as yet, entirely expended his gratitude at not being put back behind a desk in OIC.

'I get good intelligence from them,' Walsingham asserted.

'Then ask them to find out for you.'

'I need your *assurance* –'

'So much for the reliability of these Frogs, Charlie. You don't trust them to be right this time, mm?'

Walsingham shrugged. 'I want you to go tonight,' he said.

'You piss off, Charlie. Peter here and me, we'll discuss it, and see you back at the office. How about that?' Walsingham appeared to Gilliatt to be nonplussed for once. Then he nodded, almost curtly, turned on his heel and walked away. Gilliatt and McBride watched his determined stride until he turned a corner into the Strand. Then McBride looked up at Gilliatt, studying him with a suddenly intense look.

'Well, Lieutenant Peter Gilliatt – ' Gilliatt suddenly looked down at his civilian jacket and trousers as if they belied his rank. 'And what do you think to that?' McBride nodded in the direction taken by Walsingham. Gilliatt smiled. There was a charm, possibly specious, about McBride that was irresistible at that moment. Dark, medium build, good-looking in a slightly untrustworthy way, McBride was a strange and perhaps unreliable species. But Gilliatt found himself warming to the man, found within himself a penchant for future recklessness that he suspected was transmitted from the Irishman.

'I – don't know. You're the expert on Lieutenant-Commander Walsingham – what do you say?'

'Charlie is scared bloody stiff, young fellow, I know that much.'

'How come?'

'He *never* panics, always prepares. You think he's reckless with lives, mm?' Gilliatt, surprised at McBride's perceptiveness, nodded. He noticed that the fussy little office manager was doing his rounds of the typing pool once more. A rather blowsy young blonde caught Gilliatt's eye. 'Charlie's never been reckless with *my* life before, Peter – if he's started now, then he's very worried about something, that I know for certain.'

Gilliatt ignored the blonde, who by now had smiled at him, much to the irritation of the man with the nicotine-stained moustache and the half-glasses. Gilliatt saw a girl bringing out a tray full of mugs and cups of tea from the shattered interior of the offices.

'Stove's still working, Mr Hubank,' she called out.

'Thank you, Gloria.' He seemed displeased that the routine of his office-in-the-street would now be interrupted. As in a classroom, work was already dissolving into chatter.

Gilliatt looked at McBride. 'You don't think we could survive this little jaunt, then?'

He saw McBride weigh him, confirm something to himself.

'Gloria's stove is still working, and it's business as usual here. How long would that last, do you think, if the Germans had a second front in Ireland?' Gilliatt shook his head. 'Not long. There's plenty of people in Ireland who'd help the Germans, and a lot more who'd accept them. And there's nothing the British could do about it. Now, operatives are not supposed to think about things like that. That's Charlie's job, and he's scared stiff. You *know* it could happen tomorrow!'

'So, you'll go?'

McBride looked around him. An ambulance passed, bell

noisly demanding attention, but he seemed more drawn by the typing pool chattering in their tea-break.

'They had bananas yesterday, but by the time Mum got there, he'd sold out, the miserable old Jew. She says she won't go there again.'

'Got a cigarette, Sandra?'

'Smoked your ration, now you want to smoke mine. Bloody cheek!'

'He said he was doing hush-hush work, abroad and that. He might not come back, see – '

'And you let 'im? You are stupid, Norma!'

McBride turned back to Gilliatt.

'Not a lot there you'd consider dying for, is there?' He laughed. 'But then, I don't do it for anyone but myself, do I now?' He rubbed a hand through his hair. 'I'll be on the plane tonight, parachute strapped on tight. Why don't you come along for the ride? I'll look after the two of us, sure I will!' The comic brogue, the evident recklessness made McBride a stereotype for a moment.

Gilliatt shrugged. 'Why not?'

October 1980

Admiralty records were stored in half a dozen places around London still awaiting transfer to the Public Records Office at Kew. McBride had gained, via the office of the Secretary to the Admiralty, access to each one of the records offices as an historian whose latest project was a study of naval warfare in the North Atlantic and the Western Approaches during 1940 and 1941. His academic background was impeccable, his best-selling status in America no handicap. He had a different coloured pass for each of the various offices, but he had returned to the converted primary school in Hackney where he had worked the previous day and which housed mine-sweeping, anti-U-boat, and convoy duty records for the duration of the war as well as the offices of some signals branch of the navy. McBride did not bother himself with considering this department's function or legitimacy, beyond a certain comparative amusement at a converted primary school's claims to security over the massive CIA complex at Langley.

The records were kept in classrooms which had been expanded by knocking down interior walls, then filled with shelving, metal and wooden. A complex filing system, an officer close to retirement and two civilian clerks, a small reading room that might once have been the staff room of the school, and a kettle with which he could make coffee for himself comprised his surroundings.

He was allowed free access to the files, since it had been decided years earlier that all still-classified material should receive priority removal, then this records repository could be opened to researchers. McBride was not looking for classified material, merely for the indications, the half-obscured footprints, of something classified; the legitimate fingers and toes of a secret body.

He put down his copy of the *Daily Telegraph* without reluctance. He'd glanced at it on the tube train – another IRA bomb in the Midlands which had caused him to idly wonder whether he might not even have met or passed or spoken to someone in the IRA while he was in Ireland, and two IRA arrests in London. A front-page picture of the Ulster Minister, Guthrie, at Leeds Castle, waving to the cameras, accompanied by a crowd of people. He could not take an interest. He was American, not Irish.

As he hefted the first of the chosen files into the tiny reading room – a male clerk looked in, nodded and wished him a good morning – he was thinking of Claire Drummond. Now, he thought with a self-satisfied amusement, his lover. The second time, after dinner when they'd had more to drink and the food had been good and they'd talked round and round it, it had been even better. He felt himself harden now as he recaptured the image of her face above his, her slow lowering of herself on to him, her breasts just out of reach of his mouth until she wanted him to kiss them –

McBride was, he admitted to himself, besotted with the woman. He wanted to be with her now, not here with the long-dead past, the musty-smelling files and the limping footsteps of the disgruntled naval officer echoing along the corridors from time to time. Yes, he wanted her again. He'd always thought of himself as a man of limited, even minimal appetite. But he wanted her now, he'd wanted her when he awoke but she'd dismissed the idea with a laugh –

He deliberately rid himself of the thought of her, and the pleasant sensation in his genitals, and opened his notebooks, matching his previous day's notes to the relevant section of the file. Movement orders for November 1940, Western Approaches Command. A stiff card prefaced the clipped-in flimsies of the orders, on which ruled card was a digest of the orders in strict chronology. He pressed open the unyielding file at the orders concerning the minesweeping flotilla led by HMS *Bisley*, Gilliatt's ship. He remembered for a moment Gilliatt's grieving daughter, then recalled the thought that had been on the lip of his consciousness as Claire had walked into his room.

What was it? Time, time –

The sealed orders that had governed the sailing of the flotilla were not available to him, but a hand had scrawled *St George's Channel – sweep*, probably unofficially, in the margin of the record. Added by someone with a tidiness of mind that defeated security. *Bisley* and her flotilla had been absent from Milford Haven for – ?

No, he couldn't quite –

He got up, filled the kettle from the cold-water tap over an old enamel sink in the corner of the former staff room, plugged it in, and spooned instant coffee granules into a chipped mug. Something, something –

He tried to recollect his naval history, a short paper he had written perhaps eight years before on submarine activity in the Western Approaches. It had been an attempt to debunk an official British naval history he had received for review. Time, time?

The kettle boiled as he wondered. Absently, he poured the water into the mug, stirred and sipped at the scalding coffee, then carried the mug back to the table. The room was cold, didn't get the sun until afternoon. He put down his mug, rubbed his hands, and took a map from his briefcase. It was not an Admiralty chart, but he measured off distances with a ruler knowing it was sufficient. The minefield to protect the St George's Channel and the Bristol Channel was –

He marked it in roughly, then found Milford Haven. He

estimated the flotilla's speed, the duration of the sweep, the return to Milford.

And then he had it. A small, vivid excitement that became swallowed almost immediately by a sense of the work still to do, but still apparent.

Bisley's flotilla could not have carried out any kind of sweep and have returned to Milford within the times recorded in the file. Sailing time, and time of return were both recorded, and were much too close together. He flipped over flimsies eagerly, almost tearing them, Yes, *Bisley* and the rest of the flotilla – no, no! *Bisley* had returned to Milford, the rest of the flotilla had returned later. The *flotilla* would have had time to sweep St George's Channel, but *Bisley* would not. And there was no record of damage or fault that would account for her sudden return.

He thumbed through the movement orders, searching for the docket he had found the previous day. Yes, there it was. *Bisley* at anchor for three days before her captain returned. Then – yes, a week later the flotilla was ordered to a sweep of Swansea Bay, where German aircraft had dropped mines across the harbour mouth under cover of an air raid.

He picked up his coffee, sipping at it, making brief, hurried darts around the room, circling the table. St George's Channel swept – it was a British minefield, a defence? Why? *Bisley* returning early, alone –

He put down the coffee, and left the room.

It took him an hour to find the appropriate files, with the assistance of one of the civilian clerks, a grey-haired woman who seemed to regard him malevolently because he wanted access to files that had not been thoroughly reorganized and cross-referenced. Eventually, she found him two bulging, dusty box-files, and he took them back to the reading room. She huffily shrugged off his profuse thanks.

His hands were dirty, his clothes dusty, but immediately he cleared a space on the table and opened the first of the box-files. A mess of scraps of paper, notebooks, personnel forms, promotions, reassignments, casualties – the un-collated material from the office of the Department of Minesweeping filed under MILFORD HAVEN in faded type on a grubby gummed label on the front of the box-file.

He wanted two things from it – had the flotilla swept the British minefield, and had Gilliatt returned to *Bisley* with the captain?

A small excitement was growing in his stomach. There had to be, had to be a *link* with Emerald Necklace.

November 1940

It was a cottage near Kersaint-Plabennec, a small village five kilometres from Plabennec. Gilliatt – and he suspected McBride shared the instinct, though they both remained silent on the subject – sensed a pall over their mission a mere two hours after they had parachuted from the Wellington into wooded country north of Tremaouezan. The cottage where the three members of the Resistance held their Wehrmacht prisoner was half a mile from a farm where German soldiers were billeted. Gilliatt wondered whether the man's screams had carried to his comrades, and shuddered.

Lampau, the leader of the Resistance cell in the area, evidently still bore the mental scars of the summer, including a sense of having been betrayed by the British at Dunkirk. Yet, somehow, Walsingham had transformed him into a reliable source of intelligence regarding army and navy movements and dispositions in the area north of Brest and the port itself. Lampau's cell were saboteurs, and more recently assistants in escape for shot-down British airmen or torpedoed seamen. Gilliatt regarded Lampau, Fôret, and the younger Venec as undisciplined, dangerous allies, even on such a temporary basis.

McBride and he were now alone with the German prisoner they both knew would be executed as soon as he had surrendered what information he possessed. He was almost delirious, clutching his hands under his armpits because they had pulled out his fingernails; his face was swollen, reddened and cut where he had been beaten. None of the Frenchmen could speak German, the soldier could not speak English or French. The torture had been gratuitous, pointless. It sickened Gilliatt.

'Name?' McBride rapped out in German.

A long silence, ragged breathing, quiet groans, then: 'Hoffer. Johannes Hoffer.'

'Number?' It was given. 'Unit?'

Another long silence, during which time the soldier huddled in the corner of the lamp-lit room which smelled of stored meal and cooking, McBride squatted next to him on his haunches, stone-like and unmoving, and Gilliatt leaned against the door as if to keep out the rabid Frenchmen who had hurt the boy.

'Rifle Regiment, Third Fallschirmjaeger Division.' Very quiet. McBride made him repeat it, then his head swung towards Gilliatt, his eyes wide in surprise. The boy was responding to the German language, to nothing else. He'd never envisaged this, that his life could end in a dirty French cottage after they had pulled out his fingernails with a pliers and beaten him into a semi-coma. For him, the German words came out of a pain-filled void, and he wanted the voice to go on speaking, and he would answer, *make* the voice go on speaking.

'Billet?' The boy replied slowly. Gilliatt looked at the fair hair plastered close to the pink skull with sweat. He was impatient to be gone, blamed McBride because he had to go on looking at the suffering German. 'Other units in the area?' McBride asked next, his accent clipped, military, officer-like. Another long silence, as if the boy hesitated or savoured the words like ointments.

'Forty-fifth Division – Fourteenth Panzers, their grenadier and reconnaissance units – ' Silence again, then, and the growing sense of the boy slipping away from them and wanting to hear them without interruption. And the sense in both of them that Lampau waited outside the door, eager to finish what he had started.

'Thank you, Unteroffizier Hoffer,' McBride said quietly, patting the boy lightly on the shoulder, and standing up. 'Well done. You may rest now.' Then, as if he divined the boy's need, he added, 'We will come back and check on you later. *Heil Hitler!*'

Gilliatt grimaced at the violent, black farce. McBride tried to usher him from the room, but he pulled away from the Irishman.

'No – ' he hissed.

'Don't be a bloody fool, Peter!' McBride snarled almost under his breath. 'Those French would kill us if we tried to stop them killing this boy. Forget it – '

'How can I?'

'By considering what you've just heard, man!' McBride had his hand firmly on the door handle. 'Those troops have been in the Plabennec area for less than two weeks, most of them. Lampau told us that – Hoffer is in the rifle regiment of a parachute division – a whole crack infantry division here, and Panzer experts. What does it sound like to you? Well, what does it sound like?' McBride, shorter than Gilliatt, had grabbed the other man's chin in his hand, turning his face towards him, averting his gaze from the crouching, semi-conscious Hoffer.

'I suppose – '

'Yes?'

'A small, specialized invasion force – I agree with you, damn it!' Gilliatt wrenched open the door, passed Lampau who grinned mirthlessly, and went out of the cottage. McBride nodded to Lampau, who entered the room, while McBride, forgetting Hoffer almost at once, followed Gilliatt outside. Gilliatt was leaning against the wall of the cottage in the narrow passage between the house and the rickety barn, hugging himself, shivering helplessly. McBride could smell the vomit in the chill night air.

'Peter?'

'What do you want?' Hurt mistress or child.

'Forget it – or think about the people you've known who've died. Anything, but not about one Wehrmacht Unteroffizier killed for invading France – ' He put his hand on Gilliatt's shoulder, but it was shrugged away. 'Peter, Peter, I don't like it any more than you do, but I'm not going to argue with Lampau for the sake of a German.'

'You're as bad as they are!' Gilliatt accused, turning on McBride.

'I hope not, Peter,' McBride whispered. Then he lit two cigarettes and offered one to Gilliatt, who coughed on the first inhalation of smoke, then seemed not to shiver so uncontrollably. McBride saw one white hand wipe across Gilliatt's mouth, eyes. 'OK?'

'Yes. Thanks.'

'There'll be a lot more of it. This is only the beginning, Peter, the cleanest bit of it – '

'God, not really a Richard Hannay adventure, is it?' He laughed mirthlessly.

'Maybe not, but it's the only adventure we've got right now.'

'Is that why you do it – adventure?'

'Isn't it why you ran away to sea? Remember?' Both of them recalled their conversation on the bridge of the *Bisley*. 'Well, maybe I do do it for the sake of the adventure, at that. But now, we have to get into Brest and have a look for those submarines. That'll be the final bit of proof that Charlie wants.'

'An invasion of Ireland?' McBride nodded. 'What'll they do when they know for sure?'

McBride shrugged. 'God knows, Peter. Fill up the hole in the minefield for one, I should think. Maybe they'll send troops to Ireland – who knows?'

'Fill up – ?'

'Come on. Lampau will have cleared away the remains by now. He has to get us into Brest before first light. The rest will be up to us.'

A dog barked suddenly, startling them. Neither of them had heard a dog on the smallholding before. Sound carrying from the farm, Gilliatt wondered –

Then torchlight, wobbling before it was flicked off. Across the field, a hundred yards away. Nothing else to be seen in the black, moonless dark. McBride was quicker than Gilliatt to realize the danger, because Gilliatt was struggling to recall why they dare not re-sow the St George's Channel minefield, not yet –

'God, it's the Germans. Peter, Peter, come on, damn you – the Germans have come looking for Hoffer!'

Walsingham was working late in his office at the Admiralty – no more spacious than a large cupboard, as if to remind him of his temporary commission with the Royal Navy – preparing his report for the First Sea Lord. He was drafting it in the certain knowledge that his conclusions were the right and only permissible ones, and drafting it, too, in the light of possibly making his case after McBride's death. Walsingham regretted that he had had to send McBride – Gilliatt as a virtual stranger he cared far less about – but he had been near panic, desperate for proof that would be irrefutable. He was aware that a massive inertia, compounded by a nerveless fear that had grown since the cancellation of *Sea Lion,* conspired to blind the Admiralty, the War Office, possibly even the Cabinet to any version of reality that might prove catastrophic. He had to convince men who did not want to contemplate disaster or envisage any threat that might overwhelm them.

He shuffled the handwritten sheets in front of him, then leaned back in his chair and rubbed his eyes. He wondered briefly about McBride, then excised him from his mind, realizing as he did so that he was behaving with the same blinkered disregard for realities which so angered him in their Lordships. Even March, who should have been convinced by now.

He yawned.

Another reality insisted, came to light and to a sudden prominence in his mind so that he could not ignore it. The convoy. What could they do about the convoy?

And, with a colder insistence, something stirred like a nightmare he had not relived since childhood but which was now coming back with all its old force; an idea that had the terror of a shambling, nameless creature, an idea he knew, finally, would be adopted.

A war crime – would they call it that?

Yes.

October 1980
Sir Charles Walsingham, Head of the Directorate of Security, MI5, sat in his spacious civil servant's office in the Home Office, where his official rank was Permanent Under-Secretary, his fingers splayed upon the green blotter in the middle of his oak desk. He seemed possessed by an old dream or nightmare, his lips compressed to a single thin line, his forehead deeply trenched with creases, his eyes vacant yet inwardly intent and mesmerized. It was late in the evening, and outside in Parliament Street the lamps bloomed in soft, insinuating rain. His room was lit by his table-lamp and by an ornate standard lamp in one corner. He preferred the shadows at that moment.

He had slept at Leeds Castle for the last few days before

the opening of the conference, and for the first day and night of talks he had occupied himself in rechecking, rebriefing, refining. Then he had returned to London, and called at the Home Office before returning to his flat in Chesham Place. Drummond's cryptic, almost insolent telephone message was waiting for him in his aide's neat, womanish handwriting – a large question mark beneath the final words.

Drummond he had never liked, forty years before at the height of the affair. McBride's control – and yet Walsingham had possessed a deep affection for the rootless, uncaring Irishman and nothing more than civility towards the Englishman, Drummond. He remembered at one time, possibly in '41 or '42, they'd suspected Drummond of assisting German agents in Ireland – which had been patent nonsense, and nothing more than the hare-brained guesswork of one of the reckless young men who succeeded McBride . . .

Why had he remembered that about Drummond?

He would call Drummond in the morning, expecting to get no more than that out of him. But the son – McBride's son, of all people in the world. Now, at this critical time –

For a moment, he suspected an elaborate and devious plot – then dismissed the idea as ridiculous. It was nothing more than the externalizing of his own selfish fears. What the devil could young McBride drag up? Anything – *everything?* If he did, then Walsingham himself was finished, Guthrie was certainly finished – the conference, Ulster itself, even this government . . .

The ripples spread on the ruffled pond of his imagination. McBride was a heavy stone, and he had already been thrown, apparently. He would have to be watched. There ought to be nothing – no clues – for him to discover, but after forty years who could any longer be sure that there were no scraps of paper, no old memories, no loose tongues lying aroud. McBride – Walsingham had read *Gates of Hell* and disliked it – was looking for an angle, for something sensational. The *Emerald* business would be just what he would be looking for.

In that office, it was hard for Walsingham to feel genuinely fearful. Forty years of power, privilege and ascent were a barrier against fear. But, he still could not control his imagination, even though nothing of its images transferred to nerves or sweat-glands. He wasn't twitching, or getting damp, but he knew, with a kind of cold fear that went on thinking clearly, envisaging the consequences, that everything was at the hazard, that McBride could, with the right information, ruin everything.

Then the small selfish thought – *war crime*. He'd be finished, buried by an avalanche of contumely, national and international. Most of the other decision-makers and decision-takers were dead. He had decided to retire next year. He was already beyond official retirement age for his rank in the civil service. Now, he'd be the one – he and Guthrie, of course, the obedient instrument – who'd be blamed for the Emerald Decision.

He picked up one of the telephones on his desk. McBride, and quickly – whereabouts, recent enquiries, state of knowledge.

Possible solutions.

He'd ring Guthrie later, before the Minister retired for the night –

But of all people, McBride's son – now of all possible times . . .

Chapter Nine

ACCORDING TO THE RECORD

November 1940

Gilliatt had a hurried, confused impression of the smells of dung, butter, then warm hay as he followed McBride along a lightless path between cottage and barn and into the silent, dark interior of the latter. A horse whinnied softly, disturbed by the creaking of the door.

'Michael?' he called, losing sight of McBride's shadowy form almost at once when the door was shut behind them.

'Over here,' came the reply. Gilliatt moved gingerly across the uneven floor of the barn-cum-stable, catching his shin against a sharp-edged implement and swearing softly, shuffling his feet in the strewn hay. McBride's hand grabbed him, pulled him down behind a mound of hay, pressing him close to it, almost making him sneeze.

'What are they looking for?' he whispered, hearing distantly the bark of the dog, and the rapping of a fist or boot against the door of the cottage.

'With the dog – Hoffer is my guess,' McBride whispered back, irritated by his companion as by a slow-learning pupil. 'He's been reported missing. Perhaps Lampau and his goons nabbed him a couple of hours earlier than they need. Walsingham wouldn't be pleased at that. Listen!'

Gilliatt strained his hearing. Voices being raised, one French – but he couldn't pick out the words – and the other German. Then the slamming of a door. A few moments later, the fractured, eager barking of the dog.

'The scent – ' Gilliatt whispered.

'They've given it Hoffer's scent all right. I wonder where the body is?'

As if in reply or confirmation, the dog's barking became almost frantic, and had moved out of the house again, presumably behind the cottage.

'What about us?'

'Wait!'

Gilliatt was aware of the hay beneath and around him, its rich, stored smell heady, almost nauseous to the stomach he had so violently emptied. He listened, sensed McBride beside him alert and motionless. The dog went on barking, and behind its noise orders were being shouted. A French voice, raised in protest, but they could clearly hear the strained, high-pitched fear in it. Where had Lampau, Fôret, Venec *been* when they heard the knock on the door? McBride had had no time to warn them, perhaps not even the inclination. They had run immediately for the shelter of the barn.

They each heard the running footsteps, distinctly, in the moment before the first shots from a machine-pistol on automatic. The bullets thudded into the wall of the barn behind them, then something else, something heavier, collided with the same wall, slithered down in a grotesque aural impersonation of reptilian movement. Gilliatt, swallowing bile, wondered which one of them it was. He almost hoped that it was Lampau. Then he heard the revolver firing.

'What – ?' he began.

'It couldn't work out better for us, Peter. They'll get themselves killed, all three of them.' A burst from a machine-gun, the answering chatter of the Schmeissers. The horse whinnied more loudly, shuffled nervously in its stall. Gilliatt couldn't even see it as a shape in the lightless barn. Revolver again, then machine-pistols, then the machine-gun cut off in mid-sentence. The revolver three, four times, then a drowning chorus from the German machine-pistols.

Then silence, into which dripped like water the sound of boots moving about the yard, grunts of satisfaction, the noises of someone wounded who was lifted up and carried – the boot-noises became slower, heavier – and a single pistol shot as someone dying was finished off. A tidiness about the sounds of the aftermath. The dog had ceased to bark.

It might even have been dead.

Gilliatt and McBride waited for fifteen minutes, and then there were no other noises. McBride nudged Gilliatt and rose to his knees.

'Come on – our chance now.'

Gilliatt stood up, fastidiously clearing stalks of hay from his clothing. Then what McBride had said struck him.

'You wanted them to die, didn't you?'

'Not at all. But they can't talk now, can they? And, Peter, you'd have killed them all half an hour ago, just for hurting the German lad. Mm?'

McBride moved to the door of the barn, and opened it slowly and as silently as he could. It creaked with the slowness, the mounting noise of a yawn. McBride stepped outside. A minute later, he called to Gilliatt to join him.

'What do we do now?'

'Use the van they collected us in. Drive to Brest, of course.'

Gilliatt sensed the excitement in McBride. They were perhaps fifteen or twenty kilometres from the centre of the port, and from Lampau's cousin, a fisherman.

'Lampau – he was to vouch for us.'

'We'll explain – don't make difficulties, Peter. Don't give in to the sense of doom.'

'You knew – ?'

'Ah, it happens every time. One of the things you have to put to the back of your mind, every time. Come on.'

The van was waiting at the back of the cottage, where Fôret had parked it. One of its doors was open. McBride touched the door and then inspected his hand, sniffing the dark blood. He nodded, then began to examine the bodywork of the van, near the engine. He found no bullet-holes, and lifted the bonnet.

'Get in,' he said to Gilliatt, and the engine fired as he wired the ignition. Then the torches and the single searchlight came on, flooding the yard, picking out the van and McBride in a cold clear light.

All McBride could think of was that he hadn't heard the truck arrive, that its noise had been shielded from them by the cottage and by the shooting. He hadn't heard the truck with the mobile searchlight –

Then the voice, speaking in German through the megaphone.

October 1980

McBride stared into the box-file labelled MILFORD HAVEN, and his hands hovered over the mass of material it contained. Yesterday had brought nothing of any significance, and he was almost superstitious now about beginning again. If he touched it in the same way, in a different way –

The papers were cards. He needed to be dealt another hand. He discarded immediately the material he had checked the day before, lifting it out in the solid wedge he had held together with an elastic band, putting it aside. Outside, rain ran down the window of the reading room, and he felt cold. The small electric fire did not work, and he could not be bothered with it.

He flicked through the uppermost scraps of paper, discarding everything dated later than January 1941. The mound of rejected paper and notebooks and official forms and dockets grew on his left, while the scratched and doodled deal table remained bare near his right hand.

By lunchtime, he was in a fury of irritation and the first of the box-files had been refilled and dumped on the floor by his brief-case. The second one, with an identical gummed label, was open, but he had no heart to begin it on an empty stomach and in his present defeatist mood. He had lost sight of the pattern of his researches again, and wondered whether he might not have been sidetracked once more. What could this have to do with *Smaragdenhalskette,* linked as it was only by the supposition that the St George's Channel minefield would have to be breached by the Germans?

He had no evidence of that – had he been confused by the appearance of Gilliatt's name, by his father's shadowy proximity to events? He wasn't sure any longer.

The seedy pub he found was unprepossessing, but he didn't want to walk any more in the rain and opened the door to the Saloon Bar. One or two faces looked up at him, a blowsy laugh faded as he was inspected by the landlady, and he saw in one corner, by the fireplace where a tiny fire clung to life, the male clerk from the records repository. Wispy greying hair damply wiped over a bald head, dentures making much of a cheese roll. A half-pint of beer in front of him on the table. He seemed to plead silently to be joined by McBride. And McBride was aware of the style and cost of his raincoat and slacks, and the red roll-neck sweater he was wearing – and the wallet he took from his back pocket. He might have stepped back into an earlier time through the door of the bar.

'Beer,' he said. 'And the same for my friend – ' He indicated the clerk – Mr Hoskins, was it? He'd been introduced. The landlady nodded, pulled at the lever on the bar, the beer swished into a glass with a chip in it.

'Haven't had many of your lot down this way since the war,' the landlady observed. 'Lot of 'em here then, eh, Bert?' She addressed the last remark to a shrivelled man sitting at the far end of the cramped bar, reading *Sporting Life.* He merely tossed his head. The landlady's fonder memories of the Americans remained unshared. 'He didn't like 'em,' she confided. 'Always got on well with 'em meself,' she added with a wink, her preening of herself rusty, almost grotesque. McBride smiled. 'I'm glad,' he said. He picked up the beer. 'Have you anything to eat?'

'A pie, maybe.' Even the woman looked dubious. Bert snorted in his beer.

'Potato chips – sorry, crisps?' The landlady nodded, visibly brightening. 'Two bags.'

He carried the beer over to Hoskins's table, who finished his own half-pint quickly and sipped at the new glass after raising it to McBride's health.

'She makes my cheese roll for me,' he observed. 'Special order. I have to bring my own fruit.' He brought an orange from a coat pocket, and proceeded to peel it. The imagined mingled flavours of beer and orange upset McBride's palate as he opened the bag of crisps. He smiled tentatively at Hoskins, his thoughts reaching back to the second MILFORD HAVEN/DMS box-file and the hours he would have to spend sifting through its disorganized, patchwork image of mine-sweeping operations. Even records of disciplinary action taken against drunken sailors –

He tossed his head. Hoskins looked at him questioningly.

'Professor? Something the matter?' He sucked on a segment of the orange. The weak fire was still too warm for McBride, and he slipped his arms out of his raincoat. Hoskins studied the coat with unmasked envy.

'No. Just routine, is all. Dull, mm?'

'Fascinating, some of that material, Professor. What is it you're looking for, by the way?' His face was ingenious, grateful for conversation.

'Oh, this and that.'

'Minesweeping, eh?'

'That and other things.'

'November nineteen-forty, I gather, from some of the files you've requested?'

'Yes – ' McBride hid his hesitancy behind his glass, sipping at the cold thin beer.

'Ah – merchant navy myself, during the war, that is.'

'I see.'

'Atlantic convoys.'

'You've worked here a long time, Mr Hoskins?'

'Just over a year, Professor. Used to work at the

Admiralty itself, but I'm just about to retire. Easy job. I was only a boy when I did my first convoy, in nineteen-forty.' He smiled mysteriously. 'We had shore leave in New York before we set out – ' He was being deliberately mysterious. 'Three ships and a cruiser escort. Special fast run, going by the southern route round Ireland – '

McBride hardly heard him.

'Sure,' he said. Hoskins seemed about to repeat himself, then took a pocket-watch from his waistcoat and consulted it. 'Must get back, late already. See you later, Professor.'

Hoskins went out swiftly, pressing his trilby firmly down on his head, putting up his umbrella almost before he was through the door.

McBride sat until he had finished both packets of crisps and his beer, and only as he got up to leave did Hoskins's last words register. And they puzzled him. But he couldn't remember the date that Hoskins had supplied, and he rejected the coincidence. The file loomed more distinctly in his imagination, and he tried to work up some enthusiasm for his task as he walked back to the repository, its parking area still marked out as a netball court.

November 1940
McBride slammed down the bonnet of the van, and moved to the door. Gilliatt was in the passenger seat, immobile and blinded by the light. McBride slipped the .38 No 2 revolver from beneath his jacket then turned on his heel, arm out straight like a duellist, and fired twice. Glass shattered, tinkled in the sudden darkness over by the silhouette of the truck.

McBride clambered into the driving seat, revved the engine wildly, and let off the handbrake. The Citroën heaved off the mark, careering as McBride swung the wheel.

'Get down, get down!' he yelled at Gilliatt, immobile as a stunned animal in the seat next to him.

An instant later, the windscreen shattered and emptied its fragments over the shoulder and back of Gilliatt's jacket as he crouched, head covered by his arms, below the dashboard. McBride swung the wheel again, hearing the thud and tear of heavy bullets along the offside flank of the van. He was in darkness, but he knew the direction of the barn and the narrow passage between it and the cottage.

A grey shape loomed, bounced off the offside wheel arch, and McBride spun the wheel again, feeling the rear wheels bite on some lump beneath them, then rush free, skidding hideously.

'What's happening?' Gilliatt yelled.

The van's nearside struck the wooden wall of the barn, more bullets ripped through the rear doors, angling out again through the driver's side above McBride's head – tyres still good, he thought, swinging the wheel, tearing off the nearside running-board, the van sliding with a groaning wobble into the narrow space. Starlight, then blackness, a heavy thump, a scream, and something rolling wildly across the roof over McBride's head and sliding off behind the van. More bullets, and one of the double doors at the back of the van began flapping open, magnifying the shouts, the noise of engines behind them, the shots. McBride punched out the remainder of the windscreen, cutting his hand, cursing and elated.

The Citroën lurched lamely out of the narrow gap between cottage and barn, engine screeching, wheels gripping the gravel of the track to the road.

'Christ, what's happening!'

'Don't worry, Peter, we're on our way!' McBride shouted, almost gaily. Lights dazzled in the rear-view mirror for a moment, then he had turned on to the road. The village lay ahead, a few poor lights defying the blackout. He pressed the accelerator, demanding more from the protesting engine. 'Don't worry – you all right?'

Gilliatt climbed awkwardly up out of the footwell, very carefully brushed glass from the seat, and slumped next to McBride as he was overbalanced by the van's cornering speed.

'You're all right?'

'Ah, hell – I'm always like this!'

The first houses of the village. Lights behind them, spilling like ignited fuel up the road to engulf them.

'I'll try to shut the doors,' Gilliatt grinned. He accepted the adrenalin madness, felt it coursing through him like a transfusion from the Irishman. It wasn't a sane world any longer. 'Try not to shoot me out on to the road, there's a good chap.'

McBride looked at him, then nodded, sensing a transformation in Gilliatt. He might now run almost as far, almost as fast as himself.

'Hurry back, I need a navigator.'

The Citroën slowed slightly until McBride heard the doors slam, the road noise diminishing in his ears, then he accelerated again as Gilliatt clambered back over the seat. The map was in his hand. He flicked on a small torch.

'They'll know we're heading for Brest,' Gilliatt observed.

'Sure they will. How did they know we were there – did they follow us, or were they told?'

'Told? *Left here!*'

The van swerved noisily, bumping into a lane overhung with leafless trees, rutted and puddled. McBride gripped the wheel like a rally driver, stiff-armed, ready to wrestle with its vagaries. 'I don't know what I mean, either!' The noises in the van sounded as if it was tearing itself to pieces. 'Hold on, you brave tyres!' he yelled, surrendering to Gilliatt's navigation and to the stupid, senseless excitement of the chase. Lights in the mirror, dipping and swinging into the lane. McBride felt the van lurch against the bank, tear at roots and earth, then pull free.

'Another turn on the right, in maybe fifty – *there it is!*'

McBride heaved on the wheel, the van slid in the opposite direction like an unwilling animal. McBride spun the wheel, evening out the skid, then he stamped on the accelerator as he met the slope of the new track and the Citroën almost refused.

'All I know, Peter, is that they get closer to me every time I come for a visit – and they're not that clever!' Gilliatt listened but kept his eyes on the map. 'But, what the hell! They must have heard the Wellington, wondered about it, then found Hoffer and put two and two –'

The Citroën bounced off a low wall surrounding an isolated church. Gilliatt saw McBride cross himself with one hand, steering with the other, the grin never disappearing for a moment from his lips. Then they were over a rise, swinging down. McBride switched on the headlights for a moment to orient himself, then doused them again. He turned left into thicker trees that had thrown back the headlight beams in twisted, skeletal whiteness. McBride then drove totally on reaction, concentrating grimly, swerving innumerable times, hitting the boles of trees glancing blows twice, stalling the engine once, skidding frequently.

Then they were out of the trees.

'Nearest track?' he snapped.

'Keep ahead. We may have to open a gate or two, but eventually we'll find the road!'

McBride looked at him, and winked.

'That we will – we will.' He laughed.

Behind them, the first of the pursuing vehicles, an open Einheits-programme VW Type 82, entered the trees, headlights on full, followed more cautiously by an Opel Blitz 3-ton truck with a platoon aboard and the dead, glassless searchlight for which there were no spare bulbs. They were a little more than a quarter of a mile behind the Citroën van, fifteen kilometres from the outskirts of Brest.

October 1980

He'd found two items by the time the records office was due to close, and he was tempted to take them with him, knowing they would be unlikely to be missed, perhaps for years. The first was a notification from the Admiralty that Lieutenant Gilliatt had been temporarily reassigned to shore duties, and that his replacement, Sub-Lieutenant Thomas, would be arriving in forty-eight hours. There were no other details. He could not find a later reassignment of Gilliatt to the *Bisley*, or any ship at Milford Haven.

The second item was the deposition of a Leading Seaman Campbell who was charged with being drunk and disorderly while on shore leave from *Bisley* in Milford Haven. He was also accused of discussing, in a manner prejudicial to security and the safety of his ship, the sweep from which *Bisley* had just returned. After three days on board twiddling his thumbs, Campbell explained that he was disgruntled and resentful, but had not intended to breach the strict security under which he had carried out his recent duties. He claimed to be unaware of the level of security.

He referred, in his deposition, to the breach that had been found in Winnie's Welcome Mat – McBride had been puzzled by the soubriquet until Campbell had referred to it more properly later in his statement. And then he had indulged his delight. A *German* sweep of the minefield, recently carried out, running north-south between Ireland and France.

McBride, the evening closing in, cloudy and rain-threatening outside the windows, the unshaded lamp throwing a hard, dusty light on the papers and the table, wanted to leave at once, be with Claire as his just reward for successful industry. *Evidence* of Emerald Necklace – he could open up the whole can of worms with it. He looked around him, and swiftly pocketed the deposition, then closed the file. Hoskins could return it. Hoskins, something about Hoskins –

He grinned. He was seeing links everywhere. It was a popular history, a best-seller he was writing, not a mystic philosophy. He laughed, picked up his brief-case, and left.

Outside, Hoskins was watching for him. When McBride headed for the station at London Fields and disappeared from sight in the rainy evening, Hoskins entered the telephone booth beside which he had been sheltering. He arranged his five-pence pieces on the directory, wrinkled his nose at the graffiti scrawled on the small mirror in felt pen, and dialled a number. The hotel switchboard put him through to the room he requested.

'Yes?' It was Goessler.

'He's found something – probably Campbell's deposition, or something like it. Pleased as Punch, he is.'

'Good. You've made an approach?'

'Yes. He didn't seem to hear me, though.'

'Never mind. Tomorrow will do, Hoskins. Tell him in plainer terms, eh?' Goessler laughed. 'Well done, Hoskins. Report on any further progress at the same time tomorrow.'

The connection was broken. The telephone purred in Hoskins's ear, and despite his umbrella and trilby, a thin dribble of water which must have lodged in his hair ran down his collar, much to his annoyance.

Gilliatt was dog-tired, the adrenalin having seemingly vanished from his bloodstream, taking energy, willpower, consciousness with it. He watched the map, in the mesmeric pool of torchlight, move in and out of focus, taunting his eyes. Villages, hamlets, no more than spots in front of his eyes –

He rubbed his eyes.

'You OK?'

'Mm, what? Oh, sure,' Gilliatt replied, stretching his eyes, stifling a yawn. McBride smiled at him. They had crossed the River Penfeld north of Brest half an hour earlier. It was four in the morning and his own energy reserves seemed dangerously consumed. The weaving, backtracking course he had almost whimsically followed for two hours had thrown off all pursuit – they'd hidden in a stand of trees while their immediate pursuers had flashed by, headlights ablaze, the steel helmets of the platoon in the back of the Opel truck clearly visible. Then, back roads, tracks, lanes, moving north for some time away from Brest and any search or road-blocks, then cutting west. Now, McBride estimated they were no more than a few kilometres north of the fishing village of Ste. Anne-du-Portzic, where Lampau's relative, a fisherman, lived. It was time to abandon the van. Gilliatt looked all but finished, out on his feet. But McBride was satisfied with his companion, and this caused him to nudge the other man's arm, and grin.

'Come on, Christopher Robin, almost time for bed.'

Gilliatt smiled tiredly. 'Where are we?'

'On a very minor road – why am I telling you, you've got the map?' McBride laughed. 'Marshy country. We get rid of the van here.'

Gilliatt concentrated afresh on the map. 'We're somewhere off the D.105, I think.' McBride's finger tapped at the map on Gilliatt's knee.

'Just there.'

He jolted the van on down the narrow, hedged track for a time, then slowed and tugged the handbrake. The hedge had given way to open, dyke-like country, almost Dutch. The track was slightly above the level of the fields.

McBride got out of the van, and was chilled immediately by the cold, searching wind. Dead reeds rattled eerily below the road. Gilliatt joined him, rubbing his hands together.

'Great country.'

'For us, yes. Just tip the old wagon over the side of the road – have to use the headlights for a bit. Shame, that – '

They got back in the van, and McBride switched on the lights. A pale wash of light showed dead reeds, a few spindly trees lining the road at intervals, and the flat marshland smoothly sliding away into darkness. In another minute, McBride stopped again, the van turned so that its nose was at the edge of the road. Below the lights were reeds and bushes, and a dull gleam of water.

'Right, over the side with the old lady.'

They got behind the van, and heaved against it. Slowly, with a dignified reluctance, the Citroën toppled nose first down the embankment, tearing through the bushes and reeds, splashing into the water, then settling. McBride shone a torch down the embankment. The Citroën seemed impossibly small, toy-like. It was half-concealed by the bushes, and buried up to the windscreen in marshy water.

'Just some cosmetic work, I think,' McBride murmured. 'You stay here.'

McBride eased himself down the embankment until he could rest his weight against the branch of a bush. Then, removing his clasp-knife from his pocket, he proceeded to cut handfuls of reeds, and scatter them across the rear of the Citroën which now pointed up the embankment. Then he broke a large overhanging branch of the bush, pulling at it until it also helped to conceal the van. Breathing heavily, he clambered back to join Gilliatt.

'Will that do?'

'Have to. Probably no one but a local would find it anyway. And in twenty-four hours, we should be well on our way. Either that, or the discovery of the van won't matter all that much. Come on, we've got a nice walk before you climb into your own little bed again.' McBride laughed, thumping Gilliatt on the back.

'Proper caution you are,' Gilliatt said in stage-Cockney.

'I am that. You have to admit, with me there's never a dull moment, eh?'

'Too many dull moments would finish you off, would they?'

The wind whistled across the marsh, the reeds argued volubly in the silence before McBride answered.

'That question might be a little too close to the mark, Peter. I think we'll pass on that one, eh?' He increased his pace. 'Come on, otherwise we'll have the local cowmen out for early milking and wondering who we are!'

Gilliatt trotted to catch up with him.

October 1980

McBride was having a shower, whistling tunelessly and happily to himself. Claire Drummond could hear him through the open door between their rooms as she liberally applied talcum powder to herself after her bath. Her hair was tied up with a ribbon, her face devoid of make-up. Her high cheekbones and slanting eyes seemed peculiarly suited to her look of concentration and suppressed anger. Her pale skin was further whitened by powder. She looked, even to herself, curiously dead, marbled, in the dressing-table mirror. She slipped on her robe, feeling suddenly cold. The sexual bout with McBride after he had shown her what he had filched from Hackney had taken a tiring, wearing concentration, to achieve the calculated, simulated abandon which seemed required. McBride's rutting was thoughtless, self-satisfied, and he had noticed no reluctance – she was cautiously certain of that.

But she wanted to talk to Moynihan, now before they went out to dinner. It was obviously of importance in Goessler's scheme that this minefield business be exposed – either that, or McBride was on the wrong trail and she wanted to know that because if he was then they were all wasting their time and Moynihan would have to make demands of Goessler, get out of him the stuff that would dynamite the Leeds Castle fiasco.

It didn't seem like much, a drunken Scotsman's deposition before a disciplinary hearing, but that was their trouble – they didn't know what was important and what was not. Goessler had offered them a scheme he said was foolproof, had been more than a year in the making, and could not fail. They'd been greedy for it on both sides of the border, especially when Guthrie was the big prize. Guthrie was a winner, and he had to go –

She plucked the receiver off the rest as McBride went into an off-key version of an ABBA song. She hesitated, listening, then dialled rapidly, tugging the cord she held in her left hand in time to each ring of the receiver at the other end. Seven, eight, nine – she was about to put it down when Moynihan answered.

'Listen, I haven't much time. He's found something that might or might not be important. Has it anything to do with a minefield, for God's sake?'

'Minefield? Goessler just called me, told me everything was satisfactory, fat bastard –'

'Never mind that!' she whispered fiercely. 'Listen. The Germans opened a channel through the British minefield in November nineteen-forty – it must have something to do with the invasion plan. Where does that put *us*?' There was an exclusive, secretive emphasis on the last word.

'Christ, Claire, I don't know –'

'We have to get one up on Goessler. We can't afford for McBride to be following the wrong scent, that bloody conference is off the ground – ' She realized her hoarse, fierce whisper had grown louder, more intense, and glanced at the open door, paused to listen to McBride's whistling. Beethoven now. McBride the musical eclectic –

'What do you want me to do?' Moynihan was resignedly subordinate.

'How does Goessler *know* what McBride is doing? He must have someone inside –'

'Could be.'

'Find out, then. For God's sake, Sean, go over there tomorrow and find out how Goessler is keeping his eye on McBride – ' And then McBride was standing in the doorway, towelling his hair, another big towel draped round him. He was grinning perplexedly. 'That's right, McBride – eight-thirty. Thank you.' She turned to him. 'The restaurant – I was just checking the reservation,' she explained.

He crossed to her, kissed her. She eased her mouth into softness, responsiveness, as their mouths met.

'You'll have to learn, my darling, that I can organize

dinner, if we're going anywhere with this affair – ' The statement became almost a question. She kissed him again, moving her open mouth against his. His hand slipped inside her robe, kneading her breast.

She laughed, pushed him playfully away. 'I'm hungry '

'Not as hungry as I am,' he said with evident meaning, looking for something in her face, her eyes. She blenched inwardly at the intensity of his gaze. Then, even as she smiled, she dismissed him, removed him to a distance in her imagination where he was merely the instrument of her purpose.

Sir Charles Walsingham was studying papers at home. He was seated on a green-covered sofa, legs crossed, malt whisky at his elbow on a leather inset table, subdued lighting from the standard lamps and the wall-lighting falling yellowly on the material on his lap. The hands which sifted the reports and transcripts seemed little to do with him, operating robotically.

The big room, richly carpeted, elegantly appointed – Walsingham had inherited the bulk of his mother's estate some years before, and purchased the lease of this flat and a country cottage – was close as a bandage around him. He felt a pressure round his temple like the onset of a migraine. He knew that unless he drank a great deal more of the Glenmorangie he would not sleep much.

McBride had worked first from the German end, turning up clues in the Bundesarchiv in Koblenz – so said the rushed report of an SIS agent in West Germany, via a contact in the BfV. The head of the intelligence branch of the British security machine had agreed to carry out the investigation for Walsingham without question. He would expect the same co-operation from the DS, counter-intelligence. Unlike many former heads of the two branches of the service, Walsingham worked smoothly and closely with his opposite number.

Then McBride had come to England, to find that Gilliatt had died of a heart attack – no doubt about that, apparently, from the report of one of his own men who had interviewed the doctor who had signed the death certificate. Then to Ireland, and Drummond –

Walsingham shifted his body on the sofa in discomfort. McBride was homing like an arrow. What had he been doing in East Berlin, whom had he met, what discovered? That report would take a lot longer to prepare, and might never be satisfactory, though SIS were attempting the task.

Drummond sent him back to England with the daughter, who once – falsely? – had some connection with known IRA men. Another Dugdale, they'd thought, but not so Irish Special Branch had confirmed a couple of years before. Drummond had refused to amplify his telephone call, claiming when interviewed that morning by a Special Branch man from London that he merely wished Walsingham – who had been concerned in the *Emerald* affair – to know that McBride was digging into a past that might 'create certain local difficulties'.

And McBride was now at Admiralty Records, Hackney, and had been reading the MILFORD HAVEN/DMS files. Close, but how close?

Walsingham went on sitting, sipping his whisky, and staring at the papers in front of him. He arrived at his decision close to midnight. He had not spoken to Guthrie as yet, reversing his decision of the previous day. He would again postpone that conversation. Instead, clumsy and obvious though it was, he would remove temptation from McBride.

He got up heavily and crossed to the telephone. He dialled the number of the duty operations room in St John's Wood, and spoke to Clarke, the Surveillance Director.

'John – the McBride matter. I want the records removed from Hackney tonight, and McBride's notebooks must be recovered. And I want McBride watched from now on. All contacts, everything.' He paused while Clarke suggested the operatives he would deploy. 'Good. Oh, and the East Germans. I want to know whether there are *any* un-accounted for, or who've just moved on to the patch. No, I don't think anything, but I want to be sure. Oh, and watch the girl, too – just in case.'

He stood by the telephone for some moments after ending the call, remembering his one trip on a submarine, to pick up McBride's father and Gilliatt off Brest. A nasty business. He was going to wipe all trace of *Emerald* from the records, for the second time. He felt as if he were wiping out McBride – dear Michael – betraying the best field-agent he had ever known and one of his few friends.

But, better that than what he might have to do to the son if he went on with it, turned up some of the real dirt. That he could hardly bear to consider, even though it was there at the back of his mind, waiting for a summons to the forebrain. He had hated sending the father to Brest, dangerously under-briefed and under-protected, but the son –

Let him stop, he told himself almost in a prayer. Let Michael's son stop now.

Chapter Ten

MINISTERIAL RESPONSIBILITY

October 1980
Professor Thomas Michael McBride of the University of Oregon in Portland walked through the communicating door between his hotel room and that of Claire Drummond, where they had spent the night, and created for himself the conceit that he was moving between the sensual and the intellectual life. His nakedness prevented him from sustaining or elaborating the image.

His notebooks were missing. He had tidied them the previous night, before making love and after returning from the restaurant – he had dwelt on them for a few moments of self-satisfaction, a vicarious and cerebral excitement deliberately indulged. Now, realization spread through his frame as slowly as that excitement had done. Passion was a sharp, shuddering, instantaneous reaction of skin and muscle to Claire's lightly brushing fingertips. This was different, but he began to shake with it, with anger and fear. Then he moved to the wardrobe, and found that the deposition of Campbell had been taken from his wallet. He tugged open his brief-case, and found it empty of the photocopying done in Berlin and Koblenz, the notes he had made of his interviews with Menschler and Kohl.

Furiously, hands almost out of his control, he switched on his cassette-recorder. A hiss of empty tape. He played back, and again the hiss of a clean tape. His prognostications of the previous evening had been removed. Every particle of evidence concerning *Smaragdenhalskette* and the minefield and the German invasion of Ireland had been stolen.

Why?

He was still shaking, as if cold water poured from some shower-rose just above his head. He could not stop asking the question, again and again, and being frightened of the answer. He kept looking back at the communicating door as if Claire, still sleeping, might have an answer or might provide something to take away the subtly, insidiously growing sense of insecurity. Corridors, silent reading rooms, dusty files, unshaded cellar lights, small, insignificant librarians and clerks, shadows – all now possessed a patina of menace. He had been watched, followed, robbed –

Of something that had happened forty years ago, and could have little significance for anyone except a popular historian with an eye on the *New York Times* best-seller lists.

And then he was angry, very angry. They'd stolen a million dollars, maybe more. Hackney. The evidence still at Hackney – maybe more of it, waiting. He'd steal it this time.

Who? Why?

The questions now became tossed and overturned by his rising anger. Someone was trying to screw him. Some bastard. Hackney.

'I'm sorry, Professor, those files have been requisitioned for reclassification.' The naval officer with the damaged leg and the sour disposition seemed to take pleasure from McBride's shock and surprise.

'What in hell?'

'Sorry, Professor. Collected this morning by Admiralty messenger. They might end up at Kew, if you'd like to wait ten or twenty years.'

'They've been transferred somewhere else, right?'

'Sorry, Professor. Reclassified.' He leaned confidentially

over his desk. 'You weren't working on anything *sensitive*, were you, Professor?'

'Sensitive – no. Forty years old, dead as the dodo. Look, you're sure about this, uh?' McBride's anger was still there – he'd nursed it on the train like a secret passion for an unattainable woman – but he was winded now, confused and again the fear was bubbling under his heart, acid and sharp. *Official interference,* he kept repeating to himself in a bemused, unenlightened way.

'Sorry, Professor. I know it's annoying for you, but they treat us here as nothing more than clerks.' His thin face twisted, it seemed, from hair to chin to adopt the bitter line of his lips. 'Stuff lies here for years, collecting dust – when it's being of use at last, or we're just about to get round to refiling and properly documenting, they come and remove it.' McBride saw that he presumed the sudden requisition to be a comment on the running of the records repository and nothing more. A creeping, invidious sense of danger gradually assailed McBride as he sat in the man's office, the electric fire which warmed it seeming not to radiate in his direction. He felt alone, cut off by thick, almost soundproof glass from the other man.

'I see – they do it often, then?' A straw. The navy man, usually insensitive to any but his own responses, was puzzled by the thick, clogged voice that issued from McBride. McBride looked pale, too –

'You all right, Professor?'

McBride nodded. 'Yes, yes I'm OK. Just – infuriating, them taking all the stuff away just when I was working on it.' He stood up. 'Well, I guess you can't do anything, neither can I. I'll keep on looking – '

'If you could tell us what you want – '

McBride shook his head. 'I'll know it when I see it. Thanks.'

When he was back in the cold staff-room that was now a reading-room, he could no longer control the shake that had developed like a palsy in his hands and spread through his frame. He felt very cold, and very, very alone. He clasped his hands together, to still them, but his body went on shivering beneath his topcoat. He sat down, cold perspiration down his back when he felt his shirt pressed against him by the chair, and cold patches under his arms. He rubbed his face with his hands.

Everything was gone. Someone wanted to stop him, right there. Someone with official contacts, official powers. That was it. There was something he shouldn't find. The past had to stay underground, nice and buried like radioactivity. Who was going to get burned if he dug it up – apart from himself?

For a long time he sat there unmoving, his body gradually growing warmer, the shaking subsiding. And, as with a storm that has passed, there was damage and the topography of his mind and body was not quite the same, but the violence of the storm itself could no longer impinge so forcibly. The weak sun of his curiosity came out from the clouds. He wanted to know what there was to know. He wanted to know what might be left here in Hackney, overlooked in the rush to remove the evidence.

He didn't know where the bodies were buried, but he knew they hadn't died by accident. The epithet amused, calmed him. The sense of menace began to evaporate like floodwater.

Walsingham indicated McBride's notebooks and papers with his hand. Exton, his senior aide in the Executive Branch of MI5, adopted a more attentive look and sat slightly straighter in his chair in Walsingham's office.

'He was close, Exton, very close.' Exton nodded, as if silence was all that was required. 'These German papers and interviews on the one side, then our own records. He had most of it – ' Exton tried to look interested, but the old man had not put him fully in the picture, just issued orders to Clarke the previous night and had the stuff delivered direct to him. Exton, the perfect functionary, was not insulted or offended by the lack of a briefing or Walsingham's failure to consult him before they lifted this American's notebooks and raided the dust-heap at Hackney, but neither could he take the matter seriously. Which, he supposed, was what came of being only ten when the war ended. 1940 was the year he was five, and not significant for much other than that fact.

'Sir,' he murmured.

Walsingham always treated Exton, whom he disliked, with excessive formality. Noting the stiffly returned *politesse* now, he remembered Michael McBride, and a spasm passed across his mouth, lifting one corner into a crooked, ironical smile. Exton was puzzled.

'Exton, I want this German historian, Goessler, checked out. And all the other names in his notebooks. And I want Hackney gone over with a fine-tooth comb after he's got tired of mooching around there. *This* isn't going to happen again. And, while you're at it, get rid of *all* references to Guthrie in *anything* connected with nineteen-forty.'

Exton nodded, and stood up. 'I'll get straight on with it.'

'Take this stuff with you – have it all broken down and properly sifted. Then, start daily reports on McBride, direct to me.'

When Exton had gone, Walsingham kept repeating to himself a single phrase, much as if he might have been invoking some god or protective spirit. *A close-run thing*. Eventually, he was able to smile, with relief.

November 1940
The fishing smack owned by Jean Perros and his sons put out from Ste. Anne-du-Portzic in a sudden and unexpected snowstorm, and on an incoming tide. McBride and Gilliatt, dressed in blue jerseys and oilskins, assiduously checked the nets and gear with Perros's two sons, Jean-Marie and Claude. The wind-driven sleet half-obscured the shoreline and the straggling suburb that joined Brest to the fishing village. To the east, they could not see – yet – the long, low, grey line that marked the harbour wall of Lanilon where the Germans had constructed their submarine pens.

The engine of the smack was running rough, doctored by the engineer, a cousin of Perros, coughing and chugging with a worrying irregularity had the crew not expected it. McBride's hands became stiff and frozen as he fumblingly worked at checking the heavy, tangled nets, and he concentrated on what he had to do when they reached Lanilon. Occasionally, he looked up as the grey shape of a warship or submarine slid past them in the murk. Perros's boat was unlikely to be challenged, at least not until they neared the breakwater. He welcomed the weather. Gilliatt, seemingly absorbed in his task, appeared oblivious of weather or danger.

The engine cut out, dying throatily like an asthmatic old man. The boat suddenly wallowed in the tide. McBride looked beyond the bow, seeing the grey harbour wall loom in the sleet, then disappear, then re-emerge. They had rounded the Pointe de Portzic, and were drifting towards the western end of the huge harbour. At the western end were the U-boat pens.

The smack drifted under the shadow of the wall, which stretched over them like a great dam. The tide chipped whitely against its base. The minutes limped by. Perros, in the wheelhouse, used the rudder as best he could against the tide and wind, turning the boat to lurch repeatedly. Through the squalling snow, McBride could see no other vessels, and no guards on top of the breakwater. The nearest steps down to the water were also obscured.

He touched Gilliatt on the arm, startling him out of a fixed attention to the nets, and nodded. Then he went forward to the wheelhouse. Perros, hands whitened with effort on the wheel, glanced at him.

'The steps are a hundred metres or more ahead of us,' he said. Beside him, a nephew scanned the water ceaselessly for other vessels, swinging his glasses in an arc across the wheelhouse screen.

'Can you make it?'

'Maybe. This tide is doing its best to stop me!' He grinned. He'd taken Lampau's death without emotion earlier that morning, almost without comment. He evidently did not blame the two Englishmen, rather seemed to admire them, and to be flattered that they required and needed his assistance. 'If we have to start the engine, so be it. It can always cut out again!' McBride nodded, collected his own binoculars from the rear of the cramped, fuggy, fish-stenched wheelhouse – engine-oil smells seeping through the deck planking from the tiny engine-room below. 'Good luck,' Perros called after him as he went out again.

McBride looked up at the threatening wall, now only yards from the ship's deck. Ahead of them, he could see the steps. He heard the ringing of the wheelhouse telegraph as Perros called for the engine's power. A cough, stutter to life, and the smack pushed forward. The engine throbbed through the deck planking. McBride waited as the steps neared, aware that Gilliatt and the two sons were watching him intently. The engine died suddenly, and McBride wondered whether it had actually broken down. Then the boat lurched with the tide against the harbour wall, planks straining, crying out, then the boat began to move away. He jumped, glasses banging against his chest. His hands grappled with the slimy seaweed of the bottom step, water splashed over the tops of his sea-boots, then a wave drenched him up to the waist as he began to slip, his grasp loosened.

He scrabbled for a hold, catching an iron mooring-ring set in the concrete of the lowest exposed step, pushing at the same time with his feet against a seaweed-slippery step beneath the water. Then he pulled himself up, resting only when he was above the reach of the tide.

He sat down. Gilliatt gave him a thumbs-up signal from the stern of the fishing-boat, and Perros's two sons were smiling. The smack had lurched away from the breakwater, wallowing helplessly. Then Claude Perros held up the mooring-rope at the stern, and McBride, suddenly frightened by the insecurity of his perch on the steps and chilled by the wind blowing against the soaking trousers beneath his oilskins, climbed to the top of the harbour wall where the wind heaved at him, trying to throw him back into the water. He waved his arms, and the rope snaked out towards him from the stern of the smack. He caught it, but his frozen fingers could not close on it before its weight dragged it over the edge of the wall. He waited, freezing, while Claude hauled it in, looped it, then threw again. The rope landed like a heavy, arresting hand across McBride's shoulder and he grabbed it tightly, then dragged it to the nearest mooring-ring, looping it through and making it fast.

When they had bow and stern lines fast the smack wallowed only gently in the lee of the wall, the line of old car-tyres down its port side rhythmically rubbing against the concrete of the wall. Perros looked up at him through the screen of the wheelhouse, and waved him to hurry. Engine repairs was the fiction of their need to tie up, but any patrol vessel that found them would tow them away from the sensitive area of the U-boat pens.

McBride crossed to the inner lip of the breakwater, looking into the streaming sleet blowing the length of the massive harbour. The huge breakwater had been built at the end of the century parallel with the beach to enclose a huge harbour, and the port of Lanilon on the western outskirts of Brest was developed. When France had fallen in the middle of 1940, the Germans had almost immediately begun the building of the concrete submarine pens for their U-boats, from which the raiders put out into the North Atlantic to intercept the convoys from neutral America and Canada to a desperate Britain.

McBride could see, away to his left as he stood on the final section of the breakwater wall and almost a couple of hundred yards from the shoreline and the port, the crude concrete bunkers under which huddled, as if against the storm rather than an air-raid, the lines of U-boats. He could dimly make out the stern-on shapes of perhaps a dozen vessels undergoing refuelling, refits, repairs, rearming. The tunnels of the separate pens offered themselves to the view through his binoculars like open mouths containing the squat cigars of the U-boats.

He would have to get closer, changing the angle at which he could see the U-boats. Numbers alone interested him, designations in white on the conning-towers. The wind howled at him, making him lean into it to preserve his balance, but he felt gratitude towards it now that he was moving along the breakwater towards the guard-post, a grey concrete blockhouse astride the wall where it met the shoreline. Here it scanned the harbour wall and controlled traffic into the pens. If he were spotted –

Slowly, the angle of perception changed until the conning-towers of the two closest submarines began to betray tall white numbers. He could not make them out. The blockhouse was less than a hundred yards away, and he felt naked and exposed, and almost at the mercy of the storm. A gull screamed near his head, then was flung away by the wind, and he shuddered. He had to look as if he was heading for the blockhouse, in case they spotted him, and yet he had to incriminatingly use the glasses. He hunched a shoulder to the shore, raised the glasses, and looked. He could see the white stick of the figure 1, nothing more. The blockhouse was sixty yards ahead of him, and unless they were all blind or dead in there he must be spotted at any moment. He moved on slowly, hunched and leaning against the wind, glasses clenched against his chest in one frozen hand. The figure 1 was accompanied by the half-crescent that might have been the figure o. His heart jumped almost painfully. A little closer, just a little – if it was a nought, then there had to be a 1 in front as well as behind.

He could see the numbers on the boats in Guernsey. He did not need to match them. OIC knew that U-99 to U-108 were all large boats like the two of the series he had seen. Any one in the series would be the proof he needed.

Forty yards – come on, come on, they must have seen me. He could not make out the numerals without the aid of the glasses, not through the murk of sleet and wind. Was it a nought, a zero – just o?

Come on, come on –

He could see o1, he could see the two distinct numerals, o and 1. U-101. One of the series of boats that had been used for minesweeping duties in the St George's Channel. He was oblivious to his surroundings for a moment, enjoying a sense of triumph which was rare and selfish and self-congratulatory. They knew, they *knew* –

At the same instant that he recognized the numerals, he also sensed the deserted nature of the pens. No noise above the wind, no flare of acetylene, no hammer of riveting, no sign of any human being near the seaward ends of the two pens he could see most clearly. Waiting. The U-boats were waiting –

He caught the flash of welding from a distance along the pens. But here, with these nearest two, then others, there was nothing.

He felt newly chilled by the wind against his side.

'You there!' the voice called. 'Put up your hands! Come here!' the German spoke reasonable French. McBride, as he raised his hands, letting the glasses dangle from their strap against his chest, guessed he might have come from Alsace. 'Who are you?' There were two of them, each armed with a machine-pistol, coming towards him from the blockhouse.

'Charles, is indifference to human life a form of madness?'

March was seated in his office, and the slim buff folder with the single stencilled word *Emerald* lay before him on the desk. He had been reading the typed sheets – one copy only – and now he sat back, rubbed his eyes with strain or disbelief, and asked his question of Walsingham, who let no answering emotion appear on his face; a face that was wan, chalky with sleeplessness, dark stains beneath the eyes that met March's gaze levelly.

'This is simply a projection, Admiral.' All his anger, even his premonition of guilt, was squeezed into the excessive formality of his reply. He had known how it would be, had understood in advance as he worked on the draft of *Emerald* through the night and morning, that it would brand him. He would be regarded in the Admiralty corridors as a strange and dangerous species, a disease-carrier. The images whereby he presented himself to himself were melodramatic, but he did not consider them overstated or false. He could already see the glazed, suspicious look in March's eyes.

'Naturally. You couldn't murder this many people without the permission of your seniors, could you Charles?' The irony sat like an undigested meal on both of them. March wanted to disregard what he had read, even make light if it, thereby restoring a former impression of Walsingham. But this – what was he to make of it? Overwork, black humour, plain lunacy?

'Sir, you've assumed that I'm somehow *working* towards that final outcome – I'm not. What I have projected is a possible sequence of events which would produce a desirable result at a great cost. I understand the *morality* of it, Admiral, but I also understand the possible *necessity* – ' He stopped himself, drawing tight the strings on the bag of his temper. Coolness was his only ally, and would be in the days ahead. There was a long way to go.

'Are you suggesting this, or not?' His hand brushed

fiercely towards the open file as if it was infested with cobwebs.

'I'm suggesting that it might become our only feasible alternative, Admiral. If it achieves that status, then that is the operational plan we would, or might, follow.'

'My God, you know who's on board the cruiser, don't you?'

'I do.'

'We'd divert it, of course.'

'Not yet.'

'Of course not yet.'

'We must consider the effect on the Germans, though – surely?'

The dialogue snapped between them now, electrical sparks. Both men were tense, stiff in their chairs. Walsingham found himself defending the appalling logical outcome of *Emerald* even though he felt a profound loathing for it, and sensed he had begun a process in himself the end of which he could not envisage. What might he begin now to consider as no more than *a necessity of war? Emerald* was an idea that had been waiting for someone to think it. Why had it lodged in his mind?

'Of your plan?'

'Yes – my plan.' The reluctance was simply the slightest hesitation. 'It would be a significant, perhaps crucial, propaganda victory.'

'Or it might, even if it remained secret, have a profound effect on German military morale?' Walsingham nodded. 'And – the convoy to have been sunk by U-boats in the North Channel?' Again, Walsingham nodded. March seemed to wish to reiterate his ideas aloud, as if to make them the objects of a cool, rational analysis, and he had no objection to not voicing them himself. 'And if it came out, the Americans would never enter the war, might even sign a non-aggression pact with Hitler. We'd be finished.'

'Its secrecy would have to be maintained,' Walsingham commented. 'But we might only stop this invasion by destroying it. And we could lose the convoy anyway.' His face darkened further. He stared at the open file. 'We both know what cannot be done. We cannot contact the convoy. The Germans would intercept the message. We don't know their state of knowledge of our codes, but we suspect the worst – and the convoy would be doomed anyway if it was diverted by a signal from the Admiralty.'

'There are other ways – signal them by lamp from an Anson,' March said quickly.

Walsingham said, 'As long as they're not spotted first. I have mentioned that possibility on page five.'

'I *know* you have, Charles. You've been very clever all the way through this – thing.' His distaste was evident, undisguised.

'Sir. This is a projection only. Many of the factors that would make it likely, or inevitable, have not yet occurred or appeared. Will you lock it away as a projected course of action, and only as that?'

'Very well. This is the only copy?' Walsingham nodded. March seemed momentarily obsessed with the idea of destroying the file. Then he said, 'It mustn't come to this, Charles.'

'No, sir. It mustn't. Unfortunately, it might.'

March was unprepared to reply, dismissing Walsingham with a curt nod of his head.

Robert Emerson Grady was walking on the quarter-deck of the cruiser, the wind clutching at the hat he had jammed on his head, and chilling him. Yet he accepted his coldness as a relief from the days he had spent in his cramped cabin, and the noisy wind as a refreshing agent. He was alone, and most grateful for that. The sun gleamed fitfully through cloud, and the sea was grey and moving like the smooth backs of hundreds of whales, great long swells barely flecked with white, oily and somehow alive and sentient. He had gained what the British captain had called his sea-legs, he supposed, and his body rolled and angled expertly with the movement of the big ship. He had been slightly nauseous during the bad weather of the first couple of days, but not since. He was still, however, alien and a non-aquatic life-form on the ship, isolated and depressed; his state of mind an intellectual limbo in which end-less recollection of his last meetings with the President only dimmed and dulled the importance of his mission, the significance it gave a friend of Roosevelt who had been a full-time banker and a part-time special adviser.

He took off his hat, irritated with the effort to keep it in place, as if such effort were beneath his dignity. His grey hair was clipped close to his head and remained unruffled. The cold had outlined the face more sharply – the square, stiff jaw, the long lines from cheekbones to mouth and chin, the prow of a nose and the narrowed blue eyes. He strode more quickly for a few minutes as if narrowing the distance between himself and an island off Europe that he knew well.

Grady's mission was to act as Roosevelt's special envoy to Great Britain – nothing more and certainly nothing less. He was to co-ordinate the efforts and observations and advice of other Americans working inside and outside the embassy, and to assess for the eyes of the President alone the ability of Britain to go on fighting. Roosevelt could not commit the US to more than Lease-Lend; Congress would have destroyed any such effort, and Roosevelt's position would soon have become untenable. Grady he trusted, perhaps absolutely. And Grady had three months in which to assess Britain's position – to help Roosevelt decide whether Lease-Lend should be maintained, increased, or ended.

For, contrary to public opinion and the belief of the British Government, Roosevelt was beginning to regret his involvement in Lease-Lend and the possibility of the US being sucked into a European war when the Japanese had begun threatening the Pacific. That would be America's war. Grady knew that at least part of Roosevelt wanted Britain to fall, and fall quickly, so that he could turn his attention to the Japanese, this time with the full support of Congress. Grady knew that he was, in part, designed to be a hatchet-man.

Grady had spent a great deal of time during the past two decades in England. He possessed a Bostonian's affection for the country, for its landscapes, its culture, its civilization. But he was an American, and Britain – whatever his sentimental ties – was three thousand miles from his real home. Roosevelt had put the alternatives bluntly to him. If Britain is going to win, then America must continue, even increase her support. If Britain is going down, then –

Grady moved more quickly, this time perhaps to escape the bald, unfeeling *realpolitik* advanced by the President and which he knew lay in himself. He agreed with Roosevelt. If Britain was a lost cause then America must write her off as a bad debt, and turn to the Pacific.

He had chosen to travel in this experimental convoy rather than fly to Britain because he wanted first-hand encounters with British fighting-men, and the opportunity to observe their morale at his leisure.

And he was beginning to believe that Britain was beaten. Worn-down, worn-out, finished. Kept going by stubbornness, sheer bloody-mindedness, and inability to accept the defeat that loomed ahead of her. The Japanese were poised to take Burma after Indo-China, then maybe India. The Germans had Britain by the throat and Europe and North Africa under their heel. The British were finished – a sad, undeniable fact. Roosevelt, three weeks after being elected for his third term of office, was similarly saddened and similarly certain.

Robert Emerson Grady's mission gave him no pleasure, and little sense of importance. He was a grave-digger, a priest officiating at the last rites of a great and doomed empire. Suddenly, he turned on his heel, back to his cabin. He was weary of fresh air and the empty, heaving perspective of the Atlantic.

October 1980
It was late afternoon, and McBride was alternately hot and cold in the small, dusty reading room as he feverishly continued his search for corroborative evidence of the material stolen from him. He had driven himself without rest or food all day, so that he need think about nothing else – especially the consequences of the theft and the identity of the thieves. His search was fruitless, wearying, and frustrating. Whenever he paused for a moment, the chill of the room struck him forcibly, and as soon as he began poring over ledgers or sorting through box-files or ring-binders his temperature climbed again until he was sweating and agitated and flushed. He was like someone with an approaching fever-climax, distraught and barely rational.

On a wall-shelf which might once have held a teacher's books or the daily post he had collected a pitiful little heap of papers by four in the afternoon. In a new notebook there were perhaps two dozen speculative entries. Confronted by the mass of data he had extracted, with Hoskins's help, from the repository, he convinced himself that there was an answer, that a seam of gold ran through this mine of records, because he could not bear to think that what was now lost to him was the whole and entire basis of the available evidence for the German invasion of Ireland in 1940.

Hoskins carried in another two box-files, blowing dust from them as he entered, just as McBride, rubbing a dirty hand down his face and smearing his cheek, looked up from the ledger which contained the record of ships' movements in and out of Milford Haven. The flotilla of minesweepers did not appear in the ledger, leaving or returning. The record —he could not be certain that it had been amended —indicated that *Bisley*'s flotilla was in Milford Haven sound from three days before it set out until its next sailing, the mines across Swansea Harbour, when Gilliatt had already left the ship.

McBride felt a flush of anger, but refrained from directing it against Hoskins, who smiled over the box-files before putting them down on the edge of the table.

'Any luck, Professor?'

'No, dammit!' He tried to grin away his anger, but failed. His face adopted nothing more genial than a grimace. 'Sorry, Hoskins. What are these?'

'Convoys.' He made the word heavy with significance. McBride studied his face.

'Important?' he asked unhopefully.

'Could be, Professor —but it won't have anything on the convoy I was on.' Bright beads of perspiration stood out on Hoskins's pale, furrowed brow. McBride, tired now, was prepared to listen. He remembered the subject being broached the previous day.

'Your convoy?'

'Remember I told you yesterday, Professor?' Hoskins seemed to steel himself, then blurted out: 'Must be interesting to you. We were routed south of Ireland, and I

heard they'd swept a special channel for us – ' McBride's
mouth slackened in surprise, even as his body snapped to
attention in his chair.

'Go on,' he said shakily.

'They couldn't have done the job, could they? We got
sunk!' Hoskins said with sudden bitterness.

'Tell me – '

Hoskins glanced theatrically round the room. 'Not here.'
(He took a card from his pocket, on which an insurance
salesman's own address was written neatly on the reverse.)
'Come and see me this evening. I'll tell you everything I
know.'

'But – '

'Later.' And Hoskins went out, closing the door behind
him. McBride got to his feet, pacing the room, staring at
the two box-files with renewed excitement. *A special
convoy – couldn't have done the job properly* – what the hell
did it mean?

He crossed to the table, wanting to close the ledger with a
final loud noise and get on with sifting the new box-files,
the word *convoy* lurid with possibilities in his imagination,
when he read the last entry of the page he had reached.

Two minelayers arrived in Milford. November twenty-
eighth. He flicked over the page, mistaking minelayer for
minesweeper for a moment, then correcting himself even as
he read that the minelayers had sailed the following day, and
found their return as his finger slid down the ledger entries –

Minelayers.

An intuition of such force as to weaken him, make him sit
down to rest suddenly untrustworthy limbs, assailed him.
He had seen something, somewhere –

Why was it in a different handwriting in the ledger? A
new clerk, one not instructed? He flicked over pages. No –
God, no! He'd been so bored, so inattentive, so *stupid* –
This was the normal handwriting, the pages containing the
references to *Bisley* were written in a hand that was very
like but not identical. God –

He flicked through other pages, saw where a new clerk
took over the harbour records – then he flicked to the front
of the ledger, and discovered more confusion. He had
been reading, dully and mule-like and damn stupidly

the harbourmaster's ledger of shipping movements –

Handwriting, handwriting? No, Jesus but he was dumb, it was the same handwriting. *Bisley*'s flotilla was omitted, but nothing had been changed. He giggled aloud. It was stupid, suspecting a cover-up. But, someone had been instructed not to make an entry concerning *Bisley*, presumably for security, but the minelayers?

The men who had removed the Milford files had left this, if they'd found it at all, because it wasn't Admiralty records, it had belonged to the harbourmaster. During the war, all shipping had become the responsibility of the Admiralty. But the harbourmaster had gone on keeping his own log of shipping movements, apparently, separately from NOIC at Milford. And someone keeping his log failed to ignore the sailing of two minelayers from Milford to St George's Channel and their return – having reSown the passage swept by *Bisley*'s flotilla, and that swept by the Germans for their proposed invasion. God –

Hoskins, he had to talk to Hoskins immediately.

It was getting dark outside. Hoskins would already have left. He plucked the card from his pocket as if fearful someone might already have stolen it. Sansom Road, Clerkenwell. He'd need his tape-recorder from the hotel. Hoskins was on a British ship that went down in the St George's Channel because –

He could not, with any precision, form the conclusion. He was almost afraid of so doing, because it explained everything. The secrecy, Drummond's silence, the theft of his notes. The British had –

Again, a mental impediment prevented him forming the thought in precise verbal symbols. He didn't know, he told himself. He did not – he *did*. He did. It explained everything.

He stared at the ledger again. The names of the two minelayers, their tonnage, their captains. Jamieson and Guthrie. He closed the ledger as if doing so might contain its secret. He hugged the leather in his hands.

Guthrie. David Guthrie. At some castle, opening a conference on Northern Ireland. *Another* David Guthrie, he told himself. He opened the ledger again, flicking the pages feverishly, rumpling the corners of many of them.

Bisley, and the minelayers. He barely glanced at the door, then tore hurriedly and crudely at the pages until he had roughly detached them. He stuffed them into his briefcase, paused to breathe deeply once, and then went out.

He felt the tensions, the premonitions beginning almost as soon as he felt the cold air of the early evening on his face.

From inside the telephone booth, Hoskins watched him go, then made a call to Goessler. He did not notice the Vauxhall start up further down the street and pull slowly into the traffic, on McBride's trail.

Moynihan kept McBride in sight until he entered the station, and assumed that he was heading back to the hotel. Hoskins was an anonymous, mousy man he had disregarded. He was not similarly able, however, to ignore the fawn Marina with a driver and passenger who had been following McBride four cars ahead of himself. His suspicions became confirmed when the passenger alighted and followed McBride into the station. As the Marina pulled away, Moynihan looked around him for a telephone box.

November 1940
McBride put his hands above his head, and adopted a posture that he hoped was suitably cowed, frightened. In the bad weather, he had approached nearer the blockhouse than he could have hoped, and confirmed the presence in Brest of the ocean-going U-boats he had seen on Guernsey. Had the sun been shining, he would have had to march openly down the breakwater to report that the smack had broken down, and would not have been able to use the binoculars.

His satisfaction was, however, unimportant at that moment. The two German guards were angry with him because he had not been spotted earlier, and perhaps they should have been on patrol but had huddled instead round a fire, drinking coffee. Perhaps their officer had seen him first. The binoculars dangled innocently, yet betrayingly, from his neck.

'My boat,' he began in rapid French, pointing back down the breakwater towards the sea. 'Engine trouble. I came to report it. We had to tie up alongside the wall – *pardon, pardon.*'

The Germans were suspicious, and disarmed at the same time. Their machine-pistols were held more slackly, barrels angled to the ground. Just a Frenchman – McBride could see the contempt of familiarity and conquest glazing their attentiveness. An Unterfeldwebel and a Pioner from an engineer unit, the Unterfeldwebel was wearing on his uniform lemon-yellow *waffenfarben*, which meant he was from a signals regiment. And McBride knew that these men had replaced the normal infantry or police blockhouse guards. Close, it was close now –

He tried to ingratiate himself further.

'Come and see, please come – ' he babbled, even reaching a hand out for one greatcoat sleeve. A sapper and a signals NCO guarding U-boats, his mind kept repeating. 'Please, we do not mean to be here, our engine broke down – ' a machine-pistol thrust McBride's flapping hand away, but without animosity. A controlled, confident contempt seemed to animate both men. They betrayed their élite unit background by stance, smile or grimace, ease. Then the idea struck McBride – he could almost sense it growing in a smaller calculating self inside the shell that was impersonating a French fisherman – that he, and he alone, knew for certain that the Wehrmacht intended invading Ireland, and in the immediate future. And if they shot him, the surprise attack might succeed. There was no self-dramatization in the thought, no self-aggrandizement. He was terrified of the responsibility.

'What's the matter?' the Unterfeldwebel snapped in his Alsatian French as McBride stumbled over his words.

'The guns, the guns – ' he managed to say. He expelled some of the fear they would expect from a fisherman facing guns. The two Germans were alert, their eyes and stance hardly altered by his supplicatory tone.

'Engine trouble?' the Alsatian asked. The machine-pistol came up again, levelled at McBride's stomach. As if prompted by some cue, the Pioner glanced over his shoulder towards the nearest U-boat pens, then back at the binoculars round McBride's neck. 'What engine trouble?'

'I don't know – it cut out,' McBride protested, feeling the chill of the wind go away, and the sleet pattering against his cheek become distant. His body temperature began rising beneath his jersey and oilskins. 'Please, come and see for yourselves – '

They had shaken off the lethargic, welcome warmth of the blockhouse, the reluctance of coming out into the blowing sleet to investigate a mad Frenchman walking along the breakwater in full view of them. They had readopted their responsibilities.

'Move,' the Unterfeldwebel snapped, pointing with the gun. McBride hesitated, knowing that the direction they now took meant everything. The enormous consequences of going on towards the blockhouse, of the arrest of Perros, Gilliatt and the crew which would follow, the investigation of their papers, the questions – all trying to break through the mental barriers erected to help him operate on the thin surface of these successive moments. He shrugged. The Unterfeldwebel poked the barrel of the gun in his stomach, then turned him round with a slap from the machine-pistol against his side. They were going to look at the fishing smack.

'What do you think?' the Pioner asked in German as the two soldiers walked behind him, a couple of feet back, hunching into the suddenly stronger wind.

'Who knows? He doesn't look like much, does he?'

'I'll look at the engine,' the Pioner said confidently, and McBride prayed that Perros's cousin below decks would be able to bluff it out.

'Jean! Jean!' McBride called out, waving his arms as he caught sight of the ropes and the smack bobbing slowly, grindingly against the breakwater.

'Shut up, you!' the Unterfeldwebel snapped.

McBride saw Gilliatt in the stern, his face white and watchful – too watchful and not frightened enough, McBride told himself. Claude was with him, the others not in sight. Claude crossed to the hatch, and yelled down it to his father. By the time the two Germans were standing on the edge of the wall, looking down, Perros was emerging through the hatch, wiping oily hands on a filthy rag and smoking the last inch of a cigarette. McBride was grateful for his nonchalance. Gilliatt kept on watching the two soldiers, one hand close to his pocket where the gun nestled. McBride realized he did not know whether Gilliatt could bluff it out, or would panic and start firing.

'You there, you the captain of this tub?'

'It is my family's boat,' Perros replied, riding with the awkward swell, bobbing up towards them and away. He kept rubbing his hands.

'What's wrong with your engine? Why are you fishing at this time of day?'

Perros shrugged. 'We're not fishing, sergeant. We came out to test the engine, and – *phut!*' Perros raised his arms in the air, dissipating the engine's power. 'We tied up – I sent Henri there to inform you. Don't want trouble – ' He grinned.

'We'll go down,' the Unterfeldwebel said, nudging McBride with the machine-pistol. Then he raised his voice. 'We're coming aboard.' Perros shrugged.

They went down the steps, and McBride sensed the two Germans were suddenly hesitant, whether because of the water or the fact they were outnumbered on the boat he could not tell. They prodded McBride to jump first. He waited until the smack's bow swung up towards him, then jumped the gap of grey water, skidding on the wet deck, then standing upright.

One of the Germans, the Pioner, stumbled badly, but recovered, but the sergeant landed easily and confidently. The guns were immediately emphatic, dominant as soon as they were sure of their footing.

'Show him the engine,' the sergeant ordered Perros when they had moved to the stern of the smack. Again, Perros shrugged. The sapper ducked his head, disappearing behind Perros into the tiny engine-room. 'You – papers!'

McBride reached in his pocket, pulled out his forged ID card, ration book, worker-registration document and his demobilization docket. The Unterfeldwebel studied them. McBride watched Gilliatt carefully, trying to assess his mood. His face was very pale, his hand closer to his pocket. The sergeant handed back McBride's papers, then held out his hand to Gilliatt. McBride watched, saw the flicker of one eyelid, the grimace of Gilliatt's mouth – then he was handing his papers to the German.

Then Claude's papers were checked. The sergeant

seemed frustrated, but perhaps he was only angry with them for wasting his time, making him cold. Suddenly, the engine coughed into life. Claude cheered. The Pioneer emerged, wiping his hands on Perros's rag, a smear of oil on his cheek.

'The bloody French don't understand engines,' he said in German. 'Filthy. Fuel-feed was blocked with muck!' He slapped the rag into Perros's hand, who had followed him up from the engine-room. He tossed his head in mock disgust.

'Thank you,' Perros said. The engine was running smoothly. 'May we cast off now?'

'Very well, and keep clear in future.'

'Henri – ' Perros indicated, and McBride went forward again with the two soldiers. They jumped clumsily, but safely, to the steps, and McBride followed them up on to the breakwater. Here, they left him immediately, as if he might ask them to assist him.

He cast off the ropes, trotted down the steps, and jumped again for the deck. As he landed, he felt his legs go, and he sat down heavily. He was unable to move for a while, and Gilliatt came forward to check on him.

'You all right?' McBride nodded. The two Germans were thirty yards along the breakwater, watching the smack chug away towards the point. 'Thank God for that!' All Gilliatt's suppressed fears were in the words.

'It's all right, Peter. OK.'

'What?'

'The U-boats are there – and those guards are from élite units, guarding them.' McBride grinned. 'We know now. It's on, and it's soon – '

'How long?'

'Two or three days, I estimate.'

'My God – '

'Ask Him to keep the weather bad – it might slow them down, or make the U-boats travel below the surface.'

'You're sure, aren't you?' McBride nodded. 'Hell.'

'You might be right there – give me a hand up.' Gilliatt pulled McBride to his feet. 'What worries me is the Fallschirmjaeger. What the hell is their timetable?'

Sansom Street was old, narrow and dark. It lurked off the Farringdon road in Clerkenwell. McBride had taken a taxi from the Portman Hotel after collecting his cassette-recorder. Claire Drummond had not been in her room, and he was almost thankful not to be further delayed by talking to her, explaining why he was going out again. He booked a table for eight-thirty in the hotel restaurant, scribbled her a note, and left. It was seven-thirty now, and the weather was damply chill, misty around the streetlamps. McBride paid off the taxi, and studied the house that was number twenty-two.

He felt the faint tremor of a tube train passing beneath the street on the Piccadilly Line. The house had three steps up to a delapidated porch, rusty iron railings protecting scrubby remnants of grass and a few overgrown plant-pots. It looked singularly uninviting, and McBride checked Hoskins's card again, nodding reluctantly to himself to confirm the address. Sansom Street was a narrow cut-through to Saffron Hill, something to be driven through as a short-cut or used as a car park. McBride went up to the steps.

Three apartments – *flats*, he corrected himself. Probably no larger than what the British called bed-sits. He studied the names inserted on weathered card no longer white – *Hoskins*, the *Mister* placed assertively before it. Initials, *I.T.* The other cards bore only surnames, one of them written in by the present tenant over the deleted name of a former occupier – *Patel*. He could smell the curry through the door. He rang Hoskins's bell.

McBride felt that sadness that assails the well-off or the successful when confronted with the complete and utter *ordinariness* of other people's lives. Tears pricked behind his eyes at the seediness of Sansom Street, the darkness behind the cracked, dirty ornamental glass in the front door, the quarry tiles of the porch, the dulled brass doorstep. He almost felt cold assailing him from the house's interior. He dismissed the emotion, knowing it was entirely patronizing, secretly self-congratulatory, and rang the bell again.

He was getting cold. He rang more impatiently, keeping

his thumb on the bell, all his impatience now emerging as irritation with Hoskins.

Come on, come on –

A light on in the hallway, a shadow behind the glass. The door opened, and McBride was confronted by a short, thin Indian in shirt-sleeves and a patterned pullover. And a turban.

'Yes? Mr Hoskins's bell, yes?' McBride nodded. 'Sita – my wife – she heard Mr Hoskins come in, with a visitor. The visitor has now left, I am certain. I cannot understand where Mr Hoskins can be – ' The Indian seemed to be addressing a point just to the left of McBride's waist, and holding one hand in the other in front of his chest. McBride's impatience suddenly became fear.

'May I go up?' he said, pushing through the door. The Indian seemed flustered, yet attempted to stand on his dignity.

'I am the landlord here, sir. I will decide – '

'Look, it's important. I have an appointment with Mr Hoskins – ' He showed the card, and the Indian examined it carefully, carrying it to the unshaded bulb in the hall. McBride followed him in, closing the door behind him.

'Just a moment, please – I am landlord here – '

'First floor, right?' McBride said, taking the stairs two at a time, his immediate breathlessness a result of fear not effort. 'Hoskins!' he yelled.

'Just a moment, my good fellow – I am landlord here!' The Indian's voice had become a cry almost of despair.

'Hoskins!' McBride banged on the door. It swung open, and he knew what he would find inside the room. 'Hoskins?' he whispered, pleading for a reply.

Hoskins was in the bedroom, a pillow over his face, hands buried deep in it, claw-like, as if he had suffocated himself rather than been murdered.

'Oh, terrible, terrible – ' the Indian wailed behind McBride when he saw the body. McBride felt weak, could not move the pillow from Hoskins's face. Murder.

PART THREE

ACTS OF AGRESSION

Chapter Eleven

OPEN GROUND

November 1940

Robert Emerson Grady lay on his narrow bunk, staring at the ceiling of his cabin aboard the British cruiser. The long Atlantic swell reached him as a swaying, restful motion in contrast to the dreams that had visited and eventually woken him. A cold blue light above the door of the cabin dimly illuminated the cramped space. Its chilly, submarine light gave him an increased, sharper sense of the sweat on his face and brow, as if he looked down on his own face and saw its fears, its clear registration of what had become his burden.

You're my second thoughts, Bob –

Roosevelt's words, accompanied by that famous easy smile, the big hands slapping the arms of his wheelchair. *My second thoughts.* He'd repeated the phrase, the eyes behind the spectacles suddenly sombre, seeking assent and understanding in Grady. Grady had nodded, swallowing drily.

Forget Donovan and OSS, forget Lease-Lend –

Grady was to concentrate solely on estimating Britain's ability to fight through the rest of the winter into 1941, then to carry the fight to Hitler. If there was no way that was possible, then Grady had to tell his President so. Write Britain off.

In the wardroom that evening, as he dined with the ship's officers, he found himself studying their faces, as if he had asked them a serious, crucial question and was silently prompting them to give him the correct answer. Children – he wanted to prompt, give them clues, hint at the answer. But their faces answered without their knowing the question. Defeat. He knew already the answer he would give Roosevelt in three months' time. *No. They can't make it, Mr President. Europe's finished.*

Roosevelt's ambitions, Grady was sure, included making America the pre-eminent world power when this war was through. To do that, Japan would have to be defeated. Roosevelt wanted the survival of Europe, sure —

But, America first. Europe had to be savable before the President would make the attempt. Otherwise, he'd cut the umbilical with the Old World.

Grady, turning the dreams and images over in his conscious mind and feeling his heart still and the sweat on his body dry, became gradually unsurprised that his dreams were bad ones. The dreams lost their edge, their painful, black sharpness. He rolled out of the bunk, drank some water, then lay down again. He didn't want to do it, but he would. From him, Roosevelt would learn the unpleasant truth. Europe was lost. It was only a matter of time. These men on this British ship, they knew it as completely as if they could smell it in the air or taste it in their food.

Just a matter of time —

After a while, he was able to sleep, and his dreams did not come back that night.

Walsingham and Admiral March, out of uniform, were enjoying Dover sole at Prunier's in St James's Street. They were dining early so that their meal would not be interrupted, even terminated, by that night's air raid. Walsingham had no desire to seek the shelter of the nearest tube station — Green Park — and perhaps spend the night huddled against strangers, inhaling the mingled body odours that ripened in the darkness, overpowering the dry, charged air that wrinkled the nose with dust when the trains were running. He did not examine the fastidiousness of his wartime life, preferring to ignore what it hinted of his personality. At times, London pressed against him with a raucous, unwashed, grinning weight and he detested it.

Madame Prunier had given them a table near the rear of the restaurant where they could converse without interruption or the fear of being overheard. March ate his sole as if he resisted any intrusion by Walsingham, but the younger man understood that his superior merely wished to postpone discussion of the debriefing of McBride and Gilliatt — and *Emerald*. Suddenly, he was irritated by March.

'We have to face facts, sooner or later,' he observed

waspishly. Then placed a morsel of fish in his mouth, swallowed and picked up his glass. A good white Burgundy. March, disturbed, watched his actions studiously.

'We have an appointment with the First Sea Lord first thing in the morning, Charles,' he reminded Walsingham heavily, as if suggesting the discussion should not proceed.

'Yes.' Walsingham felt light-headed. It wasn't the wine, or the gin beforehand, merely some deep and surprising elation that had emerged during the debriefing and which had remained with him. He did not ask its cause, nor did he observe it in any moral light. He was, simply, right and had been all along. McBride had brought back the proof he required – no, not *he* but the others, people like March and the whole Admiralty crew. They'd needed categorical proof of what was staring them in the face. The egotism of his being right predominated among his feelings, fuelled his well-being and his attitude to March. 'But what are we going to tell the First Sea Lord?'

March looked up suddenly, stung and humiliated by the insolent edge of Walsingham's tone. 'You want to know whether we're going to take in with us that abomination I have locked in my safe?' He studied Walsingham, then shook his head. 'You're a strange person, Charles. I wonder if you're a new breed, or just an evolutionary freak – ' March broke off as someone emerged from the kitchens behind them. Walsingham smiled easily at the tall, bespectacled young industrial chemist who manufactured much of Madame Prunier's wartime vinegar for her. The chemist nodded at him. He wore his helmet and gas-mask over his shoulder, and presumably he was off fire-watching after his dinner in the kitchens. When Walsingham looked back at March, the old man seemed angry at Walsingham's distraction. 'A freak?' he added sourly, twisting his mouth to give the words emphasis.

Walsingham was angry. '*Emerald* is the only feasible plan, Admiral. You don't want to think about it, fair enough. But before long someone is going to have to. It becomes more and more *inevitable* with every passing day. Are we going to submit the operation to the First Sea Lord's scrutiny?' Perhaps it was the wine, he thought. He felt reckless, yet in control. March, he sensed, was frightened of him, felt some vague moral repulsion that rendered him impotent. 'Are we?' He sipped again at the wine.

'Very well. *Emerald* will be submitted.'

'Then you agree with me – McBride's debriefing is sufficient proof?' Walsingham sought something that would do as a substitute for approval or approbation – justification, vindication of his ideas. March nodded.

'I don't find the satisfaction in it that you do,' he observed tiredly. 'Yes, the Germans intend invading Ireland and opening up a second front against us.'

Walsingham smiled behind his wine glass. He anticipated the meeting with the First Sea Lord in the morning with a heightened, undiluted excitement.

October 1980
McBride was tired, but his head spun and buzzed with the police questions that had taken much of the night and the early morning before they had let him return to the hotel. And when he lay down he suffered a choking, asphyxiating sense of a pillow over his face and strong hands which could not be torn or pushed away pressing it down. He could physically smell the down, the linen, an imagined hair-oil on the pillow filling his nostrils.

By mid-morning, he was drunk on Scotch and an empty stomach and tiredness. Claire Drummond, at first sympathetic and almost strangely approximating to his own fear and disappointment, became irritated with him when he ceased to talk about it and had gone down to the cocktail bar. However, she reappeared after a quarter of an hour, angry and belligerent. She seemed to have decided to quarrel with him.

'Are you going to sit there all day and feel sorry for yourself?' she stormed, kicking off her elegant shoes then savagely shunting them around the carpet with her feet. 'Is that your answer to your problems?' McBride looked at her rather muzzily, unable to understand her reaction except as some tactic to lessen his burdensome reflections. The primary fear had died down with the drink, and he did not shiver with the realization that Hoskins had been killed for the simple fact that he was about to talk to him. McBride had no idea who might have done it, but his mind had forged an insoluble link between Hoskins's death and the removal of the files from Hackney. But that had gone to the back of his mind. Now, all he dwelt on was his next, unguessable step. 'What's the matter with you? I thought Americans were all balls and bullshit! You've run out of steam pretty quickly.'

He looked up at her in amazement. 'What the hell is the matter with you? What have I done to you?'

'Nothing. But you're behaving like the world had come to an end. Get up off your backside and *do* something!'

'What, for Christ's sake?'

'What were you going to see Hoskins about? Why was he so special?'

McBride fumbled for the precise information. Hoskins certainly wasn't very special. 'A convoy he says he sailed on, in nineteen-forty, which was supposed to pass through the south channel – the minefield,' he added when she looked puzzled. When he had finished, her face became concentrated, then inwardly illuminated. He did not understand the succession of emotions and felt he did not understand her at all with the easy dismissiveness of the half-drunk. But, her eyes were intent on some spot on the carpet that was her screen for an inward drama. He could not understand how she could batten so intently on his concerns.

Claire Drummond snapped out of her abstraction, aware of the next words and how they should sound. She placed her hand at her throat as if to massage away the tightness she felt there. 'A British convoy – from the States, you mean?' McBride shrugged and she wanted to hit him.

'I guess so,' he admitted, looking from his empty glass to the bottle on the writing-table. It was almost empty. She wondered whether he ought to be given another drink, or forbidden it. She was aware of every extremity of her body, aware of the fine net of nerves that might produce a tic or a twitch and give her away as she crossed the room, picked up the Scotch, and poured him a large measure. He raised his glass with a grouchy kind of gratitude, as if he had expected remonstration.

'Can't you find this information anywhere else?' she

asked, sitting down opposite him, her posture and voice those of a faithful assistant.

'I don't know.' He choked slightly on the neat spirit. Shook his head emphatically. 'He's dead.'

'My God, you think it was something to do with you?' He looked at her as if he had never considered coincidence before. 'Look, I know someone stole your notes, and they took away the material you were studying – but you *can't* think – can you?' He seemed reluctant to admit it. 'Perhaps there is something to be hidden – but no one could have thought Hoskins dangerous. Don't be so melodramatic, Tom.' He softened at the use of his first name. She smiled, then suddenly she wondered what to say next. Then it came to her. 'If they won't help you here, why not try your side of the Atlantic? Your embassy, the Naval Attaché or whatever he's called? They'd have records of a convoy sunk off the south coast of Ireland, wouldn't they?'

McBride seemed reboned by the idea. He sat up more, shrugged off the slouch of weariness and self-pity and his eyes seemed to clear of the myopia of the drink. He even put down the glass, slopping some of the Scotch on the carpet, tutting at his clumsiness.

'They would, sure. At least, they could lay hands on the records. OK,OK – ' He stood up, swaying just once before taking a firm control of himself, squaring his shoulders. 'Look, I'll call the embassy, get an appointment to see the guy.' She nodded, and he crossed to the telephone. She picked up her shoes and went into her own room, careful to leave the door open. She threw the shoes on the bed and held herself, squeezing her arms tightly across her breasts, clutching her upper arms with claw-like hands, almost bruising herself. She felt nauseous with excitement, weak in the legs, as if all her strength were in her hands and arms. She sat down on the bed.

She had made the intuitive leap, the connection between Hoskins, Goessler and the convoy. Hoskins had been intended to do no more than whet McBride's appetite. He would have pointed himself in the right direction when he sobered up, she knew that. She was very careful not to underestimate McBride. He had considerable intuitive gifts, an energy of mind for patiently following a line of enquiry, and – but she only suspected this – he might prove physically brave, tough to overcome, wear down. Which could be costly, even bloody, later on. From what her father had told her of his father, she considered there was something of Michael McBride in his son, overlaid at the present with academic soft living, sedentary barnacles.

She dismissed him, his voice on the telephone went away. She congratulated herself. They were a step ahead of Goessler now, knew more than he guessed or thought they did. A British convoy had been sunk off the Cork coast in 1940 when a path should have been swept for it by the Royal Navy. *That* was the crucial fact. She trembled with the plain verbalized idea. A scandal the British had buried, now about to blow up in their faces. If they could use McBride now, getting the proof *before* Goessler –

It was, of course – she admitted it to herself – what she had waited for. Bombs, guns, the hardware of terrorism had hardly attracted her. Control of people, strategy, tactics, orders – she craved them, the opportunity to employ her clear, detached, lucid mind on them. A woman in the Provisional IRA, however, was not allowed. Messenger, venus-trap, bomb-planter, *secretary*, was what they wanted. Sean Moynihan was considered an outstanding strategic mind in Belfast and Dublin, and she considered him a fool. There was a plain sheen to his thinking, no Byzantine chiaroscuro the like of her own. She appreciated Goessler's operation because it was so involved, so brilliantly complex – and because she had now seen through it. How did Guthrie fit? She dismissed the qualification on her enjoyment.

Ever since university she had waited for a moment like this, this intensity of self-congratulation. Ever since university and her timorous involvement with the civil rights movement in Ulster. Later the recruitment by the IRA, then the transfer to the Provisionals; the Marxism preceded the civil rights movement, almost preceded university, gathered first from the French industrialist's daughter – Claudine – at finishing school. Switzerland, 1966. What was Tom McBride doing then? she wondered. Screwing his first flower-power girl student? She wanted to giggle, to outwardly express her pleasure.

She wanted to outwit Goessler not for the Provisionals but for her own standing inside the organization. Her Marxism -- which she supposed Goessler might share -- required less obedience and loyalty than her ambition and her intellect. She was brilliant, and her talents had been wasted up to that moment. But, no longer. She remembered the summer and the Alpine meadows where Marx and Trotsky and Marcuse and hatred and impotent, passionate revulsion at class-inequalities and exploitation had not seemed out of place, but as natural and right as reading Wordsworth or Shelley in those surroundings. Vividly she remembered Claudine, and the hot days and the hotter nights of talk and feeling and growing determination.

Claudine had died in the riots of '68, beaten to death by the *flics* in some dark sidestreet in Paris. She'd heard that from a fellow-student in the Sorbonne on a student exchange to Belfast. And she'd wanted, if not the death, certainly some of the scars, the halo of violent light.

McBride looked round the door. He appeared completely sober now, and was grinning, intruding crassly on her memories. 'I have an appointment this afternoon with the attaché,' he said.

She nodded. 'Good,' she answered abstractedly. 'Good.'

Captain Brooks Gillis, USN, the Naval Attaché at the US Embassy in Grosvenor Square, was mildly puzzled by the historian, Thomas McBride, who had made and kept an appointment to consult him on some matters of naval history. McBride, seated facing the light through the open venetian blinds, appeared intense, tightly within himself as if afraid of spilling some secret from his pockets, but capable of being reduced in importance by the fact that he was an academic. Gillis had done his share of lecturing, and he felt he understood the American academic, the almost Wall Street hustling, the secretiveness applied to academic papers and researches that would not have been out of place in Standard Oil or the CIA. However, he had an easy day before a cocktail party for a Russian trade delegation at the embassy, where he would fulfil his function of psyching out any possible recruits for the Company, and so he did not resent giving his time to McBride.

'Nineteen-forty?' he said, standing at the window, half his attention on Blackburnes Mews below him. A girl got out of a Ferrari, and he studied her with the detachment of a connoisseur. The fur coat was a little ostentatious on a fine October day, but striking nonetheless. He wished his father, who'd seen action in the Pacific and the North Atlantic in that long-ago war, had been there with McBride. The old man would have loosened his tongue, and they'd have been rolling all night. The girl disappeared into Upper Grosvenor Street. 'A long time ago, Professor. How can I help?'

'British records are very sketchy for the period, and *very* disorganized.' Gillis smiled at the attempt to ingratiate. 'I thought you might have access to records of convoys that sailed during November of that year. Just the sailing dates and arrival dates in this country would be enough for the moment.'

Gillis turned to him. He preferred American cars, American girls. That one had looked Arabic, maybe. 'I guess there are records – maybe even here.' He smiled. He'd had one of his junior staff hunt them down. A lot of the records from Eisenhower's headquarters across at No 20 on the square had been dumped in the cellars of the embassy after it was completed in 1960. A lot of it had never got passage across to the States and lay still mouldering down there. Andrews had got dirty, but he seemed to have had fun down there.

'Have you had a chance to check – '. Gillis asked sharply. McBride appeared confused, impatient even, then nodded. 'OK – we'll get credit, naturally?' Again, McBride nodded. 'Man, but there's some stuff down there. Eisenhower had as much material as he could stored in his headquarters after nineteen-forty-three. Maybe he was going to write a book?' He grinned. 'All the paperwork from the clearing-houses, a lot of OSS stuff, early intelligence reports, you know the kind of thing.' He paused. 'I had one of my men go over some of the material after you called. I'll have him bring it in.' McBride's eyes blazed. Gillis spoke into the intercom, and a navy lieutenant came in, deposited some still grimy files on the desk, and left.

Gillis saw McBride's anxiety, and dismissed it as merely professorial. He had a dismissive respect for college teachers, and an anxiety to be an intelligent man of action. He considered himself superior to most of the graduate kids the CIA sent to liaise with him in London, and disliked the new *rapprochement* with the CIA embarked upon by the Office of Navy Intelligence.

'I have to stay here, naturally,' he said, 'and you can't take any of this away. But you can quote from it, take notes. Help yourself, Professor. It's called open government.'

McBride shunted his chair closer to Gillis's desk, picked up the top file fastidiously as if nervous of its grime, and opened it. Gillis walked to the percolator, poured two cups of coffee and, placing one for the unnoticing McBride, returned to the window. He was never bored with his own thoughts.

McBride read through the files as swiftly as his concentration allowed, but not so quickly that Gillis would think he was searching for just one item of information. It took him an hour or more, and the coffee cooled undrunk and Gillis occasionally scratched his head or shuffled over by the window but remained silent and somehow completely composed – like machinery switched off until again required. There was some arbitrary documentation of convoys, mostly of the invoice kind for goods received. A check-list of shipping lost, more detail regarding their cargoes than their crews. He sensed Britain hanging by a thread three thousand miles long and the Germans trying to cut it in a dozen places. Especially the North Channel, around the coast of Northern Ireland. *All* the convoys went that way round, because of the minefield.

Eventually, he found what he was seeking. An invoice which checked off what had been lost – precise tonnages – when a three-ship convoy went down late in November, together with its cruiser escort. It was clipped to a report from the Admiralty that stated the convoy was sunk still two days out from Liverpool. At the bottom of the Admiralty note, someone with an illegible signature had scribbled *'Grady lost – inform eyes only R.'* Roosevelt? he wondered.

'Captain Gillis?' Gillis turned slowly from the window as if coming to life.

'Yes?'

'Could you explain this?' He held out the two clipped-together sheets. He tapped the bottom of the page. Gillis mused silently.

'No. *R.* was the President, of course. Grady? Not a name I know. British convoy, British warship escort – no, I don't know Grady's name. Is it important?' McBride tried to appear ingenuous.

'I don't know. It's a mystery, and mysteries intrigue me. Why should someone here issue an order like that, eyes only for the President? Convoys were going down every day, and most of them were reported routinely to the Navy Department, weren't they?'

'They were. Mm. Hang on, Professor. I'll check it out.' He picked up the telephone extension, and asked for a Washington number. To hide his growing excitement, McBride pretended to study the files he had earlier discarded. It was Hoskins's convoy, heading for the southern approach to Britain, through the minefield – and expecting that minefield to be swept for them. It hadn't been, and minelayers had sailed from Milford –

Gillis was talking to a friend in the Navy Department, apparently, mincing through the social niceties of silicone cocktail waitresses and the permissive London scene and families – a sudden moralistic tone invading Gillis's voice – and old times, then Gillis asked about Grady.

'Old buddy, you were hot on the period at Annapolis. Who was Grady?' He listened. McBride caught himself straining for the reply, which was long and voluble. Then niceties again, after the explanation, then the connection severed with a chuckle by Gillis. 'That guy, I could tell you – ' He was struck by the intense, burning look in McBride's eyes. 'I got you an answer. Boston banker thick with the President. Sent over on some fact-finding mission, maybe. Anyway he was what they started calling a "Special Envoy" around that time.' He shrugged. 'Poor guy – sea-sick all the way, I bet, then he gets his ass blown off two days out from England.'

'Yes,' McBride said strangely. 'Poor guy.'

Minesweepers, minelayers, St George's Channel, an American envoy, a cover-up –

It had to be worth a million, maybe more. *It had to be –*

The man's name was Treacey. Moynihan had met him only three or four times in the last year, to receive instructions on policy initiation or to make reports on tactical progress. Treacey spent much of his time on the mainland as Operations Commandant. Ulster was not, officially, his concern or under his jurisdiction. Nevertheless, he represented Moynihan's superiors as he sat opposite him in the Bloomsbury hotel room, and Moynihan had to abide the man's anger, however much he inwardly squirmed and however unjustified he felt it to be. He concentrated on keeping his face inexpressive, neutral as Treacey's accusations stung him.

'Then Goessler had this man Hoskins killed in case you got to him – that's what you're suggesting, is it, Sean?' There was a weighted, clumsy irony, and the broad, loose face opened beneath the pudgy nose in what might have been a smile. It appeared to Moynihan as nothing more than a vehicle of threat; Treacey's smiles always did. He nodded. 'Ah, Sean, the General Staff are concerned to gain control of this business.' He paused, but not for any reply. His body and face impressed a tangible weight on the much smaller framed Moynihan. 'You've done very well up to now – ' There was a lightness of tone that denied the truth of the compliment, ' – but you're not in control here, Goessler is. Now, we may owe Herr Goessler and the organization he represents – ' Moynihan was aware once more of the affection Treacey had for his own voice, his own ideas, ' – and we're grateful to him for his present scheme. But he doesn't seem to want *us* to get hold of it. Time is getting short, as you well know, and if anything is to be done, then it will have to be done by us. We have to know the details of Goessler's scheme and put it into action ourselves. You understand me?'

Again, Moynihan nodded, despising the dryness he felt at the back of his throat. He did not want to swallow; his prominent Adam's apple would betray him if he did so. He could not even clear his throat without an admission of subordination.

'Yes, I understand.' He was grateful for the ease and volume with which the words emerged. He sat more forward in his chair, matching the hunched posture of Treacey opposite him. 'I agree with you. Goessler thinks we can't handle the operation. He's going to hand us the result like a sweet for a kid!'

'The indications are that the conference is going well – time's very short. What do you intend to do?'

'Hoskins obviously gave some indication to McBride, to lead him on. McBride's next move should be to act on what he knows or suspects. We have to go on watching him – '

'That might not be enough. What about the girl?' His face twisted in mistrust and contempt. Treacey loathed the Marxism which tinged the girl's attitudes. She was, for him, little different from Goessler and the East Germans and the PLO and the Russians – anyone who helped them for their own ends. The girl was English, anyway, even if she had been born in County Cork. Privilege, education, money enough to make her comfortable. Like Dugdale, an intellectual convert, or perhaps just a fanatical dilettante. He mistrusted her anyway. She should belong to the Irish Liberation Army not the Provisionals, with her ideology. 'What about her? She's getting into bed with McBride. What does she know about his investigations?'

'She didn't see the notebooks before they were stolen.'

'And who stole them?'

'It must have been Goessler – it *was* Goessler. Like removing Hoskins, to drive McBride along the right path.' Treacey looked doubtful, disbelieving. 'I'm certain it had to be Goessler,' he added hurriedly, angry with himself for showing even that much weakness.

'So you may be, Sean. I hope to God you're right. The girl had better start going everywhere with McBride, instead of spending her time in department stores. Tell her that, from the General Staff.' Treacey suddenly looked as if there were others behind him, physical presences who had impressed, disturbed him. He added: 'If we bomb or shoot Guthrie, then we make a martyr of him, like Neave. He's got to be disgraced. But, they're getting impatient. They've given us – you, a week and no more. Then they're threatening to pick up Goessler themselves and squeeze it out of him.'

'They can't –'

'I know. They shouldn't, but they will unless there's an alternative. Which means, you've created a Frankenstein. *You* were responsible for the adoption of this plan of Goessler's, and now you've got them so hooked on it they can't think of anything else except running it themselves. If it doesn't work, you'll be to blame, Sean.' Treacey's upper lip was damp. His own standing with the General Staff in Belfast had evidently dropped. He wasn't speaking from strength and the realization of his weakness came as no comfort to Moynihan. They were hungry for success, and afraid of the wrath of the Abteilung. They evidently saw Goessler's operation as the hammer-blow, the war-winning tactic, the final solution. Moynihan was afraid.

It was evident that Treacey blamed him exactly as he would have blamed the carrier of a disease that had infected him. He said, 'I – they've got to be patient. Goessler is someone we have to trust –'

'Is he someone we *can* trust?'

Moynihan nodded, then opened his hands. 'I think so.'

'Belfast is desperate for results, The feedback from Leeds Castle is worrying them. Guthrie is carrying the day. He's aligning most of the participants behind him, being so reasonable they can't reject his proposals. Sinn Fein are playing a weak hand, just stalling for time. That's why you only have a week. *Get* something by then.'

He stood up, as if anxious now to depart. Moynihan, busy with his own thoughts, did not bother to see him out. When Treacey had gone, however, he poured himself a large whiskey, swallowing it greedily, a suppressed tremor running through his body as if he had taken some unpalatable medicine or a poison. The room depressed and diminished him. It was no scene for grand designs, for solutions to problems. He wanted to go out, walk off his mood, but decided against it.

The General Staff – Mulligan, O'Hare, Quinn, Lennon, all of them – had indeed become his Frankenstein. They'd abandoned other plans, even slowed the mainland bombing campaign, in order to adopt Goessler's scheme to ruin Guthrie. They'd taken it on trust, like greedy children a promise of cake. Taken *his* word, because he was convinced and his was the best tactical mind in Belfast. Now they wanted results, were even afraid, perhaps, of their limelight being stolen by some insanity of the Liberation Army or one of the other deadly splinters from the movement.

He had to deliver. Inside a week. Claire Drummond had to come up with something –

He swallowed again at the whiskey, coughing on its harshness as if it did indeed contain some poison.

McBride was about to tell Claire Drummond what he had discovered at the embassy – she could see his excitement like the halo of a St Elmo's Fire, animating and enveloping his frame with electricity – when the telephone rang in his room. Her face darkened with anger.

It was Goessler.

'Professor Goessler, good to hear from you!' McBride yelled into the telephone. *Bad line,* he mouthed to Claire, grinning and hardly noticing how pale she had become. 'Yes, I'm well, and back from Ireland safely.' He chuckled at some joke of Goessler's and Claire Drummond turned in her chair so that her back was to him. She could hardly control the tension nagging her hands and feet into helpless movement. *Goessler – why?*

McBride listened as Goessler launched into a long, apologetic explanation. Goessler had rung him once in Cork, to report only mimimal progress in collating supporting evidence of the documents they had unearthed. No one else like Kohl had appeared. Now, he seemed to be trying to explain, with excessive bonhomie, that he had stopped working. McBride suspected a demand for a greater share of the potential profits, but he wasn't going to agree, bearing in mind what he had unearthed since leaving East Berlin. Goessler was out, except for the agreed percentage. Maybe not even that.

'You see,' Goessler was explaining, 'they do not have to say why, or for what reason, my friend. All they say is, stop doing this, stop helping this man or that man, don't ask those questions. And, we agree with them. We stop.'

'With who, Professor? Who are we talking about?' He had one finger in his ear to shut out all extraneous sound and was trying to hear through the excessive mush on the line. 'What?'

'The police, of course. Oh, they have many names, and ranks and jobs – but, the police. You would call them the *secret police*.'

McBride was puzzled rather than chilled, not taking Goessler more seriously at first than as another historian prying into his researches; then he went cold, and the missing files and then the pillow shutting out Hoskins's face were omnipresent.

'Why – why would they be interested, Professor?'

'Oh, they're not *interested,* my friend, not in your researches. It's me they keep an eye on. Too many contacts with Westerners, and they suspect my motives. Don't worry – I am ringing only to apologize for not being able to continue our work.' A lengthy pause, into which it seemed McBride was to pour some unobtrusive but satisfying balm.

'Our arrangement stands, Professor,' he said finally. Goessler's relief was almost audible.

'I knew I could rely upon you, my friend. Good luck with your work.'

And then the connection was cut with chilling suddenness. McBride put down the receiver slowly.

'What is it?' Claire asked.

'Mm? Oh, Goessler's backing out – some trouble with the police, or something.'

'Hag-ridden with police, those Eastern European countries,' she observed, seemingly indifferent. 'Neurotic about contact with the West. Do you need him?'

'He could have been useful – but, no, I don't need him now.' He smiled. Her answering smile invited confidentiality, and he seemed to see her more seriously. She could help him. He put aside the reluctance that bubbled up, and sat down next to her. Quickly, he told her what Gillis had found, and the explanation. Then he back-tracked, beginning with Menschler – she'd heard some of it before, but he pedantically ignored the state of her knowledge, as if a confessional necessity had overcome all reluctance – going on to her father, to Hackney and Hoskins.

When he had finished, he appeared drained. She poured him a drink, aware again of the fine net of nerves lying just below her skin and which threatened to betray her excitement, her weakness in the grip of personal and ideological passions. McBride had been pointed ahead by Goessler's withdrawal, prompted into quicker, more intense enquiry by an increased sense of being alone. Venal motive, but appealing to the ego, too. Goessler was a clever man. She handed McBride the drink, and he took it with a smile as he might have done from a wife. She had succeeded. She was now the ally, the amanuensis.

'Trinity House,' she said firmly.

'What?'

'Merchant Navy records in Trinity House. You could check there on this convoy, and whether Hoskins served on one of the ships. If *he* survived, then – '

'You're right!' He was animated again, and proud of her, she saw. Clever girl. She swallowed an irritation she had felt often with Moynihan when he was patronizing her intelligence. 'By God, girl, you're right. Witnesses are what we need. If that convoy went down in the minefield, then they'd know it. My God – ' He was galvanized now, and she enjoyed the control she had just exercised over him.

'You'd better look up their number,' she said as he embraced her. Allies.

She'd call Moynihan later, and set up a meeting. He'd have to hear it in person, what she chose to tell him. She'd make him bring Treacey. She nibbled at McBride's ear as she felt with a crawling sensation his breath on her neck.

Walsingham's duty surveillance team watched McBride enter Trinity House on Tower Hill, then parked their Vauxhall near Tower Hill Station, from which point they could observe the main portico and steps of Trinity House. To be certain they did not miss McBride when he came out again, one of them, Ryan, took a newspaper and sat on a bench in Trinity Square gardens. When McBride left, he would signal the car, then go into Trinity House and discover what McBride was doing there. To elicit the information would require no more than his CID card, one of the many organizations of security to which he was accredited.

McBride came out again near lunchtime. The woman that the man on the park bench had been observing waved to McBride, then joined him on the pavement opposite the gardens. They embraced. The watcher stood up, could almost hear the starting of the Vauxhall's engine though he knew that was impossible in the lunch hour traffic. He watched McBride and the woman – Drummond's daughter from his briefing – talking animatedly as they walked away towards Tower Hill, saw the Vauxhall tailing them down Savage Gardens, then he crossed the road to the main steps of Trinity House. In the imposing Front Hall with its numerous models of ships, he showed his CID card to the security guard, who put through a call to the Assistant Keeper of Records. In five minutes, Ryan was closeted with the Assistant Keeper, being shown the material that McBride had requested.

No, the Assistant Keeper had no way of knowing which names McBride had been concerned to check. Were there specific names? Professor McBride from the University of Oregon was interested in the kind of records, their history and comprehensiveness. Something for a paper he was to deliver to the American History of the Sea and Seafarers Society in Boston on his return to the United States. Ryan almost laughed, inwardly applauding the smokescreen McBride was capable of creating, his pulse quickening at the implications of such an elaborate subterfuge.

Records – just lists of names, sailors and the ships on which they had served. Period 1940 to '45. Trinity House, as Ryan well knew, was and is responsible for the relief of distressed and aged master mariners, but it also keeps records of all merchant seamen in distress or requiring any kind of help – all the old men with a life at sea behind them and nothing in front – together with its work in erecting and maintaining all lightships and lighthouses and being the chief pilotage authority in Britain.

Ryan clenched down on his drifting thoughts as the Assistant Keeper rambled on, repeating the information he

ad passed to McBride before leaving him alone with the
records. Names of old sailors? Would it mean anything to
Walsingham, who'd get his report direct from Exton?

As soon as politeness allowed, Ryan left Trinity House
and called in his findings. The duty officer assured him that
Exton would make sense of a visit to Trinity House.
Meanwhile, a requisition for the Trinity House records
would be issued. Would Ryan like to hang about and help
carry them to the van when it arrived?

Ryan put down the phone before his expletive could be
lopped, and stepped out of the telephone box into the warm
lunchtime sunshine, feeling hungry.

November 1940

The motor launch came close inshore, off Garrettstown
Strand in Courtmacsherry Bay, but against the tide and
they had to lower a raft to put McBride and Gilliatt ashore.
There was a high wind that streamed water over the sides of
the raft like a heavy, driving rain, and the sea was choppy
and cantankerous. Two ratings rowed inshore, but
McBride and Gilliatt still had to wade to the beach out of
waist-deep water because the raft almost overturned and its
crew could hardly hold it against the retreating tide.
McBride felt his legs go from under him the moment his
feet touched the bottom and then, as he spluttered and
splashed about with his arms, Gilliatt's hand grip his collar
and drag him upright. Gilliatt was laughing. The raft
bobbed away from them, sudden moonlight from behind
ragged cloud silhouetting it and the slim, graceful shape of
the ML beyond it.

'Come on, McBride, you really are no bloody sailor!'

'Pressed man, sir,' McBride answered in an adopted
brogue, coughing out sea-water in the wake of the remark.
They hurried through the shallows on to the smooth wet
sand. Turning, they could see the raft being hoisted aboard
the ML, then the engines moved up from idle and the
launch seemed to do no more than ease away from them in
silent apology as it turned out to sea, heading back to
England.

McBride jogged Gilliatt's arm. 'Wistful?'

'What? Oh, sorry.'

'Just rather be there than here, eh?'

'Working for Walsingham is what I can't take,' Gilliat replied with unexpected vehemence.

They walked on up the beach towards the dry sand abov the tide-line, McBride systematically wringing his sleeve and trouser-legs and jacket as they went.

'My socks are drenched. I'm surprised you feel tha strongly about him. Charlie's all right.'

Gilliatt halted, and waited until McBride was looking a him. McBride stopped wringing the last moisture from sleeve, and stilled his chattering teeth with an effort. 'Jus watch out for him, Michael. Don't let him put your head i too many lions' mouths, that's all.'

'God, I'm cold.' McBride attempted to avert the too direct remark.

'Listen to me, Michael. I've met a lot of people lik Charles Walsingham – '

'Are you going to lecture me, Uncle?' McBride sat dow like a disgruntled child and pulled off his boots, then hi socks. He twisted them in his hands and the water streame on to the sand, darkening it like blood. McBride wondere why the image had invaded his mind. He looked up a Gilliatt standing over him.

'I'm just trying to warn you – '

'You'll give me a lecture on Drummond when you'v met him, I suppose?' McBride's temper was completel under control, though he did resent Gilliatt's interferenc in his affairs.

'I might well do that.' Gilliatt obviously thought what h had to impart was important. There was an evident attemp to remain calm and not to antagonize McBride or b antagonized by him. 'My old school was full of people lik him, wearing their charm like the grass they use to cove lion-traps – '

'I like that,' McBride said mischievously.

'He does. Walsingham resents being in the navy at all and is prepared only to use this war to advance his career i intelligence. You remember that I've worked in intelli gence before. I met people like him, every week!'

'All right. I'll watch out for myself.' McBride wa abstractedly rubbing his feet warm again before putting o his socks. When he finished talking, his teeth went on chattering. 'God, I'm cold. What's the time?'

'Ten minutes to two.'

'Bloody early! No wonder Drummond isn't here with his little car and his rum ration.' He held out his hand and Gilliatt pulled him to his feet. Then he sat down and began to take off his boots. The understanding between them was almost instinctive, one on watch while the other was off-guard, easily surprised. McBride hardly remarked it, except that a sense of Gilliatt's dependability lurked at the back of his mind. McBride scanned the empty beach in another gleam of moonlight, the wind almost visible as a stream of silver. Sand pattered against his trouser-legs and the ungloved hands at his sides. 'This will be one of their beaches.'

Gilliatt looked up from chafing his feet and calves. 'What?'

'They'll land here.' He stretched his arms out to encompass the wide stretch of flat beach.

'If they have as much trouble as we did, then everybody's safe. They can be picked up while they're drying their socks.' Gilliatt looked up and down the beach. 'I agree. Flat and open.'

'How many beaches do you reckon?'

'Four or five. What do you think Walsingham wants, after we identify the most likely landing beaches?'

'God knows.' McBride was slapping his arms against his sides. 'He'll be lucky to persuade Dublin to repel boarders.'

'He can't use British troops.'

'He might. *He* would, but will Churchill?'

Gilliatt stood up. 'I could do with some of Drummond's rum.'

'Drummond's usually early himself. Come on, let's leg it up to the track and meet him. What's the time?'

'Five to.'

'I wonder where he is? Flat tyre while we freeze to death!'

They climbed a bank up off the beach on to the narrow track that ran down to the strand from the Kinsale-Clonakilty road. McBride halted and listened, but there was no engine-noise. The wind seemed colder still as it ground and snarled through hedges and bent the few stunted trees.

'How far to your place?'

'We're not going to walk that, Peter my lad. Drummond's house is only a couple of miles from here.'

He was certain that Gilliatt was going to reply. He even framed his lips in preparation for a smile in response to any witticism. But he did not hear any words because of the sudden explosion only yards from him. Gilliatt's figure was outlined in orange flame, a heavy black shape, nothing more, then it was flung on its back into the ditch alongside the track and he, too, was lifted, clouted around the body by the pressure-wave from the grenade, and deposited in a muddy pool. He was aware of a trickle of stagnant water into his mouth, the trickle of something warmer down the side of his face which made his left eye blink furiously, and of being totally deaf and removed by that deafness from the scene around him, from himself and from any real sense of danger.

More than anything, however, he was aware that only Drummond knew where they were supposed to land that night. Only Drummond in the whole of the world outside the Admiralty.

The first of the dark shapes rose from the grass thirty yards from him, moving on to the track even as the last dirt flung up by the grenade was still pattering down on the back of his jacket. McBride felt the hard shape of his gun against his hip, and tried to move his arm down. The arm seemed frozen, then was shot through with excruciating pain so that he yelped, startling the approaching figure and making him more cautious. His arm wouldn't move.

Only Drummond, he kept on thinking. He did not even consider whether Gilliatt was dead or alive. Only Drummond.

Chapter Twelve

SURVIVORS

October 1980

The Rt Hon David Guthrie's PPS, a man Walsingham hardly knew, informed the Head of the Directorate of Security that the Secretary of State was unable to talk with him at the moment because he was in closed session with the Provisional Sinn Fein representatives in an attempt to understand, and overcome, their sudden and unexpectedly silent obduracy. *A hard line,* the PPS had almost mouthed, suspecting and fearing the worst. Men sulking at the conference's progress, or men waiting for the cavalry that would rescue them from surrender. Again, the PPS's impression, confided to Walsingham as he was conducted to a small, comfortable sitting-room to await Guthrie.

Walsingham set the small cassette recorder down on the low table, and slipped the single cassette he had brought with him out of his coat pocket. It was in a buff envelope which he left beside the recorder. The tape was a transfer from reel-to-reel of the call McBride had made to the minister's office that afternoon. The envelope's innocence in the room's gathering dusk was false and uncomfortable to Walsingham. McBride was an angry man, had resented being deflected and turned away by a secretary, had spoken of the minister's wartime experiences with a cunning masked by ingenuousness. McBride was somehow no longer the straightforward academic or his eff·ontery merely that of a gauche American. It would be interesting to watch Guthrie's face as he heard McBride's words for the first time. There was, at the same time, a pressure in Walsingham to go on thinking of McBride as an historian, even as an *American*. Both ideas made something objective and unknown of him, effectively severing him from Michael McBride in his mind.

Walsingham glanced round the room, then got up and poured himself a whisky at the cocktail cabinet. Then he moved to the tall, narrow, latticed window and looked down at the darkening grounds of the castle. A gleam of water, reddened by the last of the sun, and the figures of soldiers, rifles slanting down so that they looked like park-keepers with pointed sticks seeking litter. Even the unleashed dogs appeared to scamper and gambol rather than search. The scene disturbed him throwing a mental landscape into greater relief. How dangerous was McBride? What would they have to do about him?

McBride was angry that his notebooks had been stolen from him. Walsingham now felt that move had been precipitate, an over-reaction. And he had discovered the body of the man Hoskins – would he believe that to have been some kind of official interference? Who was Hoskins, anyway, and what part was he to have played, or had he played? The questions lit his mind garishly, detonations along the hillside he had to assault.

He returned to the sofa, sitting down heavily like a fat old man. Special Branch had no leads on Hoskins's killer. Was it connected? Wasn't it all too accidental, too convenient, that McBride and the events seemingly attendant on him should appear at the precise moment of the conference? Was McBride being used?

The door opened, and Guthrie entered smiling, his hand extended to Walsingham. Walsingham studied him as they shook hands. Guthrie was tired, but there was also a combative light in his eyes, and a suggestion that he was enjoying the conference, that his reserves of energy and patience remained almost unimpaired.

He poured himself a drink, refilled Walsingham's glass, then said: 'I apologize for keeping you waiting, Charles. Bloody obstructive people – ' The smile did not go away. Infighting seemed to tone Guthrie like a cold shower. 'Your call sounded urgent, even by the time it got to me. Something the matter?'

Walsingham indicated chairs, reseated himself on the sofa, and Guthrie sat casually opposite him in an armchair, crossing his long legs, cradling his drink in both hands as if to protect the crystal glass. He was attentive, unperturbed, curious. Walsingham, with some sense of the theatrical, took the cassette from the envelope and inserted it into the recorder.

'This call was made to your office yesterday – '

'A tape?' Guthrie asked quickly. Walsingham nodded. It was evident the minister expected some death-threat from a crank with an Irish accent that might have been real or assumed.

'Listen to it, please.'

Walsingham played the tape. When he had done so, Guthrie indicated that it should be replayed. After a second hearing, the minister said: 'McBride? *Is* there an Irish connection?'

'His father was Irish. I knew him during the war.'

Guthrie was puzzled. 'What's going on, Charles?'

'This man McBride is a bona fide historian, but he's also had some success with a sensational account of Hitler's last days in the Berlin bunker. His current project concerns the proposed German invasion of Ireland in nineteen-forty – ' There was still no reaction from Guthrie, except that he nodded his head to punctuate Walsingham's narrative. 'He – has come into possession of certain information concerning the British *response* to that threat, including your name.'

Guthrie replied, in a chilly voice that gathered force from the dusky gloom: 'How did that happen, Charles?'

'Admiralty records.'

'What?' Disbelief rather than anxiety.

'There is still material in existence, material that has been overlooked up to now.'

'*My* name, Charles. How did he get my name.'

'I'm not certain. I'm having that checked. However, he has it.'

Guthrie went on nodding periodically in the silence that followed, punctuating some internal debate. Walsingham was being made to feel at fault, incompetent. All the while, however, Guthrie's face remained a smooth, inexpressive mask; unless the gloom disguised tiny flickers of emotion. Walsingham wanted a light to study him by. Eventually, Guthrie spoke. 'It would be far better than shooting me, wouldn't it?' He grinned. 'Much better.'

'Yes.'

'Is there an IRA connection?' He seemed to be asking himself, going back over his recent meeting with

Provisional Sinn Fein, perhaps re-examining their obstructiveness in another, colder light.

'I don't know. I've checked with his agents over here. They don't have much idea of what he's working on, but they do know he's aiming for a very big sale, and a lot of money.'

'Simple cupidity?'

'It could be.'

'Any connection through the father?'

'No. He was an agent of mine, that is true. But there was nothing to give rise to a motive there.' Walsingham rubbed his forehead, inspected his hand. 'Rather the reverse. He'd not like the IRA because of his father.'

'Then is it as sinister as it seems?' Guthrie held up his hand. 'I fully realize the consequences for myself and for this conference – should this matter become public. But, does it need to become public? Can't you talk to this man McBride?'

'We could, but I'm not certain that I want to do that. Oh, we are having him watched, and we know more or less how much he knows.' He paused, but did not elaborate. 'But, we know very little about him as yet, and I do not want to make any precipitate moves.'

'I understand that. There are *no* Irish hands in this pie, you suggest?'

'Not that we know. As far as we can be certain, McBride has no connection, even in the United States, with any Irish organization, and since our surveillance began there has been no contact with any suspected person.' The statement sounded dry, official as it was meant to. Walsingham now almost regretted making this personal appearance at Leeds Castle, as if he had run to Guthrie to apologize or confess. 'If we obtain evidence of any – *organized plot* against you or the conference, then we shall act. In any case, McBride can never be allowed to publish.'

'Then it might come to the same thing, might it not, whether he's alone or part of a conspiracy?' Guthrie's voice was similarly dry, official. He steepled his hands in front of his shadowed face.

Reluctantly, Walsingham nodded. He could see Michael McBride's face, imposed upon the white, featureless mask across the table from him. Hallucinatory, and un-settling.

'Yes, it might.' McBride might well have to die. He saw Guthrie nod, satisfied it seemed with the monosyllable. Walsingham wanted to tell Guthrie about Hoskins's murder, suddenly, to unsettle and disturb him, show him that events might have run away from them already. Who was Hoskins? Who had just smothered him as they might have done a Christmas puppy they had tired of amusing and feeding? Who had killed Hoskins, and was the killing connected?

The thoughts seemed to ally him more closely, even indissolubly, with Guthrie. Common interest, common enemy. He nodded, then repeated himself more strongly.

'Yes,' he said, and now the processes involved were not too covert, too removed from moral precepts to be voiced. 'McBride will, in all probability, have to be removed.'

November 1940

The dark shape of the man came steadily towards him. All his attention was focused on the shape which he could see clearly, sharply even against the night sky. He hovered on the edge of unconsciousness, fighting back the black surges that ran through his body and enveloped his thoughts in order to keep the image of the approaching man clear and unaffected. He had given up trying to move his arm, and his left eye had closed against the trickle of blood from his scalp. But he wanted to see the man's face, in the last moment. He had come to believe he would see Drummond's long, sardonic face, cheeks drawn in as against the flavour of a lemon, before he was finished off. That imperative, that his leap of suspicion should be proven, dominated his wavering awareness.

Ten yards, five. A coat against the cold, a cap. The gun hidden against the form. McBride did not see the other two figures, behind the shadow over himself. The figure paused. McBride stared up, and hopelessly tried to make out the man's face. Then, in a dislocated sequence, overlapping on his senses and understanding like a distressed sea in which he was drowning, the man above him pitched forward as if he had tripped over McBride's body and did not even put out his hands to break his fall. McBride rolled his head to watch what the man would do next even as the noise of Gilliatt's gun reached him, reverberating as if it had been fired in a small room, then he rolled his head back when the man in the coat and cap did not move, attracted by two further shots. Something whistled shrilly and angrily in the air above him but he could not focus on the nearest shapes – a man and a stunted tree – nor on the more distant shape that seemed to be running. His arm hurt too much now, and he turned his head lollingly once more to study the body on the ground near him, which did not move, then he felt everything going a long way away as the pain shuddered through him, followed by utter blackness in which the flames from Gilliatt's gun pricked on the retinae like fireflies for a moment before they, too, faded.

When he responded to the gentle slaps of Gilliatt's hand, he felt his arm quarrel with movement and consciousness immediately. Gilliatt – he was close enough for his face not to be a blank – was kneeling over him, cradling his head in one hand, slapping him lightly with the other.

'Sorry,' he said, 'but I thought you'd prefer it to ditch water.'

'I – I'm all right.'

'I know. I've had a look at you. Arm sliced open, forehead with a three-inch gash back into your hair, but otherwise OK.'

'How long – ?'

'No more than three or four minutes. I'm afraid we'd better move – '

'Yes. They'll be back. You?'

'Just stunned. The grenade exploded nearer you than me. I fell in the ditch and kept quiet until I could see how many there were. Three – one dead, another wounded I think, but two of the three have scarpered.' Gilliatt appeared suddenly reflective, and a spasm of disgust crossed his face, white in the moonlight coming suddenly from behind a cloud. McBride's teeth were chattering in the suddenly sensed cold wind, but he managed to say:

'We're all the bloody same when threatened, Peter. All the bloody same.'

'Doesn't help, finding out, does it? I enjoyed it, for God's sake. Shooting him in the back – '

'Help me up. They'll be back.'

McBride groaned as Gilliatt hauled him to his feet, then leant against the taller man, breathing raggedly, trying to control the lightheadedness that made the moonlit scene swirl and dip. He concentrated on his last rational thought as he lay on the ground, the shadowy figure whose face he half-expected moving towards him.

'Drummond,' he said through clenched teeth.

'You think they got him?'

'No!' McBride gripped Gilliatt's supporting arm fiercely. 'It's Drummond – he set the dogs on us.'

'You're delirious. Can you walk?'

'Listen to me!' McBride began a coughing fit. His arm throbbed intolerably. When his breathing was loud but steady again, he went on: 'Only Drummond *knew* – only Drummond. Don't you understand?'

Gilliatt felt he wanted to physically separate himself from McBride. The accent, the anger and hatred made him understand something beyond McBride, some spurious vision of Ireland. He tried to dismiss it, but it clung like a cold mist to muscle and bone and mind.

'Accident,' he replied without conviction.

'No. No accident. Drummond wants us dead.' Again the accent. Gilliatt wanted to side with Drummond, a man he had never met but who was a naval officer working undercover in that alien country. Hatred. It chilled him.

'Let's get out of here. Which way – to where?' Gilliatt felt alone, exposed and vulnerable as if he had walked into some disputed territory.

'Drummond – '

'No, God damn you! Your place – how far is it from here?'

'Twenty miles.'

Gilliatt looked out to sea, towards the direction in which the ML had disappeared. Vulnerability soughed against him like the chilly wind, and McBride's shaking transmitted itself like fear.

'We'll have to make it, then, won't we?' he said abruptly.

McBride studied his hanging arm. He could feel,

through the pain, the binding Gilliatt had applied realizing at the same moment that it was part of his shirt He touched his head, felt the blood congealing at the hairline, then dismissed the wound.

'OK, skipper. My place – ' He broke off, distracted, then he murmured: 'Maureen – '

'What did you say?'

'My wife.'

'You think she's – ?'

'Drummond's not such a fool. Waste of effort. Come on, then.' McBride had dismissed any fears on behalf of his wife, but he could not disguise the determination that fear had lent him. Gilliatt let go of his arm. 'We're going to be running from this moment, Peter.'

Gilliatt hesitated, as if the first step might be the most dangerous.

'What do you mean?'

'I mean you can forget the job we're supposed to do, forget the *mission* – ' He almost spat out the word. 'Forget anything except staying alive.'

'Don't be hysterical.'

'Hysterical?' McBride moved the couple of paces that separated them. 'Drummond must have been helping our friends across the Channel for a long time. If he had – and he has – then he's in with the IRA as well. Don't you understand? Drummond set up this ambush. Where is he, eh? Waiting at his bloody farm for news of our tragic demise, Peter! He'll want to finish us off now not because of the Germans, but because we know about him. He's been sitting in Ireland for the last few years with plenty of time to despise Chamberlain and plenty of time to be impressed by the Führer. Perhaps you can't live in this God-forsaken country without hating the British! Look, I *know* Drummond wants us dead. If you don't believe it, then just act as if you do. It might save your life. What's that?'

'A car?'

Both men strained to listen. The wind whipped the sound away from them, then lulled so that they could hear the almost-silence of a car engine just turning over, then being switched off.

The silence menaced them.

'The track is over there,' McBride whispered, pointing north to a line of pencilled blackness. A hedge, Gilliatt supposed. The moon disappeared behind more blown cloud. 'Cut across this way.'

McBride moved off the path they had been following up from the beach, climbing heavily into then out of the ditch, breathing stertorously. Gilliatt jumped the ditch, caught up with him. McBride dragged himself stubbornly, angrily through a gap in the thorny hedge, and Gilliatt followed him more cautiously, snagging his coat and hands. Then they heard Drummond's call from no more than thirty yards away.

'Michael? Michael, are you all right?'

Gilliatt was about to comment when McBride pulled him roughly down beside him into the shadow of the hedge.

'Shut up!' McBride whispered savagely, glaring into Gilliatt's face.

'But –'

'Shut up, damn you!'

Again, Gilliatt sensed the distance between them like an uncrossable gulf, aware of nationalities which dictated their individuality, governed it. Drummond's English tones again, then, a further assertion that Gilliatt was somehow on the wrong side in a war not of his choosing.

'Michael?' They could hear his footsteps now, coming down the track to the beach. 'Michael – where are you?' There was no hesitation and no fear in the footsteps. Gilliatt saw Drummond's form through the hedge, passing them. He listened until the footsteps stopped by the dead body. A low whistle of surprise, a grunt as Drummond got to his feet again. 'Michael?'

Gilliatt realized that McBride had his revolver in his good hand, saw his implacable face.

Gilliatt grabbed McBride's gun hand, and the Irishman looked at him with unconcealed hatred in his eyes. Gilliatt looked back at Drummond, who was casting about for any sign of them. He wanted to stand up, call out to Drummond and disprove McBride's wild suspicions. But he felt the quiver of hate running through McBride's frame, and Drummond was little more than a dark upright shadow and there was a dead IRA man on the ground only yards from them, and the impression of danger was so ominipresent that he remained silent.

Drummond hurried away, back up the track. McBride immediately got to his feet, as if to pursue him. Gilliatt stood up.

'Are we going after him?'

McBride seemed to debate the matter, then shook his head. 'No. Not yet. He's got too many helpers.'

Drummond's treachery seemed improbable, McBride's suspicions delirious. 'What do we do, then?'

'No night for us to be walking the countryside,' McBride said, grinning, leaning into Gilliatt's face. 'We'll try the beach. The tide's out, we can cross the inlet to Harbour View, maybe walk all the way to Timoleague before we join the Clonakilty road.'

'Can you make it?' Gilliatt already knew the answer.

'Oh, don't worry about me. I'm not going to die just yet. I have to see a man about a coffin and a funeral service. Come on, let's get back down to the beach before the moon comes out again.'

McBride squeezed roughly back through the hedge, and Gilliatt hesitated for a moment, in the grip of a momentous, undeniable reluctance. Then fear came with a sudden chill blast of wind, and he hurried after McBride.

The First Sea Lord turned from the tall window of his spacious office in the Admiralty, hands still behind his back. He had been looking across St James's Park to a smudge on the grey horizon which was the last sky-writing of the previous evening's Luftwaffe raid. The smoke over Battersea worked powerfully upon his imagination, suggesting the necessity of the man Walsingham's proposal, *Emerald*, while it also seemed some kind of prophetic warning, a commandment rather than a sign to follow. He unclenched his hands, then attended to March and Walsingham, who sat on the other side of his massive desk. The long room that was his office seemed to press around him once he turned from the window, almost threatening in the dull gleam of morning light from the polished dark wood and the book-shelves. The high light ceiling seemed lower. Conspiracy had entered the room. The ranks of portraits on the walls seemed to frown with disturbing unanimity. The First Sea Lord consciously did not glance in the direction of Nelson's portrait, above the fireplace.

'Commander Walsingham, while I accept the evidence you have so assiduously amassed, and believe that the Germans plan to mount an invasion of the Irish Republic – ' He glanced swiftly and keenly at Walsingham, seeing the quick passage of emotion on the man's face before he gained control of his features and they reassumed their non-committal tightness. Then his eyes, as he continued speaking, wandered again over the dark wood in the room. The light often made the wood translucent and alive, but now only depths were suggested, the absorption of light. 'But I cannot recommend to the War Cabinet the suggestion contained in your *Emerald* file. I shall, however, request a meeting with the Prime Minister later today, and I am certain the evidence you have presented will be discussed in full Cabinet either today or tomorrow.'

The hour-long meeting was suddenly over. The First Sea Lord felt no relief, for immediately he finished speaking the full weight of Walsingham's evidence seemed to settle on his shoulders. The man's solution was unthinkable –

Yet he sensed a battered city beyond his office, and a country beleaguered beyond that. Britain was powerless to prevent the invasion of Ireland and the opening up of a second front. He hoped March and Walsingham would leave his office quickly. He needed to sit down.

The thin grey trail of smoke was apparent to them as they cycled down the last half-mile of the road to Leap. McBride had borrowed two ancient and unsafe cycles in Clonakilty from his wife's cousin, and they had made good time through the last hours of the night and the slow grey dawn. Gilliatt was weary, yet the relief of having encountered none of Drummond's men remained with him until they saw the smoke beyond the last slope. He glanced at McBride, who at once began to ride furiously up the slope. His face was chalk-white, strained, tired and afraid. The hours making good time along the still-wet shoreline to Timoleague seemed to have taken little out of him, even wounded – even the jarring of his arm as he guided the cycle seemed to leave him with reserves of purpose and a kind of wild, determined pleasure in outrunning Drummond. Now, however, he appeared drained and fearful.

McBride was twenty yards ahead as Gilliatt topped the rise, pedalling furiously towards the shell of a burned-out cottage that Gilliatt knew must be McBride's home. Gilliatt paused, as if not to intrude upon an evident grief. Another, more selfish emotion occupied him gradually. The IRA had committed an atrocity, whether McBride's wife was amid the ruins of the cottage or not. Gilliatt was afraid for himself. He could hear McBride calling his wife's name as he flung down the bicycle and clambered into the smouldering ruins of the cottage – white distemper scarred and blackened, the roof fallen in, smoke wreathing the small, demented figure of McBride. Gilliatt pedalled down the slope, pulling up in front of the cottage just as McBride emerged. His hands and face were blackened, and he was sweating so that rivulets of white appeared down his cheeks. His eyes were feverishly bright.

'Is she – ?' Gilliatt began, letting his cycle fall to the ground.

'No. I can't find her.' There was no relief.

'Where could she be?'

McBride seemed not to have considered any hopeful explanation, and to be nonplussed. He rubbed the dirt on his good hand into his face, making a wilder figure of himself. The hand then flapped loosely at the air as if trying to gain some grip or purchase.

'Her father's – '

'Where, man?'

'Ross Carbery. She might be there – sometimes when I'm away she goes, sometimes not. I don't know – '

Gilliatt interrupted the leaky tap of McBride's thoughts, stopped the dribble of rusty ideas. 'Let's go there. You're sure?' He indicated the ruined cottage with a nod of his head. McBride shook his head like a wounded animal. As if to complement the image, he seemed made aware of his arm, and clutched it to stop it hurting.

'No. She's not there.'

'Come on, then.'

McBride turned to look at the remains of his home. He felt the blackened timbers, the charred walls and burst, scorched furniture wrench at him. He understood the house as a destination rather than a home, but that did not weaken its impact upon him. Broken china, charred books similarly now seemed to bear a weight of significance never previously possessed. The sight of the cottage distracted him from thoughts of his wife for some moments. Then he turned his back on it, picked up his bicycle – stifling a groan as pain shot through his damaged arm – and mounted it.

'Come on, Peter.' He saw Gilliatt's expression of bemused, anxious fear. 'It's all right,' he added gently. 'I think she'll be with her father. This – ' He tossed his head to indicate the cottage at his back, ' – is just to tell *me* the game is up, there's nowhere to hide. Quite the little Nazi, isn't he?' He grinned brokenly, swallowing as something of Gilliatt's fear reached him. He shrugged it off.

'I don't believe it could be Drummond – '

McBride studied Gilliatt in scornful silence. 'We'll have to ask him when we meet him again, won't we?' He hesitated, then some urgency seemed to press on him. 'Come on. I'm hungry.'

October 1980

The Trinity House records had supplied the present whereabouts of seamen listed as sailing on the three ships of the convoy lost in November 1940, where and if they had entered homes administered by Trinity House or an affiliated organization. McBride had a small handful of names of men still living, scattered across the country in seamen's homes. His eagerness had selected the home in Chatham, less than thirty miles from London.

The day was bright, clear and warm and he was grateful for the company of Claire Drummond. He intended to go on from Chatham to Hastings and the third name on his short list, and to spend the night with her possibly in Canterbury. He had never seen the cathedral city, and the lightness of tourism seemed appropriate – or desirous at the least. As they left London's suburb of Lewisham behind and crossed the River Darent, McBride felt the weight of recent events dimish. Hoskins's murder, the theft of his notebooks and files, receded.

He was not aware of the tail car at any point in their journey along the A2, and they arrived in Chatham just before lunch. McBride was enjoying merely the pleasure of driving and the woman's company. As they turned into the car park of the Red Dog Inn in the centre of the town, he anticipated pickle and bread and cheese as fiercely as he might have done something of much more significance Claire Drummond was aware of the mercurial changes of mood of which McBride was capable. He seemed able to shed past experience almost at will, leaving it neatly packaged against some vague time when he might need it and return to it. She had been surprised at his easiness in the aftermath of Hoskins's death, his lack of curiosity concerning the perpetrator, even his lack of fear concerning his own safety. For herself, she could not share his enthusiasm for seeking out derelict sailors who might or might not have something of interest to say. But she and Moynihan had determined that she must accompany him everywhere while they followed his trail, because he was their only chance of circumventing Goessler.

The tail car parked in the pub car park a minute after they had done so, and Ryan followed McBride into the lounge bar. He waited until McBride had ordered, then went to the bar. He sat reading the *Daily Mail* until the couple left. Then he followed them out into the car park. His driver started the engine of the Cortina as McBride's Datsun pulled out into Chatham's town-centre traffic.

McBride spent some time locating the seamen's home on a new, almost treeless estate on the outskirts of the town, near the M2. Its former building in the dockyard area had been demolished almost ten years previously. The new low building with its large picture windows looking towards the motorway and the North Downs in one direction and the estate's shopping centre in the other, huddled close to a new, ugly Catholic church and an already grimy and graffiti-bearing Leisure Centre. The car park of the Leisure Centre ran behind the seamen's home, almost overlapping its trim grass verges like a frozen concrete sea. Claire Drummond elected to remain in the car, listening to the radio. She fumed silently but knew she could not intrude upon his conversations with the men he sought without stepping out of character. She relied on her influence to prevent McBride keeping anything from her.

The tail car parked near the small supermarket across the road.

McBride had spoken over the telephone with the Warden of the home, and he was ushered into his office immediately he announced his arrival to the receptionist. He was evidently a small surprise in a deep and rutted routine. Mr Blackshaw was not discontented, but he had through the years of his work with the elderly and the dying and the past-livers lost something of his own vitality, even individuality. The inmates of the home seemed to have lived on him like vampires, or simply worn him out with their combined weight of years and extreme experiences. After he had drawn from McBride an account of the book he was researching, he reluctantly conducted him to one of the home's two television rooms where, he said, the two friends he wished to interview would be watching the afternoon racing.

'You will have to be patient,' Blackshaw offered as they clicked down a block-floored corridor, clean, neat and aseptic. None of the untidiness of a real home, McBride observed. Mr Blackshaw's recommendation of patience was that of one who had tired of the virtue, or who saw himself in some impossibly heroic alternative reality shrugging it off like a set of chains. McBride nodded in reply.

'Are they pretty cognitive?'

Blackshaw appeared puzzled, then tapped his forehead questioningly, to which McBride nodded again.

'Oh, I'm afraid not very. They are *very* old.' Blackshaw shook his head, and McBride was tempted to ask him his opinion on euthanasia.

'Ga-ga, uh?'

'Not quite. But their nuggets of wisdom are buried rather deeply these days.' Blackshaw appeared surprised at his own epithet, but, emboldened, added, 'We have begun to disbelieve the existence of the gold, Professor McBride.' He smiled, letting his lips have an unaccustomed freedom to form the expression. McBride responded with an open, easy grin.

'Thanks for the warning. How long may I have with them?'

Blackshaw looked at his watch. 'Between races, you mean? Tea will be coming round to them in half an hour. You'll not have their attention for some time after that. Here we are.'

The television room was darkened because the colour set was facing the window and the reflections of the day had to be shut out so that they did not interpose themselves between rheumy eyes and the racing. Blackshaw stood beside McBride in the doorway for a moment, as if at a loss. Then he whispered, 'The two sitting watching the TV.'

There was a third old man, impeccably tidy and wearing a collar and tie, asleep in the darkest corner of the room, apparently at ease with and unconscious of the excessive volume of the set. The commentator's voice was approaching a climax, stringing together the names of the leading horses in a meaningless gabble which did not seem to impinge on the fixed and still attention of the two old men Blackshaw had pointed out.

'I'll leave you,' he said. 'That one's Mills, and the other one's name is Laker. They've forgotten their seamen's ranks, so I shouldn't worry.'

McBride watched Blackshaw scuttle away down the corridor, then entered the television room. The race had finished. The old man pointed him out as Mills shifted in his chair, but his companion continued to stare at the screen with all the attention he might once have given to a personal crisis. McBride approached them.

'Good afternoon   Mr Mills and Mr Laker?' Both heads moved suddenly, in accord, and four preternaturally bright eyes watched him. He represented some obscure threat, the eyes exclaimed. The third old man slept on. McBride sat down, dragging a chair near them, then leaned forward towards them, displaying the cassette recorder he removed from his brief-case. The television had given him a means of impressing himself on them. 'I'm from the BBC,' he announced.

'American,' one old man said to the other, who merely

nodded, mouth open as if to catch the information like an insect on the wing. 'Bloody American.' The face puckered to an imitation of vehemence, but there was no emotion left to hold the expression and it loosened into senility almost at once.

'That's right,' McBride said brightly. 'I'm working for the BBC for a time.'

'Know that Anthea Rippon, do you?' Laker asked. 'On the news.'

'I've met her.'

There was silence. Jaws worked, masticating the morsel of information, tasting the suggested proximity to celebrity. 'And Alvar Liddell?' Mills asked. McBride was nonplussed, regretting he had adopted the role he had. He merely nodded while both pairs of eyes watching him gleamed interrogatively behind the lenses of their National Health spectacles. Mills, McBride decided, was even older than Laker. They were twinned in old age; once they might have been different in build or colouring or feature, but now they were almost identical – hairless, wrinkled, grey-skinned. Strangely, however, their hands recollected youth, and suppleness and strength, lying curled like small, sharp-toothed animals in their laps.

McBride switched on the recorder, drawing their attention immediately. Mills nudged Laker, who nudged him in return.

'I'd like to interview you two gentlemen, if I may,' he said. 'About your wartime experiences. You were both serving on the SS *Ashford* in nineteen-forty, weren't you?' Both of them looked guilty immediately, and their eyes cast about on the floor as if for identity documents or lost memories.

'Mm,' Mills offered, committed to nothing. His companion made a similar noise at the back of his throat.

'You were on convoys across the ⌐orth Atlantic, I believe?' The tape numbers rolled on into the thirties. The microphone he held towards them picked up the gentle snores of the sleeping man. *Play School* began on the television, and Mills and Laker immediately attended afresh to the set, hands stirring, clasping each other in both laps, backs more erect. Cartoon figures flashed on the screen to accompany a nonsense song. McBride bit back impatience, thrusting the microphone nearer. 'Your ship was sunk by Germans in November nineteen-forty, two days out from Liverpool.' He pronounced each word precisely, but without immediate effect.

Then Mills turned his head slowly like a compass unsure of magnetic north, and looked at McBride. Then he cackled, 'Nowhere near Liverpool.' He nudged Laker. 'Was it?'

'Was what?'

'Liverpool.'

'Near where?'

'Cork.'

McBride hesitated a moment too long, expecting an elaboration that didn't come or simply indulging the small prickle of excitement in his stomach. When he was ready to prompt them, they were watching two enlarged hands folding paper.

'You said Cork.' There was a distinct lack of interest. 'Cork is in southern Ireland. Were you in Cork?' Laker turned his head, irritated that the intruder had not yet left. The tape numbers rolled mutely into three figures. Laker appeared about to add something, then his attention was directed towards the set by another nudge from Mills. The folded paper had become a boat which was launched upon a bowl of water. Mills looked across at McBride.

'We were in the water for hours, just waiting for the Jerries to surface and machine-gun us. Oil in the lungs, a lot of 'em.' Even his voice was clearer, sharper, insistent with momentarily recaptured emotion.

'Yes?'

The camera had cut from the boat to a glove puppet. A rather supercilious sheep's head which minced its words. McBride recognized an import from his own country.

'Mint sauce,' Laker said, cackling and leaving McBride bemused.

Mills, however, seemed to dislike the puppet, or was now burdened with a memory he wished to be rid of.

'A fishing boat picked up a few of us, only because we'd been swimming all night and taken inshore by the current. Irish buggers, but all right. Saved our lives.'

'You landed in Cork?' Already McBride could envisage a journey to Cork to seek traces of British sailors brought ashore in late November 1940. Mills merely nodded in reply.

'Most of them dead,' he added. A story with pictures was being narrated by the television, and his attention slowly returned to it. McBride could sense the exact moment when he lost him, his attention slipping beneath age's dark water and drowning in an almost-life. He did not know whether a lot of men died in 1940, or had been claimed since. Reluctantly, he switched off the recorder and stood up.

Neither old man saw him leave. Mr Blackshaw, too, perhaps guilty at abandoning him to two of his charges, was nowhere in evidence. McBride emerged into the bright sunshine, waving to Claire across the car park.

Something. Not much, but enough to encourage him. Somewhere, maybe in Hastings or Great Yarmouth or Bognor Regis there would be someone who wasn't senile and who remembered exactly how the British convoy had been sunk – by British mines.

November 1940
Maureen McBride was washing up in the small downstairs kitchen at the rear of Devlin's grocery shop. Her father's assistant was serving in the shop while Devlin himself was out making deliveries. She seemed unsurprised to see her husband, Gilliatt thought, until she became fully aware of his blackened and dishevelled appearance.

'You look as if you've been dragged through a hedge backwards, Michael McBride,' she said, soap bubbles wreathing her forearms, a gleaming, willow-patterned plate in her hands. It fell and smashed on the stone floor of the kitchen as McBride grabbed hold of her and squeezed her against him. Maureen saw the tall stranger watching in relief and amusement, and was embarrassed; surprised, too, at the sudden display of affection by her husband.

'Thank God you're safe,' he murmured in her ear as she pushed out of his embrace. He, too, was suddenly aware of Gilliatt's presence.

'Safe? And why shouldn't I be safe?' She sniffed loudly,

267

scenting the burned cottage on his clothes. 'What is it?'

'They burned the cottage down – gutted it,' he said savagely, unwilling to soften the blow. Her hand went to her mouth, her eyes widened. Then she clenched both hands at her sides and looked at McBride levelly. '*Who?*'

'I don't know – some of your father's friends, Germans – who knows? But *Drummond* was behind it.'

'What?'

'Drummond. He's working for the other side, must have been all the time. He tried to kill us last night – ' He indicated Gilliatt. 'Oh, Peter Gilliatt. He's English but not bad.' He grinned. Maureen wiped her right hand, shook Gilliatt's gravely. He saw a kind of emotional bruising behind her eyes but her face remained calm. She brushed at a wisp of hair fallen from its grip, then seemed aware of her appearance – but only slowly and unimportantly.

'What will you do ?'

'Kill him,' McBride said abruptly. Maureen seemed to consider his words for a moment, then she nodded her head. 'Before he kills us,' McBride added. 'Sorry about the home.'

'Not as sorry as I am,' she returned in a way that made Gilliatt aware of his intrusion, presenting an image of a wound opening. As if to apologize, Maureen grabbed McBride's arm. He groaned and she was immediately the solicitous wife again.

'You're hurt – '

'And hungry.'

'Injuries first.'

'Yes, Mother Maureen.' She tossed her head, made him sit and then roughly pulled his sweater over his head. The strip of shirt was darkened with some dried blood, but not a great deal. Maureen looked gratefully at Gilliatt as she inspected the bandage.

'I'll cook,' Gilliatt offered. 'Where is everything?'

'Go into the shop. Seamus'll cut you some bacon, give you some eggs. Bread's in the cupboard there.'

Gilliatt disappeared back into the narrow, box-lined corridor between the living accommodation and the shop. Maureen's face immediately dissolved into a tragic mask, mouth widened and eyes narrowed.

'All right, don't take on now.'

'Everything?' McBride nodded. 'God damn them.'

She sniffed loudly and proceeded to undo the bandage on his arm, touching the stiff crusted blood on his forehead at the same time, seemingly satisfied that it could be attended to later.

'We won't be safe here,' McBride said as she washed the gash. A little streak of new blood appeared. 'Drummond wants all eight pints or more of it, and he'd use you to get hold of me.'

'What do you want, then?'

'We have to run.'

'Where?'

'We've all of Ireland, woman.'

Gilliatt reappeared with slices of bacon and eggs on a sheet of waxed paper held against his chest. Behind him, as if their conversation had summoned him, was Devlin himself, out of breath and red-faced. But his small eyes darted as if some enemy might have overtaken him even though he had hurried and be lying in wait for him in his own kitchen.

'Da!' McBride sensed the fear, the urgency at once. 'What is it, Da?'

'Michael? You're all right? There's – why are you here? They're after you, damn you, and you'll bring them here, down on my head!' Devlin glanced at each of their faces, then around the cramped kitchen. He seemed to sense impermanence wherever he looked.

'Da, I'm sorry – ' McBride began.

'Maureen, they've burned the cottage!'

'I know.'

'How did you know?' McBride asked, anticipating Gilliatt's question.

Devlin immediately became cunning, his eyes narrowing further; habits of thought and behaviour were automatically reasserted. The present, however, pressed on him.

'I was told. Someone tipped me off, for Maureen's sake.'

'So, the boys are in on it, are they?' Devlin appeared reluctant to reply. Maureen, sensing the future, quickly finished rebinding McBride's arm with a clean strip of cloth. 'Are they, Da?' Devlin merely nodded.

'You'll have to get out,' he said, almost as a plea.

'We're going. The three of us.'

'What are we up against, Michael?' Gilliatt asked, a sense of superiority given him by the nationality the others shared. He knew his mood was illusory and irrelevant, but there was a coolness of mind that assisted him even as he began frying the bacon and breaking the eggs into the pan.

'Drummond, whatever Germans are here, and the local IRA,' McBride said with a grin.

'They'll not harm us, Maureen –' Devlin began, but the look she gave him made him quail into silence.

'What are we going to do, Michael?' she asked.

'Eat breakfast, dress for the outdoors – and run,' he replied, clutching her hand, pressing it. 'Don't worry.'

'I won't. I don't know why, but I won't.' She brushed his hair aside from the scalp wound, inspected it, nodded, and went to the stove, brushing Gilliatt to one side as casually as she had parted McBride's hair. Gilliatt looked at McBride, who winked.

'Who's he?' Devlin asked, fully aware of Gilliatt for the first time, it seemed.

'No one you know, Da. Now, are you coming with us, or not?'

Devlin's face adopted a look of outraged protest, which was swiftly followed by fear, then dismissal of a slow but certain kind as he looked around the kitchen again, then at McBride and Gilliatt – marking them off from himself. He shook his head.

'They'll not harm me. And Maureen would be safe here.'

'They'll use her to get me, Da. Look, I know that Drummond is a traitor. He won't want me gossiping to London about it, now will he? Maureen comes with us – she'll be safe.' McBride's face went bleak. 'Da, they'll use you, but I won't come back for you. There's not enough leverage, you see.' He did not look at Maureen, simply concentrated on the dissolving and reforming features of her father. It was as if he looked at him through a curtain of rain or tears, so vivid were the facial movements, so flurried the quick wash and movement of emotions.

'You promised!' was all Devlin could manage. McBride nodded.

'I know I did,' he said softly. 'Come with us. I'll look after you. But not here –'

Gilliatt turned away from the scene between the two men. It was too oppressively real, too naked yet private so that it made him a voyeur, an intruder. Then Devlin went out of the kitchen, banging against some of the crates and boxes in the corridor in his hurry and disbelief. McBride had disorientated him, turned around his sign-posts, ripped up his maps.

'You didn't have to do that to him,' Maureen said softly, sliding bacon and eggs on to two plates she had warmed. She brought the plates to the table, stood looking down at McBride, her face a narrow, tight mask of displeasure. 'Why did you tell him that, Michael?'

'Because it's true, Maureen. He'll be used to get to me, and I won't give myself and you up for Da's life.'

'Then why do you play God in the first place, if you haven't His determination? Oh, Michael, you make people believe in you when really their belief doesn't make a blind bit of difference to you! Why?'

He looked up at her, his face dark, slapped by her words.

'I don't know how or why I do it, Maureen. I don't know.'

Maureen moved past him, following her father into the shop. McBride began eating the breakfast in silence, and Gilliatt kept his eyes on his plate until he had finished eating. As if on cue, Maureen entered the kitchen just as McBride swallowed his last mouthful.

'He won't listen to me,' she almost wailed, her face a crumpled ball of dirty paper. Gilliatt wanted to say something soothing, knowing that she would reject any comfort from a stranger. 'He won't listen to me.' She sat down, leaning her head and arms on the table. McBride made no move to speak or to touch her, and Gilliatt disliked him suddenly.

He looked at McBride. 'He can't stay here.'

'Haven't you heard of free will, Peter? He might even be right – the boys may leave him alone.'

Maureen looked up. 'Damn you, Michael.'

'Probably. Go and get your coat. Get some food from the shop – no, maybe not. Just get your coat.'

Maureen went out of the kitchen. McBride heard her climbing the stairs, then her footsteps on the boards of the room above them.

'Will you save *us*?' Gilliatt asked with an evident irony.

'Oh, if I can,' McBride replied with studied lightness. 'Yes, I'll save you if I can.' There was a combative, fierce light in his eyes that Gilliatt mistrusted and which disturbed him. McBride was a man obsessed and vengeful. Reckless. Gilliatt clamped down on a sense of panic, a feeling of the cosmic unfairness of his situation and a blind desire to blame, lash out. It was a question of staying alive in the company of a mad Irishman and his strange, tough wife.

McBride's head cocked, listening. Gilliatt was puzzled but even before that feeling seeped into his face he heard the car pulling up outside. McBride was on his feet, running through the narrow corridor even as the first bullets smashed the windows of the grocer's shop. Gilliatt went to the foot of the stairs, and blocked them against Maureen who came running from the upstairs room.

'Da!' he heard McBride shout. A sub-machine gun, spraying bullets, forced McBride back into the corridor. Maureen tried to push past Gilliatt, but he took hold of her. McBride ducked back towards them.

'The back way – come on!' Maureen was about to speak. 'He's dead. The only damn covenant the boys have is with death, Maureen. Only with death.' His eyes were wild, and there was spittle at the corners of his mouth. Maureen moaned. 'Get her outside!' he ordered Gilliatt as he drew the heavy revolver from his waistband. 'Get moving!'

Gilliatt dragged Maureen into the kitchen. Her head went back and a wail filled the corridor. Gilliatt clamped his hand over her mouth, heaved open the back door of the shop and dragged her out into the yard.

McBride watched them. Another burst of gunfire from in front of the shop, then silence. He wanted to wait, for the pleasurable outline in the shattered doorway, the first steps on the crunching glass, then the perfect target. He didn't. Reluctantly he turned and went back into the kitchen and out into the yard. Maureen was still in Gilliatt's grip, but didn't seem to be struggling. She was silent, appeared calmer.

They were running, McBride was enjoying it.

October 1980

The relief and colours of the heraldic shields in the cloister roof were fading as the light failed. Goessler gave up studying them. Despite his overcoat, he was cold. There was a chill about all cloisters, and those at Canterbury Cathedral were no different. Larger than some, more sombre than many, and perhaps colder than all. He regretted having had to agree to meet Moynihan and the woman, but he knew that unless he did their impatience might easily overreach itself, interfere with the operation that was proceeding so smoothly, and he therefore intended that they should now be fed a few further morsels that would stave off their hunger a little longer.

He began pacing because his feet were cold. For him there was no atmosphere of conspiracy seeping from the flagstones or lurking behind the pillars or in the arches. He was unaffected not so much by religion, which he rejected anyway, but by the past itself. His past was his own lifetime, the lifetime of his state and his rise within its security *apparat*. Canterbury Cathedral had no weight for him. He had exorcised all the ghosts, rendered himself unable to sense or feel the past – any past – when he carefully buried and destroyed and burned and erased his own Nazi past. In 1946, he had been born. Nothing before that date had any meaning for him.

He saw Moynihan emerge into the cloisters on the east side, near the huge chapter house. He did not wave to him, but continued pacing, letting the Irishman walk round the cloisters to join him. The woman appeared from the door into the nave, closer to him. He enjoyed the fleeting impression that both she and Moynihan were engaged in an attempt to overtake him that would never succeed. Then he turned to wait for them at the north-west corner of the cloisters. Their footsteps were somehow chill and damp, echoing as they did. They reached him together.

'Good evening, my friends.' Moynihan merely nodded, but the woman spoke. She had hurried and was impatient but Goessler, as formerly, found her formidable, though dangerously unreliable. She was to him that most dangerous of species, the individual self-interpreter of Marx and Lenin. She did not surrender to ideology; rather, she had absorbed it and made it something that increased her individuality, her recognition of self.

'Herr Goessler. We summoned you here – ' Goessler smiled a tight little smile in the gloom, hardly showing his dentures. She was challenging him, ' – because we're sick of being dragged around at your coat-tails. We want to know what evidence *you* already have to support a move against Guthrie.' There was a weight on the final syllables that was quite deliberate. Evidently, nothing was being kept from the woman by McBride. Silently, he complimented her.

'Ah, the Secretary of State for Northern Ireland. Indeed.' Moynihan spat on the flagstones, quite unnecessarily from Goessler's point of view. These Irish had so much wasteful, vengeful *passion* they were anathema to an intelligence operation. So many Pavlovian keys controlled their reactions and their behaviour – too many for one life or a dozen lives. 'What evidence, my dear?'

'Yes, *Herr* Goessler. Guthrie commanded one of the minelayers, didn't he? He helped to commit an act of war against a British convoy – was it sanctioned by the British government? Who – Churchill?'

She was hungry, greedy. Ideological nymphomania. Neither of them could receive, take enough history, comment, action or belief to slake their hatred. Goessler realized that this was the crucial moment of the operation. The British would be too slow to catch McBride before he had all the material, but the Irish could move too greedily, too swiftly – and spoil everything. He'd always known they'd try. Perhaps – he hoped not – he'd underestimated the woman?

He studied his words, then: 'Yes. Very well, my friends, cards on the table. Just so long as you promise that you will *not* act precipitately, and without my consent – ' He left the order hanging in the chill air. Moynihan shivered, probably because he was not wearing more than a thin sweater beneath his suede jacket. Perhaps, Goessler thought, for him the place does have ghosts. Then the Irishman spoke.

'People are beginning to disbelieve, Goessler. They're very impatient for results.'

Goessler had no intention of telling them that McBride would be theirs in no more than two or three days. The operation required now only McBride's acquisition of sufficient evidence of the sinking of the convoy for him to react strongly enough to want to make his knowledge public. Goessler believed that McBride would go public, preview his book's revelations. If Moynihan and the woman moved against him, tried to force him he would remain silent. He must not sense he was being used.

'He must not sense he is being used,' he said aloud, almost involuntarily. Then he added: 'He will make the first move, and must be allowed to. *You* must not attempt to force him into going public.' Another order.

'The evidence is already available, he's seen it.'

'I agree, my dear. But he is an historian. He must have witnesses, documentation –'

'Who stole his papers?' Claire Drummond immediately regretted her question.

'When?'

'Days ago, from the hotel.'

'Everything?' She nodded. 'MI5 are closer than I thought. Walsingham has himself to protect, of course.' Goessler was thoughtful for a moment. 'Is he being followed at the moment?'

'I don't think so.'

'Then he may be.' Moynihan looked furtively round the darkened cloisters, suspecting eavesdroppers. Goessler himself felt suddenly insecure. The operation was slipping towards the IRA's greedy hands, acquiring their passionate haste. Regrettable, but perhaps not disastrous. He went on: 'Very well. Two more days. Then, my dear, you must persuade him he must publish. If not, then you will inform the newspapers yourself, and set those dogs on him. A *cause célèbre* – vulgar but I'm afraid now unavoidable. Will that, satisfy your friends in Belfast and Dublin?'

'I hope so,' Moynihan said with a candour that Claire Drummond resented with a contemptuous glance.

'Ah, they are wolves, my friend. They eat anything.' He studied them for a moment. The moment when he had resigned his operation to their tender mercies had come and gone, and left him deflated and anxious. 'Now, goodbye. Let us meet just once more, in – ?'

'Bognor Regis,' Claire Drummond said.

'Very well. In forty-eight hours. Goodbye.'

He hurried away, disappearing through the north door of the cloisters. He was mistrustful, edgy, reluctant. It should go well, it ought to –

It had to. Men crowded at his back. He was simply another Moynihan; a subordinate. It was very cold.

Sir Charles Walsingham looked up from the papers on his desk, switching off the cassette-player that had hummed for some minutes after Ryan's verbal report had ended. Ryan had questioned the man Blackshaw in Chatham, let himself into McBride's hotel room and heard the recording he had made of the two geriatric seamen.

Exton's face was expectant, across the desk from Walsingham.

'He – almost has it all, Exton.'

'Sir.'

Walsingham felt the progress of his thoughts and words was being wrung from him.

'He must be close to going over the top with this. He's almost finished checking his coupon, and he has seven score draws so far. One lucid account of the sufferings of those men – ' Walsingham winced with imagination, – 'and he will boil over. Jackpot, a million or more. He won't be able to *contain* it!' Walsingham's hand clenched on the papers, a tight fist.

'Sir.'

'Very well. Get rid of him. Tomorrow.'

Chapter Thirteen

FALLSCHIRMJAEGER

October 1980

Drummond awoke with a piercingly clear image of the young Peter Gilliatt, weary, dishevelled and grieving, standing before him in the study of the farmhouse. He sat up, groaning with the weight of sleep and memory, his limbs suddenly restless and fidgety. The image persisted, even though the grey shape of the curtained window informed him that his eyes were open. He tried to blink the picture away, then rubbed at it to dispel it. It was only when he switched on the bedside light, however, and the familiar wallpaper vied with the shadows in the corners and the contours of his old age established themselves, that he was able to dissolve the young man's face.

He threw back the bedclothes and got up, pulling himself arthritically into his thick dressing-gown. He padded downstairs in slippers to the study and the drinks cabinet. The taste of interrupted sleep was furry in his mouth, with an acid bile waiting at the back of his throat, like a prognostication. He poured himself a large brandy, and turned on the electric fire. It glowed on the walls like distant gunfire. He sat opposite it, staring into its grilled and blank flame-pictures.

It was not the first of his dreams, and Gilliatt had never believed McBride's story that he had been betrayed, preferring the more obvious explanation of the local IRA working in conjunction with the landed German agents. Drummond had not needed to persuade him of his innocence. But now his tall figure, leaning with tiredness against the door-frame, his eyes blank with grief, was omnipresent.

Drummond swallowed at the brandy. Was Gilliatt acting as a chorus to the procession of dead people that inhabited his sleep? They crowded on him now, making him fearful of the knocking of his old heart every time they caused him to wake up – fearful, of the drink that seemed to stimulate their efforts to upset him when he returned to bed and closed his eyes. Sleep ambushed him with his past like a determined and violent gang. Sleep the terrorist.

McBride, Britain, Gilliatt, others, even Irish and German. Now McBride's son, his own daughter, Moynihan, Britain again perhaps. Anybody and anything but himself. He swallowed again at the brandy, emptying the glass, irritatedly and guiltily pouring himself another large measure immediately. Disillusion, he affirmed with a nod of his head. A young man's disillusion. The attractions of Fascism, the danger of Communism. He'd been ripe for recruitment by the Germans, Amt V, the SD-Ausland, at an embassy function in Berlin when he was attaché. Soon after Hitler came to power, and was using a miraculous, strong hand to alter the destiny of Germany. It was the only way he could share, to join secretly. Britain hollow and wormy with the Depression, Germany climbing out of vaster ruins to greatness. By the outbreak of war, Drummond was ensconced in Ireland for the sake of Admiralty Intelligence and perfectly placed to assist German agents, to help co-ordinate *Smaragdenhalskette*.

Habits of thought –

By 1940 he *was* German, in all but name and origin. He believed in the New Order, considered Churchill a damnable fool and warmonger not to accept the Führer's offer of a peace treaty and turn against the Communist barbarians with Germany. He had never wanted to escape –

So why now, after this long, interminable safety, do the faces come?

Claire.

She was his Nemesis, his punishment; blackmailing him into helping her cause. He'd been forced to point the young American who was Michael's son in the direction of the Admiralty and Walsingham; his only protest the ambiguous telephone message to Walsingham, warning him. A feeble fist moving through deep water in an attempt to land a blow. He hated his daughter, hating what she had become and how she had come to treat him. She despised his Fascism of the past, his Anglicism of the present, and she used him to further her own ends by threatening to expose his wartime treachery. She was completely and utterly uthless, and a Communist. She was uncontrollable, dedicated.

He finished the second brandy, studying the empty glass with the dedication of an alcoholic, reluctantly at last deciding that he should have no more. Brandy-strengthened dreams made him wake sweating, hands clawed near his own throat because he was being suffocated by the past. He got up from his chair, suddenly cold, and went out of the room.

Ideologues. *An intellectual hatred is the worst.* An Irish poet had said that too, he observed as he climbed the stairs like a very old and decrepit man. They'd both possessed it, that worst of things. He'd hated supine Britain and world Communism, and his only daughter hated all creeds other than her own and all the worshippers of other gods. He had only been the chrysalis stage – the small hatred, the small betrayal – she was the dark butterfly.

The bed looked cold and uninviting, an evident and threatening trap.

November 1940

McBride could not catch sight of Drummond, though he sensed with a wild, almost intangible certainty that he would be close at hand, that he would not trust either Irishman or German to finish off the threat to his safety. He'd want to see, direct, order –

Gilliatt ran ahead with Maureen, holding her arm firmly as he might have done for an older woman. Maureen seemed thankful for the support. McBride halted at every street corner, giving them a chance to get well ahead while he watched for the pursuit. Then he sprinted to catch up with them before the next corner, yelling at them the direction they should take. If there was a pursuit, then it had not yet decided which way they'd gone and was still casting about for signs of them.

A muffled explosion reached him, and he saw Maureen's white face turn to him, and he yelled: 'Get on, get on!' He knew it was the shop. Quick search, and then the gutting of the lair. They'd not be able to go back. Now they'd follow in earnest.

They emerged on to the main road near the narrow stone

bridge across the stream. The mud flats stretching away towards the bay seemed exposed, representative of their situation. The low hills to the north were treeless under a grey cold sky. Gilliatt was breathing hard and Maureen was slumped against him. There was something natural about their proximity that McBride consciously dismissed from his mind.

'Into the hills,' he said to Gilliatt, who seemed to be looking almost wistfully down the creek to the sea. Gilliatt nodded, transferring his gaze to the narrow, cobbled street down which they had come. It was empty except for a thin dog relieving itself and an old woman in black framed by an open doorway. She might have been watching them. A vague boil of grey smoke hung a few streets away from them. Devlin's shop.

Maureen breathed in deeply but the breath became a sob. Gilliatt moved his arm around her shoulders but she shrugged it off violently.

'Why, Michael – why?'

'I don't know, Maureen.' He studied her face, seeing the grief just below the tight mask of shock. There'd be no time for the grief to come out, he knew. She'd be too intent on survival. He almost regretted that she would have to become, emotionally, part of his secret, amputated world. Regretted it for her sake. 'Come on, we've no time to spare on it now. We'll head north-east, then change direction and head for Carrigfadda. They won't be able to follow us by car, not even by bicycle.' He was grinning again, and the sight of the expression angered Gilliatt unreasonably, or perhaps simply gave rise to misgivings about trusting his life to a man so evidently reckless. But he controlled his anger, and merely nodded. 'Come on, then.'

McBride began to run over the bridge, waving them to follow. The narrow road wound between two low lumps of higher ground, vanishing like a false trail. Gilliatt was aware how perilous everything was, how unlikely survival. Maureen moved away from him, aware of the shivering possessing his body. She began to run after McBride.

The first shot plucked stone chips from the bridge just as Gilliatt took his first few steps, and the bullet whined away harmlessly. Gilliatt became frozen, unable to move, as if the bullet had entered his body or was some shouted imperative. McBride, looking back to the bridge, saw the Englishman's fear possess him.

'Peter, come on!' There were two men with rifles at the edge of the village. Small puffs of smoke appeared even as bullets buzzed near them. Gilliatt still did not move. Stone spattered on his jacket as another bullet ricocheted from the parapet of the bridge. 'Get down!' he snapped at Maureen, and she sank into the shallow ditch at the side of the road in an attitude of prayer. McBride, head down, ran back to the bridge, moving as swiftly as he could, bent almost double below the level of the stonework. He grabbed Gilliatt's jacket, heaving him off-balance – the man was as stiff as a wooden crate – pulling him down beside him. The angle of the road to the bridge hid them momentarily from the riflemen. Gilliatt seemed shaken out of a trance.

'Thanks.'

'Come on, keep low and move fast.'

McBride scuttled ahead of Gilliatt. Three shots nipped through the air above the bridge as McBride paused, then straightened and ran. Gilliatt followed him. McBride's arm ached intolerably from the damage of the grenade fragment and the effort of dragging Gilliatt down into the cover of the bridge. Maureen clambered out of the ditch as they heard the noise of a small car accelerating. McBride grabbed Maureen's arm, hurrying her up the road. The car's engine idled, presumably while their two closest pursuers climbed on board, then they heard it accelerate again.

They laboured up the slope of the road. A field fell away from them towards the stream.

'Down there!' McBride yelled, pointing towards the stream through a gate in the high hedge. 'Come on!' There was a desperation close to enjoyment in his voice.

Maureen swiftly opened the white gate. A grazing cow confronted her fearfully, great brown eyes puzzled and nervous. As she began running, it turned and lumbered away towards the rest of the small dairy herd shuffling away to her left. She felt her heart struggling for space with her ragged breaths in her chest cavity, felt herself choking but pushed on, leaning backwards as the slope of the field threatened her. Gilliatt caught up with her, his face grim. She did not worry about Michael behind them. She invested him with an expertise that approximated to omniscience. She could just hear the labouring car above the pound of her feet and blood. The herd was scampering in a dozen startled directions.

Shots rang out, and bullets buzzed around her. There was an ignorant confidence about her body. She had never seen a bullet or a bullet wound. Gilliatt flinched at each report, each passage of a bullet through the air near them. Then, closer, a heavy revolver sounded twice, and there was a distant, insect cry. Then, almost immediately, McBride was running alongside them, yelling.

'Spread out, spread out!' He veered off to the right himself, and Maureen went to her left. 'Run zig-zag!' McBride gave the instructions without panic, with no sense of danger. If bullets hit them, his voice suggested, it would be like drowning in a shallow stream or swimming pool. Maureen tried to run first to left then to right, watching for betraying tussocks of grass that would trip her, sprain something.

Then she lost her balance, and the stream was cold up to her knees, and her hands plunged into the water as she tried to keep upright. She felt smooth, slimy stones, twisted around, and Gilliatt grabbed her and stopped her from falling headlong. She felt herself shivering against him, his own body shaking with effort, his heart pounding. She looked behind her, following his gaze. McBride was alongside them in the water. Three men were coming down the slope of the field, leaving something in a fawn raincoat lying near the tall hedge, perhaps blown there by the wind, brown paper or something. She felt her thoughts slipping in and out of self-deception. Michael had killed one of them – brown paper –

'Where now?' Gilliatt asked, his voice thick with phlegm. He spat to clear his mouth, and Maureen watched the phlegm move away and dissipate on the surface of the stream. McBride looked around him.

Two more men – both of them dressed in reefer jackets and carrying machine-pistols – entered the field at its southern corner, back by the bridge. For the moment they were out of range and he discounted them except as a direction in which he could not go.

'Up there,' he said, pointing towards the rising ground to the north-west of the village. The sweep of his arm took in the pencil of smoke still rising from Ross Carbery in the still grey air. Rainspots, as if occasioned by the fire and the necessity of water, splashed on the back of his hand, spattered gently against the faces of all three of them. 'Some bloody mist is what we need,' McBride muttered. 'Get going!'

Gilliatt hauled Maureen out of the stream, and they began running again. She grabbed hold of his hand as she almost lost balance, and held on to it as they began labouring up the slope again towards another tall hedge marking the field's northern boundary. The noises of the rifles seemed distant and harmless. The rain fell more steadily, dampening their hair and faces. Neither of them gave any thought to McBride, except when the reports of the revolver impinged unwelcomely on them.

Gilliatt pushed her through the gate, and she huddled into the ditch, her breathing stertorous and always threatening not to come at all. Gilliatt touched her shoulder, and she nodded because her mouth was too full for words. Then Gilliatt stood up, and she remembered with a moan that Michael was still behind them; the realization sprang on her like guilt. Gilliatt, prompted by her cry, sensed the revolver stuck uselessly into his waistband, a hard cancerous lump against his stomach. The drizzle soaked him, but refreshed him at the same time. He climbed out of the ditch, and saw McBride perhaps thirty or forty yards from him, arm out like a duellist, firing two shots back at the men who had reached the stream. One of them held his left arm limply at his side, as if he had no further use for it. A second man was kneeling, taking aim, and the third was crouching against the near bank of the stream. A tableau that he seemed to bring to life as he drew the revolver and took aim. It was an impossible distance, even in the windless conditions, but he squeezed the trigger more as a distraction. He was aware of the box of shells misshaping his left pocket, and confidently fired three more shots towards the stream. The pursuers were sufficiently distracted to seek the shelter of the stream's bank. McBride was toiling up the last of the slope to the hedge. The two men in reefer jackets were cutting the angle of the field towards them, but warily keeping out of range. 'Master race, eh?' McBride said as he leaned against him for a moment, controlling his breathing. 'Take no chances, let the local lads get themselves killed.'

'You think they're German?'

'With those guns, yes.' But McBride had lost interest already. He looked behind them, northwards. The land sloped down again towards the trees of a wood. The outliers were mere hundreds of yards from them. 'Come on, then. No rest for the wicked.'

Maureen climbed out of the ditch, shaking off their aid, and they ran together towards the dark trees. The main road beyond the wood gleamed grey and wet like a boundary. McBride remembered the first time he and Maureen had made love in the insect-clamorous wood, one summer afternoon, her body cool only for a moment before he pressed down upon her, her face white and wondering and nervous. He wondered whether she remembered the occasion.

They were into the trees before the pursuit achieved the hedge and any clear sight of them.

The First Sea Lord sat opposite the Prime Minister in the small office Churchill used habitually for his solitary moments of thought and decision. Few Cabinet colleagues were invited to join him here, but service chiefs had done, on certain dire occasions through the summer and autumn. The camp bed the Prime Minister rested on – when he could bring himself to rest – was unmade in one corner of the office. The room was thick with cigar smoke, and Churchill was in his shirt-sleeves, still unshaven and red-eyed with the consequences of a restless night. The First Sea Lord, having finished his briefing, was left fearing a reckless, even desperate decision from this tired old man whose pugnacious features seemed the solitary mask left to him, his country backed into the last corner.

Churchill paced the room, cigar clamped into his tight

lips, heavy jowls bristling as if he were parading before an audience that must be impressed. The First Sea Lord wondered how Churchill would go to his death before an SS firing squad, and regretted the thought as sharply and immediately as treachery. Yet in this small office how could Churchill gain any perspective other than a hopeless one?

As he silently asked the question, he was cognizant of the gulf between himself and the Prime Minister. He did not understand Churchill, and that lack of understanding could not be quite despised or disregarded.

Churchill paused before the First Sea Lord's chair, his blue eyes alight. He said, round the cigar, 'Your opinion?'

'Of what, Prime Minister?' The First Sea Lord had to clear his throat before he spoke. The light immediately died in Churchill's eyes, and he moved away to look out of the single small window over the gardens of No 10. He seemed to dislike the sight of the ugly brick and concrete air-raid shelter for the staff, and turned back to confront the First Sea Lord.

'This counter-measure.' He indicated Walsingham's open file on his desk. Cigar-smoke lifted to the ceiling.

'We – cannot replace the missing section of the minefield without diverting the convoy.'

Churchill's eyes flared again, as if he could see the cruiser and the three merchant ships.

'Grady – ' he murmured softly.

'Prime Minister?'

'Nothing.' He turned away again, then back. 'We must have that convoy, at all costs, Admiral. If we can get it through, Congress will go on turning a blind eye to Lease-Lend and Roosevelt will send us more. It's our main artery.' He paused, then, as if weighing some obscurer alternative, muttered again, 'Grady – ' He articulated carefully, loudly. 'Order two minelayers to Milford Haven – as a stand-by. This requires more thought. I can't see the convoy go down in the North Channel, neither can I allow the Nazis – ' He cut himself off. 'Thank you, Admiral. Leave the *Emerald* file with me for the moment.'

Robert Emerson Grady enjoyed the fierce wind much as he might have done had he been aboard a yacht or an old sailing ship. The westerly was sweeping spray across the quarter deck and gave the impression of driving the cruiser forward towards the Irish coast. That in itself might have made heavy, gloomy imagery, but the wind seemed to clean him, blow inside his head and remove the cluttered reflections which had afflicted him throughout the crossing. He wore no hat, let his grey hair be distressed, his ears and jaw go cold.

Churchill. His image persisted. Churchill would know why he was coming, know what was at stake, want to stop him. Churchill, like a schoolboy, would want to fudge his examination because he had not mastered the syllabus. He would be lost, abandoned,

Spray, whipped off the whitecaps, dashed in Grady's face and was saltily chilled by the wind at once, drying on to him. Churchill's image faded. The merchant ships astern were the first of their kind, and Grady knew they would be the last, after he made his report to Roosevelt. The wind and spray went on with their cleaning, numbing work, and a scattered, sudden sunlight splashed on the quarter deck like another good omen.

October 1980
The bright afternoon spread itself easily as a cat over the sofa and the carpet and the other furniture of the old, slightly dilapidated house on the Hastings seafront that had been converted into a seamen's home. The worn carpet was more evidently exposed by the sun's intrusion, the loose covers rendered more tasteless and chintzy, but McBride felt the room took on the character of the man to whom he was talking. Browned and worn and honourable with age. To be kept, not thrown away.

The old man rolled himself another cigarette from dark tobacco, coughed his way through the first inhalations, and shook his head, his blue eyes folded into the contour marks of age around them. Abbott's face was a mass of wrinkles, and was easy to romanticize. He looked like an old explorer, an adventurer – embayed and dragged out of the water at some high tide and stranded here, hull stripped and recaulked but never relaunched. McBride liked him, warmed to the man. And anticipated clarity of revelation.

'No,' Abbott said. 'German submarines – U-boats for certain.' Abbott had been Third Mate aboard *Southwark Rose*, and on the bridge when what he believed was a U-boat attack had commenced, and commanding one of the boat stations when the order to abandon ship had been given. According to his narrative, *Southwark Rose* had been hit for'ard and amidships by torpedoes. The boat he had managed to board in the last minutes of the ship's existence had been sighted the next day by a Coastal Command Anson and they'd been taken aboard a Royal Navy frigate in the evening.

'You're certain of that, Mr Abbott?' McBride asked softly. The old man studied him as if the question insulted his memory. But he continued smiling with all the superiority of age and greater experience. An American historian could be forgiven a great deal, apparently.

The cassette recorder wound on silently. Occasionally, cars passing along the seafront disturbed the room's autumnal calm. McBride felt himself afloat on a slow calm sea, close to his home port. Claire Drummond's passion in their Canterbury hotel room had seemed equivalent to his own as if she, too, sensed the proximity of their destination. He felt relaxed, and the memory of Hoskins's death remained below the surface of the gleaming water.

'Two torpedoes, Mr McBride. Ripped the old girl apart like a couple of tin-openers.' He shook his head, horror transmuted to something harmless by time and survival.

'What about the other ships?'

'They went for the cruiser first – terrible.' Something threatened to break through like a suddenly broken home, but he went on in the same warm, mellowed voice: 'They picked us off in turn.'

'You were in a minefield, Mr Abbott,' McBride prompted.

'Ah – that'd been swept, especially for us,' the old man said knowingly, shaking his head slightly. 'One or two of the lads joked about it, but the job had been done. They told us that.'

'Where did you go down, Mr Abbott? You were on the bridge, you'd know.'

'Off the Old Head of Kinsale, south-west of Cork Harbour.' The old man prided himself on his memory, and held this nugget of it up to his inspection, gleaming and undimmed by time.

McBride exhaled slowly. He had it all now. Everything else would be merely corroborative. He said thickly, 'And where exactly were you picked up, Mr Abbott?'

'Ah. The boat was taking on water, and the rudder was useless. We drifted out into the channel, more or less south-west. We were a bit worried about the minefield, but our shallow draught must've kept us safe enough. The sea was kind to us. Spotted by an Anson out from one of the Cornish airfields, and picked up the same day. Weather worsened the very next day.'

'What was the name of the ship that picked you up?'

'Ah.' The old man dredged along the reef of memory. His eyes brightened again. 'HMS *Saundersfoot*. Frigate.'

'Thank you, Mr Abbott, thank you.'

The old man seemed content now just to sit, and McBride shared his silence for a little time longer. The explosions, the screams, the shattered or detached limbs, the drowning, oil searing the lungs, the frenzy to launch the boats and pull away from the stricken *Southwark Rose* – all idled to the bottom of the gleaming water of his satisfaction. Nothing existed outside this sunlit room which contained the physical form that experienced nothing beyond a complete, egoistical satisfaction. The outline of his book lay in his thoughts like an unfolded map or a precise, graphed medical chart. He had it all. The German preparations, the sweeping of the minefield, the relaying of the mines, the murder by British mines of an American special envoy. An atrocity. He was made.

It was the last, and most complete, time that he was to think of money in connection with the knowledge he possessed.

Ryan watched McBride and Claire Drummond go into a café with a mock-Tudor frontage just off the Promenade, then walked to the nearest telephone box and called Walsingham.

'You're secure,' Walsingham told him, his voice

becoming slightly more distant as the scrambler was switched on. 'Go ahead.'

'He's in Eastbourne, sir. With the girl.' He laid some slight emphasis on the latter phrase.

'I'm afraid she is not to be considered separately from your assigned target,' Walsingham replied. Ryan winced silently. He disliked his superiors when they began using jargon to disguise their proposed wet operations. Blood was going to be let out, breath stopped, physical shape altered irredeemably, but they always wanted to talk about *operations* and *targets* and *necessities*. Ryan had no compunction about murder on the orders of his superiors, but no liking for euphemisms as applied to the job he did.

'Very good, sir. It would seem, from what we could pick up and his manner and the like, he knows most of it now, sir. He's like the cat who's had the cream.'

'Very well. Then the girl has to go. He may have confided in her.'

'Very good, sir. I'll have an operational report for you by this evening – eight at the latest.' He reprimanded himself for his own euphemism. *I'll have killed them by eight, sir.*

Walsingham broke the connection. Ryan stepped out of the call-box, letting the door swing shut behind him. The car was parked down the street, almost opposite the café. Walsingham, behind the induced blandness of the secure line and behind his almost imperturbable calm, was worried. Ryan sensed it like an odour in the call-box. Ripples moved out from the dropped stone that was Ryan's job and his limited view of the operation. Guthrie, Ulster, Washington –

He would not be forgiven any mistakes.

He returned to the car and nodded to the driver. Then, in order to settle the details of McBride's death in his mind, he took an OS map from the glove compartment – when the explosion ripped out the front of the Tesco supermarket three doors further down from the café where McBride and the girl were taking afternoon tea. Ryan, head snapping up even before the noise of the explosion followed the disturbance of the air and the alteration of the street's quiet perspective, saw the glass bulge in slow-motion then break into a million shards, flying across the street. Windows emptied. He ducked as the pressure-wave struck the car, rattling doors and windows then pushing in the wind-screen so that it emptied over his neck and shoulders, prickling in the backs of his hands where they covered his head. Something warm and sudden spattered against him. In the moment he had ducked, he had seen two bodies lifted and flung outwards into the street, other people subsiding in hideous slow motion,

The driver's face was lacerated, deep gashes from the shattered windscreen across his left cheek and forehead. Ryan was already assuming he would survive when he noticed the red ring like a clerical collar round the driver's neck, staining his shirt. Then the body slumped against him, and Ryan pushed it away in revulsion. He opened the passenger door and the screaming loudened immediately. The Tesco store was on fire, smoke and flame billowing from the wrecked façade. There were perhaps two dozen bodies on the pavements. A bus had run over one form, and then stopped. There was no driver visible behind the wheel. Someone staggered against the wing of the car, blinded with blood, hands pressed against the face – he could not be sure of the sex – as if preventing the features being dissolved by the flow of blood from the scalp. The high scream did not belong either to a man or a woman, not even an afflicted child or animal.

Ryan was dazed by the occurrence of the explosion and not its force, and by the destruction through which he now had to move. All that concerned him was that he had to regain contact with McBride, must not lose him.

Moynihan pressed his handkerchief against his cheek to staunch the surprising flow of blood. He imagined the gash in his cheek was longer and deeper than it could possibly be. There was no window in which he could inspect it. He was standing drunkenly where he had been when the bomb exploded, in a shop doorway well past Tesco's, watching the front of the café. Now, all he could do was curse silently the Provisional cell which had planted a bomb in an Eastbourne supermarket when McBride was in the same town, the same street, and know he would have to move before the police and ambulances arrived. Yet he wanted to know that McBride and the woman were safe, unhurt. Some growing sense in him had indicated, as he watched the café before the explosion, that the woman had something to tell him, that perhaps the time was close when Goessler would give them McBride or they would take him. He needed to *know*.

But, as he heard the first high wails of the sirens, he forced himself to move, hurrying up the street past the rows of empty shop windows, clothes and food and tailors' dummies heaped and disarranged and shattered and glass-stabbed.

Ryan shook his head, feeling glass prickling the back of his neck and his hands. He was trying to organize his thinking, reject earlier possibilities and form a fresh course of action. McBride would have to be killed now. He rejected that, but it reformed behind the qualification of the woman. Ryan could do little without the driver, and somehow the carnage thrust upon this afternoon street by the Provisional IRA made him deeply angry, made him require action – soon and sudden.

A woman lurched against him as he crossed the street, her face wide and empty with terror. There seemed nothing wrong with her, until he pushed her away and saw the blood running down her leg like helpless urine, into her shoe. The heel had snapped from the shoe, the stocking was torn on the reddened leg, and there was a gash in her skirt. Smart, young, assured. Glass in her belly. Ryan was enraged even as he was sickened. He tripped over a still form, outstretched hand holding a plastic shopping bag with the blazon of the ruined store on it. Glass had cut madly at the back of the dead woman's head, a tonsure of violence. The back of the coat she wore was opened, violated. Ryan regained his feet, his shoes crunching along the glass beach of the pavement, the heat from the frontage of the store flushing his drawn face. A legless torso wailed from the gutter where it had been blown by the bomb, wrapped in the rags of a shop assistant's uniform. A cash register had spilled on the pavement, meaninglessly. Screams and wailing howled like fire-noises from inside the store, before they were drowned by the approaching sirens.

Ryan moved out into the street again, recognizing that he

was dazed, unsteady – the situation overwhelming him – and passed the ruined store. Something like butane gas or paraffin exploded at the rear of the store, and flame gushed into the sky, smoke boiling out in pursuit of it. There were few people moving on the street – a lot of bodies, but few people moving. The bus was empty of passengers, or their bodies had slid down below the level of the window-frames. He crunched on through the glass.

He stood beside an open Mercedes that had halted against a streetlamp, and saw people begin to emerge, slowly as into an altered world, from the café. Ryan saw at the edge of his vision a child nestling in an imitation-death in the back seat of the Mercedes. Her mother's head was in an impossible position, her body only kept upright by the seatbelt. Glass from across the street had almost de-capitated the woman. But he could not understand the child's stillness until he saw the dribble of blood from the back of her head winding slowly round her neck, reaching like a small pet snake into her blouse. He thought the child might still be alive, only stunned, and that made him more angry. He felt the emotion boiling through him, wave after wave; more accurately like a kettle continuing to boil because it could not be switched off or removed from the heat.

He saw McBride mistily, staring around him at the carnage, as the first police cars screamed to a standstill only yards away. The lights of an ambulance flickered up the street, and the wail of the fire-appliances impinged on him. But McBride was the focus of his attention. The woman was hurrying him away, towards the car park where McBride's hire car had been left. Ryan went after them, everything narrowed down to the figures of McBride and the woman. Ryan patted the gun in his shoulder holster. He knew he was acting under stress, that rationality had dissipated in the flood of emotion, but the overriding irrationality of the explosion and the deaths – which might total more than a hundred if the store had been crowded – possessed him. If the IRA could get hold of McBride, if they knew what he knew –

Anger fused the circuitry there, the identification of McBride and the perpetrators of the atrocity. He saw

McBride turn into the entrance of the multi-storey car park, and hurried across the street after him. His knee pained him. He must have bruised it without realizing, perhaps against the bodywork of the silver-grey Mercedes.

The images of the car brought a nauseous bile to the back of his throat as he went up the first flight of the musty-smelling concrete steps. He paused, hearing footsteps above him, then the sighing open and shut again of a door. Next level. He hobbled up the steps, holding on to the iron rail, pausing while an elderly couple negotiated the turn in the stairs, squeezed past him, walking-sticks and old thin legs suddenly untrustworthy, betraying. A shopping-basket on wheels bounced down each step behind them, hurrying them rather than under their control.

Punk rules – OK? sprayed in blue paint on the grey wall, and the old CND symbol. *MUFC,* followed by the comment *are cunts. Rick Wakeman for King* as he went on up the steps, then in red above *Gloria does* and *What?* and *takes 14 inches,* the letters that blinded him, caused him to pause, clench his fists, reach for the 9mm Sig-Sauer P230 and feel the comfort of the butt – *Provos,* and *IRA rules.* A mindless youth with a spray-can, non-political, half-literate, meaning nothing.

And the dead in the street, the glass like a flung-down beach, the perspective changed, the town changed.

He heard as he opened the door a car engine fire, and without thought he yelled McBride's name with all the force of his lungs and throat. Red lights flicked on. The Datsun was backing out from behind a concrete pillar, and he could see the woman in the passenger seat. He ran towards the car, yelling for McBride to stop, the Sig-Sauer in his hand now, but not levelled. The woman was in the way. The Datsun had stopped, and he ran round to the driver's window. McBride was already winding it down. The man's face looked dazed and innocent, and infuriated Ryan. He raised the gun –

The woman had removed the small Astra 300 from her shoulder-bag, pointed it quickly, and fired twice into Ryan's face. He felt each of the bullets, sensed flesh opening and dissolving round the lead, sensed teeth being smashed, almost the exit of each bullet as his head lifted away from the car and he saw the grey concrete roof above him become fuzzy and unformed and dark.

November 1940

By nightfall they had reached the outskirts of Skibbereen without further contact with the pursuit. A cottage just on the edge of the village provided food and water – cheese and rough-hewn bread sticking to their palates, washed off and down into empty stomachs by the water. McBride knew the cottager, a slight acquaintance which would not prevent the old man answering any questions put to him by their pursuers. To prevent any useless bravery, he gave the man permission to answer any questions – time, condition, even direction.

They left the cottage under a cloudy night sky that suggested a moonlit night to come. The rain had petered out before darkness. McBride took them half a mile north of the village, up the bank of the River Ilen, then doubled back, skirting Skibbereen to the west and taking footpaths and bridleways through the easy farming country to the south-west of the village. The moon emerged from the last rags of cloud around ten o'clock, and the landscape was lumpy with clumps of trees and small copses, horizoned by hedges, rendered amusing and safe by the occasional disturbed lumps of sleeping cattle.

They left the lights of a hamlet behind them, navigating by the bulk of Lick Hill a mile or so ahead of them, black and humped against the stars. They walked close together as if to re-establish some community that had been lost in the grey daylight. McBride walked with his arm round Maureen, and she held Gilliatt's hand on her other side.

McBride was heading for a farm that lay snugly beneath Lick Hill, where they could sleep an undisturbed sleep in one of the barns. The farmer would know nothing of their presence. At least, that was the way McBride envisaged it. Holding the farmer hostage at gunpoint might become necessary if they were disturbed, but in that event there was nothing to consider. Guns required no forward planning.

Gilliatt heard the approaching planes first – the higher, lighter feminine note of the fighter escort above the deeper rumbling of the three-engined Junkers Ju52s. The Messerschmitts he knew by sound, the other aircraft he only recognized from their blacker silhouettes against the stars when they were almost overhead. All three of them stood, heads upraised as if in supplication or wonder, immobile as the lumbering Junkers laid strings of blooming white eggs from their bellies and the paratroopers – the Fallschirmjaeger – swung and straightened and descended all round them. A stream of blown dandelion clocks, closing on them, dropping into the fields on every side of them. Hundreds of them.

Chapter Fourteen

DECISION

November 1940

The deception of a summer night dissipated. The swinging, weighted parachutes were being jostled by a cold November wind, and the winter stars were hard and frosty. Each of them was chilled, fixed to the spot, compelled to remain in the middle of the landing ground. The Junkers and Messerschmitts droned away northwards, then banked away to the west, returning a threatening, rustling silence to the wind-soughed darkness.

The first Fallschirmjaeger landed perhaps a couple of hundred yards from them, rolling, getting up and hauling back the 'chutes that billowed and tugged them into a trot. Then others were swinging directly above their heads, and a canister thumped into the earth twenty feet away, rolling ominously towards them. It seemed to galvanize McBride. He grabbed Maureen's hand, pulling her off-balance away to their left, towards a straggling copse where already one parachutist had become entangled in a gaunt tree and was not straining to free himself but hanging limply from his harness.

'Come on!' McBride whispered fiercely, and Gilliatt broke into a run behind them.

They were running through a field of ghosts, through strange, marsh-lit spirits that appeared and rolled and moved on every side. McBride caught one parachutist in the back, bowling him over as the man dropped directly in front of him. He stumbled on the treacherous footing of the silk, skipped a few steps, almost catching his feet in the cords, all the time with one arm steering Maureen away from the billowing white mass in their path. For a moment, whiteness seemed all around them and over them, then the bustling wind whipped the 'chute into a thin, deflated fold and away from them. The small, leafless copse seemed further away than before.

Gilliatt cried out, muffled. McBride whirled around, his hurried glimpse of the field behind them one of puffs of white mist rising and boiling from the ground and the last few dandelion-clocks floating down to earth. Gilliatt was caught in the folds of a parachute that had descended on him, around him. The parachutist was regaining his feet, becoming quickly aware and dangerous. They postured, still for a half-second, like two gladiators. The net-and-trident man had his opponent enmeshed and at his mercy.

McBride avoided the embrace of the shroud, drawing his pocket knife and opening the blade. The German soldier was punching at the harness lock in the middle of his chest while his other hand brought the MP40 machine-pistol to bear on the wriggling, entangled figure on the ground who was not in uniform under the hard moonlight. Then the German saw McBride approaching, perhaps even the gleam of the knife-blade, and the harness drifted away from his shoulders and chest but caught on the MP40 as it swung towards McBride. McBride elbowed the man off-balance clumsily and as hard as he could, then knelt on top of him. The face was very young, dazed and not yet frightened. He clamped his hand over the man's mouth, and drove up beneath the breastbone with the knife. The body went rigid in its coitus with death, then suddenly limp and sack-like. McBride wiped the blade, then began chopping at the cords of the 'chute, freeing Gilliatt.

They stood up together. McBride slipped the strap of the machine-pistol from the dead man's arm and passed the MP40 to Gilliatt.

'Come on.'

Figures were moving now, all around them. The last

pleasantry of falling parachutes had vanished. Only the heavy, bulky images of troops rising from the ground, of folded silk, of guns and men collecting into units. They were fifty yards from the trees, and there were Germans rolling up their white parachutes between them and cover. The cut 'chute billowed and ghosted away with the wind, attracting attention.

'It's no good –' Gilliatt whispered.

'Don't be stupid.' McBride took Maureen's hand, and squeezed it. 'Come on.'

He began running for the trees, and Gilliatt, the MP40 cold and lumpy and uncomforting in his hand, followed them after a moment's hesitation. A cow lumbered into his path, and he ducked alongside it. The animal was disturbed rather than terrified, and was moving aimlessly wherever clear ground presented itself. While it moved towards the trees, Gilliatt moved with it, watching McBride and Maureen and waiting for them to be challenged.

'Halt!' The word was English, almost unaccented. 'Who are you?' The cow tried to shake Gilliatt's arm from its flank, its stubby horns waving just in front of his face. McBride and Maureen were just in front of two soldiers, both of whom were unencumbered and whose guns were level on the man and woman.

'I could ask you the same thing!' McBride bellowed in an outrageous brogue, putting his arm around his wife. 'This is my farm – what are you doing dropping out of the sky on my dairy herd?' Gilliatt wanted to laugh in admiration of the bluff – which he knew would not work. The cow, startled by the voices, swerved away from the trees, exposing Gilliatt.

'Down!' he yelled, waited for the second which stretched out into danger-induced images of flame and bullets emerging from the two German machine-pistols – he could almost see the bullets in slow-motion, feel his leaden limbs transfixed – then McBride had dragged Maureen below chest-level and he sprayed the two Germans with the MP40 on automatic. They were flicked aside, leaving a gap of ground and the trees where the one dead parachutist hung like an admonition. He ran to McBride even as he heard shouted orders less than fifty yards away for men to spread out, get down, locate the source of the firing –

Panic was on their side now, driving them forward while it dislocated German thinking. Ambush? The Irish army? He hardly paused to haul Maureen to her feet, running on with her arm held in a tight grip into the cover of the trees.

'Where now?' he whispered, his head moving like a clockwork toy, swivelling for sight of danger. There was a crashing through the trees and bushes away to the right, but then a mottled, startled Friesian burst out near them like a pantomime cow, head up, legs comically uncertain. It crashed through bushes and down into a ditch on the other side. McBride pointed.

'Down there.'

'Where then?'

'Towards Liss Ard – a mile, no more. Get on with it!' McBride ushered Gilliatt on his way with the MP38 he had picked up from one of the two newly dead. A thin chattering forestalled the humorous remark that would have followed. Wood chips dusted down on them from the lowest branches. 'They know where we are – get on, Peter.'

Gilliatt pressed through the bushes, and dropped surprised into the deep ditch, rolling over but saving his ankles. Then he waited until Maureen dropped, catching her and holding her on-balance. Then he helped her clamber out of the ditch on the other side. Across the fields from them the few lights of Liss Ard seemed to beckon at one moment, then float insubstantial the next. There was more firing behind them, then the noises of McBride scrabbling to the lip of the ditch.

'I hope to God they've got something better to do than chase us!' he observed, coughing with effort, as they began running across the first field between them and the lights of the hamlet of Liss Ard.

Drummond sat opposite the German officer who had come ashore from a small U-boat earlier in the evening, wishing that he would now go and consult with the company commanders who had dropped between Timoleague and Kilbrittain, one of the five designated drop-areas for the

Fallschirmjaeger which he had originally selected months before.

Drummond had met Menschler, a staff officer for *Sealowe* and then for *Smaragdenhalskette,* on a number of previous occasions, in Berlin before the war and three times when he had visited the Irish Republic as an accredited embassy official. His real purpose had been to consult with Drummond on the proposed invasion beaches and the parachute landing areas for Emerald Necklace. But Drummond had never found himself warming to the stiff, chilly Prussian with the Iron Cross always wrapped in a handkerchief in his civilian pocket. Drummond was almost certain that nationality played upon his own treachery.

Now, he wanted Menschler out of the way so that he could contact London.

Drummond felt himself diminished by his anxiety, by a pressing, enlarging sense of his duplicity. He was aware of it making the skin he was interested in saving crawl as Menschler, sitting opposite him in the study of the farmhouse, continued to discuss the movement of the airborne troops to the coast, and the possibility of counter-measures by the Irish government or Churchill. He knew now that he did not possess the commitment, that he did not wish to cast aside his mask, declare his hand. Drummond wanted to insure himself by warning the Admiralty of the landings. He assumed that the twenty-four hours before the seaborne landings was insufficient time for the British to mount any effective counter-attack – the Irish would not move, he was certain, as was the Oberkommando der Wehrmacht in Berlin – but if he reported the parachute landings he would retain the appearance of still working for the Admiralty. Then, in the event of some disaster, he would be in the clear –

And he had a great desire to be in the clear. There was this growing sense of being alone, of being in personal danger, that could not be alleviated by news of the success of the parachute landings or the suggested might of the Wehrmacht, even the genius of the Führer. McBride worked at the corner of his mind like an irritating mote. Him, or someone like him – one to one – was all that was needed, and he would be dead. The craven surrender to a sense of personal danger disappointed him, but he could not any longer ignore it.

'Very well, Drummond, now I will talk to the company commanders, then we will make our little tour, yes?' Menschler stood up with a nod, dismissive and superior, and went out of the room. Drummond, appalled at himself, strained to hear the closing of the door, even the footsteps across the yard to the barn where Menschler's staff had set up their HQ. Then, when only the wind's sound reached him from outside, he scurried to the kitchen and the cellar door, heading for the radio equipment by means of which he would warn the Admiralty of the reported landings of German parachutists in County Cork. A simple message that he was now certain would save his life.

Churchill paced the tiny, cigar-fouled office, the file labelled *Emerald* open on the desk between him and Walsingham, sitting silent and stiff on a hard upright chair. Even as he had sat there, Drummond's message from Kilbrittain had been conveyed to Churchill, interrupting their conversation. Churchill now seemed possessed of almost demonic energy, none of which he could satisfy or express or exude. It remained within him, galvanizing and bullying his frame like a seizure.

The dawn outside the one window combined with the overhead light to create starkness, even the sordid. A time for quarrels and for machinations.

Churchill picked up the telephone and in clipped, precise tones that still would not allow the captive energy to escape, ordered an emergency meeting of the Cabinet and the Chiefs of Staff for nine that morning. When he put down the receiver again, he was staring at Walsingham with glowing eyes.

'So, it's begun, young man?' he said, hands on his wide hips, belly protruding from his unbuttoned waistcoat, hardly contained by the thin gold chain of his pocket watch. Then the big cigar was waving at him, pressed between two fat fingers. 'What d'you think the Irish PM will do about it?'

'I – I don't know, Prime Minister.'

'My bet is he'll do nothing, crafty as he is, and not

without courage.' Churchill's eyes misted for a moment. '*Fait accompli,* I think about covers it, don't you? Oh, they might join in if we did something – ' He looked down at his desk. 'This scheme of yours. I think it's time to put the first stages of it into operation, don't you?'

Churchill picked up the telephone, and was connected almost at once with the First Sea Lord. He ordered the two minelayers to put to sea, and to relay the breached channel in the St George's Channel field. Then, he put down the telephone. Walsingham was breathless with the ease with which part of *Emerald* had become reality, and with the responsibility suddenly thrust upon him. *Emerald* was his scheme. It was now his Siamese twin, indivisible from him for the remainder of his life. He almost wanted to tear up the last few pages of the file. Churchill seemed to guess his feelings.

'Nervous, Commander?' he asked, almost slyly.

'I – '

'You wonder how much of *Emerald* will be put into effect, eh?' Walsingham, with a dry throat, merely nodded. 'Not your concern, young man. Thank you for coming.'

Walsingham, summarily dismissed, obediently made his way to the door. As he glanced back, he saw that Churchill was idly flicking over the pages of the *Emerald* file.

Lt Commander David Guthrie watched the slow dawn crawling across the sound and the low hills behind Milford Haven, innocent and with the promise of a fine day. Yet a greyness not entirely created by the seeping of the day into the landscape lingered across the waters of the sound, and the two minelayers, his own *Palmerston* and HMS *Gladstone* to port, seemed to be sailing towards the night which lingered out beyond St Anne's Head. He had opened the sealed envelope delivered the previous night by Admiralty guard, and pondered his orders to undo the work of the minesweeping flotilla the previous week.

The thoughtfulness, the guesswork had now, for some inexplicable reason, become foreboding. Perhaps only for the convoy which would now be rerouted through the much more dangerous North Channel to the Mersey –

Yet that seemed insufficient to account for his chilliness, for the persistent greyness of the dawn, for the sense of quiet almost unbroken by gulls' cries that seemed to hang over the sound as heavily as a blanket.

Through the remainder of the night and the early morning – which came with a grey clinging mist full of winter and a seeping drizzle that soaked them – they moved at first east until they skirted the tiny hamlet of Liss Ard, then McBride took them south, into the hills and towards the coast at Toe Head, where he had now decided they must acquire a boat of some kind. His thinking was imprecise, instinctive. Dominating everything was his betrayal by Drummond – he studiously ignored all Gilliatt's doubts and hesitations on the matter – and the need now to stay free long enough to get back to Crosswinds Farm in Kilbrittain. Both Maureen and Gilliatt receded in importance to him, considered only as encumbrances. Whenever a cooler perception of himself arose from looking at his wife, or from the workings of memory aroused by the familiar landscape, he crushed it beneath his hatred of Drummond. He was on a pinnacle of egocentricity

The hills were draped in thick mist and Gilliatt and Maureen were tired and dispirited with little or nothing to drive them. Gilliatt, like McBride, assumed that the Germans could not have landed without attracting the attention of agents – British or Irish – and the Admiralty would know within hours. Gilliatt worried about the outcome of events, but accepted his powerlessness in the face of them. More and more, he fell into step and feeling with Maureen.

They came down from the hills, where there was no sign of German troops. McBride moved through the landscape like an angry dreamer, as if he exuded the mist that blotted it out, while Maureen leaned against Gilliatt with chill and weariness. Gilliatt felt diminished by his role, and angry with McBride, yet he felt the growth of some obscure responsibility for the woman, even as he recognized that his image of her and her marriage was based on the briefest acquaintance and was probably worthless. She seemed to accept and use him like a coat or a fire.

Lickowen, the tiny scattering of cottages overlooking Toe Head Bay, where McBride expected to find a boat, had already been occupied by Germans. The mist betrayed them, allowing them a sense of unchanged calm in the hamlet until it was too late to run. One startled young soldier on guard raised one shout before they saw him at the crossroads, which brought without seeming delay three more soldiers on the run from behind a white-painted, blind-windowed cottage. McBride raised the machine-pistol, but Gilliatt knocked it from his grasp with his MP40, then threw down his gun. McBride looked at him in hatred, but Gilliatt merely shrugged and raised his arms tiredly above his head. The sleepless night, the gnawing emptiness of his stomach, Maureen's flagging body, the suddenness of the surprise – all conspired to drain him of resistance. Even as he raised his hands, he had an image of Ashe, telling him of the defeatism riddling the Admiralty. He'd thrown down his own gun in a similar mood. The Germans were here, everywhere. There was no point to it –

An Unteroffizier inspected the two machine-pistols, then stepped back, a grin on his face. He was younger than either of them, and he was enjoying their capture without thinking of the Germans they had killed to get the guns. He spoke in a thick Bavarian accent, but both McBride and Gilliatt understood him.

'We've got them. Well done, Willi. These are the bastards who turned up in the middle of the landing – ' He seemed to remember something then, and stepped half a pace towards McBride, whose face showed more defiance. McBride tensed, almost inviting some suicidal encounter. Then the Unteroffizier said in bad English, his pleasure at their easy capture unalloyed: 'We invite you to breakfast,' and laughed. He directed them, with his own MP38, towards the cottage from which they had appeared.

There was one other soldier in the cottage, already devouring bacon and eggs, cooked by an old woman with wispy grey hair trailing the shoulders of her black dress. She hardly looked up from the stove and the frying pan as they entered, merely seemed to register, waitress-like, the arrival of extra mouths to be fed, and the Unteroffizier motioned them to chairs round the table. As he sat down,

Gilliatt accepted the weariness that sidled up from his feet and ankles and calves, encasing him like an iron shroud. Maureen laid her head on the table, closing her eyes with relief. She was simply glad to stop running. The instant she laid down her head, she felt something loosen from her body and mind, received the sensation that she was physically dissolving. She hated Michael for making them run, for the night and the killings and for her tiredness and hunger and the cottage that was burned and the death of her father. Images seemed to unwind her like a mummy, peel her like the layers of an onion.

McBride sat staring at the Unteroffizier, who placed himself opposite the Irishman.

'What do we do with them?' the young guard asked him.

'Officer's business that,' the Bavarian replied.

'We're moving on in an hour – '

'Then our Irish friends will have to look after these.' He studied McBride intently, his head slightly on one side, as if mentally fitting him with various items of clothing. He nodded, eventually. 'You're not a farmer,' he observed in English.

'Drummond,' McBride replied, 'where is Drummond?' He asked the question in German which seemed only to confirm something to the Bavarian. He shook his head.

'Who is this Drummond? You are the ones in the field last night, *nicht* so?' Slowly, he leaned forward. 'But you are not a farmer, my friend. You are Irish, uh?'

'I'm Irish.' McBride added no more, returning to an inward contemplation of Drummond where he could not be distracted by the trivialities of his capture. Nevertheless, when breakfast came he fell upon it hungrily, as if restoring necessary strength.

As soon as he had finished, and Maureen and Gilliatt, too, were drinking tea from chipped mugs, the Bavarian said to the guard at the door whose MP40 had been on them all the time, 'Go and tell the Herr Hauptmann we have some guests for him to entertain.' The guard ducked out of the low door.

'It's tonight, is it?' Gilliatt suddenly asked in German, lighting a cigarette he had cautiously taken from an inside pocket. The Unteroffizier was surprised, then he smiled.

'It is tonight.'

'This will be one of the beaches, will it?' Gilliatt continued. 'The U-boats will off-load on to Toe Head Bay. How many other beaches are there – can't be more than two thousand men, surely?' He puffed smoke at the ceiling. The Bavarian looked puzzled and angry, but snapped his mouth into a steel line without replying, almost feeling that he had given something valuable to the man who already knew so much about *Smaragdenhalskette*. 'What's the operation called, by the way?' Gilliatt added.

'*Smaragdenhalskette*,' the Hauptmann said from the door. 'I obviously do not need to translate into English, or Gaelic. You are neither Irish nor innocent bystanders, I see.'

'*Emerald Necklace* – yes, it would be,' Gilliatt observed. 'And the boys from Brest come ashore tonight, mm?'

The Hauptmann appeared startled. His young face under the peaked cap seemed white and worried. 'How do you – ? You're guessing, of course.'

'What I know, the British government knows,' Gilliatt observed, marvelling at the courage transmitted by three rashers of bacon, two fried eggs and a thick slice of white bread. He was helpless, just a wasp on a windscreen at whom the driver would occasionally flick, but on whom his mind might become increasingly, dangerously concentrated.

'And what have they done with this so-called knowledge?' the captain sneered, moving closer. The old woman seemed to have melted into the flagstones.

'Ah, now I couldn't possibly tell you that. I've been on holiday in Ireland for the last few days. But, I was on the minesweeper that found your precious channel through our minefield – ' Gilliatt left the revelation floating on the air until it descended by its own weight. He smiled, and drawing on his cigarette leaned further back in his chair. McBride was watching him carefully. Maureen touched his arm as she saw the captain's face darken.

'When, eh? When did you find it?' the captain asked, dispensing with any pretence, hungry for the information.

'Oh, one day last week,' Gilliatt observed blithely.

'Get the Herr Oberst on the radio,' the captain snapped

at the Bavarian sergeant, who immediately stood up. 'Tell the Herr Oberst what this Englishman knows, and ask what is to be done with him.' The second half of the sentence seemed to come as relief and inspiration to both the captain and his sergeant. Confidence returned at once.

Gilliatt quailed inwardly, as if from some electricity that might have passed from Maureen to himself through the hand that still lay on his arm. He was a wasp, and he had just buzzed against the windscreen again. He wondered what they would do with him, and prayed that the British government was doing something. A pressing futility was as physical as a pain behind his eyes, but he rubbed at his forehead to rid himself of it. Be a wasp, he thought. Just do your little bit –

October 1980

Walsingham had reluctantly agreed to accept Guthrie's invitation to lunch at his Georgian house set in three acres of gardens and paddock, through which a trout stream ran, on the Wiltshire-Hampshire border. The Leeds Castle conference had adjourned for the weekend and Guthrie, satisfied with the concessions over recruitment into the Royal Ulster Constabulary made by the three represented Unionist Parties, had decided to spend the weekend with his wife, Marian, at his country home rather than in London. Walsingham was driven down in time for lunch on the Saturday and, as the Daimler turned into the drive of Guthrie's home, he was aware at once of the overt security that surrounded the Minister's person, family, and house. Soldiers, supplemented by police dog-handlers, were evident through the trees across the sunlit paddock and lawns, moving in pairs.

Guthrie, casual in sweater and slacks and looking ten years younger than his age, was waiting for him on the steps of the house as the Daimler came to a noisy halt on the gravel drive. Guthrie came towards him, hand extended. The warmth of the handshake seemed to require response, seek comfort. Guthrie's eyes, as if scales of confidence had dropped from them, been surgically removed by the bright autumnal sunlight, were darting, nervous, worried. Walsingham, as he was ushered into the spacious hall of the house and his light overcoat taken from him by the assiduous Guthrie, merely confirmed with a nod that McBride was to be removed from the board. Guthrie, at the desired signal, appeared instantly more affable, relaxed. He took Walsingham into the drawing-room and introduced him to his younger, still-beautiful Eurasian wife. He'd married her before he'd entered politics in the election of 1951, while he was still serving with the Royal Navy in the Far East. She was lithe, gracious, able to put men at their ease without ever inviting more than their conversation Guthrie poured the drinks.

The telephone call from Walsingham's office came while they were still eating the hors d'oeuvre, smoked chicken served with an avocado mousse and a slightly chilled white Burgundy. Walsingham took the call in Guthrie's study, which overlooked the extensive gardens at the back of the house. Two soldiers were talking to a police dog-handler on the terrace outside, but they disturbed Walsingham rather than reassured him. But the feeling was vague and obscure, and was dismissed as soon as Exton started speaking.

'Ryan is *dead*?' Walsingham repeated bemusedly. The sun obviously did not enter this room until late afternoon, and the study felt chilly. Walsingham lowered himself gingerly on to the edge of Guthrie's walnut desk and fiddled immediately with the gold pen resting near the blotter. He did not, however, make any notes. 'How?'

'Shot twice at point-blank range, through the head – '

'Wait, when was this?' Walsingham felt an urgency pluck at him.

'His body was found a couple of hours ago.'

'Where?'

'Behind a multi-storey car park in Eastbourne. It had been thrown from one of the upper floors, but he was dead before that. The pathologist's report suggests yesterday afternoon or early evening – which is why we didn't hear from him last night.'

'My God – ' Walsingham breathed. His sleepless night assailed him now with a new weariness, and the confident assertion of McBride's imminent demise he had given Guthrie seemed hollow and laughable. When they learned

Ryan's driver was dead, and Ryan not accounted for among the bombed bodies, they'd been forced to assume that Ryan was on McBride's tail on his own. A foolish assumption.

But – shot to death? And where was McBride now?

'You think he – ?' he began, but Exton appeared to have been waiting for the question.

'No, I think it was the girl.'

'Drummond's daughter? Why?'

'McBride had no history of marksmanship, didn't have a gun. It had to be the girl. Trouble is, we don't know anything about her.'

'I – I'll talk to her father. Where is McBride now?'

'We don't know, sir.' Formality masked failure, and it angered Walsingham.

'Find him – quickly.' Then, realizations overpowered him in a gang of hot, swift sensations. 'Quickly. I'll – get back to you.'

Walsingham put down the telephone. It clattered into its rest. It was damp with his palm's perspiration. He pressed his quivering hand to the blotter, leaving a pale imprint on its clear green surface. The girl, the girl –

Organization?

He was as physically aware of Guthrie as if the man had entered the room. *Organization.* McBride the pawn, digging up the dirt, the Provisional IRA's own shovel. Who? *Organization –*

It was all part of a plan. Guthrie opened the door, after knocking.

'Everything all right, Charles? Your wine's getting warm – '

'Yes, yes – just give me a few minutes!' Guthrie appeared pale and startled. 'I'll talk to you then,' Walsingham added, dismissing and mollifying him. Guthrie's face was frowned with thought and dark expectation as he went out. Walsingham picked up the telephone, dialled the operator and requested Drummond's number in Kilbrittain, County Cork.

Drummond? Rear-Admiral Sir Robert Drummond's *daughter*? It was sufficiently preposterous to be true. And they knew nothing about her. Guthrie was a dead man, the conference was a dead duck – *he* was dead. *Emerald. His idea* –

He tapped nervously on the desk, drum-rolling with his stiff, crooked fingers, until the noise was the flight of horses. Then he was told his call was through. Drummond sounded close as the next room, but wary in tone.

'Yes, Charles? What can I do for you?'

Walsingham wanted no other option than to go for the throat.

'Is your daughter a member of the Provisional IRA, Robert?' Silence, or perhaps a click in the back of Drummond's throat like fingers tapping out morse. 'Is she?' Silence, complete except for the humming of the connection. 'Robert, I think she's just killed one of my men. He was watching McBride – just keeping a friendly eye, on your advice – and now he's dead. Shot dead at point-blank range. McBride doesn't have a gun. Does she?'

The smaller admission seemed easier. 'Yes – yes, I taught her to shoot as a girl.'

'Is she a member of the IRA?'

'Yes – ' The word seemed part of a forgotten language, dredged up from deep memory. Drummond, Walsingham sensed, was going to pieces on the other end of the line, collapsing. A worm-eaten, hollow deception so old it was ready to fall down. 'Yes, she is. I – I don't know what to say – '

'Who else? Do you know anyone else in her – *cell*?'

'A man called Moynihan.' Neutral tones, blind to persons and consequences. 'Moynihan is in England now.'

'For God's sake!' Walsingham began, then cut off his blame. 'Anything else?'

'No, I don't know *anything* else!' The voice was plaintive and broken. Then the connection was severed and the receiver buzzed in Walsingham's ear. He slammed it down. He had no doubt, immediately, that Claire Drummond and the man Moynihan already had McBride. He picked up the receiver again to dial London, and recollected, with a chill, personal feeling of anxiety that created no outward-moving ripples, his first meeting with Churchill concerning *Emerald* in late November 1940.

*

McBride lay on the crumpled, unmade bed in the small
double room of the private hotel in Haywards Heath,
Sussex, his eyes still bandaged with a wet cloth, apparently
asleep at last. Claire Drummond, rubbing her strained
arm, watched him intently, as if feeding off his helplessness. She had turned inland from the coast, gone to earth in
Haywards Heath instinctively, and summoned Moynihan
to follow her from Eastbourne. Now, it was early afternoon
and he still had not arrived.

Her arms and shoulders still ached from the frantic effort
needed to drag the body across the car park, lift it and tip it
over the wall down into an enclosed, unfrequented
courtyard behind the multi-storey park. Then the ad-
ditional effort of moving the blinded, stunned McBride
over to the passenger seat of the Datsun so that she could
drive.

When they arrived at the hotel the previous evening and
she parked the car behind the converted private house in a
quiet residential street built at the turn of the century,
McBride was still in the identical, retreated state; as if time
had stopped for him, or he was suffering some catatonic
epilepsy. She fitted him with her sunglasses, walked him to
the stairs, and locked the door of their room thankfully
behind them. Now she was worried, hungry, and frightened – though she would not admit any recognition of the
last sensation. McBride's eyesight should have returned to
normal by now, he should he awake. Like this, he was
useless –

Where was Moynihan? Where?

When he knocked on the door, a little after two-thirty
and called her name softly, she pounced to the door like an
animal, afraid of her own nerves, and let him in. She took in
immediately the evidence of his sleepless night, and the
healing scar on his cheek.

'Making sure I wasn't going to be picked up?' she asked
with mustered contempt, looking at her watch. He nodded.

'No point in us both going down, is there? I'm not
wanted for murder. You are.'

'What?' Her hand fluttered round her mouth like a
wounded bird.

'Don't worry, there's nothing in the papers yet. But

hey'll guess you did it, darling, won't they now?' His eyes moved to take in McBride for the first time. 'What's the matter with him?'

'His eyes – he was blinded by the shots. And he's in shock – ' Moynihan appeared disturbed by the information. 'Don't worry. He'll come out of it.'

'He'd better.'

'Where do we take him, now we've got him?' She glanced at the bed again. McBride still appeared to be asleep, but he lowered her voice. McBride, stretched on the bed, shoeless but otherwise fully dressed, was an object, an implement. She did not even recollect their sexual encounters. She felt weary, afraid, and yet cleaner, more honest in the daylight.

'Chelmsford, Braintree, Brentwood – they're all out.' Moynihan ticked them off on his fingers. He wanted to keep the woman on edge, not in full control. 'We'll take him straight to the Cheltenham place.'

'No!'

'*Yes*. We'll have to risk the long drive. There's more chance of the pigs picking us up if we try to head back into London, or along the coast. Cheltenham.'

'Very well.' The woman seemed subdued to Moynihan, worn down beyond anything other than token resistance. He luxuriated in his new superiority. 'When will he be ready to travel?'

'In the boot? Any time.' She smiled. 'You watch him while I go and get something to eat.' She glanced at the closed window of the room. 'I could smell fish and chips two hours ago – I closed it. It was driving me up the wall.' Moynihan smiled even though he suspected she was ingratiating herself before some further attempt to take command of the situation. 'You've had food, I take it?' He nodded. 'Watch him carefully – and hire a new car. One with a big boot.'

She went out, tugging on her coat as she did so. Moynihan watched the door for a time after it had slammed behind her, then went to inspect the sleeping McBride, lifting the wet bandage. Black scorch marks, and ingrained powder in the skin round the eyes and across the cheeks like black pepper or the stubble of a beard. It was unlikely

McBride was blind, but it wasn't his eyes they wanted anyway. He strolled over to the window, and watched the quiet street until he was certain there was no one interested in his parked car or the walking woman. An Austin Princess, he thought, should satisfy her demand for a large boot to stow McBride for the journey. Stupid woman - there was no telephone in the room. He'd have to wait until her return.

Behind him as he looked out of the window, McBride could see his shadow against the light from the window. The image was wet and underwater and indistinct, but he was profoundly grateful that he wasn't blind. He went on watching Moynihan from the corner of the wet bandage that the Irishman had not properly replaced until his turning from the window caused McBride to close his eyes again. The returning darkness terrified him. Like a recent nightmare, he could not shake it off or diminish its impact.

'Rudi, my dear fellow, do stop fidgeting and sit down.' Goessler said with an affability that was half-assumed. 'Our good fortune in the sudden death of Mr Gilliatt has now been balanced by your misfortune in losing Moynihan and the Herr Professor and his mistress.'

Lobke resented the implicit blame with a pout, and an insolent slumping of his frame into the hotel room's other armchair. The room seemed to have been partially commandeered by their mutual shopping, piled in one corner and in front of the wardrobe and on the second bed. Goessler was drinking a cold beer from the room's icebox and masking his irritation and fears behind the rim of the glass. Outside, it was raining as evening came on. Lobke's arm was still in a sling. Flying glass from the Eastbourne explosion had sliced through his jacket and sweater and his flesh. He'd spent hours in hospital casualty before Goessler was able to take him back to London. He'd sat on the pavement clutching his bleeding arm while McBride and the Drummond woman headed for the car park, helpless and angry and in pain.

'But what to *do*?' he asked plaintively.

'When you have recovered your strength and your temper, Rudi, we will take a trip to Cheltenham. That is where they will take him now, I'm certain. We must meet Professor McBride just once more, I think, to ensure that Moynihan and that dammed woman have not jumped the gun.' He waved his arms expansively round the room. 'I'm certain there is nothing to worry about. McBride should be quite ready to talk to the newspapers about his discoveries – ' He broke off to finish the glass of lager. He smacked his full lips loudly. 'I do not think even the Provisional IRA can now make a mess of our scheme, Rudi. At least, I hope not. Guthrie will have resigned by the end of next week, and American pressure on Britain will raise an outcry for the total withdrawal of troops from the province.' He inspected his empty glass like a jewel or fine crystal, holding it delicately. 'A quite satisfactory conclusion, I think – don't you, Rudi?'

He'd had to appear awake eventually, to avoid suspicion. As soon as he stirred, he registered that Moynihan ducked back out of his vision. The woman gave him two sleeping pills almost immediately, and he groggily accepted them, pretending to swallow both of them but keeping one under his tongue until she and Moynihan were satisfied that he had gone to sleep once more, and left the room together to order and sign for the hire car, locking him in.

He sat up, and spat out the second tablet. His head ached dully and his neck was stiff. His eyeballs still felt peeled and bald and naked, but he could see clearly now and they no longer ached intolerably. His face felt gritty and raw with the powder burns. He groaned, stifling the sound, as he stood up and his whole body protested. Slowly, each step a new and uncertain quest for balance, he crossed to the window and looked down into the street. Some passing traffic but not much, and only a few people about. Some children playing shrill, unskilled football, in bright cagoules and yellow and red plastic boots. He leaned against the window, the cold glass cooling his head. The room was on the first floor. He unlatched the window, and raised it.

Leaning out, he could see a narrow flower-bed like a margin along the façade of the house. He had no plan, no idea of his whereabouts, and a desire to escape from Moynihan and the woman that came and went like a

313

distant, illusory mirage. Weakness and betrayal unnerved him like an anaesthetic. He could not imagine who had been using him beyond Moynihan and the woman; so keen was the sense of betrayal he felt emanating from Claire Drummond that it bounded his horizon. *She* had used him. They wanted his researches to put at the disposal of the IRA – which meant Guthrie was the real target.

He teetered in the window frame, and grabbed the sill, steadying himself. He lifted one leg tiredly over the sill, and sat astride it, looking down and registering the flower-bed winking larger and smaller, undulating in width like a moving snake. He swung his other leg out, then turned to look back into the room as if he had forgotten something. His hands gripped the sill, his arms taking his weight while his legs dangled free. Then he dropped, his feet almost immediately striking the wet earth that resisted his impact, causing him to double over and fall sideways into a sitting position. The thorns of a blown rose stabbed through his trousers, keeping his attention fixed on his immediate circumstances. He felt as if he had been sleepless for days.

Slowly, cautiously he stood up, aware of the body that might default on him rather than any danger from Moynihan and the woman. He felt chilly now that the rain was soaking through his shirt. He stepped out of the flower-bed suddenly angry, a spurt of self-pity acting like adrenalin. He was going to get away from them, he'd see the bitch in hell before –

Moynihan was standing right beside him, his automatic drawn and thrust into McBride's side. The Irishman was angry and malevolent but already McBride didn't care, the last energy draining from him so that he slumped against Moynihan who had to strain to hold him upright.

'You bastard.' Moynihan breathed in his ear, but McBride's head had slumped forward and he had regained unconsciousness.

Chapter Fifteen

PRISONERS OF CIRCUMSTANCE

October 1980

Walsingham felt caged and hampered by his room at the Home Office, sensed the heavy furnishings and dark panelling press upon his immediate concerns and make incongruous Exton's reports and his very presence. Exton, the complete functionary, was out of place there, too modern, too mechanical. Yet what he brought with him into the room promised some scarcely expected solution. At least it was a map with the names of places added, and footpaths clearly marked.

Walsingham was crippled in will by the sense of Nemesis that had assailed him all the way back from Guthrie's house – Guthrie left small and vulnerable and ridiculously youngly dressed on the steps, waving feebly – and would not leave him even here, on home ground. McBride was in the hands of the IRA, *Emerald* would come out and he would be finished. The justice of it impressed him.

'You can't trace this East German on your list – Goessler, you say?' he murmured, standing at the window watching legged umbrellas hunch down Birdcage Walk and across the Park. The sun of the early afternoon – how chilly it had been in Guthrie's study – had vanished like an omen, and the soaking, persistent drizzle had taken its place, seemingly for good.

The German connection – *origin?*

'No, sir. He hasn't flown out again, so he must still be in the UK. He hasn't booked out of his hotel room.'

'That doesn't mean he'll go back there.'

'No, sir.'

'We have nothing on him – SIS has nothing on him?' Someone slipped on wet leaves at the corner of the Walk and Horse Guards, splaying on to his back. An old man who had to be helped to his feet. To his dismay, Walsingham was appalled by the minor accident, suffered it psychosomatically.

'No, sir. He's never been in the field, he's *always* been what he pretended to be – an academic. SIS understanding of the home-birds in the Abteilung isn't what it might be, sir.'

'I appreciate that, Exton. Now, where is he?' The old man down on the wet pavement started on his way again, leaving those who had assisted him as if he had been cast adrift. His progress was painfully slow. 'We have to know where he is. He introduced McBride to the whole business of – ' He was about to say *Emerald*, and clamped his mouth round the word, stifling it, ' – this German invasion plan. It must have been *his* inspiration, this operation. There's no other explanation. Would you say?'

He turned suddenly to face the impassive Exton.

'No, sir,' Exton commented without expression.

'The object of the exercise had been achieved, Exton – the IRA now has the man with the proof it needs. But, Goessler wouldn't want to miss the end. He's not going to leave the cinema early on this occasion, just to dodge the anthem – ' Walsingham smiled, his lips curling round the metaphor. 'It's such a *devious* plan, he'll be incautiously delighted with its success. Hire cars?'

'The Branch have got men on it, sir. They're still checking. The hotel switchboard can't help, and he didn't hire one through the desk.'

'You think he's in London, don't you?'

'Most likely, sir.'

'No. I think he's somewhere out of the way, a long way away from the point of the explosion – ' His face narrowed, grew older and more cunning. An old man with a feverish grip on life. 'Find the car and we'll find him, Exton.'

'Yes, sir. What about McBride, when we find him?'

'I have – an idea for McBride, Exton. Let's find him first.'

He dismissed Exton with a gesture of his hand, then returned to the window. The build-up of traffic splashed a red tail-light glow on the wet street, and rain sparkled in headlights. The slow movement of the traffic was appropriate to some solemn occasion, a funeral. He remembered. Churchill's state funeral. *Emerald* might even have been necessary. Churchill had thought it so.

Goessler. Clever Professor Goessler of the university, and of the Abteilung. It might still not be too late –

Walsingham felt weary, and oppressed by a sense of justice moving large and blind against him, blundering down his castles of deception. He hated the need for some kind of expiation in himself. He would win, had to win.

And he knew, once he had Goessler, how to – *castrate* McBride, pull out his tongue. Eunuch and mute, never to speak of the secrets he knew. The violence of the images satisfied him, replaced the lingering fragility of the old man who had slipped on the wet pavement.

The garden was quiet, almost unreal as it slipped into night. Robert Drummond walked in it, regretting the blown roses and the drifting leaves. The house was at his back like a last line of defence, but indeed he had been driven out of its empty rooms by their heaviness of association, by the manner in which they were now only stage backcloths for the events of November forty years before. And he suspected he dwelt on those because he could not bear to consider the present, in which Claire moved like an alien life-form, entirely separate from himself yet vividly identical.

Fanatic.

She had the strength he had not been able to find in himself, when he came into contact with Menschler and the parachute troops and the invasion. The field-grey was too close, the swastikas too vivid to be saluted like a distant love. He had been afraid, and had wanted to escape. And the thought of Michael McBride had tormented him, assumed the proportions of a vengeful god. He somehow knew that McBride had seen him with the Germans, had certainly guessed he had betrayed him to them. He was afraid of McBride, even after he learned from Menschler that the three people they'd picked up had to be McBride, his wife, and Gilliatt.

Now, what had seemed so long ago, so unconnected with himself as the war progressed then peace followed and he was promoted, bemedalled, retired, grew prosperous – now, it was so omnipresent and so inescapable.

He increased his pace, as if thereby he might leave the past whispering like a group of guests he could abandon, there on the paved path by the sticks of the pruned hydrangeas. Nevertheless, the past pursued him, because Claire waited for him in the most shadowy parts of the garden and he could not bring himself to face her. What was she doing to McBride, just at that moment – ?

He felt himself breathing shallowly and rapidly, but the noise was amplified in his ears, and aged roaring of protest at effort and emotional stare. He turned back from the dark hedge at the bottom of the garden, ducking under the lowest branches of the apple trees he had planted soon after the death of his wife – the brief quiet guest in the house who had left him his daughter in his own image and then subsided into a harmless non-being – and feeling his old heart strain at that slight evocation of physical health and suppleness. When he straightened, the white house shimmered in the gloom and seemed very distant. He began to hurry towards it, feeling his chest constrict like an iron band about his lungs, and the old heart bump and shudder.

He looked around him, turning to and fro as if in a strange place, and the darkness of the garden pressed upon him, sidling closer, embracing him. His foot slipped on the edge of the paved path and his heel sank into soft dark earth. He even registered the crushing of next year's bulbs beneath the soil. Then his heart seemed to tear open, then collapse on itself like a dwarf star, drawing him into blackness. He teetered off-balance and slid sideways to the ground, his hands clutching air as if fighting off the approach of night.

November 1940

The Oberst had had them removed to a barn on the edge of Lickowen and placed under guard – the Bavarian sergeant and the young Schutze who had first spotted them at the crossroads – while he contacted Menschler at Crosswinds Farm, his co-ordination HQ. The colonel seemed at a loss as to what to do with, or to them. He was a soldier, and when Menschler ordered him to interrogate the prisoners he felt a reluctance and incompetence grow in him all the way back to the shadowy barn in the misty drizzle. He felt cold and wet and full of forebodings.

Gilliatt watched the Oberst return and made an effort to smoke his cigarette in an unconcerned manner. The German parachute colonel seemed uncertain of himself or his task, and Gilliatt drew a quiet, sedative strength from the way in which the German approached him, adopted a swagger, tried to enforce himself upon his prisoner. He ignored McBride and Maureen sitting side by side on a hay-bale a little apart from Gilliatt.

'How much do you know about our operations?' The Oberst asked.

Gilliatt smiled. 'A great deal, Colonel.' He spoke deliberately in German. 'The British government and the Admiralty have known about Emerald Necklace for some time. I myself was aboard one of the minesweepers when your channel was detected. We knew immediately what it was, what was intended – '

'So, where are your troops, where is the Irish army?' the colonel asked, regaining confidence.

Gilliatt shrugged. 'I'm not the military planner for this operation.'

'Who are you?'

'Lt Peter Gilliatt, Royal Naval Reserve.' The colonel seemed puzzled. 'Who are you, Colonel?'

'Why is a sailor here, dressed in civilian clothes?'

'Fishing holiday.' Gilliatt was amazed at his own confidence, born entirely out of their exchange. The Oberst struck him across the face, and Gilliatt's confidence crumbled because he had been too clever and the German officer was getting angry at his own impotence. Blood was warm and salty in his mouth. He wiped his lips, spat out the blood and saliva. The colonel seemed satisfied with the badge of his hurt.

'Don't be stupid. You're spying on us, mm? Who are these others?'

'Irish citizens – friends of mine. *Guides*.'

'Spies?'

'In their own country – don't be stupid.' The colonel struck Gilliatt again, snapping his head up, tipping him backwards against stacked bales of hay where he lay

drunkenly looking up at the German colonel. One of his
back teeth felt loose, amid the blood from inside his cheek
and from the dulled impressions of his bitten, swollen
tongue. It angered him unreasoningly. The whole scene
was a farce, anyway, comic-book Hun interrogating a
prisoner, lots of master-race face-slapping – a charade
whose reality he could not accept. He was telling the stupid
Kraut everything – it was the reverse of the usual prisoner-
interrogator scene anyway – and the silly man wanted to
beat him up because his nice secret plan was up the spout.
Gilliatt sat up, nursing his cheek and mouth.

'Listen, you stupid bloody Hun! I'm telling you what
you want to know, can't you understand that? You've been
rumbled, your lovely secret plan isn't a secret any more. I
don't know what the British government is doing about it,
but by now you can be sure they know you've landed. So, I
should get down to the beaches and wait for tonight and see
what turns up!'

He fell back against the bales, exhausted by his outburst.
The parachute colonel stood in front of him, mouth agape
and hands at his sides, for a long time. Then he turned
on his heel and stamped out of the barn. Gilliatt shook
his head, probing at the back tooth. Definitely loose.
Damn. He looked up, to find the Bavarian sergeant
laughing. When Gilliatt looked at him, he closed up his face
again.

Maureen moved across to him, touching his face gently,
staring into his eyes regretfully and with admonition
behind that. In a moment, she might be scolding him like a
child.

'I'm all right,' he said thickly, turning his head aside to
spit out more blood.

'Open your mouth,' she ordered. He did so. She
inspected it, then nodded. 'You'll live.' Her eyes, however,
were more tender than her voice. McBride stood behind
her.

'How am I doing?' Gilliatt asked softly.

'Brilliantly, if you want to get us all shot,' McBride
replied. Gilliatt smiled painfully. His lips were puffing out
now from the colonel's blows. 'I can see your point, but will
it do any good?'

'It might. Have you any ideas?' Gilliatt watched the Bavarian sergeant, moving slowly closer now that their voices were quiet and they were speaking in English.

'I'm going to get out of here, fairly soon. Tonight at the latest,' McBride remarked, squatting next to his wife and staring abstractedly at the strewn, crushed hay between his feet. Maureen looked viperously at him.

'You're mad, the pair of you,' she breathed angrily. 'You'll get yourselves killed, why not accept it?' She stood up, looking the Bavarian sergeant up and down. 'Men!' she snorted contemptuously. 'Little boys playing soldiers!'

The German was nonplussed. She walked away from him, arms folded across her breasts, her steps strutting and angry. Gilliatt watched her, grateful for her angry solicitousness. When he looked into McBride's eyes, there was a recognition between them. McBride's face narrowed in anger.

'You want Drummond, don't you? That's all you want, isn't it?' McBride grinned savagely, and nodded. 'You don't even know he had anything to do with the Germans, dammit! What's the matter with you?'

McBride seemed compelled to consider the question that was only intended as an insult. After a moment, he said, 'I don't know. I wonder at what I'm finding out about myself – you know that? I'm not too fond of it.'

'Stop it, then.'

McBride shook his head. 'No, I won't do that, Peter. I find it strangely satisfying.' He saw Gilliatt looking beyond him, at Maureen. 'Strange,' he said, as if he had been asked another question. 'I don't even regret Maureen all that much. I feel – under the anaesthetic, maybe.'

Gilliatt was puzzled, and appalled. Then the mood was broken by the sound of a small car approaching the barn. They listened, McBride's face contracting and expanding almost as if the muscles beneath the skin were breathing heavily. Gilliatt looked up as the car door slammed and there were footsteps across the yard outside. McBride evidently expected Drummond.

The man who stepped through the door had the raincoat and cap of one of their pursuers. It might have been another man, but he was certainly Irish. IRA. He grinned as

McBride turned and looked at him. The two men recognized each other.

When McBride turned away again, Gilliatt said, 'Who is he?'

'Riordan – he runs the Ross Carbery and district chapter. He probably shot Maureen's Da, or had him shot. If he's left to guard us, then God help him.' McBride's hands clenched and unclenched. Gilliatt felt distanced from him, further than ever before. Beneath the smiling, almost boyish adventurer's exterior there was something cold and dangerous that this situation had force-fed. He was a film star whose screen image masked a filthy or perverted private character. Gilliatt could find no more appropriate an analogy. He couldn't understand McBride and wanted a view of him that explained him in stark monochrome and not in shades of grey. He was more than a little mad, perhaps, and certainly a killer.

McBride moved away, as if sensing the bent of Gilliatt's reflections, and Gilliatt went on caricaturing him for the sake of his own mental comfort.

Churchill entered one of the small operations rooms in the command bunker beneath the Admiralty building set aside for the select team he had assembled to deal with what he now officially termed *Emerald*. He had taken personal command of the operation, and its classification for security was the highest possible. On the wall immediately in front of him was a map of the British Isles, to which a lt commander from the Tracking Room was attaching pins to show the position of the channel that the Germans had swept. Churchill allowed himself a gruff, barking laugh at the handwriting which described the minefield by its nickname. He saw Walsingham in consultation with two officers, a major and a colonel, from the War Office's Co-ordination of Intelligence Branch, and signalled him to join him. Two armchairs and a cocktail cabinet had incongruously been added to the linoleum-floored, concrete-walled room. Churchill slumped into one of these, noticing the patch of striped shirt that had pushed itself from beneath his waistcoat, tucked it back into his waistband, and placed his hat on the small table beside his chair.

Walsingham waited, and the Prime Minister indicated the drinks cabinet. Walsingham poured the old man a large brandy which Churchill swiftly demolished. Then he indicated that Walsingham should sit. Around them, the work of the room continued like the soft and constant hum of machinery. The two minelayers were indicated on the map, already well into the British-swept channel and approaching the German sweep. For its part, the army intelligence unit the War Office had assigned to *Emerald* was working at a papier-mâché relief model on a table, the Brittany coast divided by a strip of board from the Irish coast from Cork to Mizzen Head. The relief models had been hastily painted green, brown and blue, and around the sea inlets and the beaches were marker flags and along the coast were model soldiers in field grey.

Churchill studied Walsingham. The younger man felt uncomfortable under his gaze, while at the same moment he was aware of some intense inward debate, as if the old man looked inward with one eye, towards him with the other. Churchill's proximity unnerved him. The man emanated will, ruthlessness, energy. He was unsparing and unforgiving, perhaps most evidently with himself. The blue eyes were intent, dissatisfied with the corpulent, flagging body which the mind inhabited. The eyes and their gaze seemed totally an instrument of the man's intellect and nothing to do with the ageing sack of the flesh. Churchill puffed at his cigar.

'What do we know, Commander? How many troops have the Nazis dropped into County Cork?'

'The weather has been too bad for any aerial reconnaissance of the area, Prime Minister.' Churchill's face creased in irritation. 'But we have reports which suggest the number of planes they used was very small. We don't think they could have landed anything like a division in one drop.'

'How many?'

'Two or three rifle regiments, signals unit, perhaps – not much more than that.'

'A holding operation.'

'Would you like to see our guesswork as to their dispositions?'

'In a moment. What are the reports from France?'

'Sir, we can explain it better if you'd look at the models,' Walsingham persisted. Churchill looked across the room as if reluctant. Then he heaved himself out of the deep armchair, teetered for a moment but shrugged away Walsingham's supporting hand, and then crossed the room with a conscious determination in his step. The colonel from the Army Intelligence Unit snapped to attention. Walsingham noticed the way in which Churchill seemed to enjoy the subordination of the people around him, their punctilious awareness of his importance. A commander-in-chief rather than a Prime Minister. Had he painted at Chartwell all those years just for moments like this?

'Now, Colonel. Explain.' Churchill dabbed at the Brittany model. Cigar ash dropped into the blue-painted sea off Brest, and the colonel delicately blew it away, dispersing it over the flat painted paper of the Atlantic. The colonel then dabbed towards the model with a pointer. A grey toy soldier with a rifle.

'Yesterday, according to aerial reconnaissance, these units of parachute troops were moved from here down to the airfields here – ' He picked out the marked airfields one by one. 'There were a number of transport planes at each which had arrived the previous night. These units – ' He picked out two other toy soldiers, standing above Plabennec, ' – were moved down to the harbour area. As definitely as we can tell from photographs and from what the man McBride brought back with him, they are two infantry divisions. Also, we have vague reports from the local network that engineer units – Panzers – have also been on the move towards Brest. That's more or less it.'

Churchill was silent for a while then: 'What are the latest weather reports?'

'They'll sail tonight.'

'Who will come first?'

'One of the divisions will send in infantry, there'll be signals – at least a couple of *abteilungen* – recce units, engineers. They'll want a bridgehead – ' Already, it was evident that Churchill's eyes had strayed towards the Irish coast model, via the wall-map which revealed that the two minelayers had moved into the gap of the German-swept channel. He pointed with the cigar.

'What do we know about the dispositions here?' He waggled the cigar along the coast of County Cork.

'Difficult, sir,' the colonel offered apologetically. 'We've very few reports from Drummond's rather poor intelligence network, and we've no aerial reconnaissance.'

'But – ?'

'We estimate there were four landings at least, possibly five or six. To secure the beaches, since they landed so close to the coast in each case.' He pointed towards the field-grey toy soldiers. 'We know they landed here – ' Near Kilbrittain and the Old Head of Kinsale. 'And here.' Ross Carbery Bay. 'On that basis, we've selected the likeliest beaches for landings, and the easiest to hold – here, here and here.' Toe Head Bay, Clonakilty Bay, Glandore Harbour. Churchill nodded. A toy soldier loomed over each shallow inlet of the sea, carrying a rifle across his body. Churchill turned to Walsingham.

'What do you hear of the Republic's army?'

'Our intelligence sources in Dublin are indicating that the Irish are sitting tight, sir.' Churchill nodded. 'They're still gathering their own intelligence. There's an alert, all leave cancelled, a lot of meetings and consultations between the army and the government – '

'And it doesn't amount to more than piss and wind,' Churchill snapped. 'They won't want to go up against crack parachute troops. God, they saw what happened to us at Dunkirk! Who could blame them?' He rubbed his nose. They need our help, but they're not asking for it. Strict neutrality. *I* know they've been in touch with Berlin – ' He smiled at the sharing of one of his secrets. 'Apparently, the Führer is denying all knowledge of such troop landings and is assuring the Irish government he continues to recognize their neutrality. Gentlemen, it's up to us, I'm afraid. We must look out for ourselves. Now, what can we do?'

The intelligence colonel cleared his throat. 'We could land a couple of regiments today. The Dorsets and the Herefords are on full alert. They've not been told why.'

'Colonel, you know it would take today to get them to the coast and aboard suitable vessels, even if we had them. By tomorrow night, they might have begun to disembark in Cork harbour, if we were very lucky.' He paused while the colonel flushed slightly. 'Very well, get them to the coast. Bristol or Cardiff, as quickly as possible. Just *bodies* – forget heavy equipment. *I* will talk to the Prime Minster of the Irish Republic and inform him that dockside facilities will be required in Cobh or Cork tomorrow. You have a list of vessels in Bristol and Cardiff – ' Walsingham looked into Churchill's eyes, and shook his head. 'Get one!'

Walsingham crossed to the telephones ranged alongside each other on a fold-away table. Churchill watched his retreating back for a moment, then said, 'Get them on to anything, let them sail as soon as possible.' Again, he pointed with his cigar. 'They'll require Cork airport. I presume they'll try to take it tomorrow, and land equipment and the Panzergrenadiers then. Then Cork Harbour and it would be all over.' The colonel looked as if Churchill had touched a hidden nightmare or shame. 'Very well. Then our relaid minefield had better work effectively, to give us time to round up the parachutists, on behalf of the sovereign republic of Eire.' He emitted his gruff, barking laugh. The colonel realized, looking into his face, that there was a confidence that bordered on fanaticism in Churchill. The atmosphere of the War Office was cynical, depressed – even before *Emerald* – but it was as if Churchill were fighting personally, in some medieval combat with Hitler and knew his own superiority to the German leader. If *he* had no doubts, then Britain could not lose. Or was it a public-relations act, a pretence and nothing more? The colonel could not answer his own question. Churchill was speaking again.

'We have to defend Cork airport and the harbour. If we can do that – ' It was not a doubt – 'then the Nazis cannot land more troops except by parachute. And tanks are *not* dropped by parachute. Good. Walsingham – ' He called across the room. Walsingham placed his hand over the mouthpiece.

'Prime Minister?'

'I want the First Sea Lord as soon as you've ordered your

ist of shipping. This transport of two regiments to Ireland must have absolute priority. They must be there by tomorrow at the latest.'

Churchill turned back to the wall-map. Someone had added the position of the convoy carrying Robert Emerson Grady, now only a few hours' sailing from Valentia Island on the west coast of Ireland. The four pins for the cruiser and the three merchant ships were livid spots before his eyes and an interference with his thinking. Those four coloured pins were something he would have to deal with before the end of the afternoon.

He inwardly saw his own hand resting on the final pages of Walsingham's *Emerald* file. Cigar ash scattered like dandruff over its typed, double-spaced lines. Walsingham had been prepared to sacrifice the convoy for the sake of complete surprise and to ensure the destruction of the U-boat convoy that was coming that night. He'd got the wrong end of the stick. The convoy from America might have to be destroyed, but not for that reason.

There was another reason that burned at the back of Churchill's mind like a dark light, or a spillage of acid. Before that evening, he would have to allow it into the forebrain, dissect it, and act upon it.

David Guthrie watched the grey, choppy sea close over the last batch of mines from the deck of *Palmerston*. Nothing disturbed the water other than the wind which stirred and made ragged the sea-mist, and the wake of the minelayer. He felt cold inside his duffel-coat and thick sweater and uniform jacket. The sea looked forbidding, rubbed and abrased by the wind into a treacherous, insecure surface. There was no mood of satisfaction at the completion of their task, and he did not understand its absence. Nor did he comprehend the reason for his chill sense of foreboding, which lingered like the staleness of guilt in his mind.

Robert Emerson Grady thanked the officer who brought him the information that they were four hours' sailing from Valentia Island. He'd not see the coast, of course, because of the mist through which the drizzle squalled on the buffeting wind. The quarter deck was wet and treacherous, and he gripped the railing fiercely as if the sea suggested some siren call to him. He was cold, and dispirited and alone, and thankful that his journey was almost over. About the task confronting him, he was not prepared to think. He was almost ready for it, but not quite. By tomorrow, he told himself, he would be ready to go to work. By tomorrow.

Jean Perros watched from the harbour wall of St Anne-du-Portzic as the large U-boats, moving in line astern, slipped out of Brest down the Goulet de Brest towards the sea. Through the dusk and the drizzling mist he could make out their low, spectral shapes as they emerged and disappeared through the palpable, chilly air. There had been no fishing allowed by the Germans for the last two days. He'd been unable to make any accurate reports to London, via the radio set in St Pierre-Quilbignon. Now, he would be able to send the message they waited for –

And he believed, so deeply that it rendered him weak and old, that his message would be too late to make any difference.

He watched until the U-boats had finally vanished westwards, then hurried from the harbour wall to collect his bicycle to ride the mile and a half to send his signal.

October 1980

'You're going to talk to us, McBride, and not only to us. You're going to talk to the newspapers. You'll even get paid for it. We're making money for you – just look at it that way.'

Moynihan chuckled. He was sitting opposite McBride, whose hands were tied in front of him, resting on his lap. Claire Drummond was seated on an upright chair, taller than the prisoner on the battered sofa and the Irishman in the armchair by the fire, and suggesting by her posture and her silence that she was in command of the circumstances of that room. McBride, truculently silent, was still grateful for the light from the bulb above his head and for the warmth of the fire after the hours in the stifling, nightmarish boot of the car.

Gagged and bound, he had thought himself slipping into insanity. Cramp was like the gradual onset of decay, even death. The gag in his mouth seemed to be sliding down his throat, into his nostrils to suffocate him. The smell of petrol and the road noise of the tyres sickened him. Then they'd stopped, finally, and dragged him out – he'd fallen over with the cramp in his body and had lain in the long wet grass, sobbing until they'd bundled him indoors. He'd caught a brief glimpse of fields dropping away, dark copses and grazing cattle, and of a dilapidated cottage directly ahead of him. When they'd got him inside, their satisfaction made them abandon any pretence to security. He was in the Cotswolds, just outside Andoversford. Claire Drummond had laughed at his bemusement, shouting into his face that he was near Cheltenham and hadn't he ever heard of the Cotswolds, the dumb stupid Yank that he was –

Claire Drummond frightened him. The woman was high on success, on the weapon she believed he would become for her. He saw how much she hated the British, how much she despised him. She paced the room continually, until she finally settled in front of him on the hard chair. Neither the journey nor the lateness of the hour seemed to have tired her, or made her aware of any physical limitations on her driving hatred. McBride quailed inwardly. He could see no way in which he could resist them. They were determined he should talk – not to them but to the press.

'Go to hell,' he mumbled in reply to Moynihan. Moynihan crossed the room and struck him across the face. The woman seemed to enjoy the act, to anticipate a second or third blow and be disappointed when they did not come. Moynihan laughed, threatened with his open hand so that McBride flinched, and then returned to his seat.

'Don't be bloody stupid, McBride,' he said, picking up his glass of whisky from the rug beside his chair. 'You're all on your own, in this delightful weekend cottage, no one knows you're here. You'll get yourself buried in the garden if you don't co-operate.'

'Then who'll believe your story?'

'It'll still make good reading, cause quite a stir.'

'You need me – and not too knocked about, either, you dumb bunny,' McBride sneered. He didn't know where the energy, the defiance had come from. Perhaps only from the woman's silence, her withdrawal from the verbal baiting. Moynihan made as if to rise again, slopping his whisky over his trousers. 'Little wet-pants,' McBride added, laughing.

The woman suddenly stood up, and crossed to McBride. The gun in her hand, the little Astra she'd used in the car park, was close to his head. She grinned, pressing the hole of the barrel against his temple. She squeezed the trigger, very slowly and in plain sight. Her eyes were mad – she was going to kill him.

The hammer clicked, and she laughed. She showed him the magazine in her other hand. Then she leaned close to him. He could smell the grease of their fish-and-chip supper on her breath – he'd been able, with terrible hunger, to smell the fish and chips in the boot as they sat in a lay-by and ate them – and he could see tiny fragments of white fish between her bottom front teeth. She leaned to his ear, and began whispering to him. He heard the magazine click back into the gun. She pressed the barrel against his groin, moving it in a rubbing motion as if it was a part of her body, her own crotch touching his. She pressed harder and harder.

'I promise you, darling,' she whispered in a grotesque parody of seductive tones, her breath quick and shallow and obscene in his ear, 'I promise I'll let my gun make love to you, but not just yet, not just yet – ' The gun hurt now, pressing into him. He winced. 'You want it to love you, but not yet darling, not just yet – '

He screamed as she dug the barrel of the gun deeper, then drew back from him. Her eyes were alight, possessed. He clutched his bound hands over his groin, sobbing despite himself.

He heard Claire Drummond saying: 'He knows now I could do it, just as easily as anything. Blow off that thing he's had inside me. He knows his life isn't really worth a light!'

McBride looked up. 'You're mad.'

'Yes,' she said, sitting down again, putting the gun back in her shoulder-bag as primly as if it were her make-up or cigarettes. 'Oh, yes. The awful thing for you is – you know I'm aware of it, that I can *use* it, turn it on like a tap. You'll never know when I'll do it, or what effect it might have on you. Terrible, aren't I?' She lit a cigarette, exhaling the first smoke at the stained ceiling with its cracking plaster between smoke-blackened beams.

'See?' Moynihan said as if he had planned the demonstration. 'You'll co-operate.' McBride blinked back his tears of pain and fear. 'We want you to make a statement first of all, just a trailer for the main film, so to speak. On tape, and we can play it over the telephone or send it to one of the newspapers. You mention Guthrie's name, and the war, and a couple of other little items of interest, and we'll set up the meetings and make the financial arrangements. Oh, you won't be left out of it, darling. You'll stand to make – oh, fifty thousand. At least. That's about the going rate for serialization. You ought to make twice that. You can't prove Guthrie was queer as well, can you now? That'd be even better.' Moynihan was speaking through his own laughter, enjoying his joke enormously.

Then McBride was laughing, too, so that Moynihan fell silent. McBride shook his head. His voice was old and weak and tired and bereft of resistance. He said, 'You dumb bastard – I was thinking of millions, not thousands. *Millions!* Now, isn't that the funniest part of the whole thing, uh? Isn't that a real belly-laugh?'

The noise of the approaching car cut off his laughter. Claire Drummond rose swiftly from her chair.

'Put the light out!' she snapped moving to the window.

Walsingham put down the telephone with a quivering hand, rattling it in its cradle. Against all hope, against all hope –

He couldn't help it. Of course, they'd temporarily lost the car again, after they'd spotted it in a pub car park outside Cirencester, but it had been seen. They knew the area. If it moved on any road in the Cotswolds that night, they would pick it up.

But, his satisfaction and relief were almost overpowering. They'd traced the car-hire firm Goessler had used – a small one, not one of the giants – late in the afternoon, just before closing, then sent out a general alert to all police forces. By ten in the evening, a constable in a Panda patrol car of the Gloucestershire Constabulary had spotted the white Ford Escort in the pub car park. Goessler in his overconfidence had left it bathed in the white illumination of the country pub's flood lighting, unsuspicious that he was even 'wanted for questioning'. Goessler's unconcern, his illusory sense of safety, bolstered Walsingham's nerve more than any other factor. Goessler's unawareness of him put him at a disadvantage. It made him more stupid than Walsingham, slower and capable of being outwitted. He had Goessler in the palm of his hand now. He could, and would, crush him.

The hatred was pure and deep and uplifting. Goessler had been out to get him. Now, he would finish Goessler, the author and *onlie true begetter* – he smiled at the quotation – of this operation. Finish him and stalemate McBride. A stand-off.

Of course, for Goessler and for the Drummond woman and anyone else who knew, it was an end-game. That was another of the certainties he felt able to allow himself after Exton's telephone call.

He looked around his sitting-room, at the high, corniced, shadowy ceiling then at the rich carpet. The substance of the room seemed to have returned. He seemed more substantial, heavier, sitting in his favourite armchair. All would be well.

He raised his glass.

'To a gallant loser – Herr Goessler,' he mouthed, smiling, his lips seeming too thin and small to contain the vivid dentures.

He would meet Goessler just the once, when they picked him up and before –

He stopped the thought there, like breaking off chocolate to keep for later.

'Please don't be inhospitable, my friends!' the voice called from outside the door of the cottage. 'I am not a stern parent come to spoil your happiness or invade your tree-house. Open the door. We are surely still friends!'

McBride lifted his head. He couldn't believe that he recognized the voice and shook his head as if to clear it of deception. His groin ached and he was frightened and the voice seemed to belong to a calmer past. But, incredibly, Goessler went on speaking outside, addressing Claire Drummond and Moynihan. McBride, hunched over his bound wrists and aching groin, watched from under slitted lids; a physical approximation to cunning that had no inward reality. The woman opened the door, and Moynihan turned on the light as it closed again. It was Goessler, and Lobke, the so-called embassy official. The light seemed hard and dirty, making Goessler look older, fatter but with somehow hollower cheeks, stubbled and with the cheekbones emphasized like reminders of distant youth. Lobke looked wary, concentrating on Claire Drummond and Moynihan, both of whom still held their guns level on the two Germans.

'Come, come,' Goessler said with a bonhomie that made McBride's flesh creep. He was listening to the tones of someone it was easy to take for granted, even regard with a mild contempt – Goessler's academic mask that had deceived him completely. Then Goessler was standing in front of him. His pudgy hand lifted McBride's chin, inspected his face like a surgeon considering alterations. 'You look tired, Thomas.' There was no sense of irony in his words, but a kind of feminine condolence which made McBride shudder.

'Get lost, Goessler,' he said. Moynihan laughed.

'I'm sorry if they've been rough with you, Thomas – they are animals.' He turned on Claire Drummond and Moynihan. 'Don't wave those stupid guns at me. I'm your paymaster, your arms dealer, your banker, your insurance. You can't kill me. Besides, I have come merely to congratulate you on your success, and to make certain that you find Professor McBride co-operative.'

'Were you followed?' Moynihan asked. Goessler merely looked at him with contempt and sat himself against the wall where he could watch the room and its occupants. Claire Drummond put her gun away, and sat down. Moynihan was forced to sit on the narrow sofa, next to McBride, who shuffled into a corner of the seat, hunched up, frightened and sullen. Goessler studied him intently for a long time, then spread his hands.

'I'm sorry, Thomas – Professor. You should not have to

endure this. Indeed, I am sorry – ' Moynihan shuffled uncomfortably on the sofa. It was evident he hated and feared Goessler, the man's physical presence and voice disturbing him. 'But I'm afraid it was all very necessary. As our friends here have told you – unless they are being even more secretive than usual – they belong to the Provisional IRA, though Miss Drummond is really a very Left-wing Trotsky disciple, mixed in with a little Marcuse and Sartre and PLO and Italian terrorist ideology – ' Claire Drummond's face was white, her nostrils pinched into pinpricks, her mouth a bloodless single line. She was staring at Goessler, who ignored her, her eyes wide. 'A very uncomfortable mixture, and highly volatile.' Goessler smiled. 'Sean is much less complicated – he simply hates the English. Both of them have a burning desire to see the present conference on Nothern Ireland fail disastrously. You know what part the present Secretary of State, the Right Honourable David Guthrie, played in the prevention of the German invasion of Ireland. Our friends want you to tell that, to tell also what you know of the British atrocity that followed, and what you know of the death of a prominent American in the sinking of the special convoy – '

Goessler unrolled the facts of McBride's investigations one by one, ticking them off on the pudgy fingers of his left hand. A ruby ring glowed on the same hand. McBride sat, his mouth hanging stupidly open, sensing a gulf opening up beneath him and his mind spinning. Goessler knew everything, *everything* –

He could not stop the thought repeating and echoing, like something dreamed on the edge of sleep where the mind is uncontrolled and the body twists and turns to rid itself of the persistent, maddening images. Goessler knew *everything* – had always known.

Goessler recognized the process going on in his head, and waited until McBride looked balefully, defeatedly up at him again.

'Thomas,' he said softly, 'of course we've always known. There was no way we could not know. Menschler and people like him gave us everything, and we knew what must have happened to the convoy, and to the invasion, even who was involved. The present director of what they used to call MI5 evolved the plan that Churchill used – ' He smiled. 'You are the *guarantor,* the mask of accident, the façade of honour we sinister and untrustworthy people require. Of course, it would have been better had you gone ahead and published in your own time, but we could not afford to wait that long. You are the most welcome accident of all, being your father's son.'

It was evident that Goessler had another nugget of information that he wished to impart. His face became as impassive as a page of print. He wanted McBride to ask the right question. Claire Drummond frowned, watching McBride's facial reactions carefully. And McBride remembered his father, as if recalling some piece of information that had been of only tangential importance to his investigations.

'What happened to my father?'

Claire Drummond was moved by an obscure guilt, even pity – but at what or for whom she had little idea. 'Don't tell him.'

Goessler looked at her, then ignored her. 'Your father was killed by *her* father because your father discovered he was a traitor.' Claire Drummond winced at the accusation, readopting long-abandoned sensitivities for a moment. 'Oh, it wasn't unusual in Englishmen of his class and upbringing in the thirties. Many of them embraced the illusion of Russia under the benevolent government of Stalin, and others became sycophantic admirers of the Führer's New Order in Germany, the strength through joy which led to the work making free. *Arbeit macht frei.* True, many of them would not have been so fascinated if they had known about Dachau and Auschwitz and the other places, but then so many of your poets would not have loved Stalin if they had known he was liquidating millions more even than Hitler. Beliefs are strange things – it is perhaps better to live without them.' A trace of doubt flitted on Goessler's face for a moment, like a tiny cloud moving across the sun, then he nodded his head. 'Robert Drummond worked for the Germans throughout the war, most especially during November 1940. He killed your father.'

McBride looked at Claire Drummond, who snapped,

'Why did you tell him that? He'll never help us now!' There was something close to fear in her voice.

'Of course he will. It is his only chance of life, is it not, Thomas?' He smiled at McBride. 'Let him think it over for a time. Do not be in too much of a hurry to prompt him, and do not hurt him.' He stood up, hands spread in front of him, shrugging off any harm he might have done. 'That is my advice to you both.' He sounded obscenely fatherly.

Claire Drummond was puzzled. 'Is that it? Is that all you came for?'

'For now – yes. Rudi and I will be staying nearby, of course, and we will call on you again tomorrow.' He smiled expansively. Moynihan writhed visibly on the sofa next to McBride. McBride realized, through a miasma of contradictory emotions, that both the woman and Moynihan were powerless to behave independently of the East German. He controlled them, they were his employees. Even the girl, stronger than her partner, was afraid of Goessler. They'd outrun him in kidnapping McBride, but now they'd stepped back into line.

'Goodnight, Thomas,' Goessler said from the door, even as McBride's skin was still registering the change in temperature from the open door. He did not reply, and Goessler shrugged, then went out.

He had to escape. He knew that there had to be a moment, one chance, to get out and away. Otherwise he would talk, he would be working for Goessler, the man without beliefs. But the thought of escape daunted him, like a mountain he had to climb without oxygen or ropes or boots or courage. He let his head drop forward on his chest as he heard Goessler's car pull away from the cottage. He'd never make it, couldn't do it –

November 1940

The parachute troops pulled out at midday. The weather remained to their advantage, misty and drizzling persistently, the landscape grey and stifled and almost obscured. McBride and Maureen and Gilliatt were not questioned again by the Oberst. He merely dismissed them from his considerations and handed them over to Riordan and two other local IRA men – one of them Gilliatt was certain had been among their original pursuers, a short, red-headed man with a whey-coloured face that looked only half-shaped from its human clay.

Gilliatt dismissed the image of the wasp on the windscreen. It hadn't worked. It was too late for second thoughts, for reconsiderations. The plans were made, orders given, strategy rigidly defined. The parachute troops would hold the beaches for the seaborne landings early the following morning. Gilliatt had been unable to make their grasp on the situation loosen even a fraction.

Riordan seemed to take a pleasure in guarding McBride. He treated him warily, keeping a physical distance between them that admitted the danger McBride might represent, but satisfied with the docility, the unarmed innocuousness that Gilliatt knew McBride was deliberately presenting to his captors. Riordan's desultory, mindless baiting of McBride went unanswered. McBride, to all appearances, was a beaten man.

They were given bread and cheese and beer for lunch, soon after the Germans left. As the afternoon wore on, Maureen seemed least able to accept her captivity. She paced the barn continually with jerky, caged-animal steps, wearing a path in the strewn hay. McBride showed no interest in her, but Gilliatt was concerned. Her behaviour was irritating Riordan and the others, making them more edgy and watchful when they might otherwise have been lulled into carelessness. If McBride tried to escape, then he and Maureen would also have to go. At the moment, they were prisoners of war. He had no desire to become a hostage.

McBride's suspicions of Drummond had become preposterous to Gilliatt. It was far easier to believe in bad luck, in accident, than in Drummond's treachery. But McBride was obsessed, almost doom-laden. He was set apart, not even concerned to involve Gilliatt and Maureen in any plan of escape.

'Sit down, woman!' Riordan snapped out eventually, his rifle moving indecisively but dangerously on his lap. Gilliatt, as if newly aroused, looked at his watch. Four-thirty. It was getting dark outside. 'For God's sake, sit down!'

Maureen appeared stung, slapped across the face by his anger. She stood in front of him, fists clenched, her body visibly quivering with anger and the released strain of her captivity. She simply would not accept, nor exploit her situation. Gilliatt got to his feet – McBride hadn't even looked up at the scene from where he sat, which had to mean he was dangerously near making some move – and moved swiftly to Maureen's side. She shrugged off his hands on her upper arms, but he pulled her back against him in an embrace. Riordan laughed.

'He's very friendly with your wife, McBride!' he roared, highly amused at Gilliatt's overacted concern and Maureen's reluctance to be mollified. 'Just take her away,' Riordan added to Gilliatt. 'She'd wear out the patience of a saint!'

'She doesn't like being held prisoner,' Gilliatt offered affably. 'Come to that, neither do I.' His words had a studied lightness, lack of menace. Riordan smiled confidently, seated on a hay-bale, the woman between him and the man, and her face becoming more docile, bovine as her anger spent itself through her working hands and her clenched jaws. Gilliatt was leaning his head against hers in a parody of comfort.

'You'll just have to accept it, like he –'

His eyes were moving across to McBride, and widening slowly as they did so. His words cut off, and Gilliatt wondered whether McBride had left it too late. He pushed himself and Maureen forward, toppling their combined weight on to Riordan. The rifle was coming to a bead on McBride, then he lost sight of it under Maureen's body. It discharged as he fell on top of her, and she screamed. Gilliatt felt a blank emptiness as he rolled aside, striking out with his fist at Riordan's head, which bobbed into his view. His fist connected with Riordan's temple. Maureen went on screaming and screaming and Gilliatt moved slowly – too slowly it seemed – away from her body, clambering up her frame to fasten his hands on Riordan's rifle as the Irishman disentangled the Remington Mk 1 R from World War I from beneath Maureen and tried to bring it to bear on Gilliatt.

Gilliatt heard one shot, then the click of a bolt – the man

Paddy's Lee Enfield Mk III – then a second shot and a third, punctuated by the noise of the bolt-action. He let Riordan pull the rifle towards him, and then pushed, smashing the stock into his face. Riordan howled, letting go of the rifle. Gilliatt hit him again, and whirled round, fumbling with the bolt.

McBride was standing very still, the Lee Enfield in his hands. Just in front of him, Paddy lay unconscious, while across the barn the whey-faced man with the half-formed features lay on his back, three holes in close grouping in his coat, an old Mauser C96 still in his hand, unfired. Maureen, unwounded but terrified and hysterical, went on screaming. McBride crossed the barn, turned her face to his and slapped her three times across the cheek. She subsided into sobbing which racked her body like unassuageable grief. McBride looked at the unconscious Riordan, then at Gilliatt.

'I think we'd better be leaving, don't you?' he said with a grin. He was as tense as a wound spring, the pleasure of winning and killing running through his frame like electricity.

'My God,' Gilliatt muttered, feeling his legs give way. He sat down untidily alongside Riordan. 'My God, I could have killed her,' he added, looking blankly at Maureen.

'You'll have enough time to make it up to her,' McBride observed. 'When you've dropped me off, you'll take care of her.' It was like an order. Gilliatt looked up at him, bemused.

'What the hell's the matter with you?' he shouted, looking from McBride to Maureen and back again. 'We could have got your wife killed between us. Doesn't that matter to you at all?' McBride appeared unimpressed. 'What the hell's the matter with you?' he asked again, more softly.

McBride shook his head. 'Don't confuse the issue with moral speculations, Peter. I'm going to kill Drummond and you're going to look after Maureen. Those are the assigned roles. You drop me off at Kilbrittain and take her on to Cork.'

'Don't you care about her at all?'

'It isn't relevant at the moment,' McBride said without

emotion. Gilliatt saw him on an outcrop of egocentricity, not even bothering to signal to a vessel that might rescue him. McBride crossed to the body on the floor and removed the Mauser from its grasp. He weighed it in his hand and seemed satisfied with it. 'Killing him with a German gun might be more than appropriate, don't you think?'

Chapter Sixteen

PROCESS OF ELIMINATION

November 1940
McBride pulled Riordan's small Morris over to the side of the road, wrenched on the handbrake, and switched off the engine. To Gilliatt and Maureen, the silence was suddenly ominous and foreboding. McBride had skirted Clonakilty and then taken the road north before doubling back southwards towards Crosswinds Farm and Kilbrittain. They had encountered no German – or Irish – troops in the hour-and-a-half's driving. The night was heavy and wet as a facecloth when McBride wound down the window, but it had stopped raining. The sky showed black and starless through appearing tears in the cloud cover.

Crosswinds Farm was three miles away from them, across the fields that fell away from the hilltop where McBride had chosen to stop, and beyond the scattered few lights of Kilbrittain.

'You can't attempt it,' Gilliatt began, aware of the dangerous, heedless smile on McBride's face. It irritated him, and he changed his tactics. 'You haven't a shred of proof against him, Michael!' McBride's smile faded.

'Is that all you have to say, Peter? Fair play for Drummond? I'd forgotten – you're both in the Navy.'

'So are you – or supposed to be.' McBride shook his head.

'Drummond's broken the contract I had with him. God, you were *there*! What more proof do you need of his collaboration with the Germans?'

'Those weren't Germans. They were your countrymen. Irish.'

'And that's your *English* answer to everything, is it? It's only the bloody stupid Irish – let them get on with it. Is that your solution? Drummond's working for the Germans, damn you!'

Maureen interrupted them. 'Michael, come with us. Whatever the truth of it, you can't do anything by yourself.' McBride seemed abashed without being softened or dissuaded. He shook his head in a minute, determined movement.

'I'm sorry, lovey, it just won't do, you see. Drummond tried to kill me, he's tried to have all of us killed. He's not getting away with that.'

'Stupid heroics – ' she began.

'No. It's much older than heroics. Revenge.'

'For God's sake, don't do it!' she wailed. 'I'm going to have our baby. Do you think I want him to have to listen to tales about the father he never saw?' She clutched his hands convulsively, tears streaming down her face. McBride looked as if he had been cheated, that she had played to other rules than his and beaten him at the game. 'For God's sake think of the child if you won't think of me.'

McBride's face was twisted and shaped by conflicting emotions. Gilliatt found their intensity almost unbearable. Then McBride climbed swiftly out of the car.

'I'll be back,' he said.

'Damn you, Michael McBride, damn you!'

'Maybe – maybe,' he said, then nodded to Gilliatt and strode off into the night, dropping swiftly out of sight down the hillside towards the lights of the hamlet.

'Damn you – damn you!' Maureen kept calling out after him while Gilliatt got out, and went round the Morris to the driver's seat. He slammed the door angrily, started the engine – over-revving, the tyres squealing out of the dirt at the side of the road – then headed north-east again, on the road towards Ballinadee and the main road to Cork. He was angry, his nerves were being shredded by the woman's ceaseless cries, magnified in the tin box of the car, and he wanted nothing more to do with Michael McBride and his wife and the Irish. His simple duty was to reach the authorities in Cork – preferably the British authorities – and tell them what, as far as he knew, was happening. It did not matter what then happened, it did not matter what was or was not being done – that was his job. If only the bloody woman behind him would stop wailing and screaming –

He only realized that he had taken a wrong turning and was on the Kinsale road heading back towards the coast when he saw the signpost in the headlights and, almost at the same moment beyond the crossroads, a barrier of barrels across the road and grey uniforms passing to and fro just at the fringe of the glare of the lights. Then one soldier stepped into the spill of light, machine-pistol at the ready, and began walking towards the car.

'Shut up, damn you!' Gilliatt barked, and the woman subsided sobbing into the back seat. Gilliatt cursed himself, watching the German approaching the car, joined by a second soldier. Both of them were fifteen yards from the Morris. Gilliatt shoved the gear-stick into reverse, revved, and backed away down the road, switching off his headlights as he did so. He could hear the shouting over the noise of the engine, and he swung the car round on the handbrake, accelerating recklessly with the back wheels in soft dirt at the side of the road; the car suddenly jerked free and careered away down the road. 'Keep your head down!' he yelled with a dangerous elation bubbling up in his chest and a lightness, an invincibility enveloping his thoughts.

He ducked, too, and the bullets thudded into the boot of the Morris, shattered the small back window over Maureen's cowering form, and pattered on the road behind them. He kept his foot pressed down, trying to remember the road and how long the straight stretch lasted, bounced the car suddenly off the bank as the road began to descend and switched on the headlights. A bend in the road leapt at him, and he swung the wheel furiously, braking with a squeal of rubber, and went through it, the car immediately slowing on an uphill stretch.

'You all right?' he said hoarsely.

'Yes – yes, I think so,' he heard in a child-like voice from the back seat.

'Thank God for something!' Cork appeared a distant infinitely desirable oasis in the chaos of the night. No more wrong turns, he thought. Straight through, no stops.

*

McBride squeezed through a gap in the hedge, and jumped the ditch. His trouser-legs were sodden with rain from the grass, and his boots were beginning to let in water. Kilbrittain was behind him now, and he could smell the sea in the light breeze that was moving the clouds sluggishly, opening up gaps of starlit darkness. He had avoided two German patrols, each time the effect of night and secrecy and silence leaking more dangerous adrenalin into his system. The old Lee Enfield was cold and potent in his hand and the Mauser a hard-edged shape in his waistband. He was less than half a mile from Crosswinds Farm, approaching it from the north. That last hedge might even have marked the boundary of Drummond's land.

McBride felt unfettered. The cramping, desolating noises of his wife's parting curse, the wild, hampering words she had yelled at him to stop him, had diminished. He had digested them, incorporated them within his single-minded purpose. Nothing was going to prevent him from killing Drummond. Revenge whirled up in him like dry bracken set alight, consuming reason and perspective and the future. His life was a succession of immediate, vivid moments – the setting of one foot in front of another, the recognition of slopes and lines of the land, the smell of the sea, the rifle in his hand, the wetness of his trouser-legs, the images of Drummond sitting in kitchen or study or sitting-room – through which he moved like a shadow, impervious to larger, vaguer experiences or imaginings. He had even lost the capacity to judge what he was doing, to see it in any moral light. His one certainty was that Drummond had tried to kill him, but instead had spilled a corrosive desire for vengeance over brain-cells and bodily organs that made him hunger for destruction.

Drummond would expect him. Drummond was Irish enough to understand what he had started and how McBride would expect to end it. The farm would be under heavy guard. McBride bared his teeth, not with the effort of the slope but with anticipation. When he topped the gentle rise, the framework of hedges was suddenly clear in quick moonlight and in the centre of the maze-like pattern there was the white low farmhouse. And the patrols.

He slid into a hollow, ignoring the wet grass soaking his buttocks and back, and watched. Before the moon disappeared behind more distressed cloud, he counted six guards, all Germans in uniform – in three pairs, moving like figures from some ornamental clock, round and round the garden and the vegetable plot and the drive that surrounded the house. They were contained, it seemed, by the pattern of hedges and small trees, as if they required the protection of the lights from the farmhouse and the proximity of its walls. They were small, ineffectual creatures, hardly any protection at all for Drummond. He slipped out of the hollow after checking the progress of the cloud across the moon's face, and made his way carefully down the slope to the shelter of another hedge. The nearest patrol was a hundred yards away, moving across his line of sight, skirting the fruit trees at the bottom of the garden. He clicked the bolt of the Lee Enfield as gently, lovingly as he could. It made the smallest noise, but he held his breath. He could hear, on the breeze, the quiet conversation of the patrol, one of them clearing his throat, spitting.

He watched them, surrendering to the omnipotence of the moment, looking up at the moon, tensing as the edge of its disc slid from behind the cloud, then lining up the rifle sight. The backsight needed some fine adjustment, and he attended to it like a conscientious workman. Then he aligned the foresight with the two shapes a hundred yards away. He selected one of them who moved for a moment slightly away from his companion, inhaled, then squeezed the trigger with the gentlest touch. He heard the noise of the rifle in his ear, saw the German topple slowly over, and then the components of the scene moved feverishly as he snicked back the bolt, resighted and fired again as a light in the farmhouse went out and the second German, startled but already moving, was flung forward on to his face. Two huddled, moonlit shadows like sleeping animals beneath the fruit trees.

McBride got to his feet and began running along the hedge, following it as it angled towards the farmhouse. He could hear doors opening and banging shut, and the shouting of orders in German. He drew the Mauser from his waistband without pausing in his stride.

Walsingham himself decided to enter the country house that had been converted into a hotel on the outskirts of Cheltenham, after they traced Goessler's hire car to the hotel's residents' car park and checked the register. The receptionist was helpful but bemused. Two German businessmen, yes – Herr Muller and Herr Schmitt, was there anything the matter?

Exton showed her only the CID card he carried, and then asked to speak to the manager. Only the manager's wife was available, and Exton explained simply that the two men were suspected of currency illegalities and that he would cause as little disturbance as possible and he was sorry but it couldn't be postponed and he'd be grateful if the matter could be concluded immediately.

While he talked at the desk, Walsingham stood where he could see into the lounge bar without himself being seen. He located Goessler and Lobke, enjoying their after-dinner coffee and brandies, and the moment welled in him like a hot, indigestible lump. He had found them, had them in his hand, and they were unware of his presence. His plan for the two Germans stretched before him as easily and entirely as *Emerald* had come into his head, the absence of moral or human qualifications suggesting a brilliant, logical inevitability about its components. Those cold moments of clarity were Charles Walsingham's most gratifying and fulfilling experiences. He was, while they still occurred, not an old man on the verge of retirement, of being forced to relinquish his accustomed grip on clandestine power. Goessler laughed at something the more saturnine Lobke said, and Walsingham smiled in concert with him.

Exton came over to him.

'Everything satisfactory, Exton?'

'Sir. They don't like it, but they won't argue – as long as we do it discreetly, sir.' Exton smiled thinly.

'With panache and taste always, Exton. Let's go and ask Herr Goessler to accompany us.'

Walsingham crossed the half-empty lounge bar swiftly, with a youthful step. As Goessler looked up at him, there was a recognition in his eyes that was not of an individual but a type. A kindred spirit. Lobke, startled and panicked, reached inside his coat but Goessler arrested the movement with his own hand. The barman watched as he dried a pint glass, and one or two of the customers looked up, then down again as Walsingham greeted Goessler familiarly.

'Klaus, my dear fellow, how good to see you again!' He held out his hand, and Goessler took it in his own dry grip. Walsingham admitted the man's coolness, the sense of amusement that lingered in his eyes. Lobke's eyes were already darting towards doors, other people, windows.

'My assistant, Rudi Lobke,' Goessler said disarmingly.

'And mine – ah, *James* Exton.' Goessler seemed greatly amused at the hesitation while Walsingham recollected Exton's name.

'Will you sit down, gentlemen – Charles.' Walsingham was slightly taken aback, then nodded acknowledgement.

'Of course.' Walsingham's secret amusement at Goessler's behaviour increased as he saw the fat man relax, already make assumptions of diplomatic immunity, envisaging only deportation as a final solution, the ultimate weapon possessed by Walsingham. How wrong he was – 'No, I think we'd all better get off straight away, don't you?'

Goessler shrugged. 'As you wish – our luggage?'

'It will be taken care of.'

'Good. Is it a long drive?'

'No. You'll not get cold. Shall we go?'

He gestured towards the door. Lobke appeared danger-ously nervous, and Goessler touched his hand with a feminine reassurance that made Walsingham embarrassed.

'It's all right, Rudi – don't be foolish, *liebchen*.' He took Lobke by the elbow and guided him, Exton alongside them, to the door of the lounge bar. Walsingham followed, satisfied with the smoothness of events, the professionalism that Goessler had displayed, was relying on, and about which he was totally mistaken.

Outside, the night was fine and chilly, high stars pale above the halo of light from the hotel's floodlighting. Hard white light that seemed to distress Lobke. Perhaps he was picking up some kind of emitted signal from Exton or himself, Walsingham wondered, and waited until Goessler registered the absence of police cars. Just the one Granada, parked by their own Ford, with two men leaning against it but coming to alertness as they saw the party emerge from the hotel. Goessler turned to Walsingham.

'A quiet and exclusive party, yes?'

'Indeed, Herr Goessler. This way, please.' He directed them to the car, and Exton, removing Lobke's gun from his shoulder-harness, pushed the young man into the back seat. The driver and his companion waited for Walsingham's orders. 'Driver, you take us – and you, Peters, bring up the Ford. Keys, Professor?'

Goessler seemed to be reassured by another close appraisal of Walsingham's face, and handed over the keys to Walsingham, who tossed them almost carelessly to Peters, then gestured to the open rear door of the Granada. Goessler shrugged and got in. Exton squeezed in beside the two Germans. Walsingham sat next to the driver, nodded, and the Granada pulled away from the harsh floodlighting out of the car park on to the A40 towards Andoversford. For a moment, Goessler experienced the acute fear that they had already located Moynihan, the woman and their prisoner, but he had to close his face against the expression of relief when Walsingham said:

'Now, Professor, where are you keeping young McBride and his IRA friends?' Walsingham half-turned in his seat. The old man's profile was aquiline beyond the mere suggestion of a garden bird. This one preyed on meat. Lobke's leg, pressed against his on the bench seat, was throbbing with nerves, and Goessler patted the young man's thigh in warning and comfort.

'I'm sorry, Herr Walsingham – these people – *McBride?* – strangers, I'm afraid.'

'You don't deny you are a senior officer in the East German intelligence service, I hope?'

Exton, as if on cue, drew the Heckler & Koch VP-70 Parabellum from inside his coat, and laid it in a parody of innocence across his lap. Lobke was supremely aware that the gun contained eighteen cartridges in its magazine. Goessler smiled without apparent effort. Walsingham's eyes watched the lights of the Ford Escort behind them, then focused on Goessler again.

'I am covered, of course, by diplomatic immunity.'

'Naturally – under circumstances. But, it is of the utmost importance – as you well understand – that I locate Professor Thomas McBride and anyone else who may have shared his information. You understand the – *urgency* of the matter, I'm sure. Therefore, I'm sure you will understand that the ordinary rules do not apply.' Walsingham shrugged, declaring innocence and necessity and threat at the same moment. Goessler controlled the fading of the smile from his face, in the oncoming headlights of a car. Dark woods rushed by the Granada, and the half-caught gleam of a thin ribbon of reservoir water. Goessler knew they were still heading towards Andoversford.

'I'm sure I don't understand you, Herr Walsingham.'

'You will. Where are they, Goessler – or perhaps little Rudi would like to tell us?' He reached back and lifted Lobke's face by the chin. 'Well, young man?' Exton dug the pistol into Lobke's side, making him gasp with pain. Lobke shook his head. 'I see.'

'This is foolish,' Goessler said.

'Turn here,' Walsingham snapped, and the driver slowed, came level with an unmarked track, and turned into its darkness. The lights of the Escort jiggled behind them as it, too, turned off the main road. The water of the reservoir gleamed through the trees to their left. Goessler felt chilly, aware of his thin woollen suit, the silk shirt, his underwear, and the fragility and slowness of the old body beneath the clothes. The big Ford bumped and wallowed along the rutted track, puddles hissing against the underside, thin branches slashing at the windows. It unnerved Goessler, though a fatness of mind remained complacent despite the reactions of his body. 'Pull over here.'

The Granada slid between trees, down towards the gleam of the reservoir. Then it stopped well within the trees of Dowdeswell Wood, the place Walsingham had selected. He already knew that they would not volunteer the information he required. Gloucestershire Constabulary were poised to begin a search of the area at dawn, under the direction of the Assistant Chief Constable who would liaise directly with Walsingham. Army units from Cirencester were also on stand-by. It would simply be much easier if

Goessler would tell them. Walsingham was certain he knew.

'Very well, Goessler,' he said in the silence after the engine was switched off. 'I wish to know where we can find McBride, Claire Drummond, and anyone else who may be connected with this little operation of yours. I do not have a great deal of time, as you know only too well, and therefore I am impatient. Do you intend to tell me?'

'I'm sorry, Herr Walsingham. I must ask to be allowed to contact my embassy – '

'Forget the diplomatic niceties, you bloody fool!' Walsingham barked, making the driver next to him twitch with shock. 'You're going to die out here, in these woods, if you don't tell me. Understand? You are expendable – at least to me.'

Goessler, visibly disconcerted, managed to say: 'Then, as they say, you will never find out what you wish to know.'

'Take him!' Walsingham snapped, accelerating the scene through its emotional progression, creating vivid shock on Lobke's face, nervousness around Goessler's eyes. Exton dragged Lobke out of the car, across the moonlit clearing to where the Escort remained in deep shadow. Its driver, Peters, flicked on a torch. Lobke's face was white and strained.

'What – ?' Goessler began, then closed his mouth round an unpalatable reality.

'You know what comes next.' Walsingham wound down the window and rested his arm on the sill. The driver now covered Goessler with a gun, a Walther. 'I shall kill your sweetheart unless you tell me what I wish to know.'

'You *can't* kill us!'

'Oh, but I can. Indeed, one scenario would suggest I must – and blame McBride. A trade-off, his freedom for his silence. Mm?' Walsingham, in the emotional turbulence, wondered whether he had not miscalculated in revealing the scenario he intended to use, just as a threat. If Goessler *really* believed, then he might not open his mouth anyway – He added: 'Of course, he could just be blamed for Hoskins's murder. We could manage that. Now, tell me.'

'No. No, I'm afraid you are bluffing.' Goessler's throat was small and tight, but the words emerged calmly.

'Be afraid.' He raised his voice. 'Very well, Exton.'

Exton opened the door of the Escort, and pushed Lobke into the back of the car. Then he began screwing a silencer into place on the VP-70, his hands allowing both Lobke and Goessler to see what he was doing. Goessler opened his mouth to protest, then clamped his lips tight. Both men heard Lobke's gasp of fear across the tiny clearing. Goessler exhaled raggedly. Walsingham ignored Goessler, staring at the Escort with a riveted, blank-faced attention. Exton had completed fitting the silencer. He raised the gun, pointing it through the open door of the Escort. He waited.

'Well?' Walsingham asked.

For seconds, Goessler remained silent, then said simply: 'No.'

'Kill him!' Walsingham snapped, and Exton fired twice into the back of the Escort. Lobke's body twitched like a wired rabbit, his white blob of a face visible for a moment as meaningless as a rabbit's scut caught in a car's headlights, before the corpse slid down out of sight. Exton slammed the door of the Escort with suitable finality. Goessler uttered one dry, racking sob before he spoke.

'Now, Herr Walsingham, we know how far you will go to protect yourself, the author of *Emerald*.' His voice quavered with emotion, with grief and fear and defiance. Even as he listened, Walsingham, unable to interrupt, knew that Goessler would not tell him where they were hiding McBride. He had miscalculated. Goessler might not even want to live – the trouble with queers was one always underestimated their emotional involvement, saw luridly in imagination only the handclasps, the kisses, the sodomy – or he might know the only chance for his operation was to keep his secret. Perhaps he knew his own death was now inevitable. Whatever –

'Yes, Herr Walsingham. You will be ruined by the disclosures that Professor McBride will make, and so will David Guthrie. It was a very clever and subtle scheme, as I'm sure you appreciate. I shall not tell you where they are, because it would not save my life. Besides, I cannot allow the English all the heroics. You must do as you intend, and shoot me. Unless you can find McBride, you will have no trade, as you put it. Once McBride talks, no one will believe he is also a murderer.'

'Get him out of the car!' Walsingham snapped, facing the windscreen, angry and humiliated by a fat German. The driver got out, dragged Goessler out of the back of the Granada. 'Wait!' He looked up at Goessler, composed even though he was shivering with cold. With thicker underwear, Walsingham thought, he could die a brave man – and that's what it all amounted to, heroic death. Keeping the chill off with warm underwear. Michael McBride had died bravely, no doubt, so had all the Germans and all the Irish who had died. Even Lobke hadn't cried out much – now Goessler. 'Well?' he said. Goessler did not even deign to answer his question. 'Kill him!'

Walsingham shuddered at the two soft plops of the silenced shots after the crackling footsteps across the clearing and the moment of silence. The door of the Escort slammed shut again. Walsingham rubbed his face with quivering hands. He felt oppressed and driven. He loathed what he was doing, and in the same moment knew that the self-loathing would pass swiftly.

Even before Exton returned to the Granada, he was studying a map of the area on which were already marked the dispositions for the police search the following morning. McBride would not get away. And now he had his trade-off – two dead queers in their last embrace in the rear of a Ford Escort. He forced himself to shrug in amusement at the image, thereby cleansing it of all personal effect.

The woman had gone into Andoversford for food. Moynihan, red-eyed from the bravado of a sleepless night guarding him, was hungry and wanted breakfast. Claire Drummond had acquiesced reluctantly, sensing something uncalculating, vindictive about the Irishman. McBride, who was cramped and aching from sleeping on the sofa, felt dirty and helpless and angry. His sleep had been ragged and broken by dreams of his own danger and by the repetitive, insistent, humiliating impression of himself as a dupe, someone led by the nose by people cleverer than himself to this cottage and this captivity. On waking, his diminished self persisted, and he felt, too, the helplessness which would force him to fall in with Claire Drummond and Moynihan. How could he not do as they wanted?

Moynihan grudgingly filled him a glass of water, tipped it against his mouth, waited while he gulped it down. The tepid, night-tasting liquid made his empty stomach rumble audibly. Moynihan sat opposite him, slumped in his chair. He looked tired and careless, yet also the animosity he felt towards McBride emanated from him like electricity, gleamed in his red-rimmed eyes. McBride was afraid of him. He believed the hatred was sexually inspired – Claire Drummond, who Moynihan could never possess, who had slept with McBride. He wondered whether Moynihan's political fanaticism was stronger than his jealousy, his gnawing sense of humiliation which he evidently blamed on McBride.

Moynihan stood up, and walked over to McBride, who flinched as the Irishman loomed over him. The gun was very evident, lightly held but dangling meaningfully towards McBride's lap. McBride was afraid, anxious for the return of the woman.

'Was she good in bed, Yank?' Moynihan asked after a long time, as if he had reviewed the whole of his past relationship with Claire Drummond in the extended, creeping silence. The clock on the mantelpiece, rewound the previous night, ticked with a solemn hysteria.

'What can I say that's safe?' McBride heard himself saying as if the words and the casual tone belonged to someone else; a more considerable man than himself, or a figure from melodrama. 'Either way you're going to hit me. If I say no, your ego will be insulted, and if I say yes, she was fine and she climbed all over me and don't you miss it nights, you're going to – ' Moynihan hit him at that point, not with the temporarily forgotten gun but with his fist, as if he did not wish to take too much advantage, hurt too much, appear to need the gun to inflict himself on the American. Blood seeped from the corner of McBride's mouth, exciting Moynihan. His hand twitched at his side, where he hid it like something he did not wish to be accused of owning. But this was him, the Yank, the bastard who'd –

'Was she good?' he ground out.

'Yes, dammit! Why in hell's name do you want to know? What good can it do you?' McBride struggled to sit upright again, elbowing himself up, his bound hands tingling with cramp. He sensed he was on a path he had not consciously chosen, but which he had known was there for him to take. He hadn't meant to anger Moynihan, but he had done it deliberately, all the same. Suddenly, he knew that he didn't want Claire Drummond to come back yet. Not until –

'You bastard,' Moynihan breathed, leaning closer so that McBride could faintly smell his unwashed mouth and the staleness of last night's supper and his fitful sleeping. And his unwashed body exuded a discernible odour. 'You bastard.'

'Come on, Moynihan, you're just angry because your piece of tail went to someone else's bed. You're not interested in a scientific account or a consumer's report. You want to know – yeah, I screwed the ass off your woman!'

He steadied himself for the blow. Moynihan raised the gun, but then again used his clenched fist into the side of McBride's face.

'Shut up!'

McBride spat out the mouthful of blood. 'You *want* to know, dammit! You asked me, and brother, are you going to get answered!'

'Shut up, keep your filthy mouth shut!'

'What is it with you guys? You can blow people to pieces but you can't deal with your own balls? You hide in corners watching your women like you watch your bombs go off! You're a prick, Moynihan, a gutless woman-loser – Paddy Pumpkin-Eater, had a wife and couldn't keep her!' Moynihan was standing a yard or so away from the sofa with its brick-coloured stretch covers and the furious, hunched body of McBride occupying its centre. He made to move towards the American, then held off as if he wanted to go on listening while the voice lashed him. His face coloured like a lying child's. 'Jesus Christ!' McBride breathed, baring his teeth as if to attack Moynihan like a wolf. 'The big tough terrorist wants to *marry* her. Man, blow society to the moon, kill, maim, burn, explode to get what you want – but make sure you marry the girl before you sleep with her, Sean!' McBride was dangerously elated, long having abandoned caution or calculation. He could not control the urgent press of words, finding his tongue amenable, just able to cope. His stupidity, his captivity and exploitation had been going on too long.

'Shut up, shut up!' Moynihan pressed his gun against McBride's groin, just as the woman had done the previous night. 'I could blow it off for you, McBride. Then try laughing with your balls on the floor.' Moynihan's face was cold with a sheen of sweat and self-digust. McBride had shown him an image of himself the truth of which he felt compelled to acknowledge. McBride, their eyes only a foot or so apart, was afraid. The pain in his groin was minimal, to be disregarded – because now he knew why he had arranged this quarrel; it had produced this open, frontal proximity.

'You haven't got the balls to do it. She might be angry – ' Moynihan jabbed downwards, and McBride winced and cried out – and grabbed the gun with both hands, jerking upwards and to the side at once, so that the round in the chamber discharged into the ceiling. McBride felt sound go far away, and his own breath was the only noise he understood. Moynihan was yelling, or just breathing, as McBride jerked him by his gun hand to one side, toppling his weight over the arm of the sofa, rolling after him, landing on top of him, knee out into Moynihan's groin.

The desperation that would pump the adrenalin was beginning to come into Moynihan's face, but it was too late. McBride was ahead in that play, felt the hope of escape surge through him. He dropped his head, striking Moynihan across the bridge of the nose with his forehead, then lifted his head as the blood gushed and struck Moynihan's hand against the floor time after time, beating his head into the Irishman's face once more. Moynihan groaned and released the gun. McBride stood up, and his legs felt insecure and newborn under him, the frame top-heavy and overbalanced. He rocked to and fro, holding Moynihan's gun in his two bound hands. It was a big Smith & Wesson from TV police serials, awkward and heavy in his grip. Moynihan lay with his eyes closed, groaning, holding his nose and mouth in cupped hands as if drinking cool water. McBride struck him across the temple with the barrel of the revolver, and he lay still.

The room reasserted itself, returning with the sense of birdsung silence from outside the windows. No sound of a car, the woman not yet returning. He was indecisive now, the body running down like a broken spring without the injections of anger and desperation. He began quivering with shock and the realization of inflicted violence.

He went into the kitchen, scrabbled in a drawer under the enamel sink for a knife, came out with a carving knife which he tried to jam unsuccessfully into the drawer, then the door-jamb, finally squatting on the floor with the knife pressed between his thighs while he stroked the strips of cloth over the blade. They parted singly, and slowly, and he cut himself on his wrists and clenched, eager fists a number of times before he could pull the last of the cloth apart and begin to rub the bleeding wrists. Then he stood up, but cramp assailed him, making him hobble to the rear door of the cottage.

He listened. No car-noise. He paused on the edge of the fine morning, framed in the doorway, coatless and chill with the breeze already, the blue sky interrupted by some rolling white cloud with smudged grey lower edges. He studied the landscape. A farm, and village, the rulered line of the main road half a mile away, and clumps of woodland stretching across the folded, flowing countryside.

He begun running, recklessly, as fast as he could, almost overbalancing in his rapid movement down the slope. The wind yelled in his ear and his boood pounded. He was free now.

He did not hear the siren of a police-car, growing louder behind him.

Claire Drummond was anxious to get back to the cottage. The danger inherent in her appearance in Andoversford was more apparent to her because she was the one who had squeezed the trigger of the little Astra twice into the face of the pig in the multi-storey car park. Moynihan's breakfast –

Still, she had to molify Sean Moynihan somehow, at

some little cost. He hated McBride too much, and so obviously and for such a pathetic motive that he was dangerous unless she suggested – even though she hated that much compromise – that he was back in favour, that McBride had been a necessary stratagem and nothing more.

She picked up bacon, eggs, lard, two cartons of UHT milk, some more coffee – they were running low – and a bag of sugar, had to buy a plastic carrier-bag which advertised English apples, and came out of the shop regretting she had left her sunglasses in the car, shading her eyes against the bright morning sun – which gleamed off the chrome and blue-white paintwork of the police car across the main street of the village, parked outside the black-and-white pub. And a white Jaguar with the vivid orange flash of a motorway patrol stood behind the Panda car. Claire Drummond clutched her throat, stood very still, and studied the village street.

Just the four policemen from the two cars, studying a map across the bonnet of the smaller police car, two of them smoking. One of them pointed up the street out of the village, towards Cheltenham. She began walking, not too quickly, *slow down*, along the opposite pavement towards the car park at the back of the main street. She did not hurry – slow down, slow down – but something about her manner or appearance or the way she could not help hunching against recognition might have betrayed her –

But she turned the corner out of sight of the police without a restraining cry, or following heavy footsteps. She got into the car, shaking from head to foot, and fumbled the key into the ignition. She drove jerkily to the barrier, as if the choke did not function, and reached out to insert the coin, stretching her arm and cursing because she had parked badly, then dropping the tenpenny piece. She made to get out of the car, and it stalled – she'd left it in gear – picked up the coin, fed it into the coin-slot, and the barrier swung up.

She took three attempts to restart the engine, jerked the gear-stick into first, let out the clutch and jerked forward under the raised barrier. Perspiration dampened her upper lip and her hands on the wheel and made her blouse sticky inside her sweater. She pulled forward to the junction of the alley with the main street. The police car – the motorway patrol – passed her as she waited to pull out, and the policeman in the passenger seat stared at her. Her face felt naked and gleaming in the bright sunlight coming through the windscreen. His eyes transferred to the number plate of the car and then he was out of sight until she turned out into the main street. She watched her rear-view mirror as she drove out of Andoversford.

No police car followed her as she turned off the A436 up the narrow side-road to the cottage.

Walsingham listened to the radio traffic at the other end of the mobile HQ the Gloucestershire Constabulary had set up in the middle of the village of Shipton, less than two miles from the cottage which contained the people he sought. The report of a car driven by a woman who answered Claire Drummond's description had been passed immediately, on Walsingham's intervention, to the spotter helicopter diverted from motorway traffic checks on the M4. The helicopter had not, as yet, picked up the Austin Princess on any of the main roads around Andoversford, and Walsingham waited with an edginess he could not quite despise. They had narrowed the area just by sighting the car – he had no doubt it was Drummond's daughter, so obsessively single-minded had he become in the sleepless hours after the killings – and it would only be minutes before the car was spotted. Nevertheless, he shifted on his chair, and listened intently to the radio traffic. The ACC for Gloucestershire was in one of the other two caravans, checking the co-ordination of search reports inside his designated circle ten miles in diameter. Walsingham knew they would have to request army help by the afternoon, unless –

'Eagle to Mother.'

'Go ahead, Eagle.'

Walsingham savoured the code names like distinct tastes on his tongue – *Eagle* sharp, acid, *Mother* sweet with anticipation.

'Green Princess spotted turning off A436, two miles north-east of Andoversford.'

'Tell them to keep well away!' Walsingham shouted down the length of the caravan, already hot inside from the Indian-summer sun beating down on it. The police radio operator was startled, and looked up at a chief inspector in uniform who nodded without expression on his face.

'Do not close, Eagle – '

'What do you think we are? We're well back. There's a cottage up ahead of the car – '

'Where is that?' Walsingham asked, joining the chief inspector at a map pinned to board along one wall of the caravan. The police officer pointed out Andoversford, then traced the red line of the A436, then the narrow yellow thread of the track. He ran one finger-nail up the map, and tapped it.

'About there, sir.'

'The car's definitely stopping, turning into the gate of the cottage – *shit*! – we've banked away sharply, and we're out of sight. Orders, Mother?'

'Tell them to circle the cottage, but to keep as much out of sight as possible,' Walsingham instructed and while his orders were being relayed, he said to the inspector, 'Let's get men up there at once, Inspector. Guns, and tear gas.'

'Sir.'

She found Moynihan bathing his head and face with cold water, and knew at once what had happened. She could almost hear McBride needling him, bringing him closer –

'You bloody fool, where is he?'

'He's gone – Claire, I'm sorry, he – '

'You idiot! You absolute *turd*! *He* was all we had. How can we *do* anything now?' She realized she was shaking him, his hangdog face like a backward child's puzzled and hurt and about to cry. She despised him, and sensed his dependence at the same time. She turned away from him, wanting to scream, to rage. 'We've lost everything – it's all been for *nothing*!'

'Please, Claire – '

'For God's sake what's-the-matter-with-you?' She turned on him, and in the silence as she took in his hurt, beaten face almost unable to register emotional pain, so puffed and misshapen was it, she heard the first distant police siren. He seemed not to hear it, only respond blinkingly to the chalky pallor of her features, wonder at the hand that dabbed round her mouth like a bird seeking a nest. 'No – ' she murmured at last, running for the door. The siren was loud now, and there was another, more distant one accompanying it, coming from the A436. She opened the door, and saw a police Rover pulling into and across the gate. The driver and the two other policemen all descended on the far side of the car, and she could see the rifles.

She ducked back inside, slamming the door behind her, rolling her body to the shelter of the wall. Moynihan was standing in the kitchen doorway, staring at her, wet hair lank on his forehead, ridiculous broken nose and puffed lips still trying to form adequate expressions. She waited for him to blame her as the second siren wound down the scale and a third member of the sudden chorus wailed more distantly. Then he shrugged, almost pleased that they were trapped there together.

He crossed to the window, something momentous having been decided between them, and peered round the faded curtain. Two cars, one across the gateway and the other a little down the track, its nose poking up over the rise like a scouting animal's – then the police Range Rover disgorging four men who cut through the nearest trees towards the rear of the cottage. Mere details. He looked at Claire, and nodded in expectation. She had moved to the side window of the sitting-room, where she could see the old man in the heavy, burdening fawn topcoat and trilby hat. She sensed his importance, perhaps even his implacability. She returned Moynihan's nod.

Moynihan smiled, then knocked out a pane of the window, and fired immediately through the hole, two shots. Claire saw a head duck back down, the party by the Range Rover scatter, then the rifles returned fire, the heavy bullets shattering the windows, plucking plaster in shards and lumps from the far wall of the room. One whined up the chimney, after ricocheting. No warning, no call to surrender through a loudspeaker, no dispositions for a siege. Claire knew they were not intended to survive. She looked at Moynihan, who loosed off three more shots from the Browning he'd hidden in the cottage weeks before. He yelled with pleasure – she saw a police marksman holding a reddening limp arm behind the Rover. She fired through her own glassless window, bullets skittering from the Astra off the bonnet and bodywork of the Range Rover, starring the windscreen.

Another volley of shots rattled in the room, making their bodies shudder with anticipation.

'I'll watch the back!' Moynihan called, and moved on all fours out of the sitting-room. She watched him go almost with affection. She heard the kitchen window knocked out, but the fusillade of rifle shots preceded, drowned, cancelled any fire from his pistol. In the silence, she waited fearfully – then she heard one shot from the pistol, and relaxed.

The gas-shells pitched and rolled on the floor near her feet at the same moment that Moynihan stumbled through the doorway to the kitchen, blood smeared across his chest. One of the gas-shells rolled to his feet and he stared at it without recognition while the acrid tear-gas enveloped him. His single cough racked him, then he slid down the door frame into an untidy heap, sitting with his legs splayed out like a bonfire Guy. The CS gas masked his frozen, distorted features.

She began to cough. The man outside still would not speak to her. Either they already had McBride, or they assumed he was safe upstairs in the cottage. Or they wanted him dead, too. Her eyes streamed with tears and she dragged air into her lungs, head lifted to the ceiling. She couldn't see to fire through the window, and felt her way along the wall to the door. She should not open the door, but she obeyed the imperative of her lungs and eyes. She plunged through the opening, feeling the air she drew in snatched away by the impact of the first and second bullets. She had no physical sense of falling –

Walsingham's throat was tickled and his tear-ducts irritated as he walked swiftly to the body of Claire Drummond and turned it over with his foot. He thought the woman attractive, but her still-open eyes were bolting in death, suggesting the fanaticism of life. He placed his handkerchief over his mouth and nose and entered the cottage. He virtually ignored Moynihan's body, and climbed the creaking stairs.

'McBride,' he called. 'McBride, are you here?'

It took him only seconds to check the two upstairs rooms and the bathroom. McBride was not in the cottage. He opened the bathroom window, not to call down to the police but to draw in clean air. He felt weakened and nauseous, a condition he could not ascribe to the tear-gas. McBride had either been taken elsewhere, which was unlikely, or had escaped while the woman was in Andoversford. The man's face downstairs looked beaten about –

Closer, he comforted himself, closer. Just one voice left. Very well – he was still thankful the man had opened fire so conveniently – he would frighten McBride into a parley, into his trade-off. He could already see the item in the afternoon newspapers, and the nationals the following day.

Police seek American professor after double murder in Cotswolds – and then McBride's name. He'd try to trade, he'd come in. He'd have to.

Nevertheless, he felt grateful for the sweet mid-morning air as the last of the CS gas dispersed.

November 1940

Churchill stood before the mirror of the washroom, staring at his puffy, tired face, seeing his own question answered in the blue eyes. The convoy was perhaps less than an hour from the minefield, and he would allow it to sail on to its certain destruction.

He picked up the towel, and wiped his wet face. His features appeared round the edges of the towel as he dried himself, as if furtively seeking some mark that would indicate his guilt, reveal his decision to the mirror, to the world. No, he could manage to hide it.

Necessity is the mother of atrocity, he told himself with grim amusement. Grady would be lost, Roosevelt told that U-boats had sunk the convoy, and the Germans would sail into the minefield.

Churchill wished, almost futilely, that Japan would declare war on America and drag Roosevelt and his reluctant Congress into the war. The defeat of this minor

German invasion plan was only a respite. Next summer they would attempt *Sea Lion* again unless the Russians opened up another front in the east, or Hitler tired of Stalin as an ally and turned on him.

Had to be – had to be done. He finished wiping his face, and put down the towel. He nodded in confirmation to his reflection. He had made his decision. Grady had to die. He was as much an enemy as the Germans they were trying to keep out of Ireland.

He put on his waistcoat and jacket and went back into the operations room beneath the Admiralty. He looked back fleetingly from the doorway at the darkened washroom, as if he had left something behind him or his reflection still gazed out at him in accusation. Then he shut the door firmly.

Chapter Seventeen

TRADE-OFF

November 1940

McBride wriggled through the hedge to the west of the farmhouse, his jersey caught on sharp bare twigs, his hands and knees scraped on the stony earth as he forced his way underneath and through. He pushed the rifle ahead of him, clambered out after it and picked it up, fastidiously dusting its length with his hand as he began running again. The startled and confused Germans were pouring shots towards the point from where his fire had come while he was fifty yards closer to the house and approaching from another, unexpected direction. He skirted the fruit trees which now masked him from his opponents. He paused, knelt down and looked under the low branches of the trees. German soldiers, some without helmets or with uniform blouses and coats undone, were moving towards the hedge which had not returned their concentrated fire. The house was less than fifty yards away, but across a long open lawn which sloped only gently and provided no cover. There was an ornamental pool and a sundial.

He could hardly control his eagerness, the flood of

energy that the joining of battle had released; his energies seemed uncontrolled and illogical. He got up into a crouch and moved towards the last of the small trees. His foot crunched wetly on a fallen apple left to rot. He paused, waiting for breath to settle, lungs to expand to meet the effort required, body to judge its own moment. Still nerves jittered in his hands and arms, and impatience crowded him, obscured judgement. Already, his eagerness protested, they would have discovered he had moved on, already it was becoming too late –

He began running, even as he saw a dark shape emerge from the side of the house and another from the fruit trees to his left, twenty yards away. He swerved sideways, barely halting, and fired the Lee Enfield twice from the hip. The figure ducked back into the trees, and McBride did not know whether or not he had been hit. The figure by the white wall of the farmhouse – moonlight leapt betrayingly across the lawn like a finger pointing out McBride and his opponent – was kneeling, taking aim. McBride rolled to one side, coming up on to his belly and elbows and squeezing off three shots simply to distract. He heard each one pluck against the wall, and then the shouts behind him, the pack with a fresh scent.

He drew the Mauser, aimed rapidly, and squeezed off two shots. The heavy old gun jumped in his hand so that he had to compensate by aiming low before firing twice more. Then he rolled again, feeling pinned to card by the moonlight whitening the lawn. The marksman by the wall was an unmoving bundle but there were others now, hardly visible against the fretwork of the fruit trees, and awareness of them dragged at him like clinging mud until he sat up on the lawn, on the edge of the pool where lily leaves still floated but the plants had turned to dry sedge and there was wire to keep herons from the fish. The shadow of the sundial sliced across the lawn amputated one of his legs. He fired twice, swung the Mauser, held stiffly in both hands, and fired three more shots. He rolled over and got to his feet, running in a crouch until he was a fly against the white wall attracting their fire then a shadow then simply darkness as he slipped round the side of the house, out of the moonlight.

He leaned against the door for a moment, clutching his shoulder as the awareness of pain pushed through his quivering excitement, his elation, and his hand came away wet, very wet. He turned the door handle, sorry, so sorry for the mistake, for the sudden twitching aside of the cloud curtain and sorry for Maureen and the baby – and alive enough to finish Drummond.

There was a shadow in the hall, against the panelling, but the moon was gone again and he could not make it out. Then, 'Michael?' and he fired into the centre of the shadow and it fell away to one side. Then the light came on and he saw the grey uniform and heard the voice again, this time behind him, and even as he turned to the sound of his name he felt the bullets enter, their force knocking him sideways, sending his feet from under him as a rug moved. He fell over, tried to raise the Mauser at Drummond who was at the foot of the stairs, but the effort was far beyond his draining strength. Drummond looked sorry, but it was almost too late to distinguish expressions. He just heard the door bang open and the first pair of jackboots before the light faded and he rested his head lightly on the wooden floor and closed his eyes.

Drummond came and knelt by his body for a moment, feeling for the absent pulse. A German officer began to apologize, but Drummond dismissed him curtly. He was safe now, but it was too early to take comfort from the thought. McBride's dead face looked up, youthful and innocent. He looked no more than lightly asleep. Drummond was sorry – almost – that he had come back, though he had always known he would.

October 1980
'David, you simply can't do it! We are so close now. I assure you it's a matter of hours, not days.' Walsingham stared out of the window of the Cheltenham hotel he had booked into, down the length of the Promenade, wide pavements full of shoppers, the sun filtering down, barred and sliced, through the trees. Guthrie's telephone call, diverted to him by the police switchboard, came as a naked, open shock, encompassed him in a momentary futility until the ego narrowed perspective to the purely personal.

'I'm sorry, Charles. It will come out anyway, I'm certain of that. The conference can be less harmed by my resignation on the grounds of illness or overwork than it would be if I tried to carry on, and got found out. I'd not be forgiven, by *anyone*, for that.' He tried to chuckle confidently. His whole vocal presentation was a charade, Walsingham decided, and suddenly he was tired of Guthrie and the niceties above the salt. Guthrie could go to hell, but *Emerald* would never go public.

'I'm sorry you have no greater faith in my assurances, Minister,' he snapped dismissively. Guthrie sounded chastened and deflated when he replied.

'It's no reflection on you, Charles, as I'm sure you realize. I am going to do what I feel has to be done to protect my initiative in Ulster. And I can best do that by retiring from the scene – not just temporarily, but permanently.' He cleared his throat to make room for a new portentousness. 'My resignation will be with the PM this evening. I felt, however, that you should be informed.'

Walsingham wanted to tell him that people were dead to protect his precious skin and office and initiative in Ulster, but the bile that rose in him simply drained him, made him feel very old and wish only to end the conversation.

'Thank you for telling me, Minister. Goodbye.' He put down the telephone without taking his eyes from the window. Somewhere out there, in all probability, McBride was considering his next step. Walsingham looked at the afternoon edition of the local paper on the telephone table. It was folded to reveal most of the headline concerning the murders in the Cotswold cottage and the police search for Professor Thomas McBride of Portland. Was McBride reading it at that moment, was he wondering when to call? Walsingham could feel the American like another presence in the room, and he was eager for their meeting as a younger self might have been for love or fornication.

He turned his eyes back to the window. Trade-off. If not, then McBride had to be eliminated like the others.

Where was he? Where?

Thomas Sean McBride sat in the restaurant in the Cavendish House department store on the Promenade, attired in an outfit he had purchased via credit card in the men's department, drinking tea and picking idly with a fork at a huge Danish pastry. The evening newspaper was folded on the tablecloth in front of him. His nonchalance was assumed, the pastry a necessary prop. He had cleaned himself up as thoroughly as he could in the washroom of a pub in Andoversford, and had eaten bread and cheese, washed down with beer, before catching the bus into Cheltenham.

The cops were talking to him, through the newspaper. It was a threat and perhaps a plea. No, he decided, reading the details of the double murder again, it was a threat. The cops had killed the woman and Moynihan.

He still could not give her her name back, not even now she was so evidently dead – unless it was a bluff, but he had already rejected the idea because Hoskins's staring, sightless eyes had come back into his mind, looking out of the first cup of tea. It was unnerving, but something in him concentrated more vividly on the woman and on her death than on his own danger. But he still could not name her.

He felt a curious invulnerability sitting there amid the inherited formalities of afternoon tea, premature fur wraps belying the day, jewellery cording old, wrinkled throats or blazoning shrunken bosoms, chatter brittler than glass, or lumpy as the crockery. The newspaper story also served to distance the cottage at Andoversford and the police hunt for him. They had no idea where he was, the story was meant to bring him in. They wanted to trade.

His removal from the sharp, cutting edges of his recent experience made him reluctant to think about Goessler, or about Drummond. One had been the author of his predicament, the other his father's murderer. To think of either of them made him feel tired, incapable of effort. Nothing in his surroundings or his mental landscape prompted him to action. He was being told in the newspaper he could go nowhere, he was on his own – why not drop in and discuss your problem?

He didn't think he wanted to do that.

McBride finished the Danish pastry then took his bill to the cashier. He paid again by credit card. He had only a few pounds in his wallet and could not foresee how to gain access to more cash.

He passed telephones on his way to the lift. He stopped, and a smile crept on to his face, took hold, broadened. Why not? He ducked his head into the plastic bubble, and consulted the directory. He rang the police HQ in Cheltenham.

'My name is McBride,' he said. 'Don't keep me waiting or I'll hang up. *McBride* – who wants to talk to me?' Then he listened to the clicks and splutters and the muffled voices until someone spoke to him. A cool, clear old man's voice, a hint of suppressed excitement behind the bland tones.

'Professor McBride, the author of *Gates of Hell*?'

'Uh? Oh, yes, you want to check I'm no nut, right?'

'That is correct.'

'What kind of a file do you have on me?'

'We could call it sufficient – your father's name, for example?'

'Michael – and he was *murdered* before I was born, November, nineteen-forty. Now, can we get moving?'

'Thank you, Professor.'

'You had them killed, mm? Who are you, anyway'

'My name is Walsingham. I knew your father well.'

'Nice for you.' McBride began looking around him, furtively. He knew he would be long gone before anyone traced his call, but he could not prevent his physical reactions. 'Drummond told me about you – *he* killed my father.'

'What – ?' Then, with recovered aplomb, 'I didn't know that. He is dead, by the way.'

'What?' A small hole was apprehensible in McBride's stomach. 'When?'

'A heart attack last night. I got a routine report after the Admiralty was informed. So, the whirligig of time – '

'He had forty years' freedom. You had his daughter killed this morning – quite a lot of dying seems to go on around you, Mr Walsingham.'

'Will you come in and talk to us? You have only to pop into the nearest police station.'

'You want to trade, uh? But you'll never pin those two murders on me. It had to be done by a small army.'

'Ah, but there are other deaths, Professor. We would have released the story tomorrow, had you not got in touch by then. A Doktor Goessler and his assistant, two people helping you with your researches, I believe?'

McBride was silent, staring at the wall with the scribbled numbers, surprised that the occasional obscenity had spread as far as the restaurant in Cavendish House.

Walsingham was his one and only enemy, he told himself, holding the receiver away from his suddenly hot ear as if the voice at the other end might infect him. He'd killed four people who knew about the events of 1940. For Guthrie, for the goddam government?

Curiously, he no longer felt animosity for Goessler, or Lobke, or Moynihan, or for Claire. Only the man at the other end of the line was his enemy, his real enemy. A period of emotional paralysis seemed to have passed, leaving only a single object of focus for the dormant feelings that had multiplied during the past days. He was free now, and all the others were dead. This man had killed them.

'Your plan, right – it was all your idea, forty years ago?'

'I – don't think we'll discuss that now. Rather, the terms for your surrender.' The voice was cold. McBride felt flushed, excited. He wanted to raise his voice, shout down the telephone at the same time as he became suddenly more aware of his surroundings, the potential threat represented by the people around him, the waitresses, the cashier.

'I don't think I want to do that right now, Mr Walsingham.'

'Just think about Goessler and Lobke. You *can* be charged with their murders, and will be when we take you, unless you give yourself up voluntarily in the next twenty-four hours.'

'What's the deal?'

'I think we'll talk about that next time you call.'

The telephone went dead. McBride was bemused for a moment, and then he began shaking. They'd traced the call. The lift doors opened and he waited, frozen. No policeman emerged. He took to the stairs, then made his way to the rear of the store, to the delicatessen. He heard the sirens while his sense of smell was still sifting the sausages and cheeses and smoked meats and fish. One Panda car arrived outside the exit from the delicatessen, and McBride moved through into the record and TV department, and left by the side street door. He walked down to the Promenade, saw the flashing lights of two police cars parked outside the front of Cavendish House, and turned in the opposite direction, taking cover in the crowds inside W.H.Smith.

He recovered his breath and his judgement there as he browsed through the cassette tapes. Squatting on his haunches, his eyes blind to *Folk* and *TV Advertised*, he turned over the conversation in his mind. Walsingham had left him the only one alive who knew about *Smaragden-halskette* and the British response to it – the murder of Grady and hundreds of British seamen. His story was worth maybe two million, and his life.

He smiled reluctantly to himself, as if saying farewell to a good friend. His life. Maybe he could have both, but the money definitely came second. He felt assailed by sadness as sharp as a stomach cramp as he squatted there, so that he stood up, lifted out an unrecognized name, turning the cassette in his left hand. Walsingham had killed Claire Drummond, and even fat Goessler, and none of them had wanted to kill him. Walsingham would, if he had the chance. A sure and certain silence, with the dirt rattling on the lid of the box –

Genesis? The name on the cassette cover became clear, and he put it down as if it burned him. *The Lamb lies down on Broadway*. Not this one –

He shuffled along the shelving, hands in his pockets. How could he turn the tables? A determination to exploit his circumstances was as evident as a metal plate at the back of his head, preventing the incursion of doubt, or fear. He was alone now, and his enemy was identified and a single man. The police at his disposal did not count, somehow. An excitement passed through him like an earth-tremor. He needed someone else to know.

He walked away from the record department, to stationery, and picked up a writing pad and a packet of envelopes. He'd meet Walsingham, but not without

369

insurance. He saw a rack of typewriters, and replaced th
paper.

Five minutes later, he left W. H. Smith with a portabl
Japanese typewriter and a packet of bond paper and a doze
sheets of carbon paper. He felt curiously lighthearted
Doubts and trepidations hammered against the metal plat
at the back of his mind, but he knew it would hold. Hi
mind was as shallow and clear as a pool in which, clearl
visible, a pike circled a smaller fish. The small fish wa
grinning.

November 1940
Gilliatt stopped the car at the entrance to the drive o
Crosswinds Farm. The house was in darkness, except fo
one curtained light in a downstairs window. Maureen, nex
to him, stared through the windscreen intently, unseeingly
Now they had obeyed her frenetic desire to return to fin
McBride – a consuming guilt for all the years of he
marriage, Gilliatt regarded it, whether fair or unfair in it
self-blame he could not say – she seemed drained o
purpose and energy.

The minor roads and unsurfaced tracks by which the
had returned to Kilbrittain had been empty of Germans. I
was an experience on the edge of phantasmagoria, th
empty dark roads, the silent countryside, the innocen
slopes of the land, the clear moonlight. And the silent
hunched woman beside him. In the small cocoon of th
Morris he could not even care very much for the fate o
Michael McBride. Now, the farm looked as it always ha
done and McBride's lurid imagery of betrayal an
treachery seemed inappropriate.

He cleared his throat.

'I'll go up to the house,' he said. She seemed not to hea
him. 'You wait here. Get into the driving seat.' He opened
the door and swung his long legs out of the car. 'If anythin
untoward happens – anything at all – start the car and driv
away. Don't stop until you reach Cork. Understand?' Sh
looked at him, and he took hold of her cold hand. The othe
was placed across her stomach as if to protect the foetus sh
could not possibly feel. He shook her hand, waking her
'Understand?' Responsibility for her weighed on him as h

370

stared into her white, strained features. McBride had run off to play heroic games, but someone always had to be left to tidy up after heroes. His part, dustpan-and-brush for the remnants of hacked armour and the tiny shards of swords. He was angry with McBride. The silent farmhouse belied his accusations, his silly daring.

'Yes?' she said, then again, 'Yes.'

'Good, change seats then.'

When she had done so, he stood looking at her, then simply nodded and headed up the track to the farmhouse on its knoll. The moonlight illuminated the path and the lawns and the white walls of Crosswinds Farm. He turned briefly and looked out to sea. Nothing. No activity. He closed his mind to all of that. It wasn't his concern.

No one challenged him, and he knocked loudly on the front door, the assumption of innocence done deliberately, with care. After a while he knocked again and heard footsteps in the hall. Drummond opened the door. He seemed perturbed, but Gilliatt excused his expression – he was a stranger to Drummond, after all.

'I'm Peter Gilliatt – sir. I was sent from London with Michael McBride.'

'Oh, God,' Drummond breathed in an appalled voice that could have been guilt or sadness. 'Come in – Lieutenant?' Gilliatt nodded. 'Of course. I – you didn't come that night, there was shooting, but I knew Michael had to be alive, probably on the run – the Germans – he's in here –'

Drummond opened the door to his study. McBride was lying comfortably and arranged and quite dead on the sofa in front of the fire. It was obvious that Drummond had been sitting opposite him, drinking. A bottle and a single glass stood on an occasional table next to the armchair. McBride's eyes were closed, his face seemed very peaceful. Gilliatt felt emotion churn in his stomach.

'What happened?'

'He – saved my life. He must have surprised the German unit hiding in the gardens – ' Gilliatt looked at him narrowly. 'Some of the parachute troops who landed yesterday night, I imagine. He came on them, I suppose. I heard shooting, but by the time I got my own gun, after

warning London, it was all over. I found him near the doo[r]
dead, and three Germans dead in the gardens. I've seen r[...]
one since.'

Gilliatt said, 'He came back to kill you.'

'I don't understand.'

'He thought you betrayed him – the other night, when w[e]
were ambushed. We saw you then – ' He studie[d]
Drummond's face, but it was merely sorrowful, hal[f]
attentive. 'He was convinced you'd betrayed us, you wer[e]
working with the IRA for the Germans.'

'Poor Michael. He ended up saving my life.' Drummon[d]
went forward into the room and stood over the body. The[n]
he turned to Gilliatt. 'I know this has been a terrible shoc[k]
to you, Lieutenant Gilliatt, but have you anything t[o]
report? London is in a flap about these troops landing – m[y]
scouts have seen a few signs of them, but nothing mor[e.]
Why are they here?'

Gilliatt was staring at McBride's body, in valedictio[n.]
The ultimate futility of courage, he could not hel[p]
thinking. To die for an error, a stupid, bigoted mistake. H[e]
wondered what had possessed McBride –

He looked up. Drummond, a senior naval office[r]
required his report. He nodded.

'I think I'd better talk to London, sir. How much they'r[e]
aware of I don't know, but it's urgent.'

'The radio's in the cellar – come.'

Both men paused at the door to look back once [at]
McBride. Then Drummond closed the door on the bod[y]
and Gilliatt decided that Maureen could remain in the c[ar]
until he had made his report to London. He postpone[d]
sorrow until he had done his urgent duty.

As he waited for Drummond to unlock the door to th[e]
cellar, the hall window was suddenly illuminated by [a]
garish orange glow from the sea.

Grady was awoken – thrust into consciousness – by the firs[t]
explosion. He was tumbled from his bunk, and his hea[d]
banged painfully against the bulkhead. His vision becam[e]
foggy, and the weak blue light in his cabin became siniste[r]
and frightening. He scrabbled with his hands as the whol[e]
cabin lurched sideways, spilling forward, disorientatin[g]

im and making him suddenly aware of the cold water of the St George's Channel beneath the ship. The cruiser was suddenly made of paper, easily crumpled.

A second explosion, banging his shoulder against the bulkhead, rolling him along the wall of the cabin – *along the wall?* He groaned from fear rather than pain. The blue light was extinguished, and he was in complete, cold darkness. He called out, to hear his own voice. The cruiser was listing more. Footsteps outside, drumming through the bulkhead, then cursing. Dryness still beneath his hands and knees. His genitals were chilly with anticipation of the creeping, drowning water he knew must come for him. The shudder of a more distant explosion.

Blood seeped into his left eye. He wiped roughly at it like an embarrassing tear. His body was shivering, as if registering all three explosions. His mind was clear, but could not react. He knew they were under attack, even understood that the cruiser was sinking, but there seemed no urgency. Panic was still, sedative, calming.

It was some minutes – it seemed minutes, perhaps longer, perhaps only moments? – before he felt terror return, unfreezing the icy calm. He scrambled to his feet, against the sloping bulkhead, seeming alone in the silent, dark ship, and reached for the door handle. He turned it, and pulled. The door did not move. He heaved at the handle, but the door remained wedged and buckled into place by the effect of the two explosions.

He heard a siren, but could not be certain because he was screaming by that time and what he heard might have been the sound of his own demented voice. Siren – voice – hands banging on the door. The useless noises went on for some time, even after the cabin tilted forward. He heard the slither towards and past him of clothes and toilet gear and framed pictures of his wife and family and papers and the books he had been reading, then they stilled into an unseen heap against the forward bulkhead. Eventually, he had to grip the door handle with one hand to keep himself sufficiently upright to pound with increasing, weakening hopelessness on the cabin door. His voice had gone by that time, and it seemed the ship's siren was screaming for him. All his awareness seemed to be in his bare feet and ankles,

awaiting the arrival of the icy water that he somehow kne~
was already reaching through the cruiser towards him.

Churchill seemed to have acquired the company (
Walsingham more exclusively than any other office
present. None of them would openly demonstrate the
hostility to the Prime Minister, but they had overly avoide
Walsingham since the moment Churchill announced h
decision regarding the convoy. It was as if they knew th
authorship of *Emerald*. They may have done, b~
Walsingham, though he disliked the proximity of th
Prime Minister because it so clearly marked him o
physically from his companions, could not be disturbed b
their animosity. He was bound to Churchill, *Emeral*
would be with him for the remainder of his life – but he w;
beyond regretting that now. It was done, or soon would b
when the report came in, and it would have either to b
lived down or lived up to in the coming years and after th
war.

If it was not buried efficiently by the Prime Minister –

Churchill's face was blank of expression. He had drunk
good deal during the night, alternating alcohol wit
amounts of coffee, but he did not appear drunk so much a
having slipped away from himself and from any pressure
or guilts that might assail him. He seemed curiously a
peace.

A telephone rang, and it was answered by a Wren. Sh
carried the set over to Churchill.

'The Tracking Room upstairs is receiving morse fro~
the convoy, sir.'

Churchill roused himself, the face closed up around th
suddenly alert eyes. The other occupants of the roo~
stopped work, watched Churchill's broad back as he leane
over the telephone.

'Yes?'

'Prime Minister, we're getting reports that the convoy
under U-boat attack –'

'What is the convoy's position?'

'That's what's strange, sir. They're well into our ne
channel, they should be safe from attack.'

'You mean the U-boats are in our channel?' Church~

374

exploded. The intelligence colonel's face behind him wrinkled with contempt and self-digust, and he looked up at the wall-map and the marked position of the convoy.

'It must be, sir! Sir, two of the merchant ships have been hit by torpedoes, and the cruiser – !'

'You know what to do. We must save as many as we can. Report to me every half-hour.'

Churchill put down the telephone. Only the few people in this operations room, Walsingham thought, know the truth about *Emerald*. They will not be allowed to tell the truth. No one will ever know. Churchill's face was blank of all expression. He put the receiver down on the floor beside his chair. Less than two minutes, Walsingham thought, suddenly and briefly appalled, was all the time that was necessary. Upstairs, they would already be saying how shocked and moved the old man was, how terrible after the secrecy of the southern route through the minefield, even as they began the attempt to rescue the survivors. The subterranean reality in this cramped bunker room was different, but now it was robbed, somehow, of real significance. Voices on the telephone, an awaited radio report from an RAF Anson of Coastal Command, and that was how it was done. No blood anywhere near this room.

'Colonel,' Churchill called.

'Sir.' The colonel was standing in front of Churchill, his back deliberately to Walsingham, in calculated insult.

'You understand, Colonel? A tragic fact of war – we have lost a cruiser, three heavy merchantmen and God knows how many men – by U-boat attack.' The colonel nodded, his face transferring guilt to the old man in the chair, adopting the fixed lines of unthinking duty, the clear brow of necessity. Churchill could see it happening to him, and was satisfied. 'I will inform the American Ambassador in due course. That will be all, Colonel.'

'Prime Minister.' The colonel walked away with an almost light step. Churchill studied Walsingham, as if the expression on his face was of the utmost importance, just at that moment. Walsingham understood from the nod he was given that the Prime Minister was satisfied. To Walsingham, the satisfaction was a recognition of something failed or broken or missing within himself. But he dismissed the thought.

Churchill closed his eyes for a moment, as soon as Walsingham returned his gaze to the wall charts. In a sudden, clear, visionary moment, he could hear insects in the garden at Chartwell. All those years, well spent, recollected with affection, had only been an interlude. His destiny was to be the only man capable of making decisions like *Emerald*. That was why his country needed him, he acknowledged. Not for the V-sign, or the cigars, or the bulldog expression or the black homburg. Because he could make decisions like *Emerald* and not despair of himself, of his country, or of human nature. It was not having the courage, or even the ruthlessness, to do it that mattered. It was the ability to perceive necessity, to bow to that strange deity's commands.

'Sir,' the radio operator called from the other side of the room. 'I'm beginning to get a transmission.' The colonel moved to the radio, and Walsingham got to his feet. Churchill nodded his permission, but made no attempt to move himself. The volume on the radio was turned up, and the voice of the distant R/T operator aboard the Anson could be heard through a mush of static, stung and obscured occasionally by severe crackling.

Walsingham stood next to the colonel behind the radio operator. The army officer looked at him, and there was complicity in his features. A complicity of duty and transferred guilt and personal innocence. Walsingham nodded to him. The colonel seemed relieved. The authorship of *Emerald* did not matter. The old man in the chair had committed the atrocity.

'We've sighted the U-boats on the surface, but we're flying low and keeping out of sight.' The absence of jargon and the hesitancy of the words indicated that the radio operator knew he was being listened to by Churchill. No code-names, no call-signs, no references to position, just a voice on the ether, a radio commentary of an occurrence at sea. There was silence for a long time, in which only the universe spoke, then: 'There's been an explosion, no, two explosions – we're going for a look-see.' Another long silence in which each person in the room became less and less aware of the drama and significance of events and more sensible of minor irritations, hunger, a dry mouth, itching eyebrows. The outcome of the war, the fate of *Smaragdenhalskette* diminished, faded until they could cope with it as a voice commenting on distant events, a race or a Test Match. 'Two U-boats have been damaged, and another two are sinking!' Spithead Review commentary, a fireworks display. 'The remainder have altered course – there goes another one! There are hundreds of men in the water we can see – one of the damaged U-boats is rolling – *she's going!*'

'Acknowledge, and switch off!' Churchill barked from his chair, and the colonel turned the volume down almost to inaudibility. He was puzzled by the old man's behaviour – he seemed to care more for the fate of the Germans than the convoy crews.

The room returned to insulated silence, and then a telephone rang. It was the receiver still at Churchill's feet. He picked it up warily as he might have done a snake.

'It's the Irish Ambassador, sir.'

'What does he want? I'm very busy. Let me call him later, unless it's urgent.'

'He wishes to speak to you under code-name *Essex*.' Churchill paused – the Earl of Essex and his invasion of Ireland in the last years of Elizabeth's reign. The first convoyed British soldiers had landed in Cork. 'No, that isn't urgent. I'll call him later, my dear. Give him my thanks.'

He put down the telephone, heavily and clumsily. Then he lay back in the armchair, fat and helpless as an overfed baby. Walsingham felt himself to be impossibly removed from Churchill, and desperate to renounce everything to do with *Emerald*. Unlike the colonel, he could not completely and successfully transfer guilt to the corpulent figure of Churchill. He was still the author of the file.

Churchill was looking intently at him. Then he said, softly, 'Bury it, Commander. Bury it deep. You can begin tomorrow.'

October 1980
McBride placed his coins on the flat top of the call-box. The

telephone was still clammy from use by the woman in front of him, and he wiped it on the sleeve of his jacket. Andoversford was quiet in the early morning. He dialled the Cheltenham number he had used from Cavendish House the previous day.

'Come on, come on –' murmured some impatient part of him, though he felt calm, assured, even bright, despite his almost sleepless night in the small residential restaurant on Cleeve Hill above the orange, serried lights of Cheltenham and the sky-glow of Gloucester in the distance. He'd eaten well, drunk most of a bottle of claret, then retired to his room to type two letters, one to his agent in New York and the other, longer one, to his bank in Portland. He had carbon copies of both letters in the car now.

'Yes, Professor McBride? I trust you slept well?' Walsingham sounded confident, gracious in victory – and as if he was acting a part.

'I want to talk to you.'

'Of course. Will you come here?'

'Said the spider to the fly, uh? No thanks.'

Walsingham chuckled, but there was a newly cautious note in his voice when he replied. 'Of course. Where do you suggest?'

'Somewhere lonely might be nice – for you. However, if you want to shoot me dead you'll do it in the middle of London and get away with it.'

'I'm glad you understand that.'

'Let's say Foxcote Hill, in an hour. See you.' McBride put down the receiver. He stepped out of the call-box, and climbed into his car.

He drove out of Andoversford, taking minor roads until he was able, using the OS map, to approach Foxcote Hill from the south. He parked the car at the end of a track which petered out in the copse on Shill Hill, and then climbed until he was above the surrounding countryside. It was misty and autumnal in the fields, and the copses were webbed with mist. In the distance to the north, he could see the village he had left twenty minutes or so earlier, and its main roads. Trees covered the northern slopes of the hill, but he was on short, springy turf, exposed and alone. He descended into the trees again and waited. The morning was still, heavy, but the cloud was thin and transitory.

During the night he had come to the conclusion that Walsingham would let him live – just so long as he knew that the evidence for what had happened in 1940 was in hands other than McBride's alone. Whether he would ask questions first, and so elicit his powerlessness, was another matter. McBride had never possessed a gun, and he could not regret the absence of one now. Nevertheless, during the fifteen or twenty slow minutes before he heard the car approaching from the tiny hamlet of Foxcote to the north, he began to wish for the feel of one in his hand, futile though its possession would have been.

He ground out his third cigarette as he heard the undergrowth move and brush against a body, and slipped back into the shadow of the tree bole against which he had been leaning. A minute later, Walsingham appeared, struggling up the slope, his trilby hat in his hand, his topcoat unbuttoned. He appeared to be alone. He stopped for breath, dabbed his forehead with his handkerchief, felt his pounding heart, and called out.

'McBride – McBride, are you here?'

McBride said nothing. Walsingham looked back behind him, then moved on up the last of the slope to the hilltop, passing the tree that concealed McBride. McBride watched the hill below him, straining to see into the shadows beneath the trees, and listened intently. He could see and hear nothing.

Without moving from the shelter of the tree, he called out after Walsingham, 'Don't turn around for the moment, Walsingham. Are you alone?'

Walsingham stopped. 'Of course.'

'I believe you. I didn't think you'd want our little talk to be overheard. I guess *national security* covers it, uh?' He heard Walsingham chuckle. 'OK, turn around.' McBride stepped out from behind the tree. Walsingham was dabbing his brow again. He looked old and vulnerable. 'Where's the hit man?'

Walsingham raised his hands, palms outwards in innocence. 'My dear fellow – '

'Bullshit.' McBride stood higher on the slope than

Walsingham. 'Let's make it so he has to be a very good shot.'

'I'd like to sit down.' Walsingham did not appear more ruffled than simply breathless with the short climb. 'Over there? You can watch the trees, surely. And I'm not wired for sound, nor am I armed.' He held his coat open, and McBride frisked him quickly. Walsingham was aware of the slight tremor through his old body as the American's hands smoothed over his sides and chest, down his legs, between his thighs, around his ankles. Then McBride looked up at him, and the gleam of confidence in his eyes demonstrated that he had sensed the older man's fear.

'OK – a rotten log seems about right.'

They sat on the green-coated log in the spaces between the more exotic fungoid growths. Walsingham picked at one, lung-like, then at another the texture and colour of rolled pastry. His fingers were vaguely, senilely destructive. 'Entirely appropriate,' he answered softly.

'They're all dead. Just like you wanted it, really.'

'Oh, no,' Walsingham replied quickly. 'You were the one who stirred the ant-heap with a stick. On behalf of Goessler.' Walsingham's breathing refused to return to normal. Quick, short breaths, as superficial as the relationship of a mayfly to the pond water beneath it. He felt reluctant, and – yes – afraid in the company of this man. He was totally unlike Michael McBride, his father. A superficial physical resemblance, naturally, but nothing marked on the almost bland face except recent tiredness, recent extremity. Even now, he seemed somehow – *irresponsible?* His innocence as Goessler's pawn forced a comparison of guilt upon Walsingham which made him uncomfortable with himself. Self-esteem, self-confidence both seemed to evaporate.

'You should have buried it all a lot deeper – the hole wasn't big enough to hide what you had to hide. It was all your operation, from first to last, I guess?'

Walsingham's face made the admission with involuntary muscles.

'Yes,' he said after a long silence. 'I proposed the sinking of the convoy, and Churchill accepted it. It seemed to be a *necessity* to me at that moment in time, in that situation.' He paused, but then hurried on, sensing his physical proximity to Michael McBride's son like a cold wind on his frail skin. 'I had nothing to do with the death of your father. That – '

'I know. You would have, if it had helped, but Drummond got there before you. If it had become *necessary*, you'd have had him killed.'

'I liked your father – ' Walsingham's voice tailed off as he admitted the inadequacy of the statement. 'He was very likeable,' he added, almost to himself.

'Yes.' McBride looked down into the trees for a moment, but in abstraction rather than alertness. Then he returned his gaze to Walsingham. The old man felt McBride's eyes glancing over his face and body in tangible, icy contacts. There was an evident repulsion in McBride's expression. 'All men who fight wars are like you, right? Necessity. Then in peacetime it's national security. You make me sick.'

Walsingham's face was livid with anger. 'You sanctimonious American puppy! Your countrymen were collecting money for the war effort by organizing *charity bazaars* and *dances* at the very moment we were in danger of being overrun by the Nazis. You have *no* room to talk!' As soon as he paused, he seemed to become calmer by an effort of will. His anger had made him more human, more comprehensible to McBride. His thin strands of white hair and his lined face made him less dangerous. 'I'm sorry,' Walsingham continued. 'You could not be expected to understand. Let us get down to the business in hand. As you say, I did not take sufficient care to expunge the evidence of what was done. You have collected a great deal of it. You intend to write a book.' Walsingham's thin smile suddenly alerted McBride to the man's intelligence, his superiority of mind, his ruthlessness. It was the American's turn to be disturbed, edgy. He scanned the trees swiftly, knowing as he did so that he would never see the rifleman – if there was one.

Walsingham added: 'Were you in fact to write this book of yours, you would be charged with the murders of Goessler and Lobke. You would be convicted.'

McBride shivered, then nodded. 'And if I keep quiet?'

'Then there would be no need to detain you further, or to

charge you. You would be free to go. I would see you on to the aircraft at Heathrow myself.' Walsingham attempted an ingenuous smile, but it was an evident false note and he withdrew it from his features.

'Sounds easy. There's a man down there, right? Insurance?' McBride nodded down towards the thicker trees.

'Yes, there's a man down there. As you say, insurance. For my safety.'

'It's all for your safety.' McBride looked over his shoulder, then back at the trees. A noise? Squirrel or shrew, or the marksman? He wondered about Walsingham, and how desperate he was, and he felt very afraid. Then Walsingham was speaking again, with a new urgency.

'Have you deposited any evidence with anyone, McBride? I must have all your papers, your notes, lists of people you have seen – '

'What's the matter with you, Walsingham?' McBride reached very slowly into his jacket and removed the carbon copies he had made the previous evening. 'I've written to my bank in Portland, Oregon, and to my agent in New York. Also this morning I rang my agent in London enquiring about an advance against royalties for the British edition of *Gates of Hell*. I said I'd ring again this afternoon.'

He waited, his skin crawling, his hands flattened, turning white, on the damp bark of the rotten log. He could be swatted now, removed, eliminated. He had no doubt that Walsingham would do it, had planned to do it. The carbons the old man was studying appeared insubstantial, ineffectual. The bullet would pass through his frame as easily as through those papers. Come on, *come on* –

'I see. Your American agent would, in the event of your sudden demise, be authorized to receive the documents from your bank, and expose their contents. To the New York *Daily News* in the first instance, I presume?' There was a livid lightning-flash of hatred on Walsingham's face for a moment, a second of decision, and then the slow relaxing of the hand that held the papers, so that it rested nervelessly on the log beside McBride's hand. The decision had been unmade, altered. McBride wiped his green-stained hands together with relief.

'Make a beautiful noise and a very bad smell, mm?' he asked with adopted lightness, after he had cleared his throat.

What was that? Anything – nothing? Had he lost – ?

'This creates something of a problem,' Walsingham said with chilling calm. *Lost – ?* 'Fortunately, it doesn't seem to be insuperable. We should have to persuade your agent that your death was an accident. The CIA or the FBI would assist us there, I should think?' Walsingham's confidence was growing. 'Then your documents, your confessions, would moulder on in the vaults of the Citizens' Bank of Portland, undisturbed – ' Walsingham had raised his hand to mop his now dry brow. McBride watched the gesture in disbelief.

'My agent in London!' he shouted. Walsingham's hand hovered. 'If I don't call this afternoon, he talks to New York. The papers will be out of my bank before you can stop them, and it won't be an accident!'

Walsingham sat with his hand still hovering near his brow. Hate and fury crossed his old face like new streams following old, dry courses. McBride studied the trees in panic, then glanced over his shoulder. He had only a moment. Walsingham, in a few seconds, would make the irrational, irreversible decision to have him eliminated. Walsingham's face was now an agony of indecision.

'I don't believe you – ' he said.

'Can you afford not to? You're about to retire. I won't talk, to anyone, until after you're dead and in your grave, loaded with honours you don't merit. I'm leaving now. Just keep your hand on your forehead until I've gone.' Walsingham chewed his lower lip. His hand fell limply against his brow, and with an effort he held it there. Time, *time*, McBride thought. Given time, he'll see sense. He'll lose his nerve. Just let me get away from here – 'The only way you can expose me is by revealing your own rotten part in things. You won't care about the conference, or about Ulster, but you'll care about that. You won't want to have to shoot yourself to avoid the scandal.' McBride moved behind the log, watching the sweat break out along Walsingham's forehead, around the crumpled ball of the handkerchief. The old, veined hand was shaking. Slowly,

McBride backed up the last yards of the slope to the brow of the hill. 'Just take it easy, Walsingham,' he called out. 'I'll keep my word –'

He was on the long, whale-backed hilltop, and his car was only hundreds of yards away, down in the trees. He felt a curious lightness in his stomach, and began running.

Behind him, Walsingham transferred his handkerchief – glancing in distaste at its grey dampness – to his left hand, and the marksman stepped out of the trees, rifle lowered.

'What happened?' Exton asked when he reached the log. 'Why didn't you give me the signal? I could have killed him easily. You were in no danger, at any time.'

'He'd written letters,' Walsingham offered, his gaze avoiding Exton's eyes and their contempt. 'I had to settle for the original trade-off. He'll keep silent if he wants to live.'

'As you will?' Yes, it was there, in Exton's voice. The unfamiliar tinge of contempt. Walsingham felt old, older than ever before. He looked up, mustering authority, perhaps merely recollecting it.

'As I will, and you will, Exton – and so will all of us.'

Distantly, they heard an engine start, and then the noise of a car accelerating away from them. To Walsingham, the noise was both a relief in the present and a distanced humming threat from the future. But, it was settled. McBride would let him live out his days, basking in respect and honours. It would have to do. His old body, old nerves had settled for it when he faced Michael's son.

The sound of the car faded and disappeared on the morning air.